TALES OF HEROES, MYTHS & LEGENDS

CLEOPATRA

QUEEN OF EGYPT

FLAME TREE PUBLISHING
6 Melbray Mews, Fulham,
London SW6 3NS, United Kingdom
www.flametreepublishing.com

Originally published in the 451 series in 2022

26 28 30 29 27
1 3 5 7 9 10 8 6 4 2

ISBN: 978-1-80694-258-9

For Kristin:
Your resilience and fortitude would inspire an Egyptian queen.
Lindsay
Friend and business partner.

Cover and pattern art was created by Flame Tree Studio, with elements courtesy of Shutterstock.com/svekloid/miha de. Additional interior decoration courtesy of Shutterstock.com/Zvereva Yana.

Judith John (lists of Ancient Kings & Leaders) is a writer and editor specializing in literature and history. A former secondary school English Language and Literature teacher, she has subsequently worked as an editor on major educational projects, including *English A: Literature* for the Pearson International Baccalaureate series. Judith's major research interests include Romantic and Gothic literature, and Renaissance drama.

The classic text in this book derives from *Cleopatra (Makers of History)* by Jacob Abbott, published by Harper and Brothers Publishers, New York and London, 1901; in addition to extracts from: Appian, *The Civil Wars*, translated by Horace White in the Loeb Classical Library, published by William Heinemann Ltd., London, 1913; Cassius Dio, *Roman History*, translated by Earnest Cary in the Loeb Classical Library, published by William Heinemann Ltd., London, 1917; Florus, *Epitome of Roman History*, translated by E. S. Forster in the Loeb Classical Library, published by Harvard University Press, 1929; Pliny the Elder, *Natural History*, translated by John Bostock and H.T. Riley, published by Taylor and Francis, London, 1855; Plutarch, *Parallel Lives*, translated by Bernadotte Perrin in the Loeb Classical Library, Harvard University Press, dating in its entirety back to before 1923; Josephus, *Jewish Antiquities*, translated by William Whiston, published in London, 1737; Strabo, *Geography*, translated by H.L. Jones in the Loeb Classical Library, published by Harvard University Press, 1917 through 1932; Vergil, *Aeneid*, translated by Theodore C. Williams, published by Houghton Mifflin Co., 1910.

A copy of the CIP data for this book is available from the British Library.

Designed and created in the UK | Printed and bound in China

Represented in the EU for product safety and compliance by
Authorised Rep Compliance Ltd, Ground Floor,
71 Lower Baggot Street, Dublin, D02 P593, Ireland.
Contact at www.arccompliance.com

FSC
www.fsc.org
MIX
Paper | Supporting responsible forestry
FSC® C005748

COLLECTOR'S EDITIONS

TALES OF HEROES, MYTHS & LEGENDS

CLEOPATRA

QUEEN OF EGYPT

Edited and Introduced by

LINDSAY POWELL

Further Reading and

Lists of Ancient Kings & Leaders

FLAME TREE PUBLISHING

CONTENTS

CONTENTS

CONTENTS

TALES OF HEROES, MYTHS & LEGENDS

CLEOPATRA

QUEEN OF EGYPT

SERIES FOREWORD

Stretching back to the oral traditions of thousands of years ago, tales of heroes and disaster, creation and conquest have been told by many different civilizations in many different ways. Their impact sits deep within our culture even though the details in the tales themselves are a loose mix of historical record, transformed narrative and the distortions of hundreds of storytellers.

Today the language of mythology lives with us: our mood is jovial, our countenance is saturnine, we are narcissistic and our modern life is hermetically sealed from others. The nuances of myths and legends form part of our daily routines and help us navigate the world around us, with its half truths and biased reported facts.

The nature of a myth is that its story is already known by most of those who hear it, or read it. Every generation brings a new emphasis, but the fundamentals remain the same: a desire to understand and describe the events and relationships of the world. Many of the great stories are archetypes that help us find our own place, equipping us with tools for self-understanding, both individually and as part of a broader culture.

For Western societies it is Greek mythology that speaks to us most clearly. It greatly influenced the mythological heritage of the ancient Roman civilization and is the lens through which we still see the Celts, the Norse and many of the other great peoples and religions. The Greeks themselves learned much from their neighbours, the Egyptians, an older culture that became weak with age and incestuous leadership.

It is important to understand that what we perceive now as mythology had its own origins in perceptions of the divine and the rituals of the sacred. The earliest civilizations, in the crucible of the Middle East, in the Sumer of the third millennium BCE, are the source to which many of the mythic archetypes can be traced. As humankind collected together in cities for the first time, developed writing and industrial scale agriculture, started to irrigate the rivers and attempted to control rather than be at the mercy of its environment, humanity began to write down its tentative explanations of natural events, of floods and plagues, of disease.

Early stories tell of Gods (or god-like animals in the case of tribal societies such as African, Native American or Aboriginal cultures) who are crafty and use their wits to survive, and it is reasonable to suggest that these were the first rulers of the gathering peoples of the earth, later elevated to god-like status with the distance of time. Such tales became more political as cities vied with each other for supremacy, creating new Gods, new hierarchies for their pantheons. The older Gods took on primordial roles and became the preserve of creation and destruction, leaving the new gods to deal with more current, everyday affairs. Empires rose and fell, with Babylon assuming the mantle from Sumeria in the 1800s BCE, then in turn to be swept away by the Assyrians of the 1200s BCE; then the Assyrians and the Egyptians were subjugated by the Greeks, the Greeks by the Romans and so on, leading to the spread and assimilation of common themes, ideas and stories throughout the world.

The survival of history is dependent on the telling of good tales, but each one must have the 'feeling' of truth, otherwise it will be ignored. Around the firesides, or embedded in a book or a computer, the myths and legends of the past are still the living materials of retold myth, not restricted to an exploration of origins. Now we have devices and global communications that give us unparalleled access to a diversity of traditions. We can find out about Indigenous American, Indian, Chinese and tribal African mythology in a way that was denied to our ancestors, we can find connections, match the archaeology, religion and the mythologies of the world to build a comprehensive image of the human adventure.

The great leaders of history and heroes of literature have also adopted the mantle of mythic experience, because the stories of historical figures – Cyrus the Great, Alexander, Genghis Khan, Cleopatra – and mytho-poetic warriors such as Beowulf achieve a cultural significance that transcends their moment in the chronicles of humankind. Myth, history and literature have become powerful, entwined instruments of perception, with echoes of reported fact and symbolic truths that convey the sweep of human experience. In this series of books we are glad to share with you the wonderful traditions of the past.

Jake Jackson
General Editor

TALES OF HEROES, MYTHS & LEGENDS

CLEOPATRA

QUEEN OF EGYPT

INTRODUCTION
& FURTHER READING

INTRODUCTION TO CLEOPATRA

Cleopatra VII Thea Philopator (70/69–30 BCE), Queen of Egypt, is one of the most famous personalities in history. Today she is more often remembered for the affairs she had with Julius Caesar and Marcus Antonius, yet these relationships reveal her political acumen and total commitment to protecting Egypt and her dynasty. Through Caesar she was confirmed as queen. Through Antonius, she re-established Egyptian rule over territories previously governed by the pharaohs thousands of years before. Then she famously lost it all – after her defeat at the Battle of Actium (31 BCE) and the subsequent fall of Alexandria (30 BCE) – to Octavian, Julius Caesar's young and ambitious heir, who would later come to be known as Caesar Augustus. It was after his victory that the story of Cleopatra's life came to be written, creating a mostly negative narrative that has endured to this day. The manner of her death from the bite of an asp is well known, even though it may not be true. Less familiar to us is her lifelong struggle to rule her kingdom legitimately and to keep it independent. The decisions she made to achieve her goals were consequential and deserve to be studied.

The first part of this book is a lightly edited version of *Cleopatra* in the series *Makers of History*, written by Jacob Abbott in 1879 and published in 1901. His work drew upon modern scholarship, which was then extensive, and his personal study of extant works by Roman historians. Extracts from some of those ancient texts which describe key events, translated from the original Greek or Latin, are also included in this book under Contemporary Perspectives.

THE ANCIENT SOURCES AND HISTORIANS

In researching *Cleopatra* Jacob Abbott had access to good English translations of the ancient sources. Everything that is known today about Cleopatra comes from accounts recorded by foreign commentators. Key among the extant sources are: Plutarch's *Parallel Lives*, specifically the *Life of Julius Caesar* and *Life of Antony*; Appian's *Civil Wars*; and Cassius Dio's *Roman History*. There are cameo appearances of Cleopatra and snippets of information about her in: Josephus's *Jewish Antiquities*; Pliny the Elder's *Natural History*; Suetonius's *Lives of the Caesars*, specifically *Life of* Divus *Julius* and *Life of* Divus *Augustus*; and Florus's *Epitome of Roman History*. Regrettably, what would have been the most comprehensive account by the contemporary – and arguably Rome's greatest – historian Livy (Titus Livius) survives only as the so-called *Periochae* of Books 130, 131, 132 and 133.

To Roman writers the Egyptians were exotic barbarians, foreign to them in every way. Barbarians could show flashes of brilliance, but in the final analysis they were neither as smart nor as reliable as Romans. Cleopatra was also a woman and, moreover, a woman with power. She was portrayed by ancient historians as clever, determined and wily, yet also sensual, avaricious and treacherous. Strong warrior queens – Amanirenas of Kush and Boudica of the Iceni, for example – represented the threatening antithesis of a man and of his manliness (encapsulated in the revered Roman trait of *virtus*). It was a bigoted and misogynistic trope, but one universally believed by Roman historians, who were exclusively men. Getting to know the *real* Cleopatra is thus difficult: our sources are partial, partisan and patronizing.

CLEOPATRA'S FAMILY

Cleopatra's name means 'glory of her father'. It was the name of many of the women in the Ptolemaic dynasty. When Alexander the Great died in 323 BCE, his empire was fought over by rival generals, families and Alexander's friends. The *diadochoi* ('successors') emerged as leaders of their own satrapies. Ptolemy (Ptolemaios) assumed the rule of Egypt, along with the adjacent regions of Libya and Arabia. The Egyptian aristocracy accepted him as their new pharaoh and he adopted the name Ptolemy I Soter ('Saviour'). Through his children he founded a new dynasty, which reigned over Egypt with absolute power until 30 BCE.

Ptolemy I also adopted the practice of incest, a cultural norm in Egypt. An estimated one-fifth or one-sixth of all Egyptian marriages of the time were between sisters and brothers. When her father, Ptolemy XII Auletes ('Oboe-player', r. *c*. 80–58 BCE and again 55–51 BCE), stipulated in his will that his daughter Cleopatra should marry and rule Egypt with her brother Ptolemy XIII Theos Philopator ('God Father-Loving'), he was following the practice of pharaohs going back three millennia.

The identity of Cleopatra's mother is not known with certainty. Some historians believe she was Cleopatra V Tryphaea ('Dainty'), the only attested wife of Ptolemy XII. Her parentage is also unclear: she may have been a legitimate – or illegitimate – daughter of Ptolemy IX Soter or the legitimate daughter of Ptolemy X Alexander I. Either mother suggests that Cleopatra VII was descended from Macedonian Greeks and that she probably had no Egyptian or other African ancestry.

Murder of family members was also a common practice of the Ptolemies. In royal families with several siblings, political assassination was a recognized way of eliminating potential rivals. Conveniently, her brother-husband Ptolemy XIII drowned while crossing the Nile in 47 BCE, but Cleopatra likely arranged the killing of Ptolemy XIV Philopator, her next brother-husband, in 44 BCE. Arsinoë IV, her sister, was exiled and later murdered on the orders of Antonius at Cleopatra's behest in 41 BCE.

Cleopatra and Julius Caesar (*c.* 100–44 BCE) allegedly had a son, Ptolemy XV Caesarion ('Little Caesar', b. 47 BCE), although there were Romans who doubted the truth of it. In *Life of* Divus *Julius*, Suetonius writes, 'according to certain Greek writers, this child was very like Caesar in looks and carriage', and notes that 'Marcus Antonius declared to the Senate that Caesar had really acknowledged the boy, and that Caius Matius, Caius Oppius and other friends of Caesar knew this'. Suetonius adds, 'Of these Caius Oppius, as if admitting that the situation required apology and defence, published a book to prove that the child whom Cleopatra fathered on Caesar was *not* his'.

Cleopatra had three children with Antonius: the twins Alexander Helios ('Sun') and Cleopatra Selene ('Moon') II and their brother Ptolemy Philadelphus ('Brother-loving').

CLEOPATRA'S APPEARANCE

By historical reputation, Cleopatra was physically beautiful. In *Roman History* Cassius Dio writes, 'For she was a woman of surpassing beauty, and at that time, when she was in the prime of her youth, she was most striking'. In *Life of Antony*, published a century earlier, Plutarch observes less effusively, 'For her beauty, as we are told, was in itself not altogether incomparable, nor such as to strike those who saw her'. In *Civil Wars*, Appian remarks that Julius Caesar 'placed a beautiful image of Cleopatra by the side of the goddess' in the Temple of Venus Genetrix and comments that Antonius was 'amazed at her wit as well as her good looks'. In his *Epitome*, Florus records that Julius Caesar 'was moved by the beauty of the damsel, which was enhanced by the fact that, being so fair, she seemed to have been wronged'.

Coins of Cleopatra's reign minted at Alexandria during the 30s BCE show her profile on the obverse, sometimes with Antonius or an eagle on the reverse. Rather than as a glamorous queen or the goddess Isis, Cleopatra appears as a stern head of state. She has a high forehead, a prominent aquiline nose, firmly shut mouth and a strong chin. Her hair is brushed back, held in place with a diadem band and tied in a bun with a fillet. The accompanying text in Greek letters reads *ΒΑΣΙΛΙΣΣΗΣ ΚΛΕΟΠΑΤΡΑΣ* ('OF QUEEN CLEOPATRA'). Another coin, minted to celebrate Antonius's campaign in Armenia, shows a draped bust of Cleopatra wearing a diadem, along with the Latin text *CLEOPATRAE REGINAE REGVM FILIORVM REGVM* ('CLEOPATRA, QUEEN OF KINGS, OF SONS BEING KINGS'). Both issues leave no doubt as to her identity. They also project how she wished to be portrayed.

Using these coins as references, statue busts have been identified as Cleopatra. One (Inv. No. 1976.1) is in the collections of the Altes Museum, Berlin. It closely resembles the portrait on the coins, with the hair knotted at the neck and tiny curls on the forehead. Another (Inv. No. 1879,0712.15) is in the British Museum, London. In this the queen is depicted with her hair brought in waves to each side with a long plait, coiled at the back of the head.

A portrait believed to be of Cleopatra has been found painted on the wall of a house at the Roman seaside resort town of Herculaneum in Campania, Italy. The side-profile of the woman has Cleopatra's distinct facial features but with red hair, secured in place with a diadem and pearl-studded hairpins. Her skin is white. This portrait is now in the collections of the National Archaeological Museum of Naples (MANN, Inv. No. 9091).

CLEOPATRA'S EGYPT

As queen, Cleopatra took an active interest in the administration of her kingdom. Assessing and collecting the wealth of her realm, both in kind and in money, along with the process of registering and documenting it, was the purpose of the state bureaucracy. From her father she inherited the administrative service, a complex blend of Egyptian, Saite, Persian and Greek practices and procedures that had evolved over time. Headquartered in Alexandria, this service was a hierarchy of officials with various titles and differing functions. In the city were located the most senior officials, among whom was the *dioiketes*, the chief economic officer of Egypt; he was appointed directly by the king or queen. Such was Pothinus (Potheinos, early first century BCE–48 or 47 BCE), described by Plutarch as having 'most influence at court [of Ptolemy XIII]'. Cassius Dio, meanwhile, describes Pothinus as 'a eunuch who was charged with the management of Ptolemy's funds'. Plutarch also mentions the eunuch Mardion as being among the leading members of the staff of Antonius and Cleopatra.

The *nome* was the basic administrative unit, of which there were around 40 in total, each divided into toparchies and tax districts. Villages were the smallest administrative units. Officials at the *nome* level had some autonomy, but they were accountable to the central administration in Alexandria. They included the *nomarchos* (responsible for agricultural production), the *oikonomos* (finance) and the *basilikos grammateus* (record keeping), each with a staff of assistants. At the village level the office was supervised by an *epistastes* ('overseer').

The administration relied on written records, meaning that literacy was a crucial requirement for applicants for positions. An ordinance granting exemption from substantial taxes and expenses survives, written by an official on a sheet of papyrus (P.Berol. Inv. 25239). It bears the word γινέσθωι (*ginesthoi*, 'so be it'), which some believe to have been inscribed by Cleopatra herself – though it may equally have been the hand of one of her designated officials. The document is currently kept in the Ägyptisches Museum und Papyrussammlung, Berlin.

Cleopatra was intimately involved in maintaining good international relations between Egypt, Rome and other nations. Diplomatic relations were first opened with Rome in 273 BCE when Ptolemy II Philadelphus sent an embassy to the city, then a rising Mediterranean power. During the Punic Wars (264–146

BCE) Egypt remained true to its treaty obligations with the Romans. By the first century BCE Egypt was a client state with Rome as its patron. When Ptolemy XII Auletes needed help, he escaped to Rome. When Ptolemy XIII and Cleopatra vied for supremacy (marriage did not mean they ruled as a team; they still did not trust each other), they turned to Julius Caesar. To be seen sailing down the Nile with Caesar aboard the royal barge (*thalamegos*) was a public show of his support for the queen, gaining her the prestige of having the friendship of the most powerful man in Rome.

As Abbott explains, one reason Cleopatra was keen to escape from Actium was her ships, which carried the treasure of Egypt. A compelling incentive for Octavian to capture Egypt was to secure its vast wealth and productive capacity. He had financed his campaign against Antonius and Cleopatra with loans from prominent citizens and his troops were owed back-pay. With the taking of Alexandria in 30 BCE, Egypt's riches became Octavian's property.

CLEOPATRA'S GENIUS FOR POLITICAL RELATIONSHIPS

Cleopatra was skilled at diplomacy rather than military strategy. Her actions suggest that her primary aim was to preserve the independence of the kingdom of Egypt. Her secondary goal was to ensure the unbroken rule of the Ptolemaic dynasty.

Cleopatra was an intellectual and a sophisticated woman. In addition to Greek and Egyptian, Plutarch records in his *Life of Antony* that she could converse without requiring an interpreter with 'Ethiopians, Troglodytes, Hebrews, Arabians, Syrians, Medes or Parthians'. She used her talents to promote her interest with the leading powers and men of her day – Julius Caesar, Marcus Antonius and even Octavian.

She realized that Julius Caesar was crucial to her securing her position as queen. Intent on meeting him but blocked from entering the royal palace by guards of her brother, she had herself smuggled into the building. The ruse involved a bag or sack of bedclothes, not a carpet or rug as is popularly believed. Her seeming willingness to sleep with Caesar, and later with Antonius, led Roman historians to characterize her as a woman of strong desire. They claimed she was driven by 'insatiable passion [for Antonius]' (Plutarch) or 'overcome with love [for Herod the Great]' (Josephus). Sex was considered a legitimate tool for developing political relationships, just as marriages of the time were often not for love but convenient allegiances, used to bind families for political advancement or financial gain.

Cleopatra's aim may have been to become queen with Caesar, or with their son, as co-rulers of a combined empire of Egypt and Rome. However, her appearances in Rome in 46 BCE with Ptolemy XV Caesarion and in 45 BCE with Ptolemy XIV Philopator were ill-timed or ill-judged. While she was courting the leading men of Rome – senator Cicero met with her and detested her for her regal manners – her paramour Caesar was aspiring to autocratic power. When he was made *Dictator Perpetuo* (that is, for the rest of his life) in January 44 BCE, there were senators who feared that he wanted to be king. Such a concept was anathema to a society which had killed its last king in 509 BCE and founded a *Res Publica* ('Commonwealth') in reaction to it. The result was Caesar's assassination on the Ides (15) of March 44 BCE. Now without her patron, Cleopatra fled the city with her son.

In his will, Caesar had adopted his great-nephew as his heir. Known in history books as Octavian, following the deification of Caesar in 42 BCE, he adopted the name *Imperator* Caesar Divi Filius ('Commander' Caesar 'Son of God'). In the decade that followed, political turmoil arose in Rome as factions supporting Octavian and Antonius jockeyed for control of the *Res Publica*.

Following the Ides of March, civil war ensued. Brutus and Cassius (the men responsible for the assassination of Caesar) were hunted down; both died at Philippi in October 42 BCE. Emerging as a powerful man was Marcus Antonius (83–30 BCE), who had served Caesar. Together with Octavian (63 BCE–14 CE) and Marcus Aemilius Lepidus (*c.* 89–13/12 BCE), he formed a commission of three men (known as *triumviri*) to reconstitute Rome. Octavian took Italy and the provinces in the west, Lepidus Sicily and Africa, and Antonius all the territories in the east.

Antonius was ambitious to conquer Parthia. That meant he needed men, matériel and money. For these he looked to Egypt, which meant gaining the support of Cleopatra. For her it represented a new opportunity to fulfil her ambitions with support of a Roman patron. It was to prove a fateful partnership. She gave him cash, but not troops or ships. Though regarded as a talented field commander, his expeditions in Armenia and Parthia failed spectacularly. However, through Antonius, Cleopatra acquired Syria, Cyprus and Judaea for Egypt in 34 BCE, the result of the so-called 'Donations of Alexandria'. She also had children by him, founding a new Antonian-Ptolemaic dynasty.

When Octavian offered his sister Octavia to Antonius as his wife, he thought the political arrangement which split the Roman Empire three ways could be saved. However, preferring to be with Cleopatra, Antonius later sent Octavia away, insulting both her and her brother. A military conflict was bound to happen between the two men. The Roman Senate declared war against Cleopatra; by fighting a war with a foreigner, Octavian avoided the appearance of another civil war and so won support for it from the Senate. Despite having the larger force, Antonius and Cleopatra were defeated in the Actian War, with its culmination in the Battle of Actium on 2 September 31 BCE, by Octavian, assisted by the brilliant military tactician Marcus Agrippa. To save her fleet and the treasure of Egypt, Cleopatra fled the battle. Antonius followed her, abandoning the rest of the navy and the army to its fate. It proved a catastrophic decision. Following their subsequent defeat in the Alexandrian War on 1 August 30 BCE, Cleopatra's dream of a united Roman-Egyptian Empire lay in ruins. Her only remaining option was to try and save her children and so preserve the Ptolemaic dynasty.

Within a month of the fall of Alexandria, Caesarion was betrayed and murdered. Cleopatra's other children were taken to Rome and raised by Octavia. While Cleopatra was the last queen of an independent Egypt, however, she was not the last Ptolemy to rule. Her daughter Cleopatra Selene II married Juba II of Mauretania. Their son Ptolemy was the ruler and the last client king of the Romans there, dying in 40 CE.

CLEOPATRA'S DEATH

To capture Cleopatra alive had been Octavian's hope. In his *Life of* Divus *Augustus*, Suetonius describes how 'He greatly desired to save Cleopatra alive for his triumph, and even had Psylli brought to her, to suck the poison from her wound, since it was thought that she had died from the bite of an asp'. Rather than face the humiliation of such a parade, Cleopatra took her own life on 10 August 30 BCE. She was found lying on a bed, dressed in the guise of the goddess Isis and wearing the combined crown of Upper and Lower Egypt. She was 39 years old.

How she died is disputed. Famously she is reported to have been bitten by an asp, but the toxicity of the venom of that species of snake is insufficient to kill a human. The asp may have been confused with the cobra, one of the most venomous species of snakes in North Africa; it was also the symbol of Egypt, incorporated into the state crown. According to Plutarch, the snake was smuggled into the queen's chamber in a basket of figs; in Dio's account it was hidden in a basket of flowers. Plutarch specifically mentions the queen's evaluation of different poisons, even testing their efficacy on prisoners. Strabo mentions she may have died 'by applying a poisonous ointment'. The marks found on her arm could have been from a snake bite or, as Dio notes, the evidence of punctures of a poison-smeared needle. Either way, a self-administered toxin of some kind would seem to have been the cause of death.

However, rather than suicide, assassination cannot be entirely ruled out. Once Octavian had secured her treasure, he could conceivably dispense with her as a captive. However, he did welcome former kings and war chiefs who sought asylum throughout his reign and let them live peacefully in retirement.

Cleopatra still made an appearance in his Triple Triumph of 29 BCE. On 15 August her twin children, Alexander Helios and Cleopatra Selene II, were paraded as spoils of the Alexandrian War, along with a tableau of Cleopatra's death featuring an effigy of the queen on a couch.

Explorers and archaeologists have long searched for Cleopatra's tomb, assuming there is one to be found. Since 2002 Dr Kathleen Martinez, a former criminal lawyer turned maverick archaeologist from the Dominican Republic, has been directing excavations at Taposiris Magna, located to the west of Alexandria in Egypt. Though the site has produced evidence of a Temple of Isis, the supposed tomb of the celebrated queen remains elusive. However, it is quite possible that her body, along with that of Marcus Antonius, was not mummified but cremated in the Roman fashion, with the ashes then dispersed. This would have avoided the creation of a cult centre, which could later become a rallying point for protests against the Roman occupation of Egypt.

CLEOPATRA'S LEGEND

It has been said that 'History is written by victors'. Octavian's victory over Cleopatra meant that *he* decided how the Egyptian queen would be remembered. He cast the Battle of Actium as the turning point in his – and Rome's – destiny, ensuring that it became one of the iconic events in history. Monuments were erected in the city. By a vote of the Senate, a triumphal arch was erected in the Forum over the *Via Sacra* in Rome between the Temple of *Divus* Julius and the Temple of Castor. Bronze rams from captured ships of Antony's and Cleopatra's fleet were affixed to a new *Rostra* raised in front of the Temple of *Divus* Julius. Overseas, Nicopolis ('Victory City') was established on the site of Octavian's camp at Actium, together with a sanctuary to Apollo bedecked with captured ships' rams. A second Nicopolis was constructed about 8 kilometres (5 miles) east of Alexandria. A series of silver coins celebrated the victory with beautiful reverse-side motifs depicting the goddess Victoria ('Victory') standing on a ship's prow or Octavian in military panoply as the victor, and his youthful profile on the obverse.

Roman poets wrote of Octavian and the naval battle in grandiose terms. The same poets also wrote of the defeated queen in disparaging words. Vergil (Publius Vergilius Maro, 70–19 BCE) described the shield of the Trojan prince Aeneas, upon which were embossed images of Actium. He describes Cleopatra as Antonius's 'shameless Egyptian spouse' who,

In the midst, the Queen,
sounding her native timbrel, wildly calls
her minions to the fight, nor yet can see
two fatal asps behind.

Vergil, *Aeneid* 8.696–697

Aided by Apollo, Octavian and Agrippa sank the enemy's ships, but,

The vanquished Queen
made prayer to all the winds, and more and more
flung out the swelling sail: on wind-swept wave
she fled through dead and dying; her white brow
the Lord of Fire had cunningly portrayed
blanched with approaching doom. Beyond her lay
the large-limbed picture of the mournful Nile,
who from his bosom spread his garments wide,
and offered refuge in his sheltering streams
and broad, blue breast, to all her fallen power.

Vergil, *Aeneid* 8.707–713

Cleopatra was vilified as a depraved enchantress. In his *Elegies* Propertius (Sextus Propertius, 50/45 BCE–after 15 CE) calls her a 'whore queen'. In his *Odes* Horace (Quintus Horatius Flaccus, 65–8 BCE) refers to her as a 'fatal monster', while in *Pharsalia* Lucan (Marcus Annaeus Lucanus, 39–65 CE) describes her as 'Egypt's shame'.

Long after the fall of the Roman Empire, when ancient literature became available in printed books, Cleopatra was rediscovered. Inspired by the Roman historians and poets, painters of the sixteenth through the nineteenth centuries eroticized her image. They often portrayed her as a semi-naked seductress, such as in Jean-Léon Gérôme's *Cléopâtre et César* (1866). Novelists and playwrights also embellished her story to exaggerate the salacious aspects of her love affairs. Thomas North's 1519 translation of *Parallel Lives of the Noble Greeks and Romans* by Plutarch provided William Shakespeare with the inspiration for his Roman tragedies. In *Antony and Cleopatra*, first performed in London in 1607, his queen is sophisticated yet sentimental, sensual yet serious. Enobarbus describes her as having 'infinite variety' and observes that

> *Age cannot wither her, nor custom stale*
> *Her infinite variety. Other women cloy*
> *The appetites they feed, but she makes hungry*
> *Where most she satisfies. For vilest things*
> *Become themselves in her.*
> **William Shakespeare, *Antony and Cleopatra*, Act II, Scene 2**

Shakespeare's play has been performed ever since in theatres around the world. Cleopatra has been the subject of stage plays by other writers, such as *Caesar and Cleopatra* (1898) by Bernard Shaw. Her story has also been turned into screenplays. One of the very first epic movies to be made was *Cleopatra* (1917). The subject was well liked by film studios, which then produced *Cleopatra* (1934) and *Caesar and Cleopatra* (1945). Directed by Joseph L. Mankiewicz, *Cleopatra* (1963) was then the most expensive film ever made, costing Twentieth Century Fox a total of $49 million to produce and market. Attracted by its cast of Hollywood royalty, North American and worldwide audiences spent $98 million at the box office to see it. The story was even repurposed, complete with costumes and sets from the 1963 movie, as a comedy in *Carry On Cleo* (1964). More modest productions made for television followed, including *Antony and Cleopatra* (1972) and *Cleopatra* (1999). The queen has been the subject of documentaries, such as *The Real Antony and Cleopatra* by Channel 4 (2016) and *Cleopatra: Portrait of a Killer* by BBC (2019). The most recent docudrama, *Queen Cleopatra* by Netflix (2023), caused controversy when the lead role in the dramatized segments was played by a Black actor; in protest, the mini-series was banned from being broadcast in Egypt. The queen has been the subject of scholarly study in dozens of biographies, as well as fictionalized retellings in novels, in English and numerous other languages.

Cleopatra, 'The Goddess and The Father-Loving', is now partly a figure of history and partly a figure of fantasy. Her story continues to fascinate us 2,000 years after her death. She has attained immortality as completely as any pharaoh could have wished for.

FURTHER READING

ANCIENT TEXTS

Caesar (trans. Kurt A. Raaflaub), *The Landmark Julius Caesar: The Complete Works: Gallic War, Civil War, Alexandrian War, African War, and Spanish War* (Broadway Books, 2019)

Cassius Dio (trans. Ernest Cary) *Roman History*, Volumes III–VI (Loeb Classical Library, Harvard University Press, 1914–1917)

Plutarch (trans. Philip A. Stadter), *Roman Lives: A Selection of Eight Roman Lives* (Oxford University Press, 2009)

Strabo (trans. Sarah Pothecary), *Strabo's Geography: A Translation for the Modern World* (Princeton University Press, 2024)

MODERN TEXTS

Carandini, Andrea, *Atlas of Ancient Rome* (Princeton University Press, revised edition, 2017)

Chauveau, Michel (trans. David Lorton), *Egypt in the Age of Cleopatra: History and Society under the Ptolemies* (Cornell University Press, 2000)

de la Bédoyère, Guy, *The Fall of Egypt and the Rise of Rome* (Yale University Press, 2024)

Goldsworthy, Adrian, *Antony and Cleopatra* (Weidenfeld and Nicholson, 2010)

Parsons, Peter, *City of the Sharp-Nosed Fish: Greek Lives in Roman Egypt* (Weidenfeld and Nicolson, 2007)

Powell, Lindsay, *Julius Caesar* (Flame Tree Publishing Collector's Editions, 2026)

Scullard, H.H., *From the Gracchi to Nero: A History of Rome 133 BC to AD 68* (Routledge Classics, 2010)

Traina, Giusto, *The Roman World War: From the Ides of March to Cleopatra's Suicide* (Princeton University Press, 2026)

Tyldesley, Joyce, *Cleopatra: Last Queen of Egypt* (Basic Books, 2008)

Lindsay Powell (Introduction, editor) is a historian and author who writes about the conflicts, commanders and campaigns of the ancient world. He edited, and wrote the introductions for, the volumes *Hannibal of Carthage*, *Julius Caesar*, *Cleopatra: Queen of Egypt*, *Roman Ancient Origins* and *Greek Ancient Origins* for Flame Tree Publishing. His critically acclaimed books include the biographies *Marcus Agrippa*, *Eager for Glory*, *Germanicus*, *Tiberius* and *Bar Kokhba*, as well as the military histories *Augustus at War*, *Roman Soldier versus Germanic Warrior, 1st Century AD* and *The Bar Kokhba War, AD 132–136*. He is news editor of *Ancient History* and *Ancient Warfare* magazines. His articles have also appeared in *Military History*, *Strategy and Tactics* and *Desperta Ferro* magazines. Lindsay is a regular guest on the *Ancient Warfare* and *History Hit* podcasts. He is a longtime veteran of the Ermine Street Guard, the world's leading Roman army re-enactment society. He has a BSc (Hons) in managerial and administrative studies from Aston University, England. Born in Cardiff, Wales, he divides his time between Austin, Texas and Wokingham, England.

CLEOPATRA

What follows is an edited version of the text of *Cleopatra* by Jacob Abbott, written in 1879 and published in 1901. It was one of 22 historical biographies that he wrote over a busy career. Each is a complete account of the life and deeds of his famous subject, brim full of enthralling stories of growing up and of an extraordinary career in adulthood, often establishing a legend that persists after death. Spanning the Ancient World to the Renaissance, his biographical studies included Alexander the Great, Hannibal, Julius Caesar, Genghis Khan, Nero, Peter the Great and William the Conqueror.

Jacob Abbott was born on 14 November 1803 in Hallowell, Maine in the United States of America. Graduating from Bowdoin College in 1820, he went on to study at Andover Theological Seminary, then taught at Portland Academy. From 1825 he was a professor at Amhurst College, teaching mathematics and natural philosophy. Over the next 20 years he moved to other schools, becoming principal of the Mount Vernon School for Boys in New York City (1845–48).

A prolific author, Abbott wrote some 180 books and co-authored or edited 31 more. His *Rollo* books about a fictional boy, his associates and their escapades were his most popular works. Abbott's books of history and biography helped to educate and inform generations of Americans. They provided his young readers with studies not just of history, but also of people of character. Having related an episode in his subject's story, he often adds a moralizing comment as a life lesson to his reader, a practice from which modern biographers refrain.

Abbott's biography of Cleopatra is essentially sound. He sets Cleopatra in her times, beginning with the founder of the Ptolemaic dynasty. He tells his subject's life story chronologically, drawing upon the ancient sources, and shares anecdotes and interesting details that make Cleopatra's life story human and compelling. Abbott frames the story of Cleopatra as the victim of a crime. He presents her life as 'determined by the circumstances with which she was surrounded, and the influences which were brought to bear upon her in the soft and voluptuous clime where the scenes of her early life were laid'.

In the text he uses the anglicized form Mark Antony for Marcus Antonius and Octavian for *Imperator* Caesar *Divi Filius* (the official name of Julius Caesar's adopted son).

Jacob Abbott died on 31 October 1879 in Farmington, Maine, aged 75. During his lifetime he had been a witness to profound changes in the world. As the British Empire reached its zenith, the fledgling United States went through its own growth pains. His country survived the War of 1812, then suffered a wrenching Civil War (1861–65) and negotiated a fraught Reconstruction (1865–1877) to address the inequities of slavery, while its people spread from the East Coast to the West in search of gold. By the time of his death the Union had developed into a wealthy industrial nation, able to compete with the Europeans. Abbott's writings are part of the American story too.

CHAPTER I
THE VALLEY OF THE NILE

The Ancient World's Most Powerful Woman

Of all the beautiful women of history, none has left us such convincing proofs of her charms as Cleopatra, for the tide of Rome's destiny, and, therefore, that of the world, turned aside because of her beauty. Julius Caesar, whose legions trampled the conquered world from Canopus to the Thames, capitulated to her, and Mark Antony threw a fleet, an empire and his own honour to the winds to follow her to his destruction. Disarmed at last before the frigid Octavian, she found her peerless body measured by the cold eye of her captor only for the triumphal procession, and the friendly asp alone spared her Rome's crowning ignominy.

A Crime Story

The story of Cleopatra is a story of crime. It is a narrative of the course and the consequences of unlawful love. In her strange and romantic history, we see this passion portrayed with the most complete and graphic fidelity in all its influences and effects; its uncontrollable impulses, its intoxicating joys, its reckless and mad career, and the dreadful remorse and ultimate despair and ruin in which it always and inevitably ends.

Cleopatra was by birth an Egyptian; by ancestry and descent she was a Greek. Thus, while Alexandria and the Delta of the Nile formed the scene of the most important events and incidents of her history, it was the blood of Macedon which flowed in her veins. Her character and action are marked by the genius, the courage, the originality, and the impulsiveness pertaining to the stock from which she sprang. The events of her history, on the other hand, and the peculiar character of her adventures, her sufferings, and her sins, were determined by the circumstances with which she was surrounded, and the influences which were brought to bear upon her in the soft and voluptuous clime where the scenes of her early life were laid.

The Land of Egypt

Egypt has always been considered as physically the most remarkable country on the globe. It is a long and narrow valley of verdure and fruitfulness, completely insulated from the rest of the habitable world. It is more completely insulated, in fact, than any literal island could be, inasmuch as deserts are more impassable than seas. The very existence of Egypt is a most extraordinary phenomenon. If we could but soar with the wings of an eagle into the air, and look down upon the scene, so as to observe the operation of that grand and yet simple process by which this long and wonderful valley, teeming so profusely with animal and vegetable life, has been formed, and is annually revivified and renewed, in the midst of surrounding wastes of silence, desolation, and death, we should gaze upon it with never-ceasing admiration and pleasure. We have not the wings of the eagle, but the generalizations of science furnish us with a sort of substitute for them.

Egypt and the River Nile

It is found at last that both the existence of Egypt itself, and its strange insulation in the midst of boundless tracts of dry and barren sand, depend upon certain remarkable results of the general laws of rain. The water which is taken up by the atmosphere from the surface of the sea and of the land by evaporation, falls again, under certain circumstances, in showers of rain, the frequency and copiousness of which vary very much in different portions of the earth. As a general principle, rains are much more frequent and abundant near the equator than in temperate climes, and they grow less and less so as we approach the poles. This might naturally have been expected; for, under the burning sun of the equator, the evaporation of water must necessarily go on with immensely greater rapidity than in the colder zones, and all the water, which is taken up must, of course, again come down.

The Desert

The most extensive and remarkable rainless region on the earth is a vast tract extending through the interior and northern part of Africa, and the southwestern part of Asia. The Red Sea penetrates into this tract from the south, and thus breaks the outline and continuity of its form, without, however, altering, or essentially modifying its character. It divides it, however, and to the different portions which this division forms, different names have been given. The Asiatic portion is called *Arabia Deserta*; the African tract has received the name of Sahara; while between these two, in the neighbourhood of Egypt, the barren region is called simply *the desert*. The whole tract is marked, however, throughout, with one all-pervading character: the absence of vegetable, and, consequently, of animal life, on account of the absence of rain. The rising of a range of lofty mountains in the centre of it, to produce a precipitation of moisture from the air, would probably transform the whole of the vast waste into as verdant, and fertile, and populous a region as any on the globe.

The Valley of the Nile

As it is, there are no such mountains. The whole tract is nearly level, and so little elevated above the sea, that, at the distance of many hundred miles in the interior, the land rises only to the height of a few hundred feet above the surface of the Mediterranean Sea. Such an ascent as that of a few hundred feet in hundreds of miles would be wholly imperceptible to any ordinary mode of observation; and the great rainless region, accordingly, of Africa and Asia is, as it appears to the traveller, one vast plain, a thousand miles wide and five thousand miles long, with only one considerable interruption to the dead monotony which reigns, with that exception, everywhere over the immense expanse of silence and solitude. The single interval of fruitfulness and life is the Valley of the Nile.

Legendary Source of the Nile

To the south of the great rainless region of which we are speaking, there lie groups and ranges of mountains in Abyssinia, called the Mountains of the Moon. These legendary mountains are near the equator, and the relation which they sustain to the surrounding seas, and to currents of wind which blow in that quarter of the world, is such, that they bring down from the atmosphere, especially in certain seasons of the year, vast and continual torrents of rain. The water which thus falls drenches the mountainsides and deluges the valleys. There is a great portion of it which cannot flow to the southward or eastward toward the sea, as the whole country consists, in those directions, of continuous tracts of elevated land. The rush of water thus turns to the northward, and, pressing on across the desert through the great central valley which we have referred to above, it finds an outlet, at last, in the Mediterranean, at a point two thousand miles distant from the place where the immense condenser drew it from the skies. The river thus created is the Nile. It is formed, in a word, by the surplus waters of a district inundated with rains, in their progress across a rainless desert, seeking the sea.

Editor's Note: The Mountains of the Moon are mythological and date to the attempts by ancient Greek geographers to identify the source of the Nile. In fact, the Nile has two main tributaries. The White Nile has its source in Lake Victoria. The Blue Nile has its source in Lake Tana in the Gish Abay region in the Ethiopian Highlands and is where most of the water of the Nile flowing downstream originates. The two rivers meet at Khartoum, Sudan.

Antiquity of Egypt

Egypt has been occupied by man from the most remote antiquity. The oldest records of the human race, made three thousand years ago, speak of Egypt as ancient then, when they were written. Not only is Tradition silent, but even Fable herself does not attempt to tell the story of the origin of her population. Here stand the oldest and most enduring monuments that human power has ever been able to raise. It is, however, somewhat humiliating to the pride of the race to reflect that the loftiest and proudest, as well as the most permanent and stable of all the works which man has ever accomplished, are but the incidents and adjuncts of a thin stratum of alluvial fertility, left upon the sands by the subsiding waters of summer showers.

The Delta of the Nile

The most important portion of the alluvion of the Nile is the northern portion, where the valley widens and opens toward the sea, forming a triangular plain of about one hundred miles in length on each of the sides, over which the waters of the river flow in a great number of separate creeks and channels. The whole area forms a vast meadow, intersected everywhere with slow-flowing streams of water, and presenting on its surface the most enchanting pictures of fertility, abundance, and beauty. This region is called the Delta of the Nile.

The sea upon the coast is shallow, and the fertile country formed by the deposits of the river seems to have projected somewhat beyond the line of the coast; although, as the land has not advanced perceptibly for the last eighteen hundred years, it may be somewhat doubtful whether the whole of the apparent protrusion is not due to the natural conformation of the coast, rather than to any changes made by the action of the river.

The Delta of the Nile is so level itself, and so little raised above the level of the Mediterranean, that the land seems almost a continuation of the same surface with the sea, only, instead of blue waters topped with white-crested waves, we have broad tracts of waving grain, and gentle swells of land crowned with hamlets and villages. In approaching the coast, the navigator has no distant view of all this verdure and beauty. It lies so low that it continues beneath the horizon until the ship is close upon the shore. The first landmarks, in fact, which the seaman makes are the tops of trees growing apparently out of the water, or the summit of an obelisk, or the capital of a pillar, marking the site of some ancient and dilapidated city.

Pelusiac Mouth of the Nile

The most easterly of the channels by which the waters of the river find their way through the Delta to the sea is called, as it will be seen marked upon the map, the Pelusiac branch. It forms almost the boundary of the fertile region of the Delta on the eastern side. There was an ancient city named Pelusium near the mouth of it. This was, of course, the first Egyptian city reached by those who arrived by land from the eastward, travelling along the shores of the Mediterranean Sea. On account of its thus marking the eastern frontier of the country, it became a point of great importance, and is often mentioned in the histories of ancient times.

Canopic Mouth of the Nile

The westernmost mouth of the Nile, on the other hand, was called the Canopic mouth. The distance along the coast from the Canopic mouth to Pelusium was about a hundred miles. The outline of the coast was formerly, as it still continues to be, very irregular, and the water shallow. Extended banks of sand protruded into the sea, and the sea itself, as if in retaliation, formed innumerable creeks, and inlets, and lagoons in the land. Along this irregular and uncertain boundary, the waters of the Nile and the surges of the Mediterranean kept up an eternal war, with energies so nearly equal, that now, after the lapse of eighteen hundred years since the state of the contest began to be recorded, neither side has been found to have gained any perceptible advantage over the other. The river brings the sands down, and the sea drives them incessantly back, keeping the whole line of the shore in such a condition as to make it extremely dangerous and difficult of access to man.

Ancient Egypt

It will be obvious, from this description of the Valley of the Nile, that it formed a country which was in ancient times isolated and secluded, in a very striking manner, from all the rest of the world. It was wholly shut in by deserts, on every side, by land; and the shoals, and sandbars, and other dangers of navigation which marked the line of the coast, seemed to forbid approach by sea. Here it remained for many ages, under the rule of its own native ancient kings. Its population was peaceful and industrious. Its scholars were famed throughout the world for their learning, their science, and their philosophy.

It was in these ages, before other nations had intruded upon its peaceful seclusion, that the Pyramids were built, and the enormous monoliths carved, and those vast temples reared whose ruined columns are now the wonder of mankind. During these remote ages, too, Egypt was, as now, the land of perpetual fertility and abundance. There would always be corn in Egypt, wherever else famine might rage. The neighbouring nations and tribes in Arabia, Palestine, and Syria, found their way to it, accordingly, across the deserts on the eastern side, when driven by want, and thus opened a way of communication.

Conquests of the Persians and Macedonians – Dynasty of Ptolemy

At length the Persian monarchs, after extending their empire westward to the Mediterranean, found access by the same road to Pelusium, and thence overran and conquered the country. At last, about two hundred and fifty years before the time of Cleopatra, Alexander the Great, when he subverted the Persian Empire, took possession of Egypt, and annexed it, among the other Persian provinces, to his own dominions. At the division of Alexander's empire, after his death, Egypt fell to one of his generals, named Ptolemy. Ptolemy made it his kingdom, and left it, at his death, to his heirs. A long line of sovereigns succeeded him, known in history as the dynasty of the Ptolemies – Greek princes, reigning over an Egyptian realm. Cleopatra was the daughter of the eleventh in the line.

The Ptolemies and Alexandria

The capital of the Ptolemies was Alexandria. Until the time of Alexander's conquest, Egypt had no seaport. There were several landing-places along the coast, but no proper harbour. In fact, Egypt had then so little commercial intercourse with the rest of the world that she scarcely needed any. Alexander's engineers, however, in exploring the shore, found a point not far from the Canopic mouth of the Nile where the water was deep, and where there was an anchorage ground protected by an island. Alexander founded a city there, which he called by his own name. He perfected the harbour by artificial excavations and embankments. A lofty lighthouse was reared, which formed a landmark by day, and exhibited a blazing star by night to guide the galleys of the

Mediterranean in. A canal was made to connect the port with the Nile, and warehouses were erected to contain the stores of merchandise. In a word, Alexandria became at once a great commercial capital. It was the seat, for several centuries, of the magnificent government of the Ptolemies; and so well was its situation chosen for the purposes intended, that it still continues after the lapse of twenty centuries of revolution and change, one of the principal emporiums of the commerce of the East.

CHAPTER II
THE PTOLEMIES

The Dynasty of the Ptolemies, 303–30 BCE

The founder of the dynasty of the Ptolemies – the ruler into whose hands the kingdom of Egypt fell, as has already been stated, at the death of Alexander the Great – was a Macedonian general in Alexander's army. The circumstances of his birth, and the events which led to his entering into the service of Alexander, were somewhat peculiar. His mother, whose name was Arsinoë, was a personal favourite and companion of Philip, king of Macedon, the father of Alexander. Philip at length gave Arsinoë in marriage to a certain man of his court named Lagus. A very short time after the marriage, Ptolemy was born. Philip treated the child with the same consideration and favour that he had evinced toward the mother. The boy was called the son of Lagus, but his position in the royal court of Macedon was as high and honourable, and the attentions which he received were as great, as he could have expected to enjoy if he had been in reality a son of the king. As he grew up, he attained to official stations of considerable responsibility and power.

Philip of Macedon – Aridaeus and Alexander the Great

In the course of time, a certain transaction occurred by means of which Ptolemy involved himself in serious difficulty with Philip, though by the same means he made Alexander very strongly his friend. There was a province of the Persian Empire called Caria, situated in the southwestern part of Asia Minor. The governor of this province had offered his daughter to Philip as the wife of one of his sons named Aridaeus, the half-brother of Alexander. Alexander's mother, who was not the mother of Aridaeus, was jealous of this proposed marriage. She thought that it was part of a scheme for bringing Aridaeus forward into public notice, and finally making him the heir to Philip's throne; whereas she was very earnest that this splendid inheritance should be reserved for her own son. Accordingly, she proposed to Alexander that they should send a secret embassage to the Persian governor and represent to him that it would be much better, both for him and for his daughter, that she should have Alexander instead of Aridaeus for a husband, and induce him, if possible, to demand of Philip that he should make the change.

The Intrigue Discovered

Alexander entered readily into this scheme, and various courtiers, Ptolemy among the rest, undertook to aid him in the accomplishment of it. The embassy was sent. The governor of Caria was very much pleased with the change which they proposed to him. In fact, the whole plan seemed to be going on very successfully toward its accomplishment, when, by some means or other, Philip discovered the intrigue. He went immediately into Alexander's apartment, highly excited with resentment and anger. He had never intended to make Aridaeus, whose birth on the mother's side was obscure and ignoble, the heir to his throne, and he reproached Alexander in the bitterest terms for being of so debased and degenerate a spirit as to desire to marry the daughter of a Persian governor; a man who was, in fact, the mere slave, as he said, of a barbarian king.

Ptolemy Banished – Accession of Alexander the Great

Alexander's scheme was thus totally defeated; and so displeased was his father with the officers who had undertaken to aid him in the execution of it that he banished them all from the kingdom. Ptolemy, in consequence of this decree, wandered about an exile from his country for some years, until at length the death of Philip enabled Alexander to recall him. Alexander succeeded his father as King of Macedon, and immediately made Ptolemy one of his principal generals. Ptolemy rose, in fact, to a very high command in the Macedonian army, and distinguished himself very greatly in all the celebrated conqueror's subsequent campaigns. In the Persian invasion, Ptolemy commanded one of the three grand divisions of the army, and he rendered repeatedly the most signal services to the cause of his master. He was employed on the most distant and dangerous enterprises and was often entrusted with the management of affairs of the utmost importance. He was very successful in all his undertakings. He conquered armies, reduced fortresses, negotiated treaties, and evinced, in a word, the highest degree of military energy and skill. He once saved Alexander's life by discovering and revealing a dangerous conspiracy which had been formed against the king. Alexander had the opportunity to requite this favour, through a divine interposition vouchsafed to him, it was said, for the express purpose of enabling him to evince his gratitude. Ptolemy had been wounded by a poisoned arrow, and when all the remedies and antidotes of the physicians had failed, and the patient was apparently about to die, an effectual means of cure was revealed to Alexander in a dream, and Ptolemy, in his turn, was saved.

Ptolemy Elevated – Alexander the Great's Death, 323 BCE

At the great rejoicings at Susa, when Alexander's conquests were completed, Ptolemy was honoured with a golden crown, and he was married, with great pomp and ceremony, to Artacama, the daughter of one of the most distinguished Persian generals.

At length Alexander died suddenly, after a night of drinking and carousal at Babylon. He had no son old enough to succeed him, and his immense empire was divided among his generals. Ptolemy obtained Egypt for his share. He repaired immediately to Alexandria with a great army and a great number of Greek attendants and followers, and there commenced a reign which continued, in great prosperity and splendour, for forty years. The native Egyptians were reduced, of course, to subjection and bondage. All the offices in the army, and all stations of trust and responsibility in civil life, were filled by Greeks. Alexandria was a Greek city, and it became at once one of the most important commercial centres in all those seas. Greek and

Roman travellers found now a language spoken in Egypt which they could understand, and philosophers and scholars could gratify the curiosity which they had so long felt, in respect to the institutions, and monuments, and wonderful physical characteristics of the country, with safety and pleasure. In a word, the organization of a Greek government over the ancient kingdom, and the establishment of the great commercial relations of the city of Alexandria, conspired to bring Egypt out from its concealment and seclusion, and to open it in some measure to the intercourse, as well as to bring it more fully under the observation, of the rest of mankind.

Ptolemy I Soter Becomes King of Egypt

Ptolemy, in fact, made it a special object of his policy to accomplish these ends. He invited Greek scholars, philosophers, poets, and artists, in great numbers, to come to Alexandria, and to make his capital their abode. He collected an immense library, which subsequently, under the name of the Alexandrian library, became one of the most celebrated collections of books and manuscripts that was ever made. We shall have occasion to refer more particularly to this library in the next chapter.

Character of Ptolemy I's Reign – Ptolemy I's Abdication and Death – Accession of Ptolemy II Philadelphus

Besides prosecuting these splendid schemes for the aggrandizement of Egypt, King Ptolemy was engaged, during almost the whole period of his reign, in waging incessant wars with the surrounding nations. He engaged in these wars, in part, for the purpose of extending the boundaries of his empire, and in part for self-defence against the aggressions and encroachments of other powers. He finally succeeded in establishing his kingdom on the most stable and permanent basis, and then, when he was drawing toward the close of his life, being in fact over eighty years of age, he abdicated his throne in favour of his youngest son, whose name was also Ptolemy. Ptolemy the father, the founder of the dynasty, is known commonly in history by the name of Ptolemy Soter. His son is called Ptolemy Philadelphus. This son, though the youngest, was preferred to his brothers as heir to the throne on account of his being the son of the most favoured and beloved of the monarch's wives. The determination of Soter to abdicate the throne himself arose from his wish to put this favourite son in secure possession of it before his death, in order to prevent the older brothers from disputing the succession. The coronation of Philadelphus was made one of the most magnificent and imposing ceremonies that royal pomp and parade ever arranged. Two years afterwards, Ptolemy the father died and was buried by his son with a magnificence almost equal to that of his own coronation. His body was deposited in a splendid mausoleum, which had been built for the remains of Alexander; and so high was the veneration which was felt by mankind for the greatness of his exploits and the splendour of his reign, that divine honours were paid to his memory. Such was the origin of the great dynasty of the Ptolemies.

Degeneracy of the Ptolemies – Incestuous Marriages of the Ptolemy Family

Some of the early sovereigns of the line followed in some degree the honourable example set them by the distinguished founder of it; but this example was soon lost and was succeeded by the most extreme degeneracy and debasement. The successive sovereigns began soon to live and to reign solely for the gratification of their own sensual propensities and passions. Sensuality begins sometimes with kindness, but it ends always in the most reckless and intolerable cruelty. The Ptolemies became, in the end, the most abominable and terrible tyrants that the principle of absolute and irresponsible power ever produced. There was one vice in particular, a vice which they seem to have adopted from the Asiatic nations of the Persian Empire, that resulted in the most awful consequences. This vice was incest.

The Persian sovereigns were, however, above all law, and every species of incestuous marriage was practised by them without shame. The Ptolemies followed their example.

Ptolemy VIII Euergetes II Tryphon ('Physcon') – Origin of his Name

One of the most striking exhibitions of the nature of incestuous domestic life which is afforded by the whole dismal panorama of pagan vice and crime is presented in the history of the great-grandfather of the Cleopatra who is the principal subject of this narrative. He was Ptolemy Physcon, the seventh in the line. It is necessary to give some particulars of his history and that of his family, in order to explain the circumstances under which Cleopatra herself came upon the stage. The name Physcon, which afterwards became his historical designation, was originally given him in contempt and derision. He was very small of stature in respect to height, but his gluttony and sensuality had made him immensely corpulent in body, so that he looked more like a monster than a man. The term Physcon was a Greek word, which denoted opprobriously the ridiculous figure that he made.

Circumstances of Ptolemy Physcon's Accession – Cleopatra I, the Mother

The circumstances of Ptolemy Physcon's accession to the throne afford not only a striking illustration of his character, but a very faithful though terrible picture of the manners and morals of the times. He had been engaged in a long and cruel war with his brother, who was king before him, in which he had perpetrated all imaginable atrocities, when at length his brother died, leaving as his survivors his wife, who was also his sister, and a son who was yet a child. This son was properly the heir to the crown. Physcon himself, being a brother, had no claim, as against a son. The name of the queen was Cleopatra. This was, in fact, a very common name among the princesses of the Ptolemaic line. Cleopatra, besides her son, had a daughter, who was at this time a young and beautiful girl. Her name was also Cleopatra. She was, of course, the niece, as her mother was the sister, of Physcon.

Ptolemy Physcon's Perfidity

The plan of Cleopatra the mother, after her husband's death, was to make her son the king of Egypt, and to govern herself, as regent, until he should become of age. The friends and adherents of Physcon, however, formed a strong party in *his* favour. They sent for him to come to Alexandria to assert his claims to the throne. He came, and a new civil war was on the point of breaking out between the brother and sister, when at length the dispute was settled by a treaty, in which it was stipulated that Physcon should marry Cleopatra and be king; but that he should make the son of Cleopatra by her former husband his heir. This treaty was carried into effect so far as the celebration of the marriage with the mother was concerned, and the establishment of Physcon upon the throne. But the perfidious monster, instead of keeping his faith in respect to the boy, determined to murder him; and so open and brutal were his habits of violence and cruelty that he undertook to perpetrate the deed himself, in open day. The boy fled shrieking to the mother's arms for protection, and Physcon stabbed and killed him there, exhibiting the spectacle of a newly married husband murdering the son of his wife in her very arms!

Ptolemy Physcon Marries His Wife's Daughter, Cleopatra II

It is easy to conceive what sort of affection would exist between a husband and a wife after such transactions as these. In fact, there had been no love between them from the beginning. The marriage had been solely a political arrangement. Physcon hated his wife, and had murdered her son, and then, as if to complete the exhibition of the brutal lawlessness and capriciousness of his passions, he ended with falling in love with her daughter. The beautiful girl looked upon this heartless monster, as ugly and deformed in body as he was in mind, with absolute horror. But she was wholly in his power. He compelled her, by violence, to submit to his will. He repudiated the mother and forced the daughter to become his wife.

Atrocities of Ptolemy Physcon – His Flight

Physcon displayed the same qualities of brutal tyranny and cruelty in the treatment of his subjects that he manifested in his own domestic relations. The particulars we cannot here give but can only say that his atrocities became at length absolutely intolerable, and a revolt so formidable broke out that he fled from the country. In fact, he barely escaped with his life, as the mob had surrounded the palace and were setting it on fire, intending to burn the tyrant himself and all the accomplices of his crimes together. Physcon, however, contrived to make his escape. He fled to the island of Cyprus, taking with him a certain beautiful boy, his son by the Cleopatra whom he had divorced; for they had been married long enough before the divorce to have a son. The name of this boy was Memphitis. His mother was very tenderly attached to him, and Physcon took him away on this very account, to keep him as a hostage for his mother's good behaviour. He fancied that, when he was gone, she might possibly attempt to resume possession of the throne.

Cleopatra II Assumes the Government

His expectations in this respect were realized. The people of Alexandria rallied around Cleopatra and called upon her to take the crown. She did so, feeling, perhaps, some misgivings in respect to the danger which such a step might possibly bring upon her absent boy. She quieted herself, however, by the thought that he was in the hands of his own father, and that he could not possibly come to harm.

Cleopatra II's Birthday

After some little time had elapsed, and Cleopatra was beginning to be well established in her possession of the supreme power at Alexandria, her birthday approached, and arrangements were made for celebrating it in the most magnificent manner. When the day arrived, the whole city was given up to festivities and rejoicing. Grand entertainments were given in the palace, and games, spectacles, and plays in every variety, were exhibited, and performed in all quarters of the city. Cleopatra herself was enjoying a magnificent entertainment, given to the lords and ladies of the court and the officers of her army, in one of the royal palaces.

Barbarity of Ptolemy Physcon – Cleopatra II's Grief

In the midst of this scene of festivity and pleasure, it was announced to the queen that a large box had arrived for her. The box was brought into the apartment. It had the appearance of containing some magnificent present, sent in at that time by some friend in honour of the occasion. The curiosity of the queen was excited to know what the mysterious coffer might contain. She ordered it to be opened; and the guests gathered around, each eager to obtain the first glimpse of the contents. The lid was removed, and a cloth beneath it was raised, when, to the unutterable horror of all who witnessed the spectacle, there was seen the head and hands of Cleopatra's beautiful boy, lying among masses of human flesh, which consisted of the rest of his body cut into pieces. The head had been left entire, that the wretched mother might recognize in the pale and lifeless features the countenance of her son. Physcon had sent the box to Alexandria, with orders that it should be retained until the evening of the birthday, and then presented publicly to Cleopatra in the midst of the festivities of the scene. The shrieks and cries with which she filled the apartments of the palace at the first sight of the dreadful spectacle, and the agony of long continued and inconsolable grief which followed, showed how well the cruel contrivance of the tyrant was fitted to accomplish its end.

It gives us no pleasure to write, and we are sure it can give our readers no pleasure to peruse, such shocking stories of bloody cruelty as these. It is necessary, however, to a just appreciation of the character of the great subject of this history that we should understand the nature of the domestic influences that reigned in the family from which she sprang. In fact, it is due, as a matter of simple justice to her, that we should know what these influences were, and what were the examples set before her in her early life; since the privileges and advantages which the young enjoy in their early years, and, on the other hand, the evil influences under which they suffer, are to be taken very seriously into the account when we are passing judgment upon the follies and sins into which they subsequently fall.

General Character of the Ptolemy Family – Ptolemy IX Soter ('Lathyrus') – Terrible Quarrels with His Mother, Cleopatra III

The monster Physcon lived, it is true, two or three generations before the great Cleopatra; but the character of the intermediate generations, until the time of her birth, continued much the same. In fact, the cruelty, corruption, and vice which reigned in every branch of the royal family increased rather than diminished. The beautiful niece of Physcon, who, at the time of her compulsory marriage with him, evinced such an aversion to the monster, had become, at the period of her husband's death, as great a monster of ambition, selfishness, and cruelty as he. She had two sons, Lathyrus and Alexander. Physcon, when he died, left the kingdom of Egypt to her by will, authorizing her to associate with her in the government whichever of these two sons she might choose. The oldest was best entitled to this privilege, by his priority of birth; but she preferred the youngest, as she thought that her own power would be more absolute in reigning in conjunction with him, since he would be more completely under her control. The leading powers, however, in Alexandria, resisted this plan, and insisted on Cleopatra's associating her oldest son, Lathyrus, with her in the government of the realm. They compelled her to recall Lathyrus from the banishment into which she had sent him, and to put him nominally upon the throne. Cleopatra yielded to this necessity, but she forced her son to repudiate his wife, and to take, instead, another woman, whom she fancied she could make more subservient to her will. The mother and the son went on together for a time, Lathyrus being nominally king, though her determination that she would rule, and his struggles to resist her intolerable tyranny, made their wretched household the scene of terrible and perpetual quarrels. At last Cleopatra seized a number of Lathyrus's servants, the eunuchs who were employed in various offices about the palace, and after wounding and mutilating them in a horrible manner, she exhibited them to the populace, saying that it was Lathyrus that had inflicted the cruel injuries upon the sufferers, and calling upon them to arise and punish him for his crimes. In this and in other similar ways she awakened among the people of the court and of the city such an animosity against Lathyrus, that they expelled him from the country. There followed a long series of cruel and bloody wars between the mother and the son, in the course of which each party perpetrated against the other almost every imaginable deed of atrocity and crime. Alexander, the youngest son, was so afraid of his terrible mother, that he did not dare to remain in Alexandria with her but went into a sort of banishment of his own accord. He, however, finally returned to Egypt. His mother immediately supposed that he was intending to disturb her possession of power and resolved to destroy him. He became acquainted with her designs, and, grown desperate by the long-continued pressure of her intolerable tyranny, he resolved to bring the anxiety and terror in which he lived to an end by killing her. This he did, and then fled the country. Lathyrus, his brother, then returned, and reigned for the rest of his days in a tolerable degree of quietness and peace. At length Lathyrus died, and left the kingdom to his son, Ptolemy Auletes, who was the great Cleopatra's father.

Cleopatra III's Daughters, Cleopatra IV and Tryphaena – Unnatural War

Cleopatra had two daughters, who were the consistent and worthy followers of such a mother. A passage in the lives of these sisters illustrates very forcibly the kind of sisterly affection which prevailed in the family of the Ptolemies. The case was this:

There were two princes of Syria, a country lying northeast of the Mediterranean Sea, and so not very far from Egypt, who, though they were brothers, were in a state of most deadly hostility to each other. One had attempted to poison the other, and afterwards a war had broken out between them, and all Syria was suffering from the ravages of their armies. One of the sisters, of whom we have been speaking, married one of these princes. Her name was Tryphaena. After some time, while the unnatural war was still raging between the two brothers, Cleopatra, the other sister – the same Cleopatra, in fact, who had been divorced from Lathyrus at the instance of his mother – espoused the other brother. Tryphaena was exceedingly incensed against Cleopatra for marrying her husband's mortal foe, and the implacable hostility and hate of the sisters was thenceforth added to that which the brothers had before exhibited, to complete the display of unnatural and parricidal passion which this shameful contest presented to the world.

Tryphaena's Hatred of Her Sister

In fact, Tryphaena from this time seemed to feel a new and highly excited interest in the contest, from her eager desire to revenge herself on her sister. She watched the progress of it and took an active part in pressing forward the active prosecution of the war. The party of her husband, either from this or some other causes, seemed to be gaining the day. The husband of Cleopatra was driven from one part of the country to another, and at length, in order to provide for the security of his wife, he left her in Antioch, a large and strongly fortified city, where he supposed that she would be safe, while he himself was engaged in prosecuting the war in other quarters where his presence seemed to be required.

The Siege of Antioch – Cleopatra IV Flees to a Temple

On learning that her sister was at Antioch, Tryphaena urged her husband to attack the place. He accordingly advanced with a strong detachment of the army, and besieged and took the city. Cleopatra would, of course, have fallen into his hands as a captive; but, to escape this fate, she fled to a temple for refuge. A temple was considered, in those days, an inviolable sanctuary. The soldiers accordingly left her there. Tryphaena, however, made a request that her husband would deliver the unhappy fugitive into her hands. She was determined, she said, to kill her. Her husband remonstrated with her against this atrocious proposal. "It would be a wholly useless act of cruelty," said he, "to destroy her life. She can do us no possible harm in the future progress of the war, while to murder her under these circumstances will only exasperate her husband and her friends, and nerve them with new strength for the remainder of the contest. And then, besides, she has taken refuge in a temple; and if we violate that sanctuary, we shall incur, by such an act of sacrilege, the implacable displeasure of Heaven. Consider, too, that she is your sister, and for you to kill her would be to commit an unnatural and wholly inexcusable crime."

So saying, he commanded Tryphaena to say no more upon the subject, for he would on no account consent that Cleopatra should suffer any injury whatever.

Tryphaena's Resentment Increases – Cruel and Sacrilegious Murder

This refusal on the part of her husband to comply with her request only inflamed Tryphaena's insane resentment and anger the more. In fact, the earnestness with which he espoused her sister's cause, and the interest which he seemed to feel in her fate, aroused Tryphaena's jealousy. She believed, or pretended to believe, that her husband was influenced by a sentiment of love in so warmly defending her. The object of her hate, from being simply an enemy, became now, in her view, a rival, and she resolved that, at all hazards, she should be destroyed. She accordingly ordered a body of desperate soldiers to break into the temple and seize her. Cleopatra fled in terror to the altar and clung to it with such convulsive force that the soldiers cut her hands off before they could tear her away, and then, maddened by her resistance and the sight of blood, they stabbed her again and again upon the floor of the temple, where she fell. The appalling shrieks with which the wretched victim filled the air in the first moments of her flight and her terror subsided as her life ebbed away, into the most awful imprecations of the judgments of Heaven upon the head of the unnatural sister whose implacable hate had destroyed her.

CHAPTER III
ALEXANDRIA

Internal Administration of the Ptolemies

It must not be imagined by the reader that the scenes of vicious indulgence, and reckless cruelty and crime, which were exhibited with such dreadful frequency, and carried to such an enormous excess in the palaces of the Egyptian kings, prevailed to the same extent throughout the mass of the community during the period of their reign. The internal administration of government, and the institutions by which the industrial pursuits of the mass of the people were regulated, and peace and order preserved, and justice enforced between man and man, were all this time in the hands of men well qualified, on the whole, for the trusts committed to their charge, and in a good degree faithful in the performance of their duties; and thus the ordinary affairs of government, and the general routine of domestic and social life, went on, notwithstanding the profligacy of the kings, in a course of very tolerable peace, prosperity, and happiness.

The Industry of the People – Its Happy Effects

During every one of the three hundred years over which the history of the Ptolemies extends, the whole length and breadth of the land of Egypt exhibited, with comparatively few interruptions, one widespread scene of busy industry. The inundations came at their appointed season, and then regularly retired. The boundless fields which the waters had fertilized were then everywhere tilled. The lands were ploughed; the seed was sown; the canals and watercourses, which ramified from the river in every direction over the ground, were opened or closed, as the case required, to regulate the irrigation. The inhabitants were busy, and, consequently, they were virtuous. And as the sky of Egypt is seldom or never darkened by clouds and storms, the scene presented to the eye the same unchanging aspect of smiling verdure and beauty, day after day, and month after month, until the ripened grain was gathered into the storehouses, and the land was cleared for another inundation.

The Greatness of Alexandria

While the most extreme and abominable wickedness seemed to hold continual and absolute sway in the palaces of the Ptolemies, and among the nobles of their courts, the working ministers of state, and the men on whom the actual governmental functions devolved, discharged their duties with wisdom and fidelity, and throughout all the ordinary ranks and gradations of society there prevailed generally a very considerable degree of industry, prosperity and happiness. This prosperity prevailed not only in the rural districts of the Delta and along the Valley of the Nile, but also among the merchants, and navigators, and artisans of Alexandria.

The Situation of Alexandria's Port

Alexandria became, in fact, very soon after it was founded, a very great and busy city. Many things conspired to make it at once a great commercial emporium. In the first place, it was the depot of export for all the surplus grain and other agricultural produce which was raised in such abundance along the Egyptian valley. This produce was brought down in boats to the upper point of the Delta, where the branches of the river divided, and thence down the Canopic branch to the city. The city was not, in fact, situated directly upon this branch, but upon a narrow tongue of land, at a little distance from it, near the sea. It was not easy to enter the channel directly, on account of the bars and sandbanks at its mouth, produced by the eternal conflict between the waters of the river and the surges of the sea. The water was deep, however, as Alexander's engineers had discovered, at the place where the city was built, and, by establishing the port there, and then cutting a canal across to the Nile, they were enabled to bring the river and the sea at once into easy communication.

Warehouses and Granaries

The produce of the Valley was thus brought down the river and through the canal to the city. Here immense warehouses and granaries were erected for its reception, that it might be safely preserved until the ships that came into the port were ready to take it away. These ships came from Syria, from all the coasts of Asia Minor, from Greece, and from Rome. They brought the agricultural productions of their own countries, as well as articles of manufacture of various kinds; these they sold to the merchants of Alexandria and purchased the productions of Egypt in return.

The Business of the Port

The port of Alexandria presented thus a constant picture of life and animation. Merchant ships were continually coming and going or lying at anchor in the roadstead. Seamen were hoisting sails, or raising anchors, or rowing their capacious galleys through the water, singing, as they pulled, to the motion of the oars. Within the city there was the same ceaseless activity. Here groups of men were unloading the canal boats which had arrived from the river. There porters were transporting bales of merchandise or sacks of grain from a warehouse to a pier, or from one landing to another. The occasional parading of the king's guards, or the arrival and departure of ships of war to land or to take away bodies of armed men, were occurrences that sometimes intervened to interrupt, or as perhaps the people then would have said, to adorn this scene of useful industry; and now and then, for a brief period, these peaceful vocations would be wholly suspended and set aside by a revolt or by a civil war, waged by rival brothers against each other, or instigated by the conflicting claims of a mother and son. These interruptions, however, were comparatively few, and, in ordinary cases, not of long continuance. It was for the interest of all branches of the royal line to do as little injury as possible to the commercial and agricultural operations of the realm. In fact, it was on the prosperity of those operations that the revenues depended. The rulers were well aware of this, and so, however implacably two rival princes may have hated one another, and however desperately each party may have struggled to destroy all active combatants whom they should find in arms against them, they were both under every possible inducement to spare the private property and the lives of the peaceful population. This population, in fact, engaged thus in profitable industry, constituted, with the avails of their labours, the very estate for which the combatants were contending.

Seeing the subject in this light, the Egyptian sovereigns, especially Alexander and the earlier Ptolemies, made every effort in their power to promote the commercial greatness of Alexandria. They built palaces, it is true, but they also built warehouses.

The Public Buildings – Ptolemy II Philadelphus – The Lighthouse ('Pharos')

One of the most expensive and celebrated of all the edifices that they reared was the lighthouse which has been already alluded to. This lighthouse was a lofty tower, built of white marble. It was situated upon the island of Pharos, opposite the city, and at some distance from it. There was a sort of isthmus of shoals and sandbars connecting the island with the shore. Over these shallows a pier or causeway was built, which finally became a broad and inhabited neck. The principal part of the ancient city, however, was on the mainland.

The curvature of the earth requires that a lighthouse on a coast should have a considerable elevation, otherwise its summit would not appear above the horizon, unless the mariner were very nearby. To attain this elevation, the architects usually take advantage of some hill or cliff, or rocky eminence near the shore. There was, however, no opportunity to do this at Pharos; for the island was, like the mainland, level and low. The requisite elevation could only be attained, therefore, by the masonry of an edifice, and the blocks of marble necessary for the work had to be brought from a great distance. The Alexandrian lighthouse was reared in the time of Ptolemy Philadelphus, the second monarch in the line. No pains or expense were spared in its construction. The edifice, when completed, was considered one of the seven wonders of the world. It was indebted for its fame, however, in some degree, undoubtedly to the conspicuousness of its situation, rising, as it did, at the entrance of the greatest commercial emporium of its time, and standing there, like a pillar of cloud by day and of fire by night, to attract the welcome gaze of every wandering mariner whose ship came within its horizon, and to awaken his gratitude by tendering him its guidance and dispelling his fears.

The light at the top of the tower was produced by a fire, made of such combustibles as would emit the brightest flame. This fire burned slowly through the day, and then was kindled up anew when the sun went down and was continually replenished through the night with fresh supplies of fuel. In modern times, a much more convenient and economical mode is adopted to produce the requisite illumination. A great blazing lamp burns brilliantly in the centre of the lantern of the tower, and all that part of the radiation from the flame which would naturally have beamed upward, or downward, or laterally, or back toward the land, is so turned by a curious system of reflectors and polyzonal lenses, most ingeniously contrived and very exactly adjusted, as to be thrown forward in one broad and thin, but brilliant sheet of light, which shoots out where its radiance is needed, over the surface of the sea. Before these inventions were perfected, by far the largest portion of the light emitted by the illumination of lighthouse towers streamed away wastefully in landward directions or was lost among the stars.

The Architect of the Pharos – Ruins of the Pharos

Of course, the glory of erecting such an edifice as the Pharos of Alexandria, and of maintaining it in the performance of its functions, was very great; the question might, however, very naturally arise whether this glory was justly due to the architect through whose scientific skill the work was actually accomplished, or to the monarch by whose power and resources the architect was sustained. The name of the architect was Sostratus. He was a Greek. The monarch was, as has already been stated, the second Ptolemy, called commonly Ptolemy Philadelphus. Ptolemy ordered that, in completing the tower, a marble tablet should be built into the wall, at a suitable place near the summit, and that a proper inscription should be carved upon it, with his name as the builder of the edifice conspicuous thereon. Sostratus preferred inserting his own name. He accordingly made the tablet and set it in its place. He cut the inscription upon the face of it, in Greek characters, with his own name as the author of the work. He did this secretly, and then covered the face of the tablet with an artificial composition, made with lime, to imitate the natural surface of the stone. On this outer surface he cut a new inscription, in which he inserted the name of the king. In process of time the lime mouldered away, the king's inscription disappeared, and his own, which thenceforward continued as long as the building endured, came out to view.

The Pharos was said to have been four hundred feet high. It was famed throughout the world for many centuries; nothing, however, remains of it now but a heap of useless and unmeaning ruins.

The Library and Museum of Alexandria

Besides the light that beamed from the summit of this lofty tower, there was another centre of radiance and illumination in ancient Alexandria, which was in some respects still more conspicuous and renowned, namely, an immense library and museum established and maintained by the Ptolemies. The Museum, which was first established, was not, as its name might now imply, a collection of curiosities, but an institution of learning, consisting of a body of learned men, who devoted their time to philosophical and scientific pursuits. The institution was richly endowed, and magnificent buildings were erected for its use. The king who established it began immediately to make a collection of books for the use of the members of the institution. This was attended with great expense, as every book that was added to the collection required to be transcribed with a pen on parchment or papyrus with infinite labour and care. Great numbers of scribes were constantly employed upon this work at the Museum. The kings who were most interested in forming this library would seize the books that were possessed by individual scholars, or that were deposited in the various cities of their dominions, and then, causing beautiful copies of them to be made by the scribes of the Museum, they would retain the originals for the great Alexandrian library, and give the copies to the men or the cities that had been thus despoiled. In the same manner they would borrow, as they called it, from all travellers who visited Egypt, any valuable books which they might have in their possession, and, retaining the originals, give them back copies instead.

The Serapion – Serapis of Egypt – Serapis of Greece

In process of time the library increased to four hundred thousand volumes. There was then no longer any room in the buildings of the Museum for further additions. There was, however, in another part of the city, a great temple called the Serapion. This temple was a very magnificent edifice, or, rather, group of edifices, dedicated to the god Serapis. The origin and history of this temple were very remarkable. The legend was this:

It seems that one of the ancient and long-venerated gods of the Egyptians was a deity named Serapis. He had been, among other divinities, the object of Egyptian adoration ages before Alexandria was built or the Ptolemies reigned. There was also, by a curious coincidence, a statue of the same name at a great commercial town named Sinope, which was built upon the extremity of a promontory which projected from Asia Minor into the Euxine Sea. Sinope was, in some sense, the Alexandria of the north, being the centre and seat of a great portion of the commerce of that quarter of the world.

The Serapis of Sinope was considered as the protecting deity of seamen, and the navigators who came and went to and from the city made sacrifices to him, and offered him oblations and prayers, believing that they were, in a great measure, dependent upon some mysterious and inscrutable power which he exercised for their safety in storms. They carried the knowledge of his name, and tales of his imaginary interpositions, to all the places that they visited; and thus, the fame of the god became extended, first, to all the coasts of the Euxine Sea, and subsequently to distant provinces and kingdoms. The Serapis of Sinope began to be considered everywhere as the tutelary god of seamen.

Ptolemy I Soter's Dream

Accordingly, when the first of the Ptolemies was forming his various plans for adorning and aggrandizing Alexandria, he received, he said, one night, a divine intimation in a dream that he was to obtain the statue of Serapis from Sinope, and set it up in Alexandria, in a suitable temple which he was in the meantime to erect in honour of the god. It is obvious that very great advantages to the city would result from the accomplishment of this design. In the first place, a temple to the god Serapis would be a new distinction for it in the minds of the rural population, who would undoubtedly suppose that the deity honoured by it was their own ancient god. Then the whole maritime and nautical interest of the world, which had been, accustomed to adoring the god of Sinope, would turn to Alexandria as the great centre of religious attraction, if their venerated idol could be carried and placed in a new and magnificent temple built expressly for him there. Alexandria could never be the chief naval port and station of the world unless it contained the sanctuary and shrine of the god of seamen.

Ptolemy I Soter's Proposal to the King of Sinope

Ptolemy sent accordingly to the King of Sinope and proposed to purchase the idol. The embassage was, however, unsuccessful. The king refused to give up the god. The negotiations were continued for two years, but all in vain. At length, on account of some failure in the regular course of the seasons on that coast, there was a famine there, which became finally so severe that the people of the city were induced to consent to give up their deity to the Egyptians in exchange for a supply of corn. Ptolemy sent the corn and received the idol. He then built the temple, which, when finished, surpassed in grandeur and magnificence almost every sacred structure in the world.

Ptolemy II Philadelphus's Way of Acquiring Books

It was in this temple that the successive additions to the Alexandrian library were deposited when the apartments of the Museum became full. In the end there were four hundred thousand rolls or volumes in the Museum, and three hundred thousand in the Serapion. The former was called the parent library, and the latter, being, as it were, the offspring of the first, was called the daughter.

Ptolemy Philadelphus, who interested himself very greatly in collecting this library, wished to make it a complete collection of all the books in the world. He employed scholars to read and study, and travellers to make extensive tours, for the purpose of learning what books existed among all the surrounding nations; and, when he learned of their existence, he spared no pains or expense in attempting to procure either the originals themselves, or the most perfect and authentic copies of them. He sent to Athens and obtained the works of the most celebrated Greek historians, and then causing, as in other cases, most beautiful transcripts to be made, he sent the transcripts back to Athens, and a very large sum of money with them as an equivalent for the difference of value between originals and copies in such an exchange.

Various Other Plans of the Ptolemies

Besides the building of the Pharos, the Museum, and the Temple of Serapis, the early Ptolemies formed and executed a great many other plans tending to the same ends which the erection of these splendid edifices was designed to secure, namely, to concentrate in Alexandria all possible means of attraction, commercial, literary, and religious, so as to make the city the great centre of interest, and the common resort for all mankind. They raised immense revenues for these and other purposes by taxing heavily the whole agricultural produce of the Valley of the Nile. The inundations, by the boundless fertility which they annually produced, supplied the royal treasuries. Thus, the Abyssinian rains at the sources of the Nile built the Pharos at its mouth and endowed the Alexandrian library.

The Ptolemies' Means of Raising Money

The taxes laid upon the people of Egypt to supply the Ptolemies with funds were, in fact, so heavy, that only the bare means of subsistence were left to the mass of the agricultural population. In admiring the greatness and glory of the city, therefore, we must remember that there was a gloomy counterpart to its splendour in the very extended destitution and poverty to which the mass of the people was everywhere doomed. They lived in hamlets of wretched huts along the banks of the river, in order that the capital might be splendidly adorned with temples and palaces. They passed their lives in darkness and ignorance, that seven hundred thousand volumes of expensive manuscripts might be enrolled at the Museum for the use of foreign philosophers and scholars. The policy of the Ptolemies was, perhaps, on the whole, the best, for the general advancement and ultimate welfare of mankind, which could have been pursued in the age in which they lived and acted; but, in applauding the results which they attained, we must not wholly forget the cost which they incurred in attaining them.

The Splendour and Renown of Alexandria – Her Great Rival, Rome

The Ptolemies expended the revenues which they raised by this taxation mainly in a very liberal and enlightened manner, for the accomplishment of the purposes which they had in view. The building of the Pharos, the removal of the statue of Serapis, and the endowment of the Museum and the library were great conceptions, and they were carried into effect in the most complete and perfect manner. All the other operations which they devised and executed for the extension and aggrandizement of the city were conceived and executed in the same spirit of scientific and enlightened liberality. Streets were opened; the most splendid palaces were built; docks, piers, and breakwaters were constructed, and fortresses and towers were armed and garrisoned. Then every means was employed to attract to the city a great concourse from all the most highly civilized nations then existing. The highest inducements were offered to merchants, mechanics, and artisans to make the city their abode. Poets, painters, sculptors, and scholars of every nation and degree were made welcome, and every facility was afforded them for the prosecution of their various pursuits. These plans were all eminently successful. Alexandria rose rapidly to the highest consideration and importance; and, at the time when Cleopatra – born to preside over this scene of magnificence and splendour – came upon the stage, the city had but one rival in the world. That rival was Rome.

CHAPTER IV
CLEOPATRA'S FATHER, 117–51 BCE

Rome, Rival of Alexandria

Rome was perhaps the only city that could be considered the rival of Alexandria, in the estimation of mankind, in respect to interest and attractiveness as a capital. In one respect, Rome was vastly superior to the Egyptian metropolis, and that was in the magnitude and extent of the military power which it wielded among the nations of the earth. Alexandria ruled over Egypt, and over a few of the neighbouring coasts and islands; but in the course of the three centuries during which she had been acquiring her greatness and fame, the Roman Empire had extended itself over almost the whole civilized world.

The Extent of Roman Rule

Egypt had been, thus far, too remote to be directly reached; but the affairs of Egypt itself became involved at length with the operations of the Roman power, about the time of Cleopatra's birth (70/69 BCE), in a very striking and peculiar manner; and as the consequences of the transaction were the means of turning the whole course of the queen's subsequent history, a narration of it is necessary to a proper understanding of the circumstances under which she commenced her career. In fact, it was the extension of the Roman Empire to the limits of Egypt, and the connections which thence arose between the leading Roman generals and the Egyptian sovereign, which have made the story of this particular queen so much more conspicuous, as an object of interest and attention to mankind, than that of any other one of the ten Cleopatras who rose successively in the same royal line.

Cleopatra's Father, Ptolemy XII Neos Dionysus ('Auletes')

Ptolemy Auletes, Cleopatra's father, was perhaps, in personal character, the most dissipated, degraded, and corrupt of all the sovereigns in the dynasty. He spent his whole time in vice and debauchery. The only honest accomplishment that he seemed to possess was his skill in playing upon the flute; of this he was very vain. He instituted musical contests, in which the musical performers of Alexandria played for prizes and crowns; and he himself was accustomed to enter the lists with the rest as a competitor. The people of Alexandria, and the world in general, considered such pursuits as these wholly unworthy the attention of the representative of so illustrious a line of sovereigns, and the abhorrence which they felt for the monarch's vices and crimes was mingled with a feeling of contempt for the meanness of his ambition.

Ptolemy XII's Ignoble Birth

There was a doubt in respect to his title to the crown, for his birth, on the mother's side, was irregular and ignoble. Instead, however, of attempting to confirm and secure his possession of power by a vigorous and prosperous administration of the government, he wholly abandoned all concern in respect to the course of public affairs; and then, to guard against the danger of being deposed, he conceived the plan of getting himself recognized at Rome as one of the allies of the Roman people. If this were once done, he supposed that the Roman government would feel under an obligation to sustain him on his throne in the event of any threatened danger.

The Roman Republic – Pompey and Caesar – Ptolemy Buys the Alliance of Rome

The Roman government was a sort of republic, and the two most powerful men in the state at this time were Pompey and Caesar.

Caesar was in the ascendency at Rome at the time that Ptolemy made his application for an alliance. Pompey was absent in Asia Minor, being engaged in prosecuting a war with Mithradates, a very powerful monarch, who was at that time resisting the Roman power. Caesar was very deeply involved in debt, and was, moreover, very much in need of money, not only for relief from existing embarrassments, but as a means of subsequent expenditure, to enable him to accomplish certain great political schemes which he was entertaining. After many negotiations and delays, it was agreed that Caesar would exert his influence to secure an alliance between the Roman people and Ptolemy, on condition that Ptolemy paid him the sum of six thousand talents. A part of the money, Caesar said, was for Pompey.

Taxes to Raise the Money – Revolt at Alexandria

The title of ally was conferred, and Ptolemy undertook to raise the money which he had promised by increasing the taxes of his kingdom. The measures, however, which he thus adopted for the purpose of making himself the more secure in his possession of the throne, proved to be the means of overthrowing him. The discontent and disaffection of his people, which had been strong and universal before, though suppressed and concealed, broke out now into open violence. That there should be laid upon them, in addition to all their other burdens, these new oppressions, heavier than those which they had endured before, and exacted for such a purpose too, was not to be endured. To be compelled to see their country sold on any terms to the Roman people was sufficiently hard to bear; but to be forced to raise, themselves, and pay the price of the transfer, was absolutely intolerable. Alexandria commenced a revolt. Ptolemy was not a man to act decidedly against such a demonstration, or, in fact, to evince either calmness or courage in any emergency whatever. His first thought was to escape from Alexandria to save his life. His second, to make the best of his way to Rome, to call upon the Roman people to come to the succour of their ally!

Ptolemy XII's Flight from Alexandria

Ptolemy left five children behind him in his flight. The eldest was the Princess Berenice, who had already reached maturity. The second was the great Cleopatra, the subject of this history. Cleopatra was, at this time, about eleven years old. There were also two sons, but they were very young. One of them was named Ptolemy.

Bernice IV – Her Marriage with Seleucus VII Philometor

The Alexandrians determined on raising Berenice to the throne in her father's place, as soon as his flight was known. They thought that the sons were too young to attempt to reign in such an emergency, as it was very probable that Auletes, the father, would attempt to recover his kingdom. Berenice very readily accepted the honour and power which were offered to her. She established herself in her father's palace and began her reign in great magnificence and splendour. In process of time, she thought that her position would be strengthened by a marriage with a royal prince from some neighbouring realm. She first sent ambassadors to make proposals to a prince of Syria named Antiochus. The ambassadors came back, bringing word that Antiochus was dead, but that he had a brother named Seleucus, upon whom the succession fell. Berenice then sent them back to make the same offers to him. He accepted the proposals, came to Egypt, and he and Berenice were married. After trying him for a while, Berenice found that, for some reason or other, she did not like him as a husband, and accordingly she caused him to be strangled.

At length, after various other intrigues and much secret management, Berenice succeeded in a second negotiation, and married a prince, or a pretended prince, from some country of Asia Minor, whose name was Archelaus. She was better pleased with this second husband than she had been with the first, and she began, at last, to feel somewhat settled and established on her throne, and to be prepared, as she thought, to offer effectual resistance to her father in case he should ever attempt to return.

Cleopatra's Early Life

It was in the midst of the scenes, and surrounded by the influences which might be expected to prevail in the families of such a father and such a sister, that Cleopatra spent those years of life in which the character is formed. During all these revolutions, and exposed to all these exhibitions of licentious wickedness, and of unnatural cruelty and crime, she was growing up in the royal palaces a spirited and beautiful, but indulged and neglected child.

Ptolemy XII, an Object of Contempt

In the meantime, Auletes, the father, went on toward Rome. So far as his character and his story were known among the surrounding nations, he was the object of universal obloquy, both on account of his previous career of degrading vice, and now, still more, for this ignoble flight from the difficulties in which his vices and crimes had involved him.

Ptolemy XII's Interview with Cato

He stopped, on the way, at the island of Rhodes. It happened that Cato, the great Roman philosopher and general, was at Rhodes at this time. Cato was a man of stern, unbending virtue, and of great influence at that period in public affairs. Ptolemy sent a messenger to inform Cato of his arrival, supposing, of course, that the Roman general would hasten, on hearing of the fact, to pay his respects to so great a personage as he, a king of Egypt – a Ptolemy – though suffering under a temporary reverse of fortune. Cato directed the messenger to reply that, so far as he was aware, he had no particular business with Ptolemy. "Say, however, to the king," he added, "that, if he has any business with me, he may call and see me, if he pleases."

Cato's Character

Ptolemy was obliged to suppress his resentment and submit. He thought it very essential to the success of his plans that he should see Cato, and secure, if possible, his interest and co-operation; and he consequently made preparations for paying, instead of receiving, the visit, intending to go in the greatest royal state that he could command. He accordingly appeared at Cato's lodgings on the following day, magnificently dressed, and accompanied by many attendants. Cato, who was dressed in the plainest and most simple manner, and whose apartment was furnished in a style corresponding with the severity of his character, did not even rise when the king entered the room. He simply pointed with his hand, and bade the visitor take a seat.

Ptolemy XII's Reception – Cato's Advice

Ptolemy began to make a statement of his case, with a view to obtaining Cato's influence with the Roman people to induce them to interpose on his behalf. Cato, however, far from evincing any disposition to espouse his visitor's cause, censured him, in the plainest terms, for having abandoned his proper position in his own kingdom, to go and make himself a victim and a prey for the insatiable avarice of the Roman leaders. "You can do nothing at Rome," he said, "but by the influence of bribes; and all the resources of Egypt will not be enough to satisfy the Roman greediness for money." He concluded by recommending him to go back to Alexandria and rely for his hopes of extrication from the difficulties which surrounded him on the exercise of his own energy and resolution there.

Ptolemy was greatly abashed at this rebuff, but, on consultation with his attendants and followers, it was decided to be too late now to return. The whole party accordingly re-embarked on board their galleys and pursued their way to Rome.

Ptolemy XII Arrives in Rome – His Application to Pompey – Action of the Roman Senate

Ptolemy found, on his arrival at the city, that Caesar was absent in Gaul, while Pompey, on the other hand, who had returned victorious from his campaigns against Mithradates, was now the great leader of influence and power at the Capitol. This change of circumstances was not, however, particularly unfavourable; for Ptolemy was on friendly terms with Pompey, as he had been with Caesar. He had assisted him in his wars with Mithradates by sending him a squadron of horse, in pursuance of his policy of cultivating friendly relations with the Roman people by every means in his power. Besides, Pompey had received a part of the money which Ptolemy had paid to Caesar as the price of the Roman alliance and was to receive his share of the rest in case Ptolemy should ever be restored. Pompey was accordingly interested in favouring the royal fugitive's cause. He received him in his palace, entertained him in magnificent style, and took immediate measures for bringing his cause before the Roman Senate, urging upon that body the adoption of immediate and vigorous measures for effecting his restoration, as an ally whom they were bound to protect against his rebellious subjects. There was at first some opposition in the Roman Senate against espousing the cause of such a man, but it was soon put down, being overpowered in part by Pompey's authority, and in part silenced by Ptolemy's promises and bribes. The Senate determined to restore the king to his throne and began to make arrangements for carrying the measure into effect.

The Roman provinces nearest to Egypt were Cilicia and Syria, countries situated on the eastern and northeastern coast of the Mediterranean Sea, north of Judea. The forces stationed in these provinces would be, of course, the most convenient for furnishing the necessary troops for the expedition. The province of Cilicia was under the command of the consul Lentulus. Lentulus was at this time at Rome; he had repaired to the capital for some temporary purpose, leaving his province and the troops stationed there under the command, for the time, of a sort of lieutenant general named Gabinius. It was concluded that this Lentulus, with his Syrian forces, should undertake the task of reinstating Ptolemy on his throne.

Plans for Restoring Ptolemy XII to the throne of Egypt – Measures of Bernice – Her Embassy to Rome

While these plans and arrangements were yet immature, a circumstance occurred which threatened, for a time, wholly to defeat them. It seems that when Cleopatra's father first left Egypt, he had caused a report to be circulated there that he had been killed in the revolt. The object of this stratagem was to cover and conceal his flight. The government of Berenice soon discovered the truth and learned that the fugitive had gone in the direction of Rome. They immediately inferred that he was going to appeal to the Roman people for aid, and they determined that, if that were the case, the Roman people, before deciding in his favour, should have the opportunity to hear their side of the story as well as his. They accordingly made preparations at once for sending a very imposing embassage to Rome. The deputation consisted of more than a hundred persons. The object of Berenice's government in sending so large a number was not only to evince their respect for the Roman people, and their sense of the magnitude of the question at issue, but also to guard against any efforts that Ptolemy might make to intercept the embassage on the way, or to buy off the members of it by bribes. The number, however large as it was, proved insufficient to accomplish this purpose. The whole Roman world was at this time in such a condition of disorder and violence, in the hands of the desperate and reckless military leaders who then bore sway, that there were everywhere abundant facilities for the commission of any conceivable crime. Ptolemy contrived, with the assistance of the fierce partisans who had espoused his cause, and who were deeply interested in his success on account of the rewards which were promised them, to waylay and destroy a large proportion of this company before they reached Rome. Some were assassinated; some were poisoned; some were tampered with and bought off by bribes. A small remnant reached Rome; but they were so intimidated by the dangers which surrounded them that they did not dare to take any public action in respect to the business which had been committed to their charge. Ptolemy began to congratulate himself on having completely circumvented his daughter in her efforts to protect herself against his designs.

Ptolemy XII's Treachery – The Prophecy

Instead of that, however, it soon proved that the effect of this atrocious treachery was exactly the contrary of what its perpetrators had expected. The knowledge of the facts became gradually extended among the people of Rome and it awakened a universal indignation. The party who had been originally opposed to Ptolemy's cause seized the opportunity to renew their opposition; and they gained so much strength from the general odium which Ptolemy's crimes had awakened, that Pompey found it almost impossible to sustain his cause.

At length the party opposed to Ptolemy found, or pretended to find, in certain sacred books, called the Sibylline Oracles, which were kept in the custody of the priests, and were supposed to contain prophetic intimations of the will of Heaven in respect to the conduct of public affairs, the following passage:

"If a king of Egypt should apply to you for aid, treat him in a friendly manner, but do not furnish him with troops; for if you do, you will incur great danger."

Its Consequences – Opposition to Ptolemy XII

This made new difficulty for Ptolemy's friends. They attempted, at first, to evade this inspired injunction by denying the reality of it. There was no such passage to be found, they said. It was all an invention of their enemies. This point seems to have been overruled, and then they attempted to give the passage some other than the obvious interpretation. Finally, they maintained that, although it prohibited their furnishing Ptolemy himself with troops, it did not forbid their sending an armed force into Egypt under leaders of their own. *That* they could certainly do; and then, when the rebellion was suppressed, and Berenice's government overthrown, they could invite Ptolemy to return to his kingdom and resume his crown in a peaceful manner. This, they alleged, would not be "furnishing him with troops," and, of course would not be disobeying the oracle.

Attempts to Evade the Oracle – Gabinius Undertakes the Cause

These attempts to evade the direction of the oracle on the part of Ptolemy's friends only made the debates and dissensions between them and his enemies more violent than ever.

Pompey made every effort in his power to aid Ptolemy's cause; but Lentulus, after long hesitation and delay, decided that it would not be safe for him to embark on it. At length, however, Gabinius, the lieutenant who commanded in Syria, was induced to undertake the enterprise. On certain promises which he received from Ptolemy, to be performed in case he succeeded, and with a certain encouragement, not very legal or regular, which Pompey gave him, in respect to the employment of the Roman troops under his command, he resolved to march to Egypt. His route, of course, would lie along the shores of the Mediterranean Sea, and through the desert, to Pelusium, which has already been mentioned as the frontier town on this side of Egypt. From Pelusium he was to march through the heart of the Delta to Alexandria, and, if successful in his invasion, overthrow the government of Berenice and Archelaus, and then, inviting Ptolemy to return, reinstate him on the throne.

Mark Antony – His History – Antony in Greece

In the prosecution of this dangerous enterprise, Gabinius relied strongly on the assistance of a very remarkable man, then his second in command, who afterwards acted a very important part in the subsequent history of Cleopatra. His name was Mark Antony. Antony was born in Rome (83 BCE), of a very distinguished family, but his father died when he was very young, and being left subsequently much to himself, he became a very wild and dissolute young man. He wasted the property which his father had left him in folly and vice; and then going on desperately in the same career, he soon incurred enormous debts, and involved himself, in consequence, in inextricable difficulties.

His creditors continually harassed him with importunities for money, and with suits at law to compel payments which he had no means of making. He was likewise incessantly pursued by the hostility of the many enemies that he had made in the city by his violence and his crimes. At length he absconded and went to Greece.

Antony Joins Gabinius

Here Gabinius, when on his way to Syria, met him, and invited him to join his army rather than to remain where he was in idleness and destitution. Antony, who was as proud and lofty in spirit as he was degraded in morals and condition, refused to do this unless Gabinius would give him a command. Gabinius saw in the daring and reckless energy which Antony manifested the indications of the class of qualities which in those days made a successful soldier and acceded to his terms. He gave him the command of his cavalry. Antony distinguished himself in the Syrian campaigns that followed and was now full of eagerness to engage in this Egyptian enterprise. In fact, it was mainly his zeal and enthusiasm to embark in the undertaking which was the means of deciding Gabinius to consent to Ptolemy's proposals.

Danger of Crossing the Deserts

The danger and difficulty which they considered as most to be apprehended in the whole expedition was the getting across the desert to Pelusium. In fact, the great protection of Egypt had always been her isolation. The trackless and desolate sands, being wholly destitute of water, and utterly void, could be traversed, even by a caravan of peaceful travellers, only with great difficulty and danger. For an army to attempt to cross them, exposed, as the troops would necessarily be, to the assaults of enemies who might advance to meet them on the way, and sure of encountering a terrible opposition from fresh and vigorous bands when they should arrive – wayworn and exhausted by the physical hardships of the way – at the borders of the inhabited country, was a desperate undertaking. Many instances occurred in ancient times in which vast bodies of troops, in attempting marches over the deserts by which Egypt was surrounded, were wholly destroyed by famine or thirst, or overwhelmed by storms of sand.

These difficulties and dangers, however, did not at all intimidate Mark Antony. The anticipation, in fact, of the glory of surmounting them was one of the main inducements which led him to embark on the enterprise. The perils of the desert constituted one of the charms which made the expedition so attractive. He placed himself, therefore, at the head of his troop of cavalry, and set off across the sands in advance of Gabinius, to take Pelusium, in order thus to open a way for the main body of the army into Egypt. Ptolemy accompanied Antony. Gabinius was to follow.

Mark Antony – His Character

With all his faults, to call them by no severer name, Mark Antony possessed certain great excellences of character. He was ardent, but then he was cool, collected, and sagacious; and there was a certain frank and manly generosity continually evincing itself in his conduct and character which made him a great favourite among his men. He was at this time about twenty-eight years old, of a tall and manly form, and of an expressive and intellectual cast of countenance. His forehead was high, his nose aquiline, and his eyes full of vivacity and life. He was accustomed to dress in a very plain and careless manner, and he assumed an air of the utmost familiarity and freedom in his intercourse with his soldiers. He would join them in their sports, joke with them, and good-naturedly receive their jokes in return; and take his meals, standing with them around their rude tables, in the open field. Such habits of intercourse with his men in a commander of ordinary character would have been fatal to his ascendency over them; but in Mark Antony's case, these frank and familiar manners seemed only to make the military genius and the intellectual power which he possessed the more conspicuous and the more universally admired.

March Across the Nile Delta – Pelusium Taken

Antony conducted his troop of horsemen across the desert in a very safe and speedy manner and arrived before Pelusium. The city was not prepared to resist him. It surrendered at once, and the whole garrison fell into his hands as prisoners of war. Ptolemy demanded that they should all be immediately killed. They were rebels, he said, and, as such, ought to be put to death. Antony, however, as might have been expected from his character, absolutely refused to allow of any such barbarity. Ptolemy, since the power was not yet in his hands, was compelled to submit, and to postpone gratifying the spirit of vengeance which had so long been slumbering in his breast to a future day. He could the more patiently submit to this necessity since it appeared that the day of his complete and final triumph over his daughter and all her adherents was now very nigh at hand.

The Romans Victorious – Bernice Taken Prisoner – Fate of Archelaus

In fact, Berenice and her government, when they heard of the arrival of Antony and Ptolemy at Pelusium, of the fall of that city, and of the approach of Gabinius with an overwhelming force of Roman soldiers, were struck with dismay. Archelaus, the husband of Berenice, had been, in former years, a personal friend of Antony's. Antony considered, in fact, that they were friends still, though required by what the historian calls their duty to fight each other for the possession of the kingdom. The government of Berenice raised an army. Archelaus took command of it, and advanced to meet the enemy. In the meantime, Gabinius arrived with the main body of the Roman troops, and commenced his march, in conjunction with Antony, toward the capital. As they were obliged to make a circuit to the southward, in order to avoid the inlets and lagoons which, on the northern coast of Egypt, penetrate for some distance into the land, their course led them through the heart of the Delta. Many battles were fought, the Romans everywhere gaining the victory. The Egyptian soldiers were, in fact, discontented and mutinous, perhaps, in part, because they considered the government on the side of which they were compelled to engage as, after all, a usurpation. At length a great final battle was fought, which settled the controversy. Archelaus was slain upon the field, and Berenice was taken prisoner; their government was wholly overthrown, and the way was opened for the march of the Roman armies to Alexandria.

Antony's Grief – Unnatural Joy of Ptolemy XII

Mark Antony, when judged by our standards, was certainly, as well as Ptolemy, a depraved and vicious man; but his depravity was of a very different type from that of Cleopatra's father. The difference in the men, in one respect, was very clearly evinced by the objects toward which their interest and attention were respectively turned after this great battle. While the contest had been going on, the king and queen of Egypt, Archelaus and Berenice, were, of course, in the view both of Antony and Ptolemy, the two most conspicuous personages in the army of their enemies; and while Antony would naturally watch with the greatest interest the fate of his friend, the king, Ptolemy, would as naturally follow with the highest concern the destiny of his daughter. Accordingly, when the battle was over, while the mind of Ptolemy might, as we should naturally expect, be chiefly occupied by the fact that his *daughter* was made a captive, Antony's, we might suppose, would be engrossed by the tidings that his *friend* had been slain.

The one rejoiced and the other mourned. Antony sought for the body of his friend on the field of battle, and when it was found, he gave himself wholly to the work of providing for it a most magnificent burial. He seemed, at the funeral, to lament the death of his ancient comrade with real and unaffected grief. Ptolemy, on the other hand, was overwhelmed with joy at finding his daughter his captive. The long-wished-for hour for the gratification of his revenge had come at last, and the first use which he made of his power when he was put in possession of it at Alexandria was to order his daughter to be beheaded.

CHAPTER V
ACCESSION TO THE THRONE, 55–51 BCE

Cleopatra VII's Situation

At the time when the unnatural quarrel between Cleopatra's father and her sister was working its way toward its dreadful termination, as related in the last chapter, she herself was residing at the royal palace in Alexandria, a blooming and beautiful girl of about fifteen. Fortunately for her, she was too young to take any active part personally in the contention. Her two brothers were still younger than herself. They all three remained, therefore, in the royal palaces, quiet spectators of the revolution, without being either benefited or injured by it. It is singular that the name of both the boys was Ptolemy.

Excitement in Alexandria – Ptolemy XII Auletes Restored to the Throne of Egypt

The excitement in the city of Alexandria was intense and universal when the Roman army entered it to reinstate Cleopatra's father upon his throne. A very large portion of the inhabitants were pleased with having the former king restored. In fact, it appears, by a retrospect of the history of kings, that when a legitimate hereditary sovereign or dynasty is deposed and expelled by a rebellious population, no matter how intolerable may have been the tyranny, or how atrocious the crimes by which the patience of the subject was exhausted, the lapse of a very few years is ordinarily sufficient to produce a very general readiness to acquiesce in a restoration; and in this particular instance there had been no such superiority in the government of Berenice, during the period while her power continued, over that of her father, which she had displaced, as to make this case an exception to the general rule. The mass of the people, therefore – all those, especially, who had taken no active part in Berenice's government – were ready to welcome Ptolemy back to his capital. Those who had taken such a part were all summarily executed by Ptolemy's orders.

There was, of course, a great excitement throughout the city on the arrival of the Roman army. All the foreign influence and power which had been exercised in Egypt thus far, and almost all the officers, whether civil or military, had been Greek. The coming of the Romans was the introduction of a new element of interest to add to the endless variety of excitements which animated the capital.

Festivities for the Ptolemy XII

The restoration of Ptolemy was celebrated with games, spectacles, and festivities of every kind, and, of course, next to the king himself, the chief centre of interest and attraction in all these public rejoicings would be the distinguished foreign generals by whose instrumentality the end had been gained.

The Popularity of Antony – His Generosity

Mark Antony was a special object of public regard and admiration at the time. His eccentric manners, his frank and honest air, his Roman simplicity of dress and demeanour, made him conspicuous; and his interposition to save the lives of the captured garrison of Pelusium, and the interest which he took in rendering such distinguished funeral honours to the enemy whom his army had slain in battle, impressed the people with the idea of a certain nobleness and magnanimity in his character, which, in spite of his faults, made him an object of general admiration and applause. The very faults of such a man assume often, in the eyes of the world, the guise and semblance of virtues. For example, it is related of Antony that, at one time in the course of his life, having a desire to make a present of some kind to a certain person, in requital for a favour which he had received from him, he ordered his treasurer to send a sum of money to his friend – and named for the sum to be sent an amount considerably greater than was really required under the circumstances of the case – acting thus, as he often did, under the influence of a blind and uncalculating generosity. The treasurer, more prudent than his master, wished to reduce the amount, but he did not dare directly to propose a reduction; so he counted out the money, and laid it in a pile in a place where Antony was to pass, thinking that when Antony saw the amount, he would perceive that it was too great. Antony, in passing by, asked what money that was. The treasurer said that it was the sum that he had ordered to be sent as a present to such a person, naming the individual intended. Antony was quick to perceive the object of the treasurer's manoeuvre. He immediately replied, "Ah! is that all? I thought the sum I named would make a better appearance than that; send him double the amount."

To determine, under such circumstances as these, to double an extravagance merely for the purpose of thwarting the honest attempt of a faithful servant to diminish it, made, too, in so cautious and delicate a way, is most certainly a fault. But it is one of those faults for which the world, in all ages, will persist in admiring and praising the perpetrator.

Antony and Cleopatra – Antony Returns to Rome

In a word, Antony became the object of general attention and favour during his continuance at Alexandria. Whether he particularly attracted Cleopatra's attention at this time or not does not appear. She, however, strongly attracted *his*. He admired her blooming beauty, her sprightliness and wit, and her various accomplishments. She was still, however, so young – being but fifteen years of age, while Antony was nearly thirty – that she probably made no very serious impression upon him. A short time after this, Antony went back to Rome, and did not see Cleopatra again for many years.

Ptolemy XII's Murders

When the two Roman generals went away from Alexandria, they left a considerable portion of the army behind them, under Ptolemy's command, to aid him in keeping possession of his throne. Antony returned to Rome. He had acquired great renown by his march across the desert, and by the successful accomplishment of the invasion of Egypt and the restoration of Ptolemy. His funds, too, were replenished by the vast sums paid to him and to Gabinius by Ptolemy. The amount which Ptolemy is said to have agreed to pay as the price of his restoration was two thousand talents, a sum which shows on how great a scale the operations of this celebrated campaign were conducted. Ptolemy raised a large portion of the money required for his payments by confiscating the estates belonging to those friends of Berenice's government whom he ordered to be slain. It was said, in fact, that the numbers were very much increased of those that were condemned to die, by Ptolemy's standing in such urgent need of their property to meet his obligations.

Antony's New-Found Wealth – Civil War Between Pompey and Caesar – End of Ptolemy XII Auletes' Reign – Settlement of Succession – Cleopatra Marries Her Brother Ptolemy XIII, Rules as Co-Regent

Antony, through the results of this campaign, found himself suddenly raised from the position of a disgraced and homeless fugitive to that of one of the most wealthy and renowned, and, consequently, one of the most powerful personages in Rome. The great civil war broke out about this time between Caesar and Pompey. Antony espoused the cause of Caesar.

In the meantime, while the civil war between Caesar and Pompey was raging, Ptolemy succeeded in maintaining his seat on the throne, by the aid of the Roman soldiers whom Antony and Gabinius had left him, for about three years. When he found himself drawing toward the close of life, the question arose to his mind to whom he should leave his kingdom. Cleopatra was the oldest child, and she was a princess of great promise, both in respect to mental endowments and personal charms. Her brothers were considerably younger than she. The claim of a son, though younger, seemed to be naturally stronger than that of a daughter; but the commanding talents and rising influence of Cleopatra appeared to make it doubtful whether it would be safe to pass her by. The father settled the question in the way in which such difficulties were usually surmounted in the Ptolemy family. He ordained that Cleopatra should marry the oldest of her brothers, and that they two should jointly occupy the throne.

Adhering also, still, to the idea of the alliance of Egypt with Rome, which had been the leading principle of the whole policy of his reign, he solemnly committed the execution of his will and the guardianship of his children, by a provision of the instrument itself, to the Roman Senate. The Senate accepted the appointment, and appointed Pompey as the agent, on their part, to perform the duties of the trust. The attention of Pompey was, immediately after that time, too much engrossed by the civil war waged between himself and Caesar, to take any active steps in respect to the duties of his appointment. It seemed, however, that none were necessary, for all parties in Alexandria appeared disposed, after the death of the king, to acquiesce in the arrangements which he had made, and to join in carrying them into effect. Cleopatra was married to her brother – yet, it is true, only a boy. He was about ten years old. She was herself about eighteen. They were both too young to govern; they could only reign. The affairs of the kingdom were, accordingly, conducted by two ministers whom their father had designated. These ministers were Pothinus, a eunuch, who was a sort of secretary of state, and Achillas, the commander-in-chief of the armies.

First Accession of Cleopatra VII Thea Philopator as Queen of Egypt

Thus, though Cleopatra, by these events, became nominally a queen, her real accession to the throne was not yet accomplished.

There were still many difficulties and dangers to be passed through before the period arrived when she became really a sovereign. She did not, herself, make any immediate attempt to hasten this period, but seems to have acquiesced, on the other hand, very quietly, for a time, in the arrangements which her father had made.

Pothinus the Eunuch – His Character and Government

Pothinus was a eunuch. He had been, for a long time, an officer of government under Ptolemy, the father. He was a proud, ambitious, and domineering man, determined to rule, and very unscrupulous in respect to the means which he adopted to accomplish his ends. He had been accustomed to regard Cleopatra as a mere child. Now that she was queen, he was very unwilling that the real power should pass into her hands. The jealousy and ill will which he felt toward her increased rapidly as he found, in the course of the first two or three years after her father's death, that she was advancing rapidly in strength of character, and in the influence and ascendency which she was acquiring over all around her. Her beauty, her accomplishments, and a certain indescribable charm which pervaded all her demeanour, combined to give her great personal power. But, while these things awakened in other minds feelings of interest in Cleopatra and attachment to her, they only increased the jealousy and envy of Pothinus. Cleopatra was becoming his rival. He endeavoured to thwart and circumvent her. He acted toward her in a haughty and overbearing manner, in order to keep her down to what he considered her proper place as his ward; for he was yet the guardian both of Cleopatra and her husband, and the regent of the realm.

Machinations of Pothinus

Cleopatra had a great deal of what is sometimes called spirit, and her resentment was aroused by this treatment. Pothinus took pains to enlist her young husband, Ptolemy, on his side, as the quarrel advanced. Ptolemy was younger, and of a character much less marked and decided than Cleopatra. Pothinus saw that he could maintain control over him much more easily and for a much longer time than over Cleopatra. He contrived to awaken the young Ptolemy's jealousy of his wife's rising influence, and to induce him to join in efforts to thwart and counteract it. These attempts to turn her husband against her only aroused Cleopatra's resentment the more. Hers was not a spirit to be coerced. The palace was filled with the dissensions of the rivals. Pothinus and Ptolemy began to take measures for securing the army on their side. An open rupture finally ensued, and Cleopatra was expelled from the kingdom.

Cleopatra is Expelled from Egypt

She went to Syria. Syria was the nearest place of refuge, and then, besides, it was the country from which the aid had been furnished by which her father had been restored to the throne when he had been expelled, in a similar manner, many years before. Her father, it is true, had gone first to Rome; but the succours which he had negotiated for had been sent from

Syria. Cleopatra hoped to obtain the same assistance by going directly there.

Cleopatra's Army – Approaching Contest

Nor was she disappointed. She obtained an army, and commenced her march toward Egypt, following the same track which Antony and Gabinius had pursued in coming to reinstate her father. Pothinus raised an army and went forth to meet her. He took Achillas as the commander of the troops, and the young Ptolemy as the nominal sovereign; while he, as the young king's guardian and prime minister, exercised the real power. The troops of Pothinus advanced to Pelusium. Here they met the forces of Cleopatra coming from the east. The armies encamped not very far from each other, and both sides began to prepare for battle.

Caesar and Pompey fight at the Battle of Pharsalus, 9 August 48 BCE

The battle, however, was not fought. It was prevented by the occurrence of certain great and unforeseen events which at this crisis suddenly burst upon the scene of Egyptian history and turned the whole current of affairs into new and unexpected channels. The breaking out of the civil war between the great Roman generals Caesar and Pompey, and their respective partisans, has already been mentioned as having occurred soon after the death of Cleopatra's father, and as having prevented Pompey from undertaking the office of executor of the will. This war had been raging ever since that time with terrible fury. Its distant thundering had been heard even in Egypt, but it was too remote to awaken there any special alarm. The immense armies of these two mighty conquerors had moved slowly – like two ferocious birds of prey, flying through the air, and fighting as they fly – across Italy into Greece, and from Greece, through Macedon, into Thessaly, contending in dreadful struggles with each other as they advanced, and trampling down and destroying everything in their way. At length a great final battle had been fought at Pharsalus. Pompey had been totally defeated. He had fled to the seashore, and there, with a few ships and a small number of followers, he had pushed out upon the Mediterranean, not knowing whither to fly, and overwhelmed with wretchedness and despair. Caesar followed him in eager pursuit. He had a small fleet of galleys with him, on board of which he had embarked two or three thousand men. This was a force suitable, perhaps, for the pursuit of a fugitive, but wholly insufficient for any other design.

Pompey at Pelusium – Treachery of Pothinus

Pompey thought of Ptolemy. He remembered the efforts which he himself had made for the cause of Ptolemy Auletes, at Rome, and the success of those efforts in securing that monarch's restoration – an event through which alone the young Ptolemy had been enabled to attain the crown. He came, therefore, to Pelusium, and, anchoring his little fleet off the shore, sent to the land to ask Ptolemy to receive and protect him. Pothinus, who was really the commander in Ptolemy's army, made answer to this application that Pompey should be received and protected, and that he would send out a boat to bring him to the shore. Pompey felt some misgivings in respect to this proffered hospitality, but he finally concluded to go to the shore in the boat which Pothinus sent for him. As soon as he landed, the Egyptians, by Pothinus's orders, stabbed and beheaded him on the sand. Pothinus and his council had decided that this would be the safest course. If they were to receive Pompey, they reasoned, Caesar would be made their enemy; if they refused to receive him, Pompey himself would be offended, and they did not know which of the two it would be safe to displease; for they did not know in what way, if both the generals were to be allowed to live, the war would ultimately end. "But by killing Pompey," they said, "we shall be sure to please Caesar and Pompey himself will *lie still*."

Caesar's Pursuit of Pompey – His Danger

In the meantime, Caesar, not knowing to what part of Egypt Pompey had fled, pressed on directly to Alexandria. He exposed himself to great danger in so doing, for the forces under his command were not sufficient to protect him in case of his becoming involved in difficulties with the authorities there. Nor could he, when once arrived on the Egyptian coast, easily go away again; for, at the season of the year in which these events occurred, there was a periodical wind which blew steadily toward that part of the coast, and, while it made it very easy for a fleet of ships to go to Alexandria, rendered it almost impossible for them to return.

Caesar at Alexandria

Caesar was very little accustomed to shrink from danger in any of his enterprises and plans, though still he was usually prudent and circumspect. In this instance, however, his ardent interest in the pursuit of Pompey overruled all considerations of personal safety. He arrived at Alexandria, but he found that Pompey was not there. He anchored his vessels in the port, landed his troops, and established himself in the city. These two events, the assassination of one of the great Roman generals on the eastern extremity of the coast, and the arrival of the other, at the same moment, at Alexandria, on the western, burst suddenly upon Egypt together, like simultaneous claps of thunder. The tidings struck the whole country with astonishment, and immediately engrossed universal attention. At the camps both of Cleopatra and Ptolemy, at Pelusium, all was excitement and wonder. Instead of thinking of a battle, both parties were wholly occupied in speculating on the results which were likely to accrue, to one side or to the other, under the totally new and unexpected aspect which public affairs had assumed.

Caesar Presented with Pompey's Head – Pompey's Seal – Cleopatra at Pelusium

Of course, the thoughts of all were turned toward Alexandria. Pothinus immediately proceeded to the city, taking with him the young king. Achillas, too, either accompanied them, or followed soon afterwards. They carried with them the head of Pompey, which they had cut off on the shore where they had killed him, and also a seal which they took from his finger. When they arrived at Alexandria, they sent the head, wrapped up in a cloth, and also the seal, as presents to Caesar. Accustomed as they were to the brutal deeds and heartless cruelties of the Ptolemies, they supposed that Caesar would exult at the spectacle of the dissevered and ghastly head of his great rival and enemy.

Instead of this, he was shocked and displeased, and ordered the head to be buried with the most solemn and imposing funeral ceremonies. He, however, accepted and kept the seal. The device engraved upon it was a lion holding a sword in his paw – a fit emblem of the characters of the men, who, though in many respects magnanimous and just, had filled the whole world with the terror of their quarrels.

The army of Ptolemy, while he himself and his immediate counsellors went to Alexandria, was left at Pelusium, under the command of other officers, to watch Cleopatra. Cleopatra herself would have been pleased, also, to repair to Alexandria and appeal to Caesar, if it had been in her power to do so; but she was beyond the confines of the country, with a powerful army of her enemies ready to intercept her on any attempt to enter or pass through it. She remained, therefore, at Pelusium, uncertain what to do.

Caesar's Situation – His Demands

In the meantime, Caesar soon found himself in a somewhat embarrassing situation at Alexandria. He had been accustomed, for many years, to the possession and the exercise of the most absolute and despotic power, wherever he might be; and now that Pompey, his great rival, was dead, he considered himself the monarch and master of the world. He had not, however, at Alexandria, any means sufficient to maintain and enforce such pretensions, and yet he was not of a spirit to abate, on that account, in the slightest degree, the advancing of them. He established himself in the palaces of Alexandria as if he were himself the king. He moved, in state, through the streets of the city, at the head of his guards, and displaying the customary emblems of supreme authority used at

Rome. He claimed the six thousand talents which Ptolemy Auletes had formerly promised him for procuring a treaty of alliance with Rome, and he called upon Pothinus to pay the balance due. He said, moreover, that by the will of Auletes the Roman people had been made the executor; and that it devolved upon him as the Roman consul, and, consequently, the representative of the Roman people, to assume that trust, and in the discharge of it to settle the dispute between Ptolemy and Cleopatra, and he called upon Ptolemy to prepare and lay before him a statement of his claims, and the grounds on which he maintained his right to the throne to the exclusion of Cleopatra.

Pothinus's Conduct – Quarrels – Policy of Pothinus

On the other hand, Pothinus, who had been as little accustomed to acknowledge a superior as Caesar, though his supremacy and domination had been exercised on a somewhat humbler scale, was obstinate and pertinacious in resisting all these demands, though the means and methods which he resorted to were of a character corresponding to his weak and ignoble mind. He fomented quarrels in the streets between the Alexandrian populace and Caesar's soldiers. He thought that, as the number of troops under Caesar's command in the city, and of vessels in the port, was small, he could tease and worry the Romans with impunity, though he had not the courage openly to attack them. He pretended to be a friend, or, at least, not an enemy, and yet he conducted himself toward them in an overbearing and insolent manner. He had agreed to make arrangements for supplying them with food, and he did this by procuring damaged provisions of a most wretched quality; and when the soldiers remonstrated, he said to them, that they who lived at other people's cost had no right to complain of their fare. He caused wooden and earthen vessels to be used in the palace, and said, in explanation, that he had been compelled to sell all the gold and silver plate of the royal household to meet the exactions of Caesar. He busied himself, too, about the city, in endeavouring to excite odium against Caesar's proposal to hear and decide the question at issue between Cleopatra and Ptolemy. Ptolemy was a sovereign, he said, and was not amenable to any foreign power whatever. Thus, without the courage or the energy to attempt any open, manly, and effectual system of hostility, he contented himself with making all the difficulty in his power, by urging an incessant pressure of petty, vexatious, and provoking, but useless annoyances. Caesar's demands may have been unjust, but they were bold, manly, and undisguised. The eunuch may have been right in resisting them; but the mode was so mean and contemptible, that mankind have always taken part with Caesar in the sentiments which they have formed as spectators of the contest.

Caesar Sends to Syria for Additional Troops

With the very small force which Caesar had at his command and shut up as he was in the midst of a very great and powerful city, in which both the garrison and the population were growing more and more hostile to him every day, he soon found his situation was beginning to be attended with very serious danger. He could not retire from the scene. He probably would not have retired if he could have done so. He remained, therefore, in the city, conducting himself all the time with prudence and circumspection, but yet maintaining, as at first, the same air of confident self-possession and superiority which always characterized his demeanour. He, however, dispatched a messenger forthwith into Syria, the nearest country under the Roman sway, with orders that several legions which were posted there should be embarked and forwarded to Alexandria with the utmost possible celerity.

CHAPTER VI
CLEOPATRA AND CAESAR, 50–48 BCE

Cleopatra's Predicament

In the meantime, while the events related in the last chapter were taking place at Alexandria, Cleopatra remained anxious and uneasy in her camp, quite uncertain, for a time, what it was best for her to do. She wished to be at Alexandria. She knew very well that Caesar's power in controlling the course of affairs in Egypt would necessarily be supreme. She was, of course, very earnest in her desire to be able to present her cause before him. As it was, Ptolemy and Pothinus were in communication with the arbiter, and, for aught she knew, assiduously cultivating his favour, while she was far away, her cause unheard, her wrongs unknown, and perhaps even her existence forgotten. Of course, under such circumstances, she was very earnest to get to Alexandria.

Cleopatra Resolves to Go to Alexandria

But how to accomplish this purpose was a source of great perplexity. She could not march thither at the head of an army, for the army of the king was strongly entrenched at Pelusium, and effectually barred the way. She could not attempt to pass alone, or with few attendants, through the country, for every town and village was occupied with garrisons and officers under the orders of Pothinus, and she would be certainly intercepted. She had no fleet, and could not, therefore, make the passage by sea. Besides, even if she could by any means reach the gates of Alexandria, how was she to pass safely through the streets of the city to the palace where Caesar resided, since the city, except in Caesar's quarters, was wholly in the hands of Pothinus's government? The difficulties in the way of accomplishing her object seemed thus almost insurmountable.

Cleopatra's Message to Caesar – Caesar's Reply – Apollodorus's Stratagem

She was, however, resolved to make the attempt. She sent a message to Caesar, asking permission to appear before him and plead her own cause. Caesar replied, urging her by all means to come. She took a single boat, and with the smallest number of attendants possible, made her way along the coast to Alexandria. The man on whom she principally relied in this hazardous expedition was a domestic named Apollodorus. She had, however, some other attendants besides. When the party reached Alexandria, they waited until night, and then advanced to the foot of the walls of the citadel. Here Apollodorus rolled the queen up in a piece of carpeting, and, covering the whole package with a cloth, he tied it with a thong, so as to give it the appearance of a bale of ordinary merchandise, and then throwing the load across his shoulder, he advanced into the city. Cleopatra was at this time about twenty-one years of age, but she was of a slender and graceful form, and the burden was, consequently, not very heavy. Apollodorus came to the gates of the palace where Caesar was residing. The guards at the gates asked him what it was that he was carrying. He said that it was a present for Caesar. So, they allowed him to pass, and the pretended porter carried his package safely in.

Cleopatra and Caesar

When it was unrolled, and Cleopatra came out to view, Caesar was perfectly charmed with the spectacle. In fact, the various conflicting emotions which she could not but feel under such circumstances as these, imparted a double interest to her beautiful and expressive face, and to her naturally bewitching manners. She was excited by the adventure through which she had passed, and yet pleased with her narrow escape from its dangers. The curiosity and interest which she felt on the one hand, in respect to the great personage into whose presence she had been thus strangely ushered, was very strong; but then, on the other hand, it was chastened and subdued by that feeling of timidity which, in new and unexpected situations like these, and under a consciousness of being the object of eager observation to the other sex, is inseparable from the nature of woman.

First Impressions of Cleopatra – Caesar's Attachment – Caesar's Wife

The conversation which Caesar held with Cleopatra deepened the impression which her first appearance had made upon him. Her intelligence and animation, the originality of her ideas, and the point and pertinency of her mode of expressing them, made her, independently of her personal charms, an exceedingly entertaining and agreeable companion. She, in fact, completely won the great conqueror's heart; and, through the strong attachment to her which he immediately formed, he became wholly disqualified to act impartially between her and her brother in regard to their respective rights to the crown. We call Ptolemy Cleopatra's brother; for, though he was also, in fact, her husband, still, as he was only ten or twelve years of age at the time of Cleopatra's expulsion from Alexandria, the marriage had been probably regarded, thus far, only as a mere matter of form. Caesar was now about fifty-two. He had a wife, named Calpurnia, to whom he had been married about ten years. She was living, at this time, in an unostentatious and quiet manner at Rome. She was a lady of an amiable and gentle character, devotedly attached to her husband, patient and forbearing in respect to his faults, and often anxious and unhappy at the thought of the difficulties and dangers in which his ardent and unbounded ambition so often involved him.

Caesar's Fondness for Cleopatra – She Commits Her Cause to Caesar

Caesar immediately began to take a very strong interest in Cleopatra's cause. He treated her personally with the fondest attention, and it was impossible for her not to reciprocate in some degree the kind feeling with which he regarded her. It was, in fact, something altogether new to her to have a warm and devoted friend, espousing her cause, tendering her protection, and seeking in every way to promote her happiness. Her father had all his life neglected her. Her brother, of years and understanding totally inferior to hers, whom she had been compelled to make her husband, had become her mortal enemy. It is true that, in depriving her of her inheritance and expelling her from her native land, he had been only the tool and instrument of more designing men. This, however, far from improving the point of view from which she regarded him, made him appear not only hateful, but contemptible too. All the officers of government, also, in the Alexandrian court had turned against her, because they had supposed that they could control her brother more easily if she were away. Thus, she had always been surrounded by selfish, mercenary, and implacable foes. Now, for the first time, she seemed to have a friend. A protector had suddenly arisen to support and defend her – a man of very alluring person and manners, of a very noble and generous spirit, and of the very highest station. He loved her, and she could not refrain from loving him in return. She committed her cause entirely into his hands, confided to him all her interests, and gave herself up wholly into his power.

Caesar's Pretentions

Nor was the unbounded confidence which she reposed in him undeserved, so far as related to his efforts to restore her to her throne. The legions which Caesar had sent for into Syria had not yet arrived, and his situation in Alexandria was still very defenceless and very precarious. He did not, however, on this account, abate in the least degree the loftiness and self-confidence of the position which he had assumed, but he commenced immediately the work of securing Cleopatra's restoration. This quiet assumption of the right and power to arbitrate and decide such a question as that of the claim to the throne, in a country where he had accidentally landed and found rival claimants disputing for the succession, while he was still wholly destitute of the means of enforcing the superiority which he so coolly assumed, marks the immense ascendency which the Roman power had attained at this time in the estimation of mankind, and is, besides, specially characteristic of the genius and disposition of Caesar.

Caesar Sends for Ptolemy XIII – Ptolemy's Indignation – His Complaints Against Caesar

Very soon after Cleopatra had come to him, Caesar sent for the young Ptolemy, and urged upon him the duty and expediency of restoring Cleopatra. Ptolemy was beginning now to attain an age at which he might be supposed to have some opinion of his own on such a question. He declared himself utterly opposed to any such design. In the course of the conversation, he learned that Cleopatra had arrived at Alexandria, and that she was then concealed in Caesar's palace. This intelligence awakened in his mind the greatest excitement and indignation. He went away from Caesar's presence in a rage. He tore the diadem which he was accustomed to wear in the streets, from his head, threw it down, and trampled it under his feet. He declared to the people that he was betrayed and displayed the most violent indications of vexation and chagrin. The chief subject of his complaint, in the attempts which he made to awaken the popular indignation against Caesar and the Romans, was the disgraceful impropriety of the position which his sister had assumed in surrendering herself as she had done to Caesar. It is most probable, however, unless his character was very different from that of every other Ptolemy in the line, that what really awakened his jealousy and anger was fear of the commanding influence and power to which Cleopatra was likely to attain through the agency of so distinguished a protector, rather than any other consequences of his friendship, or any real considerations of delicacy in respect to his sister's good name or his own marital honour.

Tumult in Alexandria – Excitement of the Population

However, this may be, Ptolemy, together with Pothinus and Achillas, and all his other friends and adherents, who joined him in the terrible outcry that he made against the coalition which he had discovered between Cleopatra and Caesar, succeeded in producing a very general and violent tumult throughout the city. The populace was aroused, and began to assemble in great crowds, and full of indignation and anger. Some knew the facts and acted under something like an understanding of the cause of their anger. Others only knew that the aim of this sudden outbreak was to assault the Romans, and were ready, on any pretext, known or unknown, to join in any deeds of violence directed against these foreign intruders. There were others still, and these, probably, far the larger portion, who knew nothing and understood nothing but that there was to be tumult and a riot in and around the palaces, and were, accordingly, eager to be there.

Ptolemy's Forces – Caesar's Forces – Ptolemy XIII Captured

Ptolemy and his officers had no large body of troops in Alexandria; for the events which had thus far occurred since Caesar's arrival had succeeded each other so rapidly, that a very short time had yet elapsed, and the main army remained still at Pelusium. The main force, therefore, by which Caesar was now attacked, consisted of the population of the city, headed, perhaps, by the few guards which the young king had at his command.

Caesar, on his part, had but a small portion of his forces at the palace where he was attacked. The rest were scattered about the city. He, however, seems to have felt no alarm. He did not even confine himself to acting on the defensive. He sent out a detachment of his soldiers with orders to seize Ptolemy and bring him in a prisoner. Soldiers trained, disciplined, and armed as the Roman veterans were, and nerved by the ardour and enthusiasm which seemed always to animate troops which were under Caesar's personal command, could accomplish almost any undertaking against a mere populace, however numerous or however furiously excited they might be. The soldiers sallied out, seized Ptolemy, and brought him in.

Caesar's Address to the People

The populace was, at first, astounded at the daring presumption of this deed, and then exasperated at the indignity of it, considered as a violation of the person of their sovereign. The tumult would have greatly increased, had it not been that Caesar – who had now attained all his ends in thus having brought Cleopatra and Ptolemy both within his power – thought it most expedient to allay it. He accordingly ascended to the window of a tower, or of some other elevated portion of his palace, so high that missiles from the mob below could not reach him and began to make signals expressive of his wish to address them.

When silence was obtained, he made them a speech well calculated to quiet the excitement. He told them that he did not pretend to any right to judge between Cleopatra and Ptolemy as their superior, but only in the performance of the duty solemnly assigned by Ptolemy Auletes, the father, to the Roman people, whose representative he was. Other than this he claimed no jurisdiction in the case; and his only wish, in the discharge of the duty which devolved upon him to consider the cause, was to settle the question in a manner just and equitable to all the parties concerned, and thus arrest the progress of the civil war, which, if not arrested, threatened to involve the country in the most terrible calamities. He counselled them, therefore, to disperse, and no longer disturb the peace of the city. He would immediately take measures for trying the question between Cleopatra and Ptolemy, and he did not doubt but that they would all be satisfied with his decision.

The Impact of Caesar's Speech – The Mob Disperses

This speech, made, as it was, in the eloquent and persuasive, and yet dignified and imposing manner for which Caesar's harangues to turbulent assemblies like these were so famed, produced a great effect. Some were convinced, others were silenced; and those whose resentment and anger were not appeased found themselves deprived of their power by the pacification of the rest. The mob was dispersed, and Ptolemy remained with Cleopatra in Caesar's custody.

Caesar Convenes an Assembly – Caesar's Decision – Cleopatra VII and Ptolemy XIII to Rule Egypt Jointly

The next day, Caesar, according to his promise, convened an assembly of the principal people of Alexandria and officers of state, and then brought out Ptolemy and Cleopatra, that he might decide their cause. The original will which Ptolemy Auletes had executed had been deposited in the public archives of Alexandria, and carefully preserved there. An authentic copy of it had been sent to Rome. Caesar caused the original will to be brought out and read to the assembly. The provisions of it were perfectly explicit and clear. It required that Cleopatra and Ptolemy should be married, and then settled the sovereign power upon them jointly, as king and queen. It recognized the Roman commonwealth as the ally of Egypt and constituted the Roman government the executor of the will, and the guardian of the king and queen. In fact, so clear and explicit was this document that the simple reading of it seemed to be of itself a decision of the question. When, therefore, Caesar announced that, in his judgment, Cleopatra was entitled to share the supreme power with Ptolemy, and that it was his duty, as the representative of the Roman power and the executor of the will, to protect both the king and the queen in their respective rights, there seemed to be nothing that could be said against his decision.

Besides Cleopatra and Ptolemy, there were two other children of Ptolemy Auletes in the royal family at this time. One was a girl, named Arsinoë. The other, a boy, was, singularly enough, named, like his brother, Ptolemy. These children were quite young, but Caesar thought that it would perhaps gratify the Alexandrians and lead them to acquiesce more readily in his decision if he were to make some royal provision for them. He accordingly proposed to assign the island of Cyprus as a realm for them. This was literally a gift, for Cyprus was at this time a Roman possession.

Satisfaction of the Assembly

The whole assembly seemed satisfied with this decision except Pothinus. He had been so determined and inveterate an enemy to Cleopatra that, as he was well aware, her restoration must end in his downfall and ruin. He went away from the assembly moodily determining that he would not submit to the decision but would immediately adopt efficient measures to prevent its being carried into effect.

Festivals and Rejoicings

Caesar made arrangements for a series of festivals and celebrations, to commemorate and confirm the reestablishment of a good understanding between the king and the queen, and the consequent termination of the war. Such celebrations, he judged, would have great influence in removing any remaining animosities from the minds of the people, and restore the dominion of a kind and friendly feeling throughout the city.

Pothinus's and Achillas's Plot

The people fell in with these measures, and cordially co-operated to give them effect; but Pothinus and Achillas, though they suppressed all outward expressions of discontent, made incessant efforts in secret to organize a party, and to form plans for overthrowing the influence of Caesar, and making Ptolemy again the sole and exclusive sovereign.

Pothinus represented to all whom he could induce to listen to him that Caesar's real design was to make Cleopatra queen alone, and to depose Ptolemy, and urged them to combine with him to resist a policy which would end in bringing Egypt under the dominion of a woman. He also formed a plan, in connection with Achillas, for ordering the army back from Pelusium. The army consisted of thirty thousand men. If that army could be brought to Alexandria and kept under Pothinus's orders, Caesar and his three thousand Roman soldiers would be, they thought, wholly at their mercy.

Achillas's Escape

There was, however, one danger to be guarded against in ordering the army to march toward the capital, and that was that Ptolemy, while under Caesar's influence, might open communication with the officers, and so obtain command of its movements, and thwart all the conspirators' designs. To prevent this, it was arranged between Pothinus and Achillas that the latter should make his escape from Alexandria, proceed immediately to the camp at Pelusium, resume the command of the troops there, and conduct them himself to the capital; and that in all these operations, and also subsequently on his arrival, he should obey no orders unless they came to him through Pothinus himself.

Although sentinels and guards were probably stationed at the gates and avenues leading from the city Achillas contrived to effect his escape and to join the army. He placed himself at the head of the forces and commenced his march toward the capital. Pothinus remained all the time within the city as a spy, pretending to acquiesce in Caesar's decision, and to be on friendly terms with him, but really plotting for his overthrow, and obtaining all the information which his position enabled him to command, in order that he might co-operate with the army and Achillas when they should arrive.

March of the Army of Egypt

All these things were done with the utmost secrecy, and so cunning and adroit were the conspirators in forming and executing their plots that Caesar seems to have had no knowledge of the measures which his enemies were taking, until he suddenly heard that the main body of Ptolemy's army was approaching the city, at least twenty thousand strong. In the meantime, however, the forces which he had sent for from Syria had not arrived, and no alternative was left but to defend the capital and himself as well as he could with the very small force which he had at his disposal.

He determined, however, first, to try the effect of orders sent out in Ptolemy's name to forbid the approach of the army to the city. Two officers were accordingly entrusted with these orders and sent out to communicate them to Achillas. The names of these officers were Dioscorides and Serapion.

Achillas Murders the Messengers – Achillas's Intentions

It shows in a very striking point of view to what an incredible exaltation the authority and consequence of a sovereign king rose in those ancient days, in the minds of men, that Achillas, at the moment when these men made their appearance in the camp, bearing evidently some command from Ptolemy in the city, considered it more prudent to kill them at once, without hearing their message, rather than to allow the orders to be delivered and then take the responsibility of disobeying them. If he could succeed in marching to Alexandria and in taking possession of the city, and then in expelling Caesar and Cleopatra and restoring Ptolemy to the exclusive possession of the throne, he knew very well that the king would rejoice in the result, and would overlook all irregularities on his part in the means by which he had accomplished it, short of absolute disobedience of a known command. Whatever might be the commands that these messengers were bringing him, he supposed that they doubtless originated, not in Ptolemy's own free will, but that they were dictated by the authority of Caesar. Still, they would be commands coming in Ptolemy's name, and the universal experience of officers serving under the military despots of those ancient days showed that, rather than to take the responsibility of directly disobeying a royal order once received, it was safer to avoid receiving it by murdering the messengers.

Achillas therefore directed the officers to be seized and slain. They were accordingly taken off and speared by the soldiers, and then the bodies were borne away. The soldiers, however, it was found, had not done their work effectually. There was no interest for them in such a cold-blooded assassination, and perhaps something like a sentiment of compassion restrained their hands. At any rate, though both the men were desperately wounded, one only died. The other lived and recovered.

Caesar's Measures – Caesar's Arrangements for Defence of Alexandria

Achillas continued to advance toward the city. Caesar, finding that the crisis which was approaching was becoming very serious in its character, took, himself, the whole command within the capital, and began to make the best arrangements possible under the circumstances of the case to defend himself there. His numbers were altogether too small to defend the whole city against the overwhelming force which was advancing to assail it. He accordingly entrenched his troops in the palaces and in the citadel, and in such other parts of the city as it seemed practicable to defend. He barricaded all the streets and avenues leading to these points and fortified the gates. Nor did he, while thus doing all in his power to employ the insufficient means of defence already in his hands to the best advantage, neglect the proper exertions for obtaining succour from abroad. He sent off galleys to Syria, to Cyprus, to Rhodes, and to every other point accessible from Alexandria where Roman troops might be expected to be found, urging the authorities there to forward reinforcements to him with the utmost possible dispatch.

Cleopatra VII and Ptolemy XIII

During all this time Cleopatra and Ptolemy remained in the palace with Caesar, both ostensibly co-operating with him in his councils and measures for defending the city from Achillas. Cleopatra, of course, was sincere and in earnest in this co-operation; but Ptolemy's adhesion to the common cause was very little to be relied upon. Although, situated as he was, he was compelled to seem to be on Caesar's side, he must have secretly desired that Achillas should succeed, and Caesar's plans be overthrown. Pothinus was more active, though not less cautious in his hostility to them. He opened secret communication with Achillas, sending him information, from time to time, of what took place within the walls, and of the arrangements made there for the defence of the city against him, and gave him also directions how to proceed. He was very wary and sagacious in all these movements, feigning all the time to be on Caesar's side. He pretended to be very zealously employed in aiding Caesar to secure more effectually the various points where attacks were to be expected, and in maturing and completing the arrangements for defence.

Pothinus's Double Dealing – He is Detected

But, notwithstanding all his cunning, he was detected in his double dealing, and his career was suddenly brought to a close, before the great final conflict came on. There was a barber in Caesar's household, who, for some cause or other, began to suspect Pothinus; and, having little else to do, he employed himself in watching the eunuch's movements and reporting them to Caesar. Caesar directed the barber to continue his observations. He did so; his suspicions were soon confirmed, and at length a letter, which Pothinus had written to Achillas, was intercepted and brought to Caesar. This furnished the necessary proof of what they called his guilt, and Caesar ordered him to be beheaded.

Pothinus is Beheaded – Arsinoë and Ganymede

This circumstance produced, of course, a great excitement within the palace, for Pothinus had been for many years the great ruling minister of state – the king, in fact, in all but in name. His execution alarmed a great many others, who, though in Caesar's power, were secretly wishing that Achillas might prevail. Among those most disturbed by these fears was a man named Ganymede. He was the officer who had charge of Arsinoë, Cleopatra's sister. The arrangement which Caesar had proposed for establishing her in conjunction with her brother Ptolemy over the island of Cyprus had not gone into effect; for, immediately after the decision of Caesar, the attention of all concerned had been wholly engrossed by the tidings of the advance of the army, and by the busy preparations which were required on all hands for the impending contest. Arsinoë, therefore, with her governor Ganymede, remained in the palace. Ganymede had joined Pothinus in his plots; and when Pothinus was beheaded, he concluded that it would be safest for him to fly.

Arsinoë's Flight

He accordingly resolved to make his escape from the city, taking Arsinoë with him. It was a very hazardous attempt, but he succeeded in accomplishing it. Arsinoë was very willing to go, for she was now beginning to be old enough to feel the impulse of that insatiable and reckless ambition which seemed to form such an essential element in the character of every son and daughter in the whole Ptolemaic line. She was insignificant and powerless where she was, but at the head of the army she might become immediately a queen.

Arsinoë IV Proclaimed Queen by the Army

It resulted, in the first instance, as she had anticipated. Achillas and his army received her with acclamations. Under Ganymede's influence they decided that, as all the other members of the royal family were in durance, being held captive by a foreign general, who had by chance obtained possession of the capital, and were thus incapacitated for exercising the royal power, the crown devolved upon Arsinoë; and they accordingly proclaimed her queen.

Ptolemy XIII's Predicament

Everything was now prepared for a desperate and determined contest for the crown between Cleopatra, with Caesar for her minister and general, on the one side, and Arsinoë, with Ganymede and Achillas for her chief officers, on the other. The young Ptolemy, in the meantime, remained Caesar's prisoner, confused with the intricacies in which the quarrel had become involved, and scarcely knowing now what to wish in respect to the issue of the contest. It was very difficult to foresee whether it would be best for him that Cleopatra or that Arsinoë should succeed.

CHAPTER VII
THE ALEXANDRIAN WAR, 48–47 BCE

War for Supremacy

The war which ensued as the result of the intrigues and manoeuvres described in the last chapter is known in the history of Rome and Julius Caesar as the Alexandrian War. The events which occurred during the progress of it, and its termination at last in the triumph of Caesar and Cleopatra, will form the subject of this chapter.

Caesar's Forces – The Army of Egypt – Fugitive Slaves

Achillas had greatly the advantage over Caesar at the outset of the contest, in respect to the strength of the forces under his command. Caesar, in fact, had with him only a detachment of three or four thousand men, a small body of troops which he had hastily put on board a little squadron of Rhodian galleys for pursuing Pompey across the Mediterranean. When he set sail from the European shores with this inconsiderable fleet, it is probable that he had no expectation even of landing in Egypt at all, and much less of being involved in great military undertakings there. Achillas, on the other hand, was at the head of a force of twenty thousand effective men. His troops were, it is true, of a somewhat miscellaneous character, but they were all veteran soldiers, inured to the climate of Egypt, and skilled in all the modes of warfare which were suited to the character of the country. Some of them were Roman soldiers, men who had come with the army of Mark Antony from Syria when Ptolemy Auletes, Cleopatra's father, was reinstated on the throne, and had been left in Egypt, in Ptolemy's service, when Antony returned to Rome. Some were native Egyptians. There was also in the army of Achillas a large number of fugitive slaves – refugees who had made their escape from various points along the shores of the Mediterranean, at different periods, and had been from time to time incorporated into the Egyptian army. These fugitives were all men of the most determined and desperate character.

Achillas had also in his command a force of two thousand horse. Such a body of cavalry made him, of course, perfect master of all the open country outside the city walls. At the head of these troops Achillas gradually advanced to the very gates of Alexandria, invested the city on every side, and shut Caesar closely in.

Presence of Caesar – The Influence of Cleopatra

The danger of the situation in which Caesar was placed was extreme; but he had been so accustomed to succeed in extricating himself from the most imminent perils that neither he himself nor his army seem to have experienced any concern in respect to the result. Caesar personally felt a special pride and pleasure in encountering the difficulties and dangers which now beset him, because Cleopatra was with him to witness his demeanour, to admire his energy and courage, and to reward by her love the efforts and sacrifices which he was making in espousing her cause. She confided everything to him, but she watched all the proceedings with the most eager interest, elated with hope in respect to the result, and proud of the champion who had thus volunteered to defend her. In a word, her heart was full of gratitude, admiration, and love.

The immediate effect, too, of the emotions which she felt so strongly was greatly to heighten her natural charms. The native force and energy of her character were softened and subdued. Her voice, which always possessed a certain inexpressible charm, was endued with new sweetness through the influence of affection.

Her countenance beamed with fresh animation and beauty, and the sprightliness and vivacity of her character, which became at later periods of her life boldness and eccentricity, now being softened and restrained within proper limits by the respectful regard with which she looked upon Caesar, made her an enchanting companion. Caesar was, in fact, entirely intoxicated with the fascinations which she unconsciously displayed.

Under other circumstances than these, a personal attachment so strong, formed by a military commander while engaged in active service, might have been expected to interfere in some degree with the discharge of his duties; but in this case, since it was for Cleopatra's sake and on her behalf that the operations which Caesar had undertaken were to be prosecuted, his love for her only stimulated the spirit and energy with which he engaged in them.

Caesar's First Measures – Caesar's Stores – Siege Weapons

The first measure to be adopted was, as Caesar plainly perceived, to concentrate and strengthen his position in the city, so that he might be able to defend himself there against Achillas until he should receive reinforcements from abroad. For this purpose. he selected a certain group of palaces and citadels which lay together near the head of the long pier or causeway which led to the Pharos, and, withdrawing his troops from all other parts of the city, established them there. The quarter which he thus occupied contained the great city arsenals and public granaries. Caesar brought together all the arms and munitions of war which he could find in other parts of the city, and also all the corn and other provisions which were contained either in the public depots or in private warehouses and stored the whole within his lines. He then enclosed the whole quarter with strong defences. The avenues leading to it were barricaded with walls of stone. Houses in the vicinity, which might have afforded shelter to an enemy, were demolished and the materials used in constructing walls wherever they were needed, or in strengthening the barricades. Prodigious military engines, made to throw heavy stones, and beams of wood, and other ponderous missiles, were set up within his lines, and openings were made in the walls and other defences of the citadel, wherever necessary, to facilitate the action of these machines.

The Mole and the Island Fortress

There was a strong fortress situated at the head of the pier or mole leading to the island of Pharos, which was without Caesar's lines, and still in the hands of the Egyptian authorities. The Egyptians thus commanded the entrance to the mole. The island itself, also, with the fortress at the other end of the pier, was still in the possession of the Egyptian authorities, who seemed disposed to hold it for Achillas. The mole was very long, as the island was nearly a mile from the shore. There was quite a little town upon the island itself, besides the fortress or castle built there to defend the place. The garrison of this castle was strong, and the inhabitants of the town, too, constituted a somewhat formidable population, as they consisted of fishermen, sailors, wreckers, and such other desperate characters, as usually congregate about such a spot. Cleopatra and Caesar, from the windows of their palace within the city, looked out upon this island, with the tall light house rising in the centre of it and the castle at its base, and upon the long and narrow isthmus connecting it with the mainland, and concluded that it was very essential that they should get possession of the post, commanding, as it did, the entrance to the harbour.

Strategic Importance of Taking the Mole

In the harbour, which was on the south side of the mole, and, consequently, on the side opposite to that from which Achillas was advancing toward the city, there were lying a large number of Egyptian vessels, some dismantled, and others manned and armed more or less effectively. These vessels had not yet come into Achillas's hands, but it would be certain that he would take possession of them as soon as he should gain admittance to those parts of the city which Caesar had abandoned. This it was extremely important to prevent; for, if Achillas held this fleet, especially if he continued to command the island of Pharos, he would be perfect master of all the approaches to the city on the side of the sea. He could then not only receive reinforcements and supplies himself from that quarter, but he could also effectually cut off the Roman army from all possibility of receiving any. It became, therefore, as Caesar thought, imperiously necessary that he should protect himself from this danger. This he did by sending out an expedition to burn all the shipping in the harbour, and, at the same time, to take possession of a certain fort upon the island of Pharos which commanded the entrance to the port. This undertaking was abundantly successful. The troops burned the shipping, took the fort, expelled the Egyptian soldiers from it, and put a Roman garrison into it instead, and then returned in safety within Caesar's lines. Cleopatra witnessed these exploits from her palace windows with feelings of the highest admiration for the energy and valour which her Roman protectors displayed.

The Egyptian Fleet – Caesar Burns the Ships – Fire Spreads to the City – The Library Destroyed

The burning of the Egyptian ships in this action, however fortunate for Cleopatra and Caesar, was attended with a catastrophe which has ever since been lamented by the whole civilized world. Some of the burning ships were driven by the wind to the shore, where they set fire to the buildings which were contiguous to the water. The flames spread and produced an extensive conflagration, in the course of which the largest part of the great library was destroyed. This library was the only general collection of the ancient writings that ever had been made, and the loss of it was never repaired.

Achillas Captured – Achillas Beheaded

The destruction of the Egyptian fleet resulted also in the downfall and ruin of Achillas. From the time of Arsinoë's arrival in the camp there had been a constant rivalry and jealousy between himself and Ganymede, the eunuch who had accompanied Arsinoë in her flight. Two parties had been formed in the army, some declaring for Achillas and some for Ganymede. Arsinoë advocated Ganymede's interests, and when, at length, the fleet was burned, she charged Achillas with having been, by his neglect or incapacity, the cause of the loss. Achillas was tried, condemned, and beheaded. From that time Ganymede assumed the administration of Arsinoë's government as her minister of state and the commander-in-chief of her armies.

Ganymede's Plan

About the time that these occurrences took place, the Egyptian army advanced into those parts of the city from which Caesar had withdrawn, producing those terrible scenes of panic and confusion which always attend a sudden and violent change of military possession within the precincts of a city. Ganymede brought up his troops on every side to the walls of Caesar's citadels and entrenchments, and hemmed him closely in. He cut off all avenues of approach to Caesar's lines by land and commenced vigorous preparations for an assault. He constructed engines for battering down the walls. He opened shops and established forges in every part of the city for the manufacture of darts, spears, pikes, and all kinds of military machinery. He built towers supported upon huge wheels, with the design of filling them with armed men when finally ready to make his assault upon Caesar's lines and moving them up to the walls of the citadels and palaces, so as to give to his soldiers the advantage of a lofty elevation in making their attacks. He levied contributions on the rich citizens for the necessary funds and provided himself with men by pressing all the artisans, labourers, and men capable of bearing arms into his service. He sent messengers back into the interior of the country, in every direction, summoning the people to arms, and calling for contributions of money and military stores.

Ganymede's Messengers – Their Instructions

These messengers were instructed to urge upon the people that, unless Caesar and his army were at once expelled from Alexandria, there was imminent danger that the national independence of Egypt would be for ever destroyed. The Romans, they were to say, had extended their conquests over almost all the rest of the world. They had sent one army into Egypt before, under the command of Mark Antony, under the pretence of restoring Ptolemy Auletes to the throne. Now another commander, with another force, had come, offering some other pretexts for interfering in their affairs. These Roman encroachments, the messengers were to say, would end in the complete subjugation of Egypt to a foreign power, unless the people of the country roused themselves to meet the danger manfully, and to expel the intruders.

Ganymede Cuts Off Caesar's Access to Fresh Water

As Caesar had possession of the island of Pharos and of the harbour, Ganymede could not cut him off from receiving such reinforcements of men and arms as he might make arrangements for obtaining beyond the sea; nor could he curtail his supply of food, as the granaries and magazines within Caesar's quarter of the city contained almost inexhaustible stores of corn. There was one remaining point essential to the subsistence of an army besieged, and that was an abundant supply of water. The palaces and citadels which Caesar occupied were supplied with water by means of numerous subterranean aqueducts, which conveyed the water from the Nile to vast cisterns built underground, whence it was raised by buckets and hydraulic engines for use. In reflecting upon this circumstance, Ganymede conceived the design of secretly digging a canal, so as to turn the waters of the sea by means of it into these aqueducts. This plan he carried into effect. The consequence was that the water in the cisterns was gradually changed. It became first brackish, then more and more salt and bitter, until, at length, it was wholly impossible to use it. For some time, the army within could not understand these changes; and when, at length, they discovered the cause the soldiers were panic-stricken at the thought that they were now apparently wholly at the mercy of their enemies, since, without supplies of water, they must all immediately perish. They considered it hopeless to attempt any longer to hold out, and urged Caesar to evacuate the city, embark on board his galleys, and proceed to sea.

Caesar Orders Wells Dug

Instead of doing this, however, Caesar, ordering all other operations to be suspended, employed the whole labouring force of his command, under the direction of the captains of the several companies, in digging wells in every part of his quarter of the city. Fresh water, he said, was almost invariably found, at a moderate depth, upon seacoasts, even upon ground lying in very close proximity to the sea. The digging was successful. Fresh water, in great abundance, was found. Thus, this danger was passed, and the men's fears effectually relieved.

Arrival of the Transports – Transports in Distress

A short time after these transactions occurred, there came into the harbour one day, from along the shore west of the city, a small sloop, bringing the intelligence that a squadron of transports had arrived upon the coast to the westward of Alexandria, and had anchored there, being unable to come up to the city on account of an easterly wind which prevailed at that season of the year. This squadron was one which had been sent across the Mediterranean with arms, ammunition, and military stores for Caesar, in answer to requisitions which he had made immediately after he had landed. The transports being thus windbound on the coast, and having nearly exhausted their supplies of water, were in distress; and they accordingly sent forward the sloop, which was probably propelled by oars, to make known their situation to Caesar, and to ask for succour. Caesar immediately went, himself, on board of one of his galleys, and ordering the remainder of his little fleet to follow him, he set sail out of the harbour, and then turned to the westward, with a view of proceeding along the coast to the place where the transports were lying.

Lowness of the Coast – Caesar's Fleet

All this was done secretly. The land is so low in the vicinity of Alexandria that boats or galleys are out of sight from it at a very short distance from the shore. In fact, travellers say that, in coming upon the coast, the illusion produced by the spherical form of the surface of the water and the low and level character of the coast is such that one seems actually to descend from the sea to the land. Caesar might therefore have easily kept his expedition a secret, had it not been that, in order to be provided with a supply of water for the transports immediately on reaching them, he stopped at a solitary part of the coast, at some distance from Alexandria, and sent a party a little way into the interior in search for water. This party were discovered by the country people and were intercepted by a troop of horse and made prisoners. From these prisoners the Egyptians learned that Caesar himself was on the coast with a small squadron of galleys. The tidings spread in all directions. The people flocked together from every quarter. They hastily collected all the boats and vessels which could be obtained at the villages in that region and from the various branches of the Nile. In the meantime, Caesar had gone on to the anchorage ground of the squadron and had taken the transports in tow to bring them to the city; for the galleys, being propelled by oars, were in a measure independent of the wind. On his return, he found quite a formidable naval armament assembled to dispute the passage.

A Naval Conflict – Caesar Victorious

A severe conflict ensued, but Caesar was victorious. The navy which the Egyptians had so suddenly got together was as suddenly destroyed. Some of the vessels were burned, others sunk, and others captured; and Caesar returned in triumph to the port with his transports and stores. He was welcomed with the acclamations of his soldiers, and, still more warmly, by the joy and gratitude of Cleopatra, who had been waiting during his absence in great anxiety and suspense to know the result of the expedition, aware as she was that her hero was exposing himself in it to the most imminent personal danger.

Ganymede Equips a Fleet – Caesar in Danger

The arrival of these reinforcements greatly improved Caesar's condition, and the circumstance of their coming forced upon the mind of Ganymede a sense of the absolute necessity that he should gain possession of the harbour if he intended to keep Caesar in check. He accordingly determined to take immediate measures for forming a naval force. He sent along the coast, and ordered every ship and galley that could be found in all the ports to be sent immediately to Alexandria. He employed as many men as possible in and around the city in building more. He unroofed some of the most magnificent edifices to procure timber as a material for making benches and oars. When all was ready, he made a grand attack upon Caesar in the port, and a terrible contest ensued for the possession of the harbour, the mole, the island, and the citadels and fortresses commanding the entrances from the sea. Caesar well knew this contest would be a decisive one in respect to the final result of the war, and he accordingly went forth himself to take an active and personal part in the conflict. He felt doubtless, too, a strong emotion of pride and pleasure in exhibiting his prowess in the sight of Cleopatra, who could watch the progress of the battle from the palace windows, full of excitement at the dangers which he incurred, and of admiration at the feats of strength and valour which he performed. During this battle the life of the great conqueror was several times in the most imminent danger. He wore a habit or mantle of the imperial purple, which made him a conspicuous mark for his enemies; and, of course, wherever he went, in that place was the hottest of the fight. Once, in the midst of a scene of most dreadful confusion and din, he leaped from an overloaded boat into the water and swam for his life, holding his cloak between his teeth and drawing it through the water after him, that it might not fall into the hands of his enemies. He carried, at the same time, as he swam, certain valuable papers which he wished to save, holding them above his head with one hand, while he propelled himself through the water with the other.

Another Victory for Caesar

The result of this contest was another decisive victory for Caesar. Not only were the ships which the Egyptians had collected defeated and destroyed, but the mole, with the fortresses at each extremity of it, and the island, with the light house and the town of Pharos, all fell into Caesar's hands.

The Egyptians Discouraged – Secret Messengers

The Egyptians now began to be discouraged. The army and the people, judging, as mankind always do, of the virtue of their military commanders solely by the criterion of success, began to be tired of the rule of Ganymede and Arsinoë. They sent secret messengers to Caesar avowing their discontent, and saying that, if he would liberate Ptolemy – who, it will be recollected, had been all this time held as a sort of prisoner of state in Caesar's palaces – they thought that the people generally would receive him as their sovereign, and that then an arrangement might easily be made for an amicable adjustment of the whole controversy. Caesar was strongly inclined to accede to this proposal.

Dissimulation of Ptolemy XIII – Arrival of Mithradates

He accordingly called Ptolemy into his presence and, taking him kindly by the hand, informed him of the wishes of the people of

Egypt, and gave him permission to go. Ptolemy, however, begged not to be sent away. He professed the strongest attachment to Caesar, and the utmost confidence in him, and he very much preferred, he said, to remain under his protection. Caesar replied that, if those were his sentiments, the separation would not be a lasting one. "If we part as friends," he said, "we shall soon meet again." By these and similar assurances he endeavoured to encourage the young prince, and then sent him away. Ptolemy was received by the Egyptians with great joy and was immediately placed at the head of the government. Instead, however, of endeavouring to promote a settlement of the quarrel with Caesar, he seemed to enter into it now himself, personally, with the utmost ardour, and began at once to make the most extensive preparations both by sea and land for a vigorous prosecution of the war. What the result of these operations would have been can now not be known, for the general aspect of affairs was, soon after these transactions, totally changed by the occurrence of a new and very important event which suddenly intervened, and which turned the attention of all parties, both Egyptians and Romans, to the eastern quarter of the kingdom. The tidings arrived that a large army under the command of a general named Mithradates, whom Caesar had dispatched into Asia for this purpose, had suddenly appeared at Pelusium, had captured that city and were now ready to march to Alexandria.

Defeat of Ptolemy XIII – Terror and Confusion – Death of Ptolemy XIII by Drowning

The Egyptian army immediately broke up its encampments in the neighbourhood of Alexandria and marched to the eastward to meet these new invaders. Caesar followed them with all the forces that he could safely take away from the city. He left the city in the night, and unobserved, and moved across the country with such celerity that he joined Mithradates before the forces of Ptolemy had arrived. After various marches and manoeuvres, the armies met, and a great battle was fought. The Egyptians were defeated. Ptolemy's camp was taken. As the Roman army burst in upon one side of it, the guards and attendants of Ptolemy fled upon the other, clambering over the ramparts in the utmost terror and confusion. The foremost fell headlong into the ditch below, which was thus soon filled to the brim with the dead and the dying; while those who came behind pressed on over the bridge thus formed, trampling remorselessly, as they fled, on the bodies of their comrades, who lay writhing, struggling, and shrieking beneath their feet. Those who escaped reached the river. They crowded together into a boat which lay at the bank and pushed off from the shore. The boat was overloaded, and it sank as soon as it left the land. The Romans drew the bodies which floated to the shore upon the bank again, and they found among them one, which, by the royal cuirass which was upon it, the customary badge and armour of the Egyptian kings, they knew to be the body of Ptolemy.

Second Reign of Cleopatra VII Thea Philopator – She Marries Ptolemy XIV Philopator – Arsinoë Captured

The victory which Caesar obtained in this battle and the death of Ptolemy ended the war. Nothing now remained but for him to place himself at the head of the combined forces and march back to Alexandria. The Egyptian forces which had been left there made no resistance, and he entered the city in triumph. He took Arsinoë prisoner. He decreed that Cleopatra should reign as queen, and that she should marry her youngest brother, the other Ptolemy – a boy at this time about eleven years of age. A marriage with one so young was, of course, a mere form. Cleopatra remained, as before, the companion of Caesar.

General Disapproval of Caesar's Course

Caesar had, in the meantime, incurred great censure at Rome, and throughout the whole Roman world, for having thus turned aside from his own proper duties as the Roman consul, and the commander-in-chief of the armies of the empire, to embroil himself in the quarrels of a remote and secluded kingdom with which the interests of the Roman commonwealth were so little connected. His friends and the authorities at Rome were continually urging him to return. They were especially indignant at his protracted neglect of his own proper duties, from knowing that he was held in Egypt by a guilty attachment to the queen – thus not only violating his obligations to the state, but likewise inflicting upon his wife Calpurnia, and his family at Rome, an intolerable wrong. But Caesar was so fascinated by Cleopatra's charms, and by the mysterious and unaccountable influence which she exercised over him, that he paid no heed to any of these remonstrances. Even after the war was ended, he remained some months in Egypt to enjoy his favourite's society. He would spend whole nights in her company, in feasting and revelry. He made a splendid royal progress with her through Egypt after the war was over, attended by a numerous train of Roman guards. He formed a plan for taking her to Rome and marrying her there; and he took measures for having the laws of the city altered so as to enable him to do so, though he was already married.

Ptolemy XV Caesarion, Cleopatra's Son by Caesar

All these things produced great discontent and disaffection among Caesar's friends and throughout the Roman army. The Egyptians, too, strongly censured the conduct of Cleopatra. A son was born to her about this time, whom the Alexandrians named, from his father, Caesarion. Cleopatra was regarded in the new relation of mother, which she now sustained, not with interest and sympathy, but with feelings of reproach and condemnation.

Public Opinion of Cleopatra's Conduct

Cleopatra was all this time growing more and more accomplished, and more and more beautiful; but her vivacity and spirit, which had been so charming while it was simple and childlike, now began to appear more forward and bolder. It is the characteristic of pure and lawful love to soften and subdue the heart, and infuse a gentle and quiet spirit into all its action; while that which breaks over the barriers that God and nature have marked out for it, tends to make woman masculine and bold, to indurate all her sensibilities, and to destroy that gentleness and timidity of demeanour which have so great an influence in heightening her charms. Cleopatra was beginning to experience these effects. She was indifferent to the opinions of her subjects and was only anxious to maintain as long as possible her guilty ascendency over Caesar.

Caesar Departs for Rome – Takes Arsinoë with Him

Caesar, however, finally determined to set out on his return to the capital. Leaving Cleopatra, accordingly, a sufficient force to secure the continuance of her power, he embarked the remainder of his forces in his transports and galleys and sailed away. He took the unhappy Arsinoë with him, intending to exhibit her as a trophy of his Egyptian victories on his arrival at Rome.

CHAPTER VIII
CLEOPATRA, A QUEEN, 47–43 BCE

Short Conflict, Big Consequences

The war by which Caesar reinstated Cleopatra upon the throne was not one of very long duration. Caesar arrived in Egypt in pursuit of Pompey about the first of August 48 BCE; the war was ended, and Cleopatra established in secure possession by the end of January; so that the conflict, violent as it was while it continued, was very brief, the peaceful and commercial pursuits of the Alexandrians having been interrupted by it only for a few months.

Extent of the Alexandrian War

Nor did either the war itself, or the derangements consequent upon it, extend very far into the interior of the country. The city of Alexandria itself and the neighbouring coasts were the chief scenes of the contest until Mithradates arrived at Pelusium. He, it is true, marched across the Delta, and the final battle was fought in the interior of the country. It was, however, after all, but a very small portion of the Egyptian territory that was directly affected by the war. The great mass of the people, occupying the rich and fertile tracts which bordered the various branches of the Nile, and the long and verdant valley which extended so far into the heart of the continent, knew nothing of the conflict but by vague and distant rumours. The pursuits of the agricultural population went on, all the time, as steadily and prosperously as ever; so that when the conflict was ended, and Cleopatra entered upon the quiet and peaceful possession of her power, she found that the resources of her empire were very little impaired.

Revenues of Egypt – The City Repaired – The Library Rebuilt

She availed herself, accordingly, of the revenues which poured in very abundantly upon her, to enter upon a career of the greatest luxury, magnificence, and splendour. The injuries which had been done to the palaces and other public edifices of Alexandria by the fire, and by the military operations of the siege, were repaired. The bridges which had been broken down were rebuilt. The canals which had been obstructed were opened again. The seawater was shut off from the palace cisterns; the rubbish of demolished houses was removed; the barricades were cleared from the streets; and the injuries which the palaces had suffered either from the violence of military engines or the rough occupation of the Roman soldiery, were repaired. In a word, the city was speedily restored once more, so far as was possible, to its former order and beauty. The five hundred thousand manuscripts of the Alexandrian library, which had been burned, could not, indeed, be restored; but, in all other respects, the city soon resumed in appearance all its former splendour. Even in respect to the library, Cleopatra made an effort to retrieve the loss. She repaired the ruined buildings, and afterwards, in the course of her life, she brought together, it was said, in a manner hereafter to be described, one or two hundred thousand rolls of manuscripts, as the commencement of a new collection. The new library, however, never acquired the fame and distinction that had pertained to the old.

Luxury and Splendour

The former sovereigns of Egypt, Cleopatra's ancestors, had generally, as has already been shown, devoted the immense revenues which they extorted from the agriculturalists of the Valley of the Nile to purposes of ambition. Cleopatra seemed now disposed to expend them in luxury and pleasure. They, the Ptolemies, had employed their resources in erecting vast structures, or founding magnificent institutions at Alexandria, to add to the glory of the city, and to widen and extend their own fame. Cleopatra, on the other hand, as was, perhaps, naturally to be expected of a young, beautiful, and impulsive woman suddenly raised to so conspicuous a position, and to the possession of such unbounded wealth and power, expended her royal revenues in plans of personal display, and in scenes of festivity, gaiety, and enjoyment. She adorned her palaces, built magnificent barges for pleasure excursions on the Nile, and expended enormous sums for dress, for equipages, and for sumptuous entertainments. In fact, so lavish were her expenditures for these and similar purposes during the early years of her reign that she is considered as having carried the extravagance of sensual luxury, and personal display, and splendour, beyond the limits that had ever before or have ever since been attained.

Deterioration of Cleopatra's Character – Cleopatra Murders her Brother, Ptolemy XIV Philopator, by Poison

Whatever of simplicity of character, and of gentleness and kindness of spirit she might have possessed in her earlier years, of course gradually disappeared under the influences of such a course of life as she now was leading. She was beautiful and fascinating still, but she began to grow selfish, heartless, and designing. Her little brother – he was but eleven years of age, it will be recollected, when Caesar arranged the marriage between them – was an object of jealousy to her. He was now, of course, too young to take any actual share in the exercise of the royal power, or to interfere at all in his sister's plans or pleasures. But then he was growing older. In a few years he would be fifteen – which was the period of life fixed upon by Caesar's arrangements, and, in fact, by the laws and usages of the Egyptian kingdom – when he was to come into possession of power as king, and as the husband of Cleopatra. Cleopatra was extremely unwilling that the change in her relations to him and to the government, which this period was to bring, should take place. Accordingly, just before the time arrived, she caused him to be poisoned. His death released her, as she had intended, from all restraints, and thereafter she continued to reign alone. During the remainder of her life, so far as the enjoyment of wealth and power, and of all other elements of external prosperity could go, Cleopatra's career was one of uninterrupted success. She had no conscientious scruples to interfere with the most full and unrestrained indulgence of every propensity of her heart, and the means of indulgence were before her in the most unlimited profusion. The only bar to her happiness was the impossibility of satisfying the impulses and passions of the human soul when they once break over the bounds which the laws both of God and of nature ordain for restraining them.

Caesar's Career – Rapid Course of Conquests – Cleopatra Decides to Go to Rome

In the meantime, while Cleopatra was spending the early years of her reign in all this luxury and splendour, Caesar was pursuing his career, as the conqueror of the world, in the most successful manner. On the death of Pompey, he would naturally have succeeded at once to the enjoyment of the supreme power; but his delay in Egypt, and the extent to which it was known that he was entangled with Cleopatra, encouraged and strengthened his enemies in various parts of the world. In fact, a revolt which broke out in Asia Minor, and which it was absolutely necessary that he should proceed at once to quell, was the immediate cause of his leaving Egypt at last. Other plans for making head against Caesar's power were formed in Spain, in Africa, and in Italy. His military skill and energy, however, were so great, and the ascendency which he exercised over the minds of men by his personal presence was so unbounded, and so astonishing, moreover, was the celerity with which he moved from continent to continent, and from kingdom to kingdom, that in a very short period from the time of his leaving Egypt, he had conducted most brilliant and successful campaigns in all the three quarters of the world then known, had put down effectually all opposition to his power, and then had returned to Rome the acknowledged master of the world. Cleopatra, who had, of course, watched his career during all this time with great pride and pleasure, concluded, at last, to go to Rome and make a visit to him there.

Feelings of the Romans Toward Cleopatra

The people of Rome were, however, not prepared to receive her very cordially. It was an age in which vice of every kind was regarded with great indulgence, but the moral instincts of mankind were too strong to be wholly blinded to the true character of so conspicuous an example of wickedness as this. Arsinoë was at Rome, too, during this period of Caesar's life. He had brought her there, it will be recollected, on his return from Egypt, as a prisoner, and as a trophy of his victory. His design was, in fact, to reserve her as a captive to grace his *triumph*.

Caesar's Four Triumphs – Roman Triumphal Processions

A triumph, according to the usages of the ancient Romans, was a grand celebration decreed by the Senate to great military commanders of the highest rank, when they returned from distant campaigns in which they had made great conquests or gained extraordinary victories. Caesar concentrated all his triumphs into one. They were celebrated on his return to Rome for the last time, after having completed the conquest of the world. The processions of this triumph occupied four days. In fact, there were four triumphs, one on each day for the four days. The wars and conquests which these ovations were intended to celebrate were those of Gaul, of Egypt, of Asia, and of Africa; and the processions on the several days consisted of endless trains of prisoners, trophies, arms, banners, pictures, images, convoys of wagons loaded with plunder, captive princes and princesses, animals wild and tame, and everything else which the conqueror had been able to bring home with him from his campaigns, to excite the curiosity or the admiration of the people of the city and illustrate the magnitude of his exploits. Of course, the Roman generals, when engaged in distant foreign wars, were ambitious of bringing back as many distinguished captives and as much public plunder as they were able to obtain, in order to add to the variety and splendour of the triumphal procession by which their victories were to be honoured on their return. It was with this view that Caesar brought Arsinoë from Egypt; and he had retained her as his captive at Rome until his conquests were completed and the time for his triumph arrived. She, of course, formed a part of the triumphal train on the *Egyptian* day. She walked immediately before the chariot in which Caesar rode. She was in chains, like any other captive, though her chains, in honour of her lofty rank, were made of gold.

Sympathy of the Roman Population Towards Arsinoë

The effect, however, upon the Roman population of seeing the unhappy princess, overwhelmed as she was with sorrow and chagrin, as she moved slowly along in the train, among the other emblems and trophies of violence and plunder, proved to be by no means favourable to Caesar. The population were inclined to pity her, and to sympathize with her in her sufferings. The sight of her distress recalled, too, to their minds, the dereliction from duty which Caesar had been guilty of in his yielding to the enticements of Cleopatra and remaining so long in Egypt to the neglect of his proper duties as a Roman minister of state. In a word, the tide of admiration for Caesar's military exploits which had been setting so strongly in his favour, seemed inclined to turn, and the city was filled with murmurs against him even in the midst of his triumphs.

Caesar Overacts His Part

In fact, the pride and vainglory which led Caesar to make his triumphs more splendid and imposing than any former conqueror had ever enjoyed, caused him to overact his part so as to produce effects the reverse of his intentions. The case of Arsinoë was one example of this. Instead of impressing the people with a sense of the greatness of his exploits in Egypt, in deposing one queen and bringing her captive to Rome, in order that he might place another upon the throne in her stead, it only reproduced anew the censures and criminations which he had deserved by his actions there, but which, had it not been for the pitiable spectacle of Arsinoë in the train, might have been forgotten.

Feasts and Festivals

There were other examples of a similar character. There were the feasts, for instance. From the plunder which Caesar had obtained in his various campaigns, he expended the most enormous sums in making feasts and spectacles for the populace at the time of his triumph. A large portion of the populace was pleased, it is true, with the boundless indulgences thus offered to them; but the better part of the Roman people was indignant at the waste and extravagance which were everywhere displayed. For many days the whole city of Rome presented to the view nothing but one widespread scene of riot and debauchery. The people, instead of being pleased with this abundance, said that Caesar must have practised the most extreme and lawless extortion to have obtained the vast amount of money necessary to enable him to supply such unbounded and reckless waste.

Spectacles for the Roman People – Gladiator Combats – Mock Naval Combats

There was another way, too, by which Caesar turned public opinion strongly against himself, by the very means which he adopted for creating a sentiment in his favour. The Romans, among the other barbarous amusements which were practised in the city, were especially fond of combats. These combats were of various kinds. They were fought sometimes between ferocious beasts of the same or of different species, as dogs against each other, or against bulls, lions, or tigers. Any animals, in fact, were employed for this purpose, that could be teased or goaded into anger and ferocity in a fight. Sometimes men were employed in these combats – captive soldiers, that had been taken in war, and brought to Rome to fight in the amphitheatres there as gladiators. These men were compelled to contend sometimes with wild beasts, and sometimes with one another.

Caesar, knowing how highly the Roman assemblies enjoyed such scenes, determined to afford them the indulgence on a most magnificent scale, supposing, of course, that the greater and the more dreadful the fight, the higher would be the pleasure which the spectators would enjoy in witnessing it. Accordingly, in making preparations for the festivities attending his triumph, he caused a large artificial lake to be formed at a convenient place in the vicinity of Rome, where it could be surrounded by the populace of the city, and there he made arrangements for a naval battle. A great number of galleys were introduced into the lake. They were of the usual size employed in war. These galleys were manned with numerous soldiers. Tyrian captives were put upon one side, and Egyptian upon the other; and when all was ready, the two squadrons were ordered to approach and fight a real battle for the amusement of the enormous throngs of spectators that were assembled around. As the nations from which the combatants in this conflict were respectively taken were hostile to each other, and as the men fought, of course, for their lives, the engagement was attended with the usual horrors of a desperate naval encounter. Hundreds were slain. The dead bodies of the combatants fell from the galleys into the lake and the waters of it were dyed with their blood.

Combats on Land with Elephants

There were land combats, too, on the same grand scale. In one of them five-hundred foot soldiers, twenty elephants, and a troop of thirty horse were engaged on each side. The horror of these scenes proved to be too much even for the populace, fierce and merciless as it was, which they were intended to amuse. Caesar, in his eagerness to outdo all former exhibitions and shows, went beyond the limits within which the seeing of men butchered in bloody combats and dying in agony and despair would serve for a pleasure and a pastime. The people were shocked; and condemnations of Caesar's cruelty were added to the other suppressed reproaches and criminations which everywhere arose.

Cleopatra Visits Rome

Cleopatra, during her visit to Rome, lived openly with Caesar at his residence, and this excited very general displeasure. In fact, while the people pitied Arsinoë, Cleopatra, notwithstanding her beauty and her thousand personal accomplishments and charms, was an object of general displeasure, so far as public attention was turned toward her at all. The public mind was, however, much engrossed by the great political movements made by Caesar and the ends toward which he seemed to be aiming. Men accused him of designing to be made a king. Parties were formed for and against him; and though men did not dare openly to utter their sentiments, their passions became the more violent in proportion to the external force by which they were suppressed. Mark Antony was at Rome at this time. He warmly espoused Caesar's cause and encouraged his design of making himself king. He once, in fact, offered to place a royal diadem upon Caesar's head at some public celebration; but the marks of public disapprobation which the act elicited caused him to desist.

Caesar, Dictator in Perpetuity – Conspiracy Against Caesar – Assassination of Caesar

At length, however, the time arrived when Caesar determined to cause himself to be proclaimed *Dictator Perpetuo*. He took advantage of a certain remarkable conjuncture of public affairs, which cannot here be particularly described, but which seemed to him specially to favour his designs, and arrangements were made for having him invested with the regal power by the Senate. The murmurs and the discontent of the people at the indications that the time for the realization of their fears was drawing nigh, became more and more audible, and at length a conspiracy was formed to put an end to the danger by destroying the ambitious aspirant's life. Two stern and determined men, Brutus and Cassius, were the leaders of this conspiracy. They matured their plans, organized their band of associates, provided themselves secretly with arms, and when the Senate convened, on the day in which the decisive vote was to have been passed, Caesar himself presiding, they came up boldly around him in his presidential chair, and murdered him with their daggers on the Ides of March (15th) 44 BCE.

Antony, from whom the plans of the conspirators had been kept profoundly secret, stood by, looking on stupefied and confounded while the deed was done, but utterly unable to render his friend any protection.

Cleopatra immediately fled from the city and returned to Egypt.

Arsinoë Released – Goes to Syria

Arsinoë had gone away before. Caesar, either taking pity on her misfortunes, or impelled, perhaps, by the force of public sentiment, which seemed inclined to take part with her against him, set her at liberty immediately after the ceremonies of his triumph were over. He would not, however, allow her to return into Egypt, for fear, probably, that she might in some way or other be the means of disturbing the government of Cleopatra. She proceeded, accordingly, into Syria, no longer as a captive, but still as an exile from her native land. We shall hereafter learn what became of her there.

Calpurnia Looks to Mark Antony for Protection

Calpurnia mourned the death of her husband with sincere and unaffected grief. She bore the wrongs which she suffered as a wife with a very patient and unrepining spirit and loved her husband with the most devoted attachment to the end. Nothing can be more affecting than the proofs of her tender and anxious regard on the night immediately preceding the assassination. There were certain slight and obscure indications of danger which her watchful devotion to her husband led her to observe, though they eluded the notice of all Caesar's other friends, and they filled her with apprehension and anxiety; and when at length the bloody body was brought home to her from the Senate-house, she was overwhelmed with grief and despair.

She had no children. She accordingly looked upon Mark Antony as her nearest friend and protector, and in the confusion and terror which prevailed the next day in the city, she hastily packed together the money and other valuables contained in the house, and all her husband's books and papers, and sent them to Antony for safe keeping.

CHAPTER IX
THE BATTLE OF PHILIPPI, 3 AND 23 OCTOBER 42 BCE

Avenging Caesar

When the tidings of the assassination of Caesar were first announced to the people of Rome, all ranks and classes of men were struck with amazement and consternation. No one knew what to say or do. A very large and influential portion of the community had been Caesar's friends. It was equally certain that there was a very powerful interest opposed to him. No one could foresee which of these two parties would now carry the day, and, of course, for a time, all was uncertainty and indecision.

Caesar's Will – Mark Antony's Rivals as the Successor to Caesar

Mark Antony came forward at once and assumed the position of Caesar's representative and the leader of the party on that side. A will was found among Caesar's effects, and when the will was opened it appeared that large sums of money were left to the Roman people, and other large amounts to a nephew of the deceased, named Octavian, who will be more particularly spoken of hereafter. Antony was named in the will as the executor of it. This and other circumstances seemed to authorize him to come forward as the head and the leader of the Caesar party. Brutus and Cassius, who remained openly in the city after their desperate deed had been performed, were the acknowledged leaders of the other party; while the mass of the people was at first so astounded at the magnitude and suddenness of the revolution which the open and public assassination of a Roman emperor by a Roman Senate denoted, that they knew not what to say or do. In fact, the killing of Julius Caesar, considering the exalted position which he occupied, the rank and station of the men who perpetrated the deed, and the very extraordinary publicity of the scene in which the act was performed, was, doubtless, the most conspicuous and most appalling case of assassination that has ever occurred. The whole population of Rome seemed for some days to be amazed and stupefied by the tidings. At length, however, parties began to be more distinctly formed. The lines of demarcation between them were gradually drawn, and men began to arrange themselves more and more unequivocally on the opposite sides.

For a short time, the supremacy of Antony over the Caesar party was readily acquiesced in and allowed. At length, however, and before his arrangements were finally matured, he found that he had two formidable competitors upon his own side. These were Octavian and Lepidus.

Octavian Leaves Apollonia for Rome – Claims His Rights to Julius Caesar's Name and Legacy

Octavian, who was the nephew of Caesar, already alluded to, was a very accomplished and elegant young man, now about nineteen years of age. He was the son of Julius Caesar's niece.

He had always been a great favourite with his uncle. Every possible attention had been paid to his education, and he had been advanced by Caesar, already, to positions of high importance in public life. Caesar, in fact, adopted him as his son, and made him his heir. At the time of Caesar's death he was at Apollonia, a city of Illyricum, north of Greece. The troops under his command there offered to march at once with him, if he wished it, to Rome, and avenge his uncle's death. Octavian, after some hesitation, concluded that it would be most prudent for him to proceed thither first himself, alone, as a private person, and demand his rights as his uncle's heir, according to the provisions of the will. He accordingly did so. He found, on his arrival, that the will, the property, the books and parchments, and the substantial power of the government, were all in Antony's hands. Antony, instead of putting Octavian into possession of his property and rights, found various pretexts for evasion and delay. Octavian was too young yet, he said, to assume such weighty responsibilities. He was himself also too much pressed with the urgency of public affairs to attend to the business of the will. With these and similar excuses as his justification, Antony seemed inclined to pay no regard whatever to Octavian's claims.

Octavian's Character

Octavian, young as he was, possessed a character that was marked with great intelligence, spirit, and resolution. He soon made many powerful friends in the city of Rome and among the Roman Senate. It became a serious question whether he or Antony would gain the greatest ascendency in the party of Caesar's friends. The contest for this ascendency was, in fact, protracted for two or three years, and led to a vast complication of intrigues, and manoeuvres, and civil wars, which cannot, however, be here particularly detailed.

Lepidus Takes Command of the Army

The other competitor who Antony had to contend with was a distinguished Roman general named Lepidus. Lepidus was an officer of the army, in very high command at the time of Caesar's death. He was present in the Senate-chamber on the day of the assassination. He stole secretly away when he saw that the deed was done, and repaired to the camp of the army without the city and immediately assumed the command of the forces. This gave him great power, and in the course of the contests which subsequently ensued between Antony and Octavian, he took an active part, and held in some measure the balance between them.

Octavian, Antony and Lepidus, 'Three Men for Organizing the Republic'

At length the contest was finally closed by a coalition of the three rivals. Finding that they could not either of them gain a decided victory over the others, they combined together, and formed the celebrated *triumvirate*, which continued afterwards for some time to wield the supreme command in the Roman world. In forming this league of reconciliation, the three rivals held their conference on an island situated in one of the branches of the Po, in the north of Italy. They manifested extreme jealousy and suspicion of each other in coming to this interview. Two bridges were built leading to the island, one from each bank of the stream. The army of Antony was drawn up upon one side of the river, and that of Octavian upon the other. Lepidus went first to the island by one of the bridges. After examining the ground carefully, to make himself sure that it contained no ambuscade, he made a signal to the other generals, who then came over, each advancing by his own bridge, and accompanied by three hundred guards, who remained upon the bridge to secure a retreat for their masters in case of treachery. The conference lasted three days, at the expiration of which time the articles were all agreed upon and signed.

This league being formed, the three confederates turned their united force against the party of the conspirators. Of this party Brutus and Cassius were still at the head.

The Conspirators Demand Aid from Cleopatra – Cleopatra Espouses Antony's Cause – Her Motives

The scene of the contests between Octavian, Antony, and Lepidus had been chiefly Italy and the other central countries of Europe. Brutus and Cassius, on the other hand, had gone across the Adriatic Sea into the East immediately after Caesar's assassination. They were now in Asia Minor, and were employed in concentrating their forces, forming alliances with the various Eastern powers, raising troops, bringing over to their side the Roman legions which were stationed in that quarter of the world, seizing magazines, and exacting contributions from all who could be induced to favour their cause. Among other embassies which they sent, one went to Egypt to demand aid from Cleopatra. Cleopatra, however, was resolved to join the other side in the contest. It was natural that she should feel grateful to Caesar for his efforts and sacrifices on her behalf, and that she should be inclined to favour the cause of his friends. Accordingly, instead of sending troops to aid Brutus and Cassius, as they had desired her to do, she immediately fitted out an expedition to proceed to the coast of Asia, with a view of rendering all the aid in her power to Antony's cause.

Cassius's Plan to Seize Egypt – Plan Abandoned – Brutus and Cassius Go to Thrace

Cassius, on his part, finding that Cleopatra was determined on joining his enemies, immediately resolved on proceeding at once to Egypt and taking possession of the country. He also stationed a military force at Taenarus, the southern promontory of Greece, to watch for and intercept the fleet of Cleopatra as soon as it should appear on the European shores. All these plans, however – both those which Cleopatra formed against Cassius, and those which Cassius formed against her – failed of accomplishment. Cleopatra's fleet encountered a terrible storm, which dispersed and destroyed it. A small remnant was driven upon the coast of Africa, but nothing could be saved which could be made available for the purpose intended. As for Cassius's intended expedition to Egypt, it was not carried into effect. The dangers which began now to threaten him from the direction of Italy and Rome were so imminent, that, at Brutus's urgent request, he gave up the Egyptian plan, and the two generals concentrated their forces to meet the armies of the *triumvirate* which were now rapidly advancing to attack them. They passed for this purpose across the Hellespont from Sestos to Abydos and entered Thrace.

Brutus and Cassius Assemble Their Armies at Philippi

After various marches and countermarches, and a long succession of those manoeuvres by which two powerful armies, approaching a contest, endeavour each to gain some position of advantage against the other, the various bodies of troops belonging, respectively, to the two powers, came into the vicinity of each other near Philippi. Brutus and Cassius arrived there first. There was a plain in the neighbourhood of the city, with a rising ground in a certain portion of it. Brutus took possession of this elevation, and entrenched himself there. Cassius posted his forces about three miles distant, near the sea. There was a line of entrenchments between the two camps, which formed a chain of communication by which the positions of the two commanders were connected. The armies were thus very advantageously posted. They had the River Strymon and a marsh on the left of the ground that they occupied, while the plain was before them, and the sea behind. Here they awaited the arrival of their foes.

Antony and Octavian Arrive at Philippi

Antony, who was at this time at Amphipolis, a city not far distant from Philippi, learning that Brutus and Cassius had taken their positions in anticipation of an attack, advanced immediately and encamped upon the plain. Octavian was detained by sickness at the city of Dyrrachium, not very far distant. Antony waited for him. It was ten days before he came. At length he arrived, though in coming he had to be borne upon a litter, being still too sick to travel in any other way. Antony approached, and established his camp opposite that of Cassius, near the sea, while Octavian took post opposite Brutus. The four armies then paused, contemplating the probable results of the engagement that was about to ensue.

Difference of Opinion Between Brutus and Cassius – Council of War's Decision

The forces on the two sides were nearly equal; but on the Republican side, that is, on the part of Brutus and Cassius, there was great inconvenience and suffering for want of a sufficient supply of provisions and stores. There was some difference of opinion between Brutus and Cassius in respect to what it was best for them to do. Brutus was inclined to give the enemy battle. Cassius was reluctant to do so, since, under the circumstances in which they were placed, he considered it unwise to hazard, as they necessarily must do, the whole success of their cause to the chances of a single battle. A council of war was convened, and the various officers were asked to give their opinions. In this conference, one of the officers having recommended to postpone the conflict to the next winter, Brutus asked him what advantage he hoped to attain by such delay. "If I gain nothing else," replied the officer, "I shall live so much the longer." This answer touched Cassius's pride and military sense of honour. Rather than concur in a counsel which was thus, on the part of one of its advocates at least, dictated by what he considered an inglorious love of life, he preferred to retract his opinion. It was agreed by the council that the army should maintain its ground and give the enemy battle. The officers then repaired to their respective camps.

Brutus Elated – Cassius Despondent

Brutus was greatly pleased at this decision. To fight the battle had been his original desire, and as his counsels had prevailed, he was, of course, gratified with the prospect for the morrow. He arranged a sumptuous entertainment in his tent and invited all the officers of his division of the army to sup with him. The party spent the night in convivial pleasures, and in mutual congratulations at the prospect of the victory which, as they believed, awaited them on the morrow. Brutus entertained his guests with brilliant conversation all the evening and inspired them with his own confident anticipations of success in the conflict which was to ensue.

Cassius, on the other hand, in his camp by the sea, was silent and desponding. He supped privately with a few intimate friends. On rising from the table, he took one of his officers aside, and, pressing his hand, said to him that he felt great misgivings in respect to the result of the contest. "It is against my judgment," said he, "that we thus hazard the liberty of Rome on the event of one battle, fought under such circumstances as these. Whatever is the result, I wish you to bear me witness hereafter that I was forced into this measure by circumstances that I could not control. I suppose, however, that I ought to take courage, notwithstanding the reasons that I have for these gloomy forebodings. Let us, therefore, hope for the best; and come and sup with me again to-morrow night. Tomorrow is my birthday."

Brutus's Resolution

The next morning, the scarlet mantle – the customary signal displayed in Roman camps on the morning of a day of battle – was seen at the tops of the tents of the two commanding generals, waving there in the air like a banner. While the troops, in obedience to this signal, were preparing themselves for the conflict, the two generals went to meet each other at a point midway between their two encampments, for a final consultation and agreement in respect to the arrangements of the day. When this business was concluded, and they were about to separate, in order to proceed each to his own sphere of duty, Cassius asked Brutus what he intended to do in case the day should go against them. "We hope for the best," said he, "and pray that the gods may grant us the victory in this most momentous crisis. But we must remember that it is the greatest and the most momentous of human affairs that are always the most uncertain, and we cannot foresee what is to-day to be the result of the battle. If it goes against us, what do you intend to do? Do you intend to escape, or to die?"

"When I was a young man," said Brutus, in reply, "and looked at this subject only as a question of theory, I thought it wrong for a man ever to take his own life. However great the evils that threatened him, and however desperate his condition, I considered it his duty to live, and to wait patiently for better times. But now, placed in the position in which I am, I see the subject in a different light. If we do not gain the battle this day, I shall consider all hope and possibility of saving our country for ever gone, and I shall not leave the field of battle alive."

Cassius Similarly Resolved

Cassius, in his despondency, had made the same resolution for himself before, and he was rejoiced to hear Brutus utter these sentiments. He grasped his colleague's hand with a countenance expressive of the greatest animation and pleasure, and bade him farewell, saying, "We will go out boldly to face the enemy. For we are certain either that we shall conquer them, or that we shall have nothing to fear from their victory over us."

Cassius's dejection, and the tendency of his mind to take a despairing view of the prospects of the cause in which he was engaged, were owing, in some measure, to certain unfavourable omens which he had observed. These omens, though really frivolous and wholly unworthy of attention, seem to have had great influence upon him, notwithstanding his general intelligence, and the remarkable strength and energy of his character. They were as follows:

Omens Before Battle

In offering certain sacrifices, he was to wear, according to the usage prescribed on such occasions, a garland of flowers, and it happened that the officer who brought the garland, by mistake or accident, presented it wrong side up. Again, in some procession which was formed, and in which a certain image of gold, made in honour of him, was borne, the bearer of it stumbled and fell, and the image was thrown upon the ground. This was a very dark presage of impending calamity. Then a great number of vultures and other birds of prey were seen for a number of days before the battle, hovering over the Roman army; and several swarms of bees were found within the precincts of the camp. So alarming was this last indication that the officers altered the line of the entrenchments so as to shut out the ill-omened spot from the camp. These and other such things had great influence upon the mind of Cassius, in convincing him that some great disaster was impending over him.

Brutus Receives Warnings

Nor was Brutus himself without warnings of this character, though they seem to have had less power to produce any serious impression upon his mind than in the case of Cassius. The most extraordinary warning which Brutus received, according to the story of his ancient historians, was by a supernatural apparition which he saw, some time before, while he was in Asia Minor. He was encamped near the city of Sardis at that time. He was always accustomed to sleep very little, and would often, it was said, when all his officers had retired, and the camp was still, sit alone in his tent, sometimes reading, and sometimes revolving the anxious cares which were always pressing upon his mind. One night he was thus alone in his tent, with a small lamp burning before him, sitting lost in thought, when he suddenly heard a movement as of someone entering the tent. He looked up, and saw a strange, unearthly, and monstrous shape, which appeared to have just entered the door and was coming toward him. The spirit gazed upon him as it advanced, but it did not speak.

Brutus is Visited by Julius Caesar's Spirit

Brutus, who was not much accustomed to fear, boldly demanded of the apparition who and what it was, and what had brought it there. "I am your evil spirit," said the apparition. "I shall meet you at Philippi." "Then, it seems," said Brutus, "that, at any rate, I shall see you again." The spirit made no reply to this, but immediately vanished.

Brutus arose, went to the door of his tent, summoned the sentinels, and awakened the soldiers who were sleeping nearby. The sentinels had seen nothing; and, after the most diligent search, no trace of the mysterious visitor could be found.

Brutus Discusses What He Saw with Cassius

The next morning Brutus related to Cassius the occurrence which he had witnessed. Cassius, though very sensitive, it seems, to the influence of omens affecting himself, was quite philosophical in his views in respect to those of other men. He argued very rationally with Brutus to convince him that the vision which he had seen was only a phantom of sleep, taking its form and character from the ideas and images which the situation in which Brutus was then placed, and the fatigue and anxiety which he had endured, would naturally impress upon his mind.

Battle of Philippi, 3 October 42 BCE – Initial Defeat of Octavian

But to return to the battle. Brutus fought against Octavian, while Cassius, two or three miles distant, encountered Antony, that having been, as will be recollected, the disposition of the respective armies and their encampments upon the plain. Brutus was triumphantly successful in his part of the field. His troops defeated the army of Octavian and got possession of his camp. The men forced their way into Octavian's tent, and pierced the litter in which they supposed that the sick general was lying through and through with their spears. But the object of their desperate hostility was not there. He had been borne away by his guards a few minutes before, and no one knew what had become of him.

Defeat of Cassius

The result of the battle was, however, unfortunately for those whose adventures we are now more particularly following, very different in Cassius's part of the field. When Brutus, after completing the conquest of his own immediate foes, returned to his elevated camp, he looked toward the camp of Cassius, and was surprised to find that the tents had disappeared. Some of the officers around perceived weapons glancing and glittering in the sun in the place where Cassius's tents ought to appear. Brutus now suspected the truth, which was that Cassius had been defeated, and his camp had fallen into the hands of the enemy. He immediately collected together as large a force as he could command and marched to the relief of his colleague. He found him, at last, posted with a small body of guards and attendants upon the top of a small elevation to which he had fled for safety. Cassius saw the troop of horsemen which Brutus sent forward coming toward him and supposed that it was a detachment from Antony's army advancing to capture him. He, however, sent a messenger forward to meet them, and ascertain whether they were friends or foes. The messenger, whose name was Titinius, rode down. The horsemen recognized Titinius, and, riding up eagerly around him, they dismounted from their horses to congratulate him on his safety, and to press him with enquiries in respect to the result of the battle and the fate of his master.

Death of Cassius

Cassius, seeing all this, but not seeing it very distinctly, supposed that the troop of horsemen were enemies, and that they had surrounded Titinius, and had cut him down or made him prisoner. He considered it certain, therefore, that all was now finally lost. Accordingly, in execution of a plan which he had previously formed, he called a servant, named Pindarus, whom he directed to follow him, and went into a tent which was nearby. When Brutus and his horsemen came up, they entered the tent. They found no living person within; but the dead body of Cassius was there, the head being totally dissevered from it. Pindarus was never afterwards to be found.

Battle of Philippi, 23 October 42 BCE – Defeat of Brutus

Brutus was overwhelmed with grief at the death of his colleague; he was also oppressed by it with a double burden of responsibility and care, since now the whole conduct of affairs devolved upon him alone. He found himself surrounded with difficulties which became more and more embarrassing every day. At length he was compelled to fight a second battle. The details of the contest itself we cannot give, but the result of it was that, notwithstanding the most unparalleled and desperate exertions made by Brutus to keep his men to the work, and to maintain his ground, his troops were borne down and overwhelmed by the irresistible onsets of his enemies, and his cause was irretrievably and hopelessly ruined.

Brutus's Retreat

When Brutus found that all was lost, he allowed himself to be conducted off the field by a small body of guards, who, in their retreat, broke through the ranks of the enemy on a side where they saw that they should meet with the least resistance.

Death of Brutus

Brutus then asked first one and then another of his friends to aid him in the last duty, as he seems to have considered it, of destroying his life; but one after another declared that they could not do anything to assist him in carrying into effect so dreadful a determination. Finally, he took with him an old and long-tried friend named Strato, and went away a little, apart from the rest. Here he solicited once more the favour which had been refused him before – begging that Strato would hold out his sword. Strato still refused. Brutus then called one of his slaves. Upon this Strato declared that he would do anything rather than that Brutus should die by the hand of a slave. He took the sword, and with his right hand held it extended in the air. With the left hand he covered his eyes, that he might not witness the horrible spectacle. Brutus rushed upon the point of the weapon with such fatal force that he fell and immediately expired.

Thus ended the great and famous Battle of Philippi, celebrated in history as marking the termination of the great conflict between the friends and the enemies of Caesar, which agitated the world so deeply after the conqueror's death. This battle established the ascendency of Antony and made him for a time the most conspicuous man, as Cleopatra was the most conspicuous woman, in the world.

CHAPTER X
CLEOPATRA AND ANTONY, 41–32 BCE

Cleopatra Espouses Antony's Cause

How far Cleopatra was influenced, in her determination to espouse the cause of Antony rather than that of Brutus and Cassius, in the civil war described in the last chapter, by gratitude to Caesar, and how far, on the other hand, by personal interest in Antony, the reader must judge. Cleopatra had seen Antony, it will be recollected, some years before, during his visit to Egypt, when she was a young girl. She was doubtless well acquainted with his character. It was a character peculiarly fitted, in some respects, to captivate the imagination of a woman so ardent, and impulsive, and bold as Cleopatra was fast becoming.

Antony's Early Life and Character

Antony had, in fact, made himself an object of universal interest throughout the world, by his wild and eccentric manners and reckless conduct, and by the very extraordinary vicissitudes which had marked his career. In moral character he was as utterly abandoned and depraved as it was possible to be. In early life, as has already been stated, he plunged into such a course of dissipation and extravagance that he became utterly and hopelessly ruined; or, rather, he would have been so, had he not, by the influence of that magic power of fascination which such characters often possess, succeeded in gaining a great ascendency over a young man of immense fortune, named Curio, who for a time upheld him by becoming surety for his debts. This resource, however, soon failed, and Antony was compelled to abandon Rome, and to live for some years as a fugitive and exile, in dissolute wretchedness and want. During all the subsequent vicissitudes through which he passed in the course of his career, the same habits of lavish expenditure continued, whenever he had funds at his command. This trait of character took the form sometimes of a noble generosity. In his campaigns, the plunder which he acquired he usually divided among his soldiers, reserving nothing for himself. This made his men enthusiastically devoted to him and led them to consider his prodigality as a virtue, even when they did not themselves derive any direct advantage from it. A thousand stories were always in circulation in camp of acts on his part illustrating his reckless disregard of the value of money, some ludicrous, and all eccentric and strange.

Antony's Personal habits

In his personal habits, too, he was as different as possible from other men. He prided himself on being descended from Hercules, and he affected a style of dress and a general air and manner in accordance with the savage character of this his pretended ancestor. His features were sharp, his nose was arched and prominent, and he wore his hair and beard very long – as long, in fact, as he could make them grow. These peculiarities imparted to his countenance a very wild and ferocious expression. He adopted a style of dress, too, which, judged of with reference to the prevailing fashions of the time, gave to his whole appearance a rough, savage, and reckless air. His manner and demeanour corresponded with his dress and appearance. He lived in habits of the most unreserved familiarity with his soldiers. He associated freely with them, ate and drank with them in the open air, and joined in their noisy mirth and rude and boisterous hilarity. His commanding powers of mind, and the desperate recklessness of his courage, enabled him to do all this without danger. These qualities inspired in the minds of the soldiers a feeling of profound respect for their commander; and this good opinion he was enabled to retain, notwithstanding such habits of familiarity with his inferiors as would have been fatal to the influence of an ordinary man.

Antony's Indulgences and Vices

In the most prosperous portion of Antony's career – for example, during the period immediately preceding the death of Caesar – he addicted himself to vicious indulgences of the most open, public, and shameless character. He had around him a sort of court, formed of jesters, tumblers, mountebanks, play-actors, and other similar characters of the lowest and most disreputable class. Many of these companions were singing and dancing girls, very beautiful, and very highly accomplished in the arts of their respective professions, but all totally corrupt and depraved. Public sentiment, even in that age and nation, strongly condemned this conduct.

Public Condemnation of Antony

But, notwithstanding the influence of Antony's rank and power in shielding him from public censure, he carried his excesses to such an extreme that his conduct was very loudly and very generally condemned. He would spend all the night in carousals, and then, the next day, would appear in public, staggering in the streets. Sometimes he would enter the tribunals for the transaction of business when he was so intoxicated that it would be necessary for friends to come to his assistance to conduct him away. In some of his journeys in the neighbourhood of Rome, he would take a troop of companions with him of the worst possible character, and travel with them openly and without shame. There was a certain actress, named Cytheride, whom he made his companion on one such occasion. She was borne upon a litter in his train, and he carried about with him a vast collection of gold and silver plate, and of splendid table furniture, together with an endless supply of luxurious articles of food and of wine, to provide for the entertainments and banquets which he was to celebrate with her on the journey. He would sometimes stop by the roadside, pitch his tents, establish his kitchens, set his cooks at work to prepare a feast, spread his tables, and make a sumptuous banquet of the most costly, complete, and ceremonious character – all to make men wonder at the abundance and perfection of the means of luxury which he could carry with him wherever he might go. In fact, he always seemed to feel a special pleasure in doing strange and extraordinary things in order to excite surprise. Once on a journey he had lions harnessed to his carts to draw his baggage, in order to create a sensation.

Antony's Energy – Powers of Endurance

Notwithstanding the heedlessness with which Antony abandoned himself to these luxurious pleasures when at Rome, no man could endure exposure and hardship better when in camp or on the field. In fact, he rushed with as much headlong precipitation into difficulty and danger when abroad, as into expense and dissipation when at home. During his contests with Octavian and Lepidus, after Caesar's death, he once had occasion to pass the Alps, which, with his customary recklessness, he attempted to traverse without any proper supplies of stores or means of transportation. He was reduced, on the passage, together with the troops under his command, to the most extreme destitution and distress. They had to feed on roots and herbs, and finally on the bark of trees; and they barely preserved themselves, by these means, from actual starvation. Antony seemed, however, to care nothing for all this, but pressed on through the difficulty and danger, manifesting the same daring and determined unconcern to the end. In the same campaign he found himself at one time reduced to extreme destitution in respect to men. His troops had been gradually wasted away until his situation had become very desperate. He conceived, under these circumstances, the most extraordinary idea of going over alone to the camp of Lepidus and enticing away his rival's troops from under the very eyes of their commander. This bold design was successfully executed. Antony advanced alone, clothed in wretched garments, and with his matted hair and beard hanging about his breast and shoulders, up to Lepidus's lines. The men, who knew him well, received him with acclamations; and pitying the sad condition to which they saw that he was reduced, began to listen to what he had to say. Lepidus, who could not attack him, since he and Antony were not at that time in open hostility to each other, but were only rival commanders in the same army, ordered the trumpeters to sound in order to make a noise which should prevent the words of Antony from being heard. This interrupted the negotiation; but the men immediately disguised two of their number in female apparel and sent them to Antony to make arrangements with him for putting themselves under his command, and offering, at the same time, to murder Lepidus, if he would but speak the word. Antony charged them to do Lepidus no injury. He, however, went over and took possession of the camp, and assumed the command of the army. He treated Lepidus himself, personally, with extreme politeness, and retained him as a subordinate under his command.

Antony's Wife, Fulvia – Her Influence Over Antony

Not far from the time of Caesar's death, Antony was married. The name of the lady was Fulvia. She was a widow at the time of her marriage with Antony and was a woman of very marked and decided character. She had led a wild and irregular life previous to that time, but she conceived a very strong attachment to her new husband and devoted herself to him from the time of her marriage with the most constant fidelity. She soon acquired a very great ascendency over him and was the means of effecting a very considerable reform in his conduct and character. She was an ambitious and aspiring woman and made many very efficient and successful efforts to promote the elevation and aggrandizement of her husband. She appeared, also, to take a great pride and pleasure in exercising over him, herself, a great personal control. She succeeded in these attempts in a manner that surprised everybody. It seemed astonishing to all mankind that such a tiger as he had been could be subdued by any human power. Nor was it by gentleness and mildness that Fulvia gained such power over her husband. She was of a very stern and masculine character, and she seems to have mastered Antony by surpassing him in the use of his own weapons. In fact, instead of attempting to soothe and mollify him, she reduced him, it seems, to the necessity of resorting to various contrivances to soften and propitiate her. Once, for example, on his return from a campaign in which he had been exposed to great dangers, he disguised himself and came home at night in the garb of a courier bearing dispatches. He caused himself to be ushered, muffled and disguised as he was, into Fulvia's apartments, where he handed her some pretended letters, which, he said, were from her husband; and while Fulvia was opening them in great excitement and trepidation, he threw off his disguise, and revealed himself to her by clasping her in his arms and kissing her in the midst of her amazement.

Change in Antony's Character

Antony's marriage with Fulvia, besides being the means of reforming his morals in some degree, softened and civilized him in respect to his manners. His dress and appearance now assumed a different character. In fact, his political elevation after Caesar's death soon became very exalted, and the various democratic arts by which he had sought to raise himself to it, being now no longer necessary, were, as usual in such cases, gradually discarded. He lived in great style and splendour when at Rome, and when absent from home, on his military campaigns, he began to exhibit the same pomp and parade in his equipage and in his arrangements as were usual in the camps of other Roman generals.

Antony Approves a Funeral for Brutus

After the Battle of Philippi, described in the last chapter, Antony – who, with all his faults, was sometimes a very generous foe – as soon as the tidings of Brutus's death were brought to him, repaired immediately to the spot, and appeared to be quite shocked and concerned at the sight of the body. He took off his own military cloak or mantle – which was a very magnificent and costly garment, being enriched with many expensive ornaments – and spread it over the corpse. He then gave directions to one of the officers of his household to make arrangements for funeral ceremonies of a very imposing character, as a testimony of his respect for the memory of the deceased. In these ceremonies it was the duty of the officer to have burned the military cloak which Antony had appropriated to the purpose of a pall, with the body. He did not, however, do so. The cloak being very valuable, he reserved it; and he withheld, also, a considerable part of the money which had been given him for the expenses of the funeral. He supposed that Antony would probably not enquire very closely into the details of the arrangements made for the funeral of his most inveterate enemy. Antony, however, did enquire into them, and when he learned what the officer had done, he ordered him to be killed.

Antony's Movements After Philippi – His Summons to Cleopatra

The various political changes which occurred, and the movements which took place among the several armies after the Battle of Philippi, cannot be here detailed. It is sufficient to say that Antony proceeded to the eastward through Asia Minor, and in the course of the following year came into Cilicia. From this place he sent a messenger to Egypt to Cleopatra, summoning her to appear before him. There were charges, he said, against her of having aided Cassius and Brutus in the late war instead of rendering assistance to him. Whether there really were any such charges, or whether they were only fabricated by Antony as pretexts for seeing Cleopatra, the fame of whose beauty was very widely extended, does not certainly appear. However this may be, he sent to summon the queen to come to him. The name of the messenger whom Antony dispatched on this errand was Dellius. Fulvia, Antony's wife, was not with him at this time. She had been left behind at Rome.

Dellius the Messenger

Dellius proceeded to Egypt and appeared at Cleopatra's court. The queen was at this time about twenty-eight, but more beautiful, as was said, than ever before. Dellius was very much struck with her beauty and with a certain fascination in her voice and conversation, of which her ancient biographers often speak as one of the most irresistible of her charms. He told her that she need have no fear of Antony. It was of no consequence, he said, what charges there might be against her. She would find that, in a very few days after she had entered into Antony's presence, she would be in great favour. She might rely, in fact, he said, on gaining, very speedily, an unbounded ascendency over the general. He advised her, therefore, to proceed to Cilicia without fear; and to present herself before Antony in as much pomp and magnificence as she could command. He would answer, he said, for the result.

Cleopatra Resolves to Meet Antony – Her Preparations

Cleopatra determined to follow this advice. In fact, her ardent and impulsive imagination was fired with the idea of making, a second time, the conquest of the greatest general and highest potentate in the world. She began immediately to make provision for the voyage. She employed all the resources of her kingdom in procuring for herself the most magnificent means of display, such as expensive and splendid dresses, rich services of plate, ornaments of precious stones and of gold, and presents in great variety and of the most costly description for Antony. She appointed, also, a numerous retinue of attendants to accompany her, and, in a word, made all the arrangements complete for an expedition of the most imposing and magnificent character. While these preparations were going forward, she received new and frequent communications from Antony, urging her to hasten her departure; but she paid very little attention to them. It was evident that she felt quite independent and was intending to take her own time.

Cleopatra Enters the Cydnus – Her Splendid Barge

At length, however, all was ready, and Cleopatra set sail. She crossed the Mediterranean Sea and entered the mouth of the River Cydnus. Antony was at Tarsus, a city upon the Cydnus, a small distance above its mouth. When Cleopatra's fleet had entered the river, she embarked on board a most magnificent barge which she had constructed for the occasion and had brought with her across the sea. This barge was the most magnificent and highly ornamented vessel that had ever been built. It was adorned with carvings and decorations of the finest workmanship, and elaborately gilded. The sails were of purple, and the oars were inlaid and tipped with silver. Upon the deck of this barge Queen Cleopatra appeared, under a canopy of cloth of gold. She was dressed very magnificently in the costume in which Venus, the goddess of Beauty, was then generally represented. She was surrounded by a company of beautiful boys, who attended upon her in the form of Cupids, and fanned her with their wings, and by a group of young girls representing the Nymphs and the Graces. There was a band of musicians stationed upon the deck. This music guided the oarsmen, as they kept time to it in their rowing; and, soft as the melody was, the strains were heard far and wide over the water and along the shores, as the beautiful vessel advanced on its way. The performers were provided with flutes, lyres, viols, and all the other instruments customarily used in those times to produce music of a gentle and voluptuous kind.

A Scene of Enchantment at Tarsus – Cleopatra Declines Antony's Invitation – Her Reception for Antony

In fact, the whole spectacle seemed like a vision of enchantment. Tidings of the approach of the barge spread rapidly around, and the people of the country came down in crowds to the shores of the river to gaze upon it in admiration as it glided slowly along. At the time of its arrival at Tarsus, Antony was engaged in giving a public audience at some tribunal in his palace, but everybody ran to see Cleopatra and the barge, and the great triumvir was left consequently alone, or, at least, with only a few official attendants near him. Cleopatra, on arriving at the city, landed, and began to pitch her tents on the shores. Antony sent a messenger to bid her welcome, and to invite her to come and sup with him. She declined the invitation, saying that it was more proper that he should come and sup with her. She would accordingly expect him to come, she said, and her tents would be ready at the proper hour. Antony complied with her proposal and came to her entertainment. He was received with a magnificence and splendour which amazed him. The tents and pavilions where the entertainment was made were illuminated with an immense number of lamps. These lamps were arranged in a very ingenious and beautiful manner, so as to produce an illumination of the most surprising brilliancy and beauty. The immense number and variety, too, of the meats and wines, and of the vessels of gold and silver, with which the tables were loaded, and the magnificence and splendour of the dresses worn by Cleopatra and her attendants, combined to render the whole scene one of bewildering enchantment.

Antony Outdone

The next day, Antony invited Cleopatra to come and return his visit; but though he made every possible effort to provide a banquet as sumptuous and as sumptuously served as hers, he failed entirely in this attempt, and acknowledged himself completely outdone. Antony was, moreover, at these interviews, perfectly fascinated with Cleopatra's charms. Her beauty, her wit, her thousand accomplishments, and, above all, the tact, and adroitness, and self-possession which she displayed in assuming at once so boldly, and carrying out so adroitly, the idea of her social superiority over him, that he yielded his heart almost immediately to her undisputed sway.

Execution of Arsinoë

The first use which Cleopatra made of her power was to ask Antony, for her sake, to order her sister Arsinoë to be slain. Arsinoë had gone, it will be recollected, to Rome, to grace Caesar's triumph there, and had afterwards retired to Asia, where she was now living an exile. Cleopatra, either from a sentiment of past revenge, or else from some apprehensions of future danger, now desired that her sister should die. Antony readily acceded to her request. He sent an officer in search of the unhappy princess. The officer slew her where he found her, within the precincts of a temple to which she had fled, supposing it a sanctuary which no degree of hostility, however extreme, would have dared to violate.

Cleopatra's Life at Tarsus – Her Munificence – Story of the Pearls

Cleopatra remained at Tarsus for some time, revolving in an incessant round of gaiety and pleasure, and living in habits of unrestrained intimacy with Antony. She was accustomed to spending whole days and nights with him in feasting and revelry. The immense magnificence of these entertainments, especially on Cleopatra's part, were the wonder of the world. She seems to have taken special pleasure in exciting Antony's surprise by the display of her wealth and the boundless extravagance in which she indulged. At one of her banquets, Antony was expressing his astonishment at the vast number of gold cups, enriched with jewels, that were displayed on all sides. "Oh," said she, "they are nothing; if you like them, you shall have them all." So saying, she ordered her servants to carry them to Antony's house. The next day she invited Antony again, with a large number of the chief officers of his army and court. The table was spread with a new service of gold and silver vessels, more extensive and splendid than that of the preceding day; and at the close of the supper, when the company was about to depart, Cleopatra distributed all these treasures among the guests who had been present at the entertainment. At another of these feasts, she carried her ostentation and display to the astonishing extreme of taking off from one of her earrings a pearl of immense value and dissolving it in a cup of vinegar, which she afterwards made into a drink, such as was customarily used in those days, and then drank it. She was proceeding to do the same with the other pearl, when some of the company arrested the proceeding, and took the remaining pearl away.

Position of Fulvia – Her Anxiety and Distress – Antony Proposes to Go to Rome

In the meantime, while Antony was thus wasting his time in luxury and pleasure with Cleopatra, his public duties were neglected, and everything was getting into confusion. Fulvia remained in Italy. Her position and her character gave her a commanding political influence, and she exerted herself in a very energetic manner to sustain, in that quarter of the world, the interests of her husband's cause. She was surrounded with difficulties and dangers, the details of which cannot, however, be here particularly described. She wrote continually to Antony, urgently entreating him to come to Rome, and displaying in her letters all those marks of agitation and distress which a wife would naturally feel under the circumstances in which she was placed. The thought that her husband had been so completely drawn away from her by the guilty arts of such a woman and led by her to abandon his wife and his family, and leave in neglect and confusion concerns of such momentous magnitude as those which demanded his attention at home, produced an excitement in her mind bordering upon frenzy. Antony was at length so far influenced by the urgency of the case that he determined to return. He broke up his quarters at Tarsus and moved south toward Tyre, which was a great naval port and station in those days. Cleopatra went with him. They were to separate at Tyre. She was to embark there for Egypt, and he for Rome.

Antony's Plans Frustrated by Cleopatra

At least that was Antony's plan, but it was not Cleopatra's. She had determined that Antony should go with her to Alexandria. As might have been expected, when the time came for the decision, the woman gained the day. Her flatteries, her arts, her caresses, her tears, prevailed. After a brief struggle between the sentiment of love on the one hand and those of ambition and of duty combined on the other, Antony gave up the contest. Abandoning everything else, he surrendered himself wholly to Cleopatra's control, and went with her to Alexandria. He spent the winter there, giving himself up with her to every species of sensual indulgence that the most remorseless license could tolerate, and the most unbounded wealth procure.

Antony's Infatuation – Feasting and Revelry

There seemed, in fact, to be no bounds to the extravagance and infatuation which Antony displayed during the winter in Alexandria. Cleopatra devoted herself to him incessantly, day and night, filling up every moment of time with some new form of pleasure, in order that he might have no time to think of his absent wife, or to listen to the reproaches of his conscience.

Antony, on his part, surrendered himself a willing victim to these wiles, and entered with all his heart into the thousand plans of gaiety and merry-making which Cleopatra devised. They had each a separate establishment in the city, which was maintained at an enormous cost, and they made a regular arrangement by which each was the guest of the other on alternate days. These visits were spent in games, sports, spectacles, feasting, drinking, and in every species of riot, irregularity, and excess.

Philotas – The Story of the Eight Boats

A curious instance is afforded of the accidental manner in which intelligence in respect to the scenes and incidents of private life in those ancient days is sometimes obtained, in a circumstance which occurred at this time at Antony's court. It seems that there was a young medical student at Alexandria that winter, named Philotas, who happened, in some way or other, to have formed an acquaintance with one of Antony's domestics, a cook. Under the guidance of this cook, Philotas went one day into the palace to see what was to be seen. The cook took his friend into the kitchens, where, to Philotas's great surprise, he saw, among an infinite number and variety of other preparations, eight wild boar roasting before the fires, some being more and some less advanced in the process. Philotas asked what great company was to dine there that day. The cook smiled at this question and replied that there was to be no company at all, other than Antony's ordinary party. "But," said the cook, in explanation, "we are obliged always to prepare several suppers, and to have them ready in succession at different hours, for no one can tell at what time they will order the entertainment to be served. Sometimes, when the supper has been actually carried in, Antony and Cleopatra will get engaged in some new turn of their diversions and conclude not to sit down just then to the table, and so we have to take the supper away, and presently bring in another."

Antony's Son Antony – The Garrulous Guest

Antony had a son with him at Alexandria at this time, the child of his wife Fulvia. The name of the son, as well as that of the father, was Antony. He was old enough to feel some sense of shame at his father's dereliction from duty, and to manifest some respectful regard for the rights and the honour of his mother. Instead of this, however, he imitated his father's example, and, in his own way, was as reckless and extravagant as he. The same Philotas who is above referred to was, after a time, appointed to some office or other in the young Antony's household, so that he was accustomed to sit at his table and share in his convivial enjoyments. He relates that once, while they were feasting together, there was a guest present, a physician, who was a very vain and conceited man, and so talkative that no one else had any opportunity to speak. All the pleasure of conversation was spoiled by his excessive garrulity. Philotas, however, at length puzzled him so completely with a question of logic, – of a kind similar to those often discussed with great interest in ancient days, – as to silence him for a time; and young Antony was so much delighted with this feat that he gave Philotas all the gold and silver plate that there was upon the table, and sent all the articles home to him, after the entertainment was over, telling him to put his mark and stamp upon them, and lock them up.

The Puzzle

The question with which Philotas puzzled the self-conceited physician was this. It must be premised, however, that in those days it was considered that cold water in an intermittent fever was extremely dangerous, except in some peculiar cases, and in those the effect was good. Philotas then argued as follows: "In cases of a certain kind it is best to give water to a patient in an ague. All cases of ague are cases of a certain kind. Therefore, it is best in all cases to give the patient water." Philotas having propounded his argument in this way, challenged the physician to point out the fallacy of it; and while the physician sat perplexed and puzzled in his attempts to unravel the intricacy of it, the company enjoyed a temporary respite from his excessive loquacity.

The Gold and Silver Returned to Young Antony

Philotas adds, in his account of this affair, that he sent the gold and silver plate back to young Antony again, being afraid to keep them. Antony said that perhaps it was as well that this should be done, since many of the vessels were of great value on account of their rare and antique workmanship, and his father might possibly miss them and wish to know what had become of them.

Debasing Pleasures – Antony and Cleopatra in Disguise

As there were no limits, on the one hand, to the loftiness and grandeur of the pleasures to which Antony and Cleopatra addicted themselves, so there were none to the low and debasing tendencies which characterized them on the other. Sometimes, at midnight, after having been spending many hours in mirth and revelry in the palace, Antony would disguise himself in the dress of a slave, and sally forth into the streets, excited with wine, in search of adventures. In many cases, Cleopatra herself, similarly disguised, would go out with him. On these excursions Antony would take pleasure in involving himself in all sorts of difficulties and dangers – in street riots, drunken brawls, and desperate quarrels with the populace – all for Cleopatra's amusement and his own. Stories of these adventures would circulate afterwards among the people, some of whom would admire the free and jovial character of their eccentric visitor, and others would despise him as a prince degrading himself to the level of a brute.

Fishing Excursions

Some of the amusements and pleasures which Antony and Cleopatra pursued were innocent in themselves, though wholly unworthy to be made the serious business of life by personages on whom such exalted duties rightfully devolved. They made various excursions upon the Nile and arranged parties of pleasure to go out on the water in the harbour, and to various rural retreats in the environs of the city. Once they went out on a fishing-party, in boats, in the port. Antony was unsuccessful; and feeling chagrined that Cleopatra should witness his ill-luck, he made a secret arrangement with some of the fishermen to dive down, where they could do so unobserved, and fasten fishes to his hook under the water. By this plan he caught very large and fine fish very fast. Cleopatra, however, was too wary to be easily deceived by such a stratagem as this. She observed the manoeuvre, but pretended not to observe it; she expressed, on the other hand, the greatest surprise and delight at Antony's good luck, and the extraordinary skill which it indicated.

Cleopatra's Stratagem

The next day she wished to go a fishing again, and a party was accordingly made as on the day before. She had, however, secretly instructed another fisherman to procure a dried and salted fish from the market, and, watching his opportunity, to get down into the water under the boats and attach it to the hook, before Antony's divers could get there. This plan succeeded, and Antony, in the midst of a large and gay party that were looking on, pulled out an excellent fish, cured and dried, such as was known to everyone as an imported article, bought in the market. It was a fish of a kind that was brought originally from Asia Minor. The boats and the water all around them resounded with the shouts of merriment and laughter which this incident occasioned.

Fulvia's Plan to Compel Antony to Return – Antony's Departure – Cleopatra's Chagrin

In the meantime, while Antony was thus spending his time in low and ignoble pursuits and in guilty pleasures at Alexandria, his wife Fulvia, after exhausting all other means of inducing her husband to return to her, became desperate, and took measures for fomenting an open war, which she thought would compel him to return. The extraordinary energy, influence, and talent which Fulvia possessed enabled her to do this in an effectual manner. She organized an army, formed a camp, placed herself at the head of the troops, and sent such tidings to Antony of the dangers which threatened his cause as greatly alarmed him. At the same time news came of great disasters in Asia Minor, and of alarming insurrections among the provinces which had been committed to his charge there. Antony saw that he must arouse himself from the spell which had enchanted him and break away from Cleopatra, or that he would be wholly and irretrievably ruined. He made, accordingly, a desperate effort to get free. He bade the queen farewell, embarked hastily in a fleet of galleys, and sailed away to Tyre, leaving Cleopatra in her palace, vexed, disappointed, and chagrined.

CHAPTER XI
THE BATTLE OF ACTIUM, 2 SEPTEMBER 31 BCE

Antony Distracted and Perplexed

Cleopatra, in parting with Antony as described in the last chapter, lost him for two or three years. During this time Antony himself was involved in a great variety of difficulties and dangers, and passed through many eventful scenes, which, however, cannot here be described in detail. His life, during this period, was full of vicissitude and excitement, and was spent probably in alternations of remorse for the past and anxiety for the future.

Antony's Meeting with Fulvia in Athens – Fulvia's Death

On landing at Tyre, he was at first extremely perplexed whether to go to Asia Minor or to Rome. His presence was imperiously demanded in both places. The war which Fulvia had fomented was caused, in part, by the rivalry of Octavian, and the collision of his interests with those of her husband. Antony was very angry with her for having managed his affairs in such a way as to bring about a war. After a time Antony and Fulvia met at Athens. Fulvia had retreated to that city, and was very seriously sick there, either from bodily disease, or from the influence of long-continued anxiety, vexation, and distress. They had a stormy meeting. Neither party was disposed to exercise any mercy toward the other. Antony left his wife rudely and roughly, after loading her with reproaches. A short time afterwards, she sank down in sorrow to the grave.

Antony Reconciles with Octavian

The death of Fulvia was an event which proved to be of advantage to Antony. It opened the way to a reconciliation between him and Octavian. Fulvia had been extremely active in opposing Octavian's designs, and in organizing plans for resisting him. He felt, therefore, a special hostility against her, and, through her, against Antony. Now, however, that she was dead, the way seemed to be in some sense opened for a reconciliation.

Antony Marries Octavian's Sister, Octavia

Octavian had a sister, Octavia, who had been the wife of a Roman general named Marcellus. She was a very beautiful and a very accomplished woman, and of a spirit very different from that of Fulvia. She was gentle, affectionate, and kind, a lover of peace and harmony, and not at all disposed, like Fulvia, to assert and maintain her influence over others by an overbearing and violent demeanour. Octavia's husband died about this time, and, in the course of the movements and negotiations between Antony and Octavian, the plan was proposed of a marriage between Antony and Octavia, which, it was thought, would ratify and confirm the reconciliation. This proposal was finally agreed upon. Antony was glad to find so easy a mode of settling his difficulties. The people of Rome, too, and the authorities there, knowing that the peace of the world depended upon the terms on which these two men stood with regard to each other, were extremely desirous that this arrangement should be carried into effect. There was a law of the commonwealth forbidding the marriage of a widow within a specified period after the death of her husband. That period had not, in Octavia's case, yet expired. There was, however, so strong a desire that no obstacle should be allowed to prevent this proposed union, or even to occasion delay, that the law was altered expressly for this case, and Antony and Octavia were married. The empire was divided between Octavian and Antony, Octavian receiving the western portion as his share, while the eastern was assigned to Antony.

Octavia's Influence Over Antony and Octavian – She Pleads for Antony

It is not probable that Antony felt any very strong affection for his new wife, beautiful and gentle as she was. A man, in fact, who had led such a life as his had been must have become by this time incapable of any strong and pure attachment. He, however, was pleased with the novelty of his acquisition, and seemed to forget for a time the loss of Cleopatra. He remained with Octavia a year.

After that he went away on certain military enterprises which kept him some time from her. He returned again, and again he went away. All this time Octavia's influence over him and over her brother was of the most salutary and excellent character. She soothed their animosities, quieted their suspicions and jealousies, and at one time, when they were on the brink of open war, she effected a reconciliation between them by the most courageous and energetic, and at the same time, gentle and unassuming efforts. At the time of this danger, she was with her husband in Greece; but she persuaded him to send her to her brother at Rome, saying that she was confident that she could arrange a settlement of the difficulties impending. Antony allowed her to go. She proceeded to Rome and procured an interview with her brother in the presence of his two principal officers of state. Here she pleaded her husband's cause with tears in her eyes; she defended his conduct, explained what seemed to be against him, and entreated her brother not to take such a course as should cast her down from being the happiest of women to being the most miserable. "Consider the circumstances of my case," said she. "The eyes of the world are upon me. Of the two most powerful men in the world, I am the wife of one and the sister of another. If you allow rash counsels to go on and war to ensue, I am hopelessly ruined; for, whichever is conquered, my husband or my brother, my own happiness will be for ever gone."

Octavian Agrees to Meet Antony – Their Difficulties Settled

Octavian sincerely loved his sister, and he was so far softened by her entreaties that he consented to appoint an interview with Antony in order to see if their difficulties could be settled. This interview was accordingly held. The two generals came to a river, where, at the opposite banks, each embarked in a boat and, being rowed out toward each other, they met in the middle of the stream. A conference ensued, at which all the questions at issue were, for a time at least, very happily arranged.

Antony Grows Tired of Octavia – He Sails to Egypt

Antony, however, after a time, began to become tired of his wife, and to sigh for Cleopatra once more. He left Octavia at Rome and proceeded to the eastward, under pretence of attending to the affairs of that portion of the empire; but, instead of doing this, he went to Alexandria, and there renewed again his former intimacy with the Egyptian queen.

Octavian's Indignation – His Hostility Towards Antony Renewed

Octavian was very indignant at this. His former hostility to Antony, which had been in a measure appeased by the kind influence of Octavia, now broke forth anew, and was heightened by the feeling of resentment naturally awakened by his sister's wrongs public sentiment in Rome, too, was setting very strongly against Antony. Lampoons were written against him to ridicule him and Cleopatra, and the most decided censures were passed upon his conduct. Octavia was universally beloved, and the sympathy which was everywhere felt for her increased and heightened very much the popular indignation which was felt against the man who could wrong so deeply such sweetness, and gentleness, and affectionate fidelity as hers.

Antony Again with Cleopatra – He Campaigns in the East

After remaining for some time in Alexandria, and renewing his connection and intimacy with Cleopatra, Antony went away again, crossing the sea into Asia, with the intention of prosecuting certain military undertakings there which imperiously demanded his attention. His plan was to return as soon as possible to Egypt after the object of his expedition should be accomplished. He found, however, that he could not bear even a temporary absence from Cleopatra. His mind dwelled so much upon her, and upon the pleasures which he had enjoyed with her in Egypt, and he longed so much to see her again, that he was wholly unfit for the discharge of his duties in the camp. He became timid, inefficient, and remiss, and almost everything that he undertook ended disastrously. The army, who understood perfectly well the reason of their commander's remissness and consequent ill fortune, were extremely indignant at his conduct, and the camp was filled with suppressed murmurs and complaints. Antony, however, like other persons in his situation, was blind to all these indications of dissatisfaction; probably he would have disregarded them if he had observed them. At length, finding that he could bear his absence from his mistress no longer, he set out to march across the country, in the depth of the winter, to the seashore, to a point where he had sent for Cleopatra to come to join him. The army endured incredible hardships and exposures in this march. When Antony had once commenced the journey, he was so impatient to get forward that he compelled his troops to advance with a rapidity greater than their strength would bear. They were, besides, not provided with proper tents or with proper supplies of provisions. They were often obliged, therefore, after a long and fatiguing march during the day, to bivouac at night in the open air among the mountains, with scanty means of appeasing their hunger, and very little shelter from the cold rain, or from the storms of driving snow. Eight thousand men died on this march, from cold, fatigue, and exposure; a greater sacrifice, perhaps, than had ever been made before to the mere ardour and impatience of a lover.

Antony's March to Sidon – Suffering of the Troops

When Antony reached the shore, he advanced to a certain seaport, near Sidon, where Cleopatra was to land. At the time of his arrival but a very small part of his army was left, and the few men who survived were in a miserably destitute condition. Antony's eagerness to see Cleopatra became more and more excited as the time drew nigh. She did not come so soon as he had expected, and during the delay he seemed to pine away under the influence of love and sorrow. He was silent, absent-minded, and sad. He had no thoughts for anything but the coming of Cleopatra and felt no interest in any other plans. He watched for her incessantly, and would sometimes leave his place at the table, in the midst of the supper, and go down alone to the shore, where he would stand gazing out upon the sea, and saying mournfully to himself, "Why does not she come?" The animosity and the ridicule which these things awakened against him, on the part of the army, were extreme; but he was so utterly infatuated that he disregarded all the manifestations of public sentiment around him and continued to allow his mind to be wholly engrossed with the single idea of Cleopatra's coming.

Cleopatra's Arrival

She arrived at last. She brought a great supply of clothes and other necessaries for the use of Antony's army, so that her coming not only gratified his love, but afforded him, also, a very essential relief, in respect to the military difficulties in which he was involved.

Octavia Intercedes for Antony – She Brings Him Reinforcements

After some time spent in the enjoyment of the pleasure which being thus reunited to Cleopatra afforded him, Antony began again to think of the affairs of his government, which every month more and more imperiously demanded his attention. He began to receive urgent calls from various quarters, rousing him to action. In the meantime, Octavia – who had been all this while waiting in distress and anxiety at Rome, hearing continually the most gloomy accounts of her husband's affairs, and the most humiliating tidings in respect to his infatuated devotion to Cleopatra – resolved to make one more effort to save him. She interceded with her brother to allow her to raise troops and to collect supplies, and then proceed to the eastward to reinforce him. Octavian consented to this. He, in fact, assisted Octavia in making her preparations. It is said, however, that he was influenced in this plan by his confident belief that this noble attempt of his sister to reclaim her husband would fail, and that, by the failure of it, Antony would be put in the wrong, in the estimation of the Roman people, more absolutely and hopelessly than ever, and that the way would thus be prepared for his complete and final destruction.

Octavia was rejoiced to obtain her brother's aid to her undertaking, whatever the motive might be which induced him to afford it. She accordingly levied a considerable body of troops, raised a large sum of money, provided clothes, and tents, and military stores for the army; and when all was ready, she left Italy and put to sea, having previously dispatched a messenger to her husband to inform him that she was coming.

Cleopatra's Alarm – Her Arts

Cleopatra began now to be afraid that she was to lose Antony again, and she at once began to resort to the usual artifices employed in such cases, in order to retain her power over him. She said nothing but assumed the appearance of one pining under the influence of some secret suffering or sorrow. She contrived to be often surprised in tears. In such cases she would hastily brush her tears away, and assume a countenance of smiles and good humour, as if making every effort to be happy, though really oppressed with a heavy burden of anxiety and grief. When Antony was near her, she would seem overjoyed at his presence, and gaze upon him with an expression of the most devoted fondness. When absent from him, she spent her time alone, always silent and dejected, and often in tears; and she took care that the secret sorrows and sufferings that she endured should be duly made known to Antony, and that he should understand that they were all occasioned by her love for him, and by the danger which she apprehended that he was about to leave her.

Cleopatra's Friends and Secret Agents – Their Representations to Antony – Cleopatra's Sacrifices

The friends and secret agents of Cleopatra, who reported these things to Antony, made, moreover, direct representations to him, for the purpose of inclining his mind in her favour. They had, in fact, the astonishing audacity to argue that Cleopatra's claims upon Antony for a continuance of his love were paramount to those of Octavia. She, that is, Octavia, had been his wife, they said, only for a very short time. Cleopatra had been most devotedly attached to him for many years. Octavia was married to him, they alleged, not under the impulse of love, but from political considerations alone, to please her brother, and to ratify and confirm a political league made with him. Cleopatra, on the other hand, had given herself up to him in the most absolute and unconditional manner, under the influence solely of a personal affection which she could not control. She had surrendered and sacrificed everything to him. For him she had lost her good name, alienated the affections of her subjects, made herself the object of reproach and censure to all mankind, and now she had left her native land to come and join him in his adverse fortunes. Considering how much she had done, and suffered, and sacrificed for his sake, it would be extreme and unjustifiable cruelty in him to forsake her now. She never would survive such an abandonment. Her whole soul was so wrapped up in him that she would pine away and die if he were now to forsake her.

Antony's Message to Octavia – Her Devotion to Antony

Antony was distressed and agitated beyond measure by the entanglements in which he found that he was involved. His duty, his inclination perhaps, certainly his ambition, and every dictate of prudence and policy required that he should break away from these snares at once and go to meet Octavia. But the spell that bound him was too mighty to be dissolved. He yielded to Cleopatra's sorrows and tears. He dispatched a messenger to Octavia, who had by this time reached Athens, in Greece, directing her not to come any farther. Octavia, who seemed incapable of resentment or anger against her husband, sent back to ask what she should do with the troops, and money, and the military stores which she was bringing. Antony directed her to leave them in Greece. Octavia did so, and mournfully returned to her home.

Indignation at Antony – Antony with Cleopatra

As soon as she arrived at Rome, Octavian, her brother, whose indignation was now thoroughly aroused at the baseness of Antony, sent to his sister to say that she must leave Antony's house and come to him. A proper self-respect, he said, forbade her remaining any longer under the roof of such a man. Octavia replied that she would not leave her husband's house. That house was her post of duty, whatever her husband might do, and there she would remain. She accordingly retired within the precincts of her old home and devoted herself in patient and uncomplaining sorrow to the care of the family and the children. Among these children was one young son of Antony's, born during his marriage with her predecessor Fulvia. In the meantime, while Octavia was thus faithfully though mournfully fulfilling her duties as wife and mother, in her husband's house at Rome, Antony himself had gone with Cleopatra to Alexandria, and was abandoning himself once more to a life of guilty pleasure there. The greatness of mind which this beautiful and devoted wife thus displayed, attracted the admiration of all mankind. It produced, however, one other effect, which Octavia must have greatly deprecated. It aroused a strong and universal feeling of indignation against the unworthy object toward whom this extraordinary magnanimity was displayed.

Antony Goes Native – Octavian's Accusations Against Antony

In the meantime, Antony gave himself up wholly to Cleopatra's influence and control, and managed all the affairs of the Roman Empire in the East in the way best fitted to promote her aggrandizement and honour. He made Alexandria his capital, celebrated triumphs there, arranged ostentatious expeditions into Asia and Syria with Cleopatra and her train, gave her whole provinces as presents, and exalted her two sons, Alexander and Ptolemy, children born during the period of his first acquaintance with her, to positions of the highest rank and station, as his own acknowledged sons. The consequences of these and similar measures at Rome were fatal to Antony's character and standing. Octavian reported everything to the Roman Senate and people, and made Antony's misgovernment and his various misdemeanours the ground of the heaviest accusations against him. Antony, hearing of these things, sent his agents to Rome and made accusations against Octavian; but these counter accusations were of no avail. Public sentiment was very strong and decided against him at the capital, and Octavian began to prepare for war.

Antony's Preparations – Cleopatra Supports Him

Antony perceived that he must prepare to defend himself. Cleopatra entered into the plans which he formed for this purpose with great ardour. Antony began to levy troops, and collect and equip galleys and ships of war, and to make requisitions of money and military stores from all the eastern provinces and kingdoms. Cleopatra put all the resources of Egypt at his disposal. She furnished him with immense sums of money, and with an inexhaustible supply of corn, which she procured for this purpose from her dominions in the Valley of the Nile. The various divisions of the immense armament which was thus provided for were ordered to rendezvous at Ephesus, where Antony and Cleopatra were awaiting to receive them, having proceeded there when their arrangements in Egypt were completed, and they were ready to commence the campaign.

Canidius Bribed – His Advice to Antony Regarding Cleopatra

When all was ready for the expedition to set sail from Ephesus, it was Antony's judgment that it would be best for Cleopatra to return to Egypt and leave him to go forth with the fleet to meet Octavian alone. Cleopatra was, however, determined not to go away. She did not dare to leave Antony at all to himself, for fear that in some way or other a peace would be effected between himself and Octavian, which would result in his returning to Octavia and abandoning *her*. She accordingly contrived to persuade Antony to retain her with him, by bribing his chief counsellor to advise him to do so. His counsellor's name was Canidius. Canidius, having received Cleopatra's money, while yet he pretended to be wholly disinterested in his advice, represented to Antony that it would not be reasonable to send Cleopatra away, and deprive her of all participation in the glory of the war, when she was defraying so large a part of the expense of it. Besides, a large portion of the army consisted of Egyptian troops, who would feel discouraged and disheartened if Cleopatra were to leave them and would probably act far less efficiently in the conflict than they would do if animated by the presence of their queen. Then, moreover, such a woman as Cleopatra was not to be considered, as many women would be, an embarrassment and a source of care to a military expedition which she might join, but a very efficient counsellor and aid to it. She was, he said, a very sagacious, energetic, and powerful queen, accustomed to the command of armies and to the management of affairs of state, and her aid in the conduct of the expedition might be expected to conduce very materially to its success.

Antony was easily won by such persuasions as these, and it was at length decided that Cleopatra should accompany him.

Antony's Fleet at Samos – His Infatuation – Riot and Revelry

Antony then ordered the fleet to move forward to the island of Samos. Here it was brought to anchor and remained for some time, waiting for the coming in of new reinforcements, and for the completion of the other arrangements. Antony, as if becoming more and more infatuated as he approached the brink of his ruin, spent his time while the expedition remained at Samos, not in maturing his plans and perfecting his arrangements for the tremendous conflict which was approaching, but in festivities, games, revellings, and every species of riot and dissolute excess. This, however, is not surprising. Men almost always, when in a situation analogous to his, fly to similar means of protecting themselves, in some small degree, from the pangs of remorse, and from the forebodings which stand ready to terrify and torment them at every instant in which these gloomy spectres are not driven away by intoxication and revelry. At least Antony found it so. Accordingly, an immense company of players, tumblers, fools, jesters, and mountebanks were ordered to assemble at Samos, and to devote themselves with all zeal to the amusement of Antony's court. The island was one universal scene of riot and revelry. People were astonished at such celebrations and displays, wholly unsuitable, as they considered them, to the occasion. If such are the rejoicings, said they, which Antony celebrates before going into the battle, what festivities will he contrive on his return, joyous enough to express his pleasure if he shall gain the victory?

Antony and Cleopatra at Athens – Octavia's Fidelity and Modesty Contrast with Cleopatra's Jealousy and Ostentation – Honours Bestowed on the Egyptian Queen

After a time, Antony and Cleopatra, with a magnificent train of attendants, left Samos, and, passing across the Aegean Sea, landed in Greece, and advanced to Athens, while the fleet, proceeding westward from Samos, passed around Taenarus, the southern promontory of Greece, and then moved northward along the western coast of the peninsula. Cleopatra wished to go to Athens for a special reason. It was there that Octavia had stopped on her journey toward her husband with reinforcements and aid; and while she was there, the people of Athens, pitying her sad condition, and admiring the noble spirit of mind which she displayed in her misfortunes, had paid her great attention, and during her stay among them had bestowed upon her many honours. Cleopatra now wished to go to the same place, and to triumph over her rival there, by making so great a display of her wealth and magnificence, and of her ascendency over the mind of Antony, as should entirely transcend and outshine the more unassuming pretensions of Octavia. She was not willing, it seems, to leave to the unhappy wife whom she had so cruelly wronged even the possession of a place in the hearts of the people of this foreign city but must go and enviously strive to efface the impression which injured innocence had made, by an ostentatious exhibition of the triumphant prosperity of her own shameless wickedness. She succeeded well in her plans. The people of Athens were amazed and bewildered at the immense magnificence that Cleopatra exhibited before them. She distributed vast sums of money among the people. The city, in return, decreed to her the most exalted honours. They sent a solemn embassy to her to present her with these decrees. Antony himself, in the character of a citizen of Athens, was one of the ambassadors. Cleopatra received the deputation at her palace. The reception was attended with the most splendid and imposing ceremonies.

Antony Divorces Octavia

One would have supposed that Cleopatra's cruel and unnatural hostility to Octavia might now have been satisfied; but it was not. Antony, while he was at Athens, and doubtless at Cleopatra's instigation, sent a messenger to Rome with a notice of divorcement to Octavia, and with an order that she should leave his house. Octavia obeyed. She went forth from her home, taking the children with her, and bitterly lamenting her cruel destiny.

Octavian Makes Preparations for War – Antony's Will – Charges Levelled Against Him

In the meantime, while all these events had been transpiring in the East, Octavian had been making his preparations for the coming crisis and was now advancing with a powerful fleet across the sea. He was armed with authority from the Roman Senate and people, for he had obtained from them a decree deposing Antony from his power. The charges made against him all related to misdemeanours and offences arising out of his connection with Cleopatra. Octavian contrived to get possession of a will which Antony had written before leaving Rome, and which he had placed there in what he supposed a very sacred place of deposit. The custodians who had it in charge replied to Octavian, when he demanded it, that they would not give it to him, but if he wished to take it they would not hinder him. Octavian then took the will and read it to the Roman Senate. It provided, among other things, that at his death, if his death should happen at Rome, his body should be sent to Alexandria to be given to Cleopatra; and it evinced in other ways a degree of subserviency and devotedness to the Egyptian queen which was considered wholly unworthy of a Roman chief magistrate. Antony was accused, too, of having plundered cities and provinces, to make presents to Cleopatra; of having sent a library of two hundred thousand volumes to her from Pergamus, to replace the one which Julius Caesar had accidentally burned; of having raised her sons, ignoble as their birth was, to high places of trust and power in the Roman government, and of having in many ways compromised the dignity of a Roman officer by his unworthy conduct in reference to her. He used, for example, when presiding at a judicial tribunal, to receive love-letters sent him from Cleopatra, and then at once turn off his attention from the proceedings going forward before him to read the letters.

Antony Accused of Neglecting His Duties

Sometimes he did this when sitting in the chair of state, giving audience to ambassadors and princes. Cleopatra probably sent these letters in at such times under the influence of a wanton disposition to show her power. At one time, as Octavian said in his arguments before the Roman Senate, Antony was hearing a cause of the greatest importance, and during a time in the progress of the cause when one of the principal orators of the city was addressing him, Cleopatra came passing by, when Antony suddenly arose, and, leaving the court without any ceremony, ran out to follow her. These and a thousand similar tales exhibited Antony in so odious a light that his friends forsook his cause, and his enemies gained a complete triumph. The decree was passed against him, and Octavian was authorized to carry it into effect; and accordingly, while Antony, with his fleet and army, was moving westward from Samos and the Aegean Sea, Octavian was coming eastward and southward down the Adriatic to meet him.

Opinions of the War Council of Antony and Cleopatra – Their Fleet Clashes with Octavian's at Actium, 2 September 31 BCE

In process of time, after various manoeuvres and delays, the two armaments came into the vicinity of each other at a place called Actium, which will be found upon the map on the western coast of Epirus, north of Greece. Both of the commanders had powerful fleets at sea, and both had great armies upon the land. Antony was strongest in land troops, but his fleet was inferior to that of Octavian, and he was himself inclined to remain on the land and fight the principal battle there. But Cleopatra would not consent to this. She urged him to give Octavian battle at sea. The motive which induced her to do this has been supposed to be her wish to provide a surer way of escape in case of an unfavourable issue to the conflict. She thought that in her galleys she could make sail at once across the sea to Alexandria in case of defeat, whereas she knew not what would become of her if beaten at the head of an army on the land. The ablest counsellors and chief officers in the army urged Antony very strongly not to trust himself to the sea. To all their arguments and remonstrances, however, Antony turned a deaf ear. Cleopatra must be allowed to have her way. On the morning of the battle, when the ships were drawn up in array, Cleopatra held the command of a division of fifty or sixty Egyptian vessels, which were all completely manned, and well equipped with masts and sails. She took good care to have everything in perfect order for flight, in case flight should prove to be necessary. With these ships she took a station in reserve, and for a time remained there a quiet witness of the battle. The ships of Octavian advanced to the attack of those of Antony, and the men fought from deck to deck with spears, boarding-pikes, flaming darts, and every other destructive missile which the military art had then devised. Antony's ships had to contend against great disadvantages. They were not only outnumbered by those of Octavian but were far surpassed by them in the efficiency with which they were manned and armed. Still, it was a very obstinate conflict. Cleopatra, however, did not wait to see how it was to be finally decided. As Antony's forces did not immediately gain the victory, she soon began to yield to her fears in respect to the result, and, finally, fell into a panic and resolved to fly. She ordered the oars to be manned and the sails to be hoisted, and then forcing her way through a portion of the fleet that was engaged in the contest, and throwing the vessels into confusion as she passed, she succeeded in getting to sea, and then pressed on, under full sail, down the coast to the southward. Antony, as soon as he perceived that she was going, abandoning every other thought, and impelled by his insane devotedness to her, hastily called up a galley of five banks of oarsmen to pull with all their force after Cleopatra's flying squadron.

Cleopatra Flees the Battle

Cleopatra, looking back from the deck of her vessel, saw this swift galley pressing on toward her. She raised a signal at the stern of the vessel which she was in, that Antony might know for which of the fifty flying ships he was to steer. Guided by the signal, Antony came up to the vessel, and the sailors hoisted him up the side and helped him in. Cleopatra had, however, disappeared. Overcome with shame and confusion, she did not dare, it seems, to meet the look of the wretched victim of her arts whom she had now irretrievably ruined. Antony did not seek her. He did not speak a word. He went forward to the prow of the ship, and, throwing himself down there alone, pressed his head between his hands, and seemed stunned and stupefied, and utterly overwhelmed with horror and despair.

Antony Follows Cleopatra – He Gains Her Galley – A Severe Conflict – Avenger of a Father

He was, however, soon aroused from his stupor by an alarm raised on board his galley that they were pursued. He rose from his seat, seized a spear, and, on ascending to the quarter-deck, saw that there were a number of small light boats, full of men and of arms, coming up behind them, and gaining rapidly upon his galley. Antony, now free for a moment from his enchantress's sway, and acting under the impulse of his own indomitable boldness and decision, instead of urging the oarsmen to press forward more rapidly in order to make good their escape, ordered the helm to be put about, and thus, turning the galley around, he faced his pursuers, and drove his ship into the midst of them. A violent conflict ensued, the din and confusion of which was increased by the shocks and collisions between the boats and the galley. In the end, the boats were beaten off, all excepting one: that one kept still hovering near, and the commander of it, who stood upon the deck, poising his spear with an aim at Antony, and seeking eagerly an opportunity to throw it, seemed by his attitude and the expression of his countenance to be animated by some peculiarly bitter feeling of hostility and hate. Antony asked him who he was that dared so fiercely to threaten *him*. The man replied by giving his name and saying that he came to avenge the death of his father. It proved that he was the son of a man whom Antony had at a previous time, on some account or other, caused to be beheaded.

Antony Pursued – His Anguish

There followed an obstinate contest between Antony and this fierce assailant, in the end of which the latter was beaten off. The boats then, having succeeded in making some prizes from Antony's fleet, though they had failed in capturing Antony himself, gave up the pursuit and returned. Antony then went back to his place, sat down in the prow, buried his face in his hands, and sank into the same condition of hopeless distress and anguish as before.

Antony and Cleopatra Shun Each Other

When husband and wife are overwhelmed with misfortune and suffering, each instinctively seeks a refuge in the sympathy and support of the other. It is, however, far otherwise with such connections as that of Antony and Cleopatra. Conscience, which remains calm and quiet in prosperity and sunshine, rises up with sudden and unexpected violence as soon as the hour of calamity comes; and thus, instead of mutual comfort and help, each finds in the thoughts of the other only the means of adding the horrors of remorse to the anguish of disappointment and despair. So extreme was Antony's distress that for three days he and Cleopatra neither saw nor spoke to each other. She was overwhelmed with confusion and chagrin, and he was in such a condition of mental excitement that she did not dare to approach him. In a word, reason seemed to have wholly lost its sway – his mind, in the alternations of his insanity, rising sometimes to fearful excitement, in paroxysms of uncontrollable rage, and then sinking again for a time into the stupor of despair.

Arrival at Taenarus – Antony and Cleopatra Flee Together to Alexandria

In the meantime, the ships were passing down as rapidly as possible on the western coast of Greece. When they reached Taenarus, the southern promontory of the peninsula, it was necessary to pause and consider what was to be done. Cleopatra's women went to Antony and attempted to quiet and calm him. They brought him food. They persuaded him to see Cleopatra. A great number of merchant ships from the ports along the coast gathered around Antony's little fleet and offered their services. His cause, they said, was by no means desperate. The army on the land had not been beaten. It was not even certain that his fleet had been conquered. They endeavoured thus to revive the ruined commander's sinking courage, and to urge him to make a new effort to retrieve his fortunes. But all was in vain. Antony was sunk in a hopeless despondency. Cleopatra was determined on going to Egypt, and he must go too. He distributed what treasure remained at his disposal among his immediate followers and friends and gave them advice about the means of concealing themselves until they could make peace with Octavian. Then, giving up all as lost, he followed Cleopatra across the sea to Alexandria.

CHAPTER XII
THE END OF CLEOPATRA, 10 AUGUST 30 BCE

Antony's Infatuation

The case of Mark Antony affords one of the most extraordinary examples of the power of unlawful love to lead its deluded and infatuated victim into the very jaws of open and recognized destruction that history records. Cases similar in character occur by the thousands in common life; but Antony's, though perhaps not more striking in itself than a great multitude of others have been, is the most conspicuous instance that has ever been held up to the observation of mankind.

Antony's Character in Early Life – Powerful Influence of Cleopatra Over Him

In early life, Antony was remarkable, as we have already seen, for a certain savage ruggedness of character, and for a stern and indomitable recklessness of will, so great that it seemed impossible that anything human should be able to tame him. He was under the control, too, of an ambition so lofty and aspiring that it appeared to know no bounds; and yet we find him taken possession of, in the very midst of his career, and in the height of his prosperity and success, by a woman, and so subdued by her arts and fascinations as to yield himself wholly to her guidance, and allow himself to be led about by her entirely at her will. She displaces whatever there might have been that was noble and generous in his heart and substitutes therefor her own principles of malice and cruelty. She extinguishes all the fires of his ambition, originally so magnificent in its aims that the world seemed hardly large enough to afford it scope, and instead of this lofty passion, fills his soul with a love of the lowest, vilest, and most ignoble pleasures. She leads him to betray every public trust, to alienate from himself all the affections of his countrymen, to repel most cruelly the kindness and devotedness of a beautiful and faithful wife, and, finally to expel this wife and all of his own legitimate family from his house; and now, at last, she conducts him away in a most cowardly and ignoble flight from the field of his duty as a soldier – he knowing, all the time, that she is hurrying him to disgrace and destruction, and yet utterly without power to break from the control of his invisible chains.

Indignation at Antony's Conduct

The indignation which Antony's base abandonment of his fleet and army at the Battle of Actium excited, over all that part of the empire which had been under his command, was extreme. There was not the slightest possible excuse for such a flight. His army, in which his greatest strength lay, remained unharmed, and even his fleet was not defeated. The ships continued the combat until night, notwithstanding the betrayal of their cause by their commander. They were at length, however, subdued. The army, also, being discouraged, and losing all motive for resistance, yielded too. In a very short time, the whole country went over to Octavian's side.

Cleopatra's Plan

In the meantime, Cleopatra and Antony, on their first return to Egypt, were completely beside themselves with terror. Cleopatra formed a plan for having all the treasures that she could save, and a certain number of galleys sufficient for the transportation of these treasures and a small company of friends, carried across the isthmus of Suez and launched upon the Red Sea, in order that she might escape in that direction, and find some remote hiding-place and safe retreat on the shores of Arabia or India, beyond the reach of Octavian's dreaded power. She actually commenced this undertaking and sent one or two of her galleys across the isthmus; but the Arabs seized them as soon as they reached their place of destination, and killed or captured the men who had them in charge, so that this desperate scheme was soon abandoned. She and Antony then finally concluded to establish themselves at Alexandria, and made preparation, as well as they could, for defending themselves against Octavian there.

Antony Becomes a Misanthrope – He Builds a Hut on the Island of Pharos

Antony, when the first effects of his panic subsided, began to grow mad with vexation and resentment against all mankind. He determined that he would have nothing to do with Cleopatra or with any of her friends, but went off in a fit of sullen rage, and built a hermitage in a lonely place, on the island of Pharos, where he lived for a time, cursing his folly and his wretched fate, and uttering the bitterest invectives against all who had been concerned in it. Here tidings came continually in, informing him of the defection of one after another of his armies, of the fall of his provinces in Greece and Asia Minor, and of the irresistible progress which Octavian was now making toward universal dominion. The tidings of these disasters coming incessantly upon him kept him in a continual fever of resentment and rage.

Antony's Reconciliation with Cleopatra – Scenes of Revelry

At last he became tired of his misanthropic solitude, a sort of reconciliation ensued between himself and Cleopatra, and he went back again to the city. Here he joined himself once more to Cleopatra, and, collecting together what remained of their joint resources, they plunged again into a life of dissipation and vice, with the vain attempt to drown in mirth and wine the bitter regrets and the anxious forebodings which filled their souls. They joined with them a company of revellers as abandoned as themselves and strove very hard to disguise and conceal their cares in their forced and unnatural gaiety. They could not, however, accomplish this purpose. Octavian was gradually advancing in his progress, and they knew very well that the time of his dreadful reckoning with them must soon come; nor was there any place on earth in which they could look with any hope of finding a refuge in it from his vindictive hostility.

Cleopatra Makes a Collection of Poisons – Her Experiments with Them

Cleopatra, warned by dreadful presentiments of what would probably at last be her fate, amused herself in studying the nature of poisons – not theoretically, but practically – making experiments with them on wretched prisoners and captives whom she compelled to take them in order that she and Antony might see the effects which they produced. She made a collection of all the poisons which she could procure, and administered portions of them all, that she might see which were sudden and which were slow in their effects, and also learn which produced the greatest distress and suffering, and which, on the other hand, only benumbed and stupefied the faculties, and thus extinguished life with the least infliction of pain. These experiments were not confined to such vegetable and mineral poisons as could be mingled with the food or administered in a potion. Cleopatra took an equal interest in the effects of the bite of venomous serpents and reptiles. She procured specimens of all these animals, and tried them upon her prisoners, causing the men to be stung and bitten by them, and then watching the effects. These investigations were made, not directly with a view to any practical use, which she was to make of the knowledge thus acquired, but rather as an agreeable occupation, to divert her mind, and to amuse Antony and her guests. The variety in the forms and expressions which the agony of her poisoned victims assumed – their writhings, their cries, their convulsions, and the distortions of their features when struggling with death – furnished exactly the kind and degree of excitement which she needed to occupy and amuse her mind.

Antony's Suspicions – Cleopatra's Strategem

Antony was not entirely at ease, however, during the progress of these terrible experiments. His foolish and childish fondness for Cleopatra was mingled with jealousy, suspicion, and distrust; and he was so afraid that Cleopatra might secretly poison him that he would never take any food or wine without requiring that she should taste it before him. At length, one day, Cleopatra caused the petals of some flowers to be poisoned, and then had the flowers woven into the chaplet which Antony was to wear at supper. In the midst of the feast, she pulled off the leaves of the flowers from her own chaplet and put them playfully into her wine, and then proposed that Antony should do the same with his chaplet, and that they should then drink the wine, tinctured, as it would be, with the colour and the perfume of the flowers. Antony entered very readily into this proposal, and when he was about to drink the wine, she arrested his hand, and told him that it was poisoned. "You see now," said she, "how vain it is for you to watch against me. If it were possible for me to live without you, how easy it would be for me to devise ways and means to kill you." Then, to prove that her words were true, she ordered one of the servants to drink Antony's wine. He did so and died before their sight in dreadful agony.

The Bite of the Asp

The experiments which Cleopatra thus made on the nature and effects of poison were not, however, wholly without practical result. Cleopatra learned from them, it is said, that the bite of the asp was the easiest and least painful mode of death. The effect of the venom of that animal appeared to her to be the lulling of the sensorium into a lethargy or stupor, which soon ended in death, without the intervention of pain. This knowledge she seems to have laid up in her mind for future use.

Cleopatra's Tomb

The thoughts of Cleopatra appear, in fact, to have been much disposed, at this time, to flow in gloomy channels, for she occupied herself a great deal in building for herself a sepulchral monument in a certain sacred portion of the city. This monument had, in fact, been commenced many years ago, in accordance with a custom prevailing among Egyptian sovereigns, of expending a portion of their revenues during their lifetime in building and decorating their own tombs. Cleopatra now turned her mind with new interest to her own mausoleum. She finished it, provided it with the strongest possible bolts and bars, and, in a word, seemed to be preparing it in all respects for occupation.

Octavian Reaches Pelusium – Antony Seeks Terms with Octavian – Octavian Refuses

In the meantime, Octavian, having made himself master of all the countries which had formerly been under Antony's sway, now advanced, meeting none to oppose him, from Asia Minor into Syria, and from Syria toward Egypt. Antony and Cleopatra made one attempt, while he was thus advancing toward Alexandria, to avert the storm which was impending over them, by sending an embassy to ask for some terms of peace. Antony proposed, in this embassy, to give up everything to his conqueror on condition that he might be permitted to retire unmolested with Cleopatra to Athens and allowed to spend the remainder of their days there in peace; and that the kingdom of Egypt might descend to their children. Octavian replied that he could not make any terms with Antony, though he was willing to consent to anything that was reasonable on behalf of Cleopatra. The messenger who came back from Octavian with this reply spent some time in private interviews with Cleopatra. This aroused Antony's jealousy and anger. He accordingly ordered the unfortunate messenger to be scourged and then sent back to Octavian, all lacerated with wounds, with orders to say to Octavian that if it displeased him to have one of his servants thus punished, he might revenge himself by scourging a servant of Antony's who was then, as it happened, in Octavian's power.

Antony and Cleopatra Prepare to Meet Their Doom

The news at length suddenly arrived at Alexandria that Octavian had appeared before Pelusium, and that the city had fallen into his hands. The next thing Antony and Cleopatra well knew would be, that they should see him at the gates of Alexandria. Neither Antony nor Cleopatra had any means of resisting his progress, and there was no place to which they could fly. Nothing was to be done but to await, in consternation and terror, the sure and inevitable doom which was now so near.

Cleopatra Gathers Her Treasure at the Tomb

Cleopatra gathered together all her treasures and sent them to her tomb. These treasures consisted of great and valuable stores of gold, silver, precious stones, garments of the highest cost, and weapons, and vessels of exquisite workmanship and great value, the hereditary possessions of the Egyptian kings. She also sent to the mausoleum an immense quantity of flax, tow, torches, and other combustibles. These she stored in the lower apartments of the monument, with the desperate determination of burning herself and her treasures together rather than to fall into the hands of the Romans.

Octavian Reaches Alexandria – He Negotiates with Cleopatra

In the meantime, the army of Octavian steadily continued its march across the desert from Pelusium to Alexandria. On the way, Octavian learned, through the agents in communication with him from within the city what were the arrangements which Cleopatra had made for the destruction of her treasure whenever the danger should become imminent of its falling into his hands. He was extremely unwilling that this treasure should be lost. Besides its intrinsic value, it was an object of immense importance to him to get possession of it for the purpose of carrying it to Rome as a trophy of his triumph. He accordingly sent secret messengers to Cleopatra, endeavouring to separate her from Antony, and to infuse her mind with the profession that he felt only friendship for her, and did not mean to do her any injury, being in pursuit of Antony only.

These negotiations were continued from day to day while Octavian was advancing. At last, the Roman army reached Alexandria, and invested it on every side.

Antony's Sally from Alexandria – He Skirmishes with Octavian's Cavalry – The Unfaithful Captain

As soon as Octavian was established in his camp under the walls of the city, Antony planned a sally, and he executed it, in fact, with considerable energy and success. He issued suddenly from the gates, at the head of as strong a force as he could command and attacked a body of Octavian's horsemen. He succeeded in driving these horsemen away from their position, but he was soon driven back in his turn, and compelled to retreat to the city, fighting as he fled, to beat back his pursuers. He was extremely elated at the success of this skirmish. He came to Cleopatra with a countenance full of animation and pleasure, took her in his arms and kissed her, all accoutred for battle as he was, and boasted greatly of the exploit which he had performed. He praised, too, in the highest terms, the valour of one of the officers who had gone out with him to the fight, and whom he had now brought to the palace to present to Cleopatra. Cleopatra rewarded the faithful captain's prowess with a magnificent suit of armour made of gold. Notwithstanding this reward, however, the man deserted Antony that very night, and went over to the enemy. Almost all of Antony's adherents were in the same state of mind. They would have gladly gone over to the camp of Octavian, if they could have found an opportunity to do so.

Battle of Alexandria, 1 October 30 BCE – Antony's Fleet Defects to Octavian

In fact, when the final battle was fought, the fate of it was decided by a grand defection in the fleet, which went over in a body to the side of Octavian. Antony was planning the operations of the day and, reconnoitring the movements of the enemy from an eminence which he occupied at the head of a body of foot soldiers – all the land forces that now remained to him – and looking off, from the eminence on which he stood, toward the harbour, he observed a movement among the galleys. They were going out to meet the ships of Octavian, which were lying at anchor not very far from them. Antony supposed that his vessels were going to attack those of the enemy, and he looked to see what exploits they would perform. They advanced toward Octavian's ships, and when they met them, Antony observed, to his utter amazement, that, instead of the furious combat that he had expected to see, the ships only exchanged friendly salutations, by the use of the customary naval signals; and then his ships, passing quietly round, took their positions in the lines of the other fleet. The two fleets had thus become merged and mingled into one.

Antony Suspects Betrayal by Cleopatra – She Withdraws to Her Tomb

Antony immediately decided that this was Cleopatra's treason. She had made peace with Octavian, he thought, and surrendered the fleet to him as one of the conditions of it.

Antony ran through the city, crying out that he was betrayed, and in a frenzy of rage sought the palace. Cleopatra fled to her tomb. She took in with her one or two attendants, and bolted and barred the doors, securing the fastenings with the heavy catches and springs that she had previously made ready. She then directed her women to call out through the door that she had killed herself within the tomb.

False Rumour of Cleopatra's Death Reaches Antony

The tidings of her death were borne to Antony. It changed his anger to grief and despair. His mind, in fact, was now wholly lost to all balance and control, and it passed from the dominion of one stormy passion to another with the most capricious facility. He cried out with the most bitter expressions of sorrow, mourning, he said, not so much Cleopatra's death, for he should soon follow and join her, as the fact that she had proved herself so superior to him in courage at last, in having thus anticipated him in the work of self-destruction.

Antony's Despair – Eros the Slave

He was at this time in one of the chambers of the palace, whither he had fled in despair, and was standing by a fire, for the morning was cold. He had a favourite servant named Eros, whom he greatly trusted, and whom he had made to take an oath long before, that whenever it should become necessary for him to die, Eros should kill him. This Eros he now called to him, and telling him that the time was come, ordered him to take the sword and strike the blow.

Antony Attempts to Commit Suicide

Eros took the sword while Antony stood up before him. Eros turned his head aside as if wishing that his eyes should not see the deed which his hands were about to perform. Instead, however, of piercing his master with it, he plunged it into his own breast, fell down at Antony's feet, and died.

Antony gazed a moment at the shocking spectacle, and then said, "I thank thee for this, noble Eros. Thou hast set me an example. I must do for myself what thou couldst not do for me." So saying, he took the sword from his servant's hands, plunged it into his body, and staggering to a little bed that was near, fell over upon it in a swoon. He had received a mortal wound.

Antony Taken to Cleopatra

The pressure, however, which was produced by the position in which he lay upon the bed, stanched the wound a little, and stopped the flow of blood. Antony came presently to himself again, and then began to beg and implore those around him to take the sword and put him out of his misery. But no one would do it. He lay for a time suffering great pain, and moaning incessantly, until, at length, an officer came into the apartment and told him that the story which he had heard of Cleopatra's death was not true; that she was still alive, shut up in her monument, and that she desired to see him there. This intelligence was the source of new excitement and agitation. Antony implored the by-standers to carry him to Cleopatra, that he might see her once more before he died. They shrank from the attempt; but, after some hesitation and delay, they concluded to undertake to remove him. So, taking him in their arms, they bore him along, faint and dying, and marking their track with his blood, toward the tomb.

Cleopatra Refuses to Open the Door of the Tomb – Her Grief

Cleopatra would not open the gates to let the party in. The city was all in uproar and confusion through the terror of the assault which Octavian was making upon it, and she did not know what treachery might be intended. She therefore went up to a window above, and letting down ropes and chains, she directed those below to fasten the dying body to them, that she and the two women with her might draw it up. This was done. Those who witnessed it said that it was a most piteous sight to behold – Cleopatra and her women above exhausting their strength in drawing the wounded and bleeding sufferer up the wall, while he, when he approached the window, feebly raised his arms to them, that they might lift him in. The women had hardly strength sufficient to draw the body up. At one time it seemed that the attempt would have to be abandoned; but Cleopatra reached down from the window as far as she could to get hold of Antony's arms, and thus, by dint of great effort, they succeeded at last in taking him in. They bore him to a couch which was in the upper room from which the window opened, and laid him down, while

Cleopatra wrung her hands and tore her hair, and uttered the most piercing lamentations and cries. She leaned over the dying Antony, crying out incessantly with the most piteous exclamations of grief. She bathed his face, which was covered with blood, and vainly endeavoured to stanch his wound.

Death of Antony, 1 August 30 BCE

Antony urged her to be calm, and not to mourn his fate. He asked for some wine. They brought it to him and he drank it. He then entreated Cleopatra to save her life, if she possibly could do so, and to make some terms or other with Octavian, so as to continue to live. Very soon after this he expired.

Octavian Arrives – He Parleys with Cleopatra

In the meantime, Octavian had heard of the mortal wound which Antony had given himself; for one of the by-standers had seized the sword the moment that the deed was done, and had hastened to carry it to Octavian, and to announce to him the death of his enemy. Octavian immediately desired to get Cleopatra into his power. He sent a messenger, therefore, to the tomb, who attempted to open a parley there with her. Cleopatra talked with the messenger through the keyholes or crevices but could not be induced to open the door. The messenger reported these facts to Octavian. Octavian then sent another man with the messenger, and while one was engaging the attention of Cleopatra and her women at the door below, the other obtained ladders, and succeeded in gaining admission into the window above. Cleopatra was warned of the success of this stratagem by the shrieks of her women, who saw the officer coming down the stairs. She looked around, and observing at a glance that she was betrayed, and that the officer was coming to seize her, she drew a little dagger from her robe, and was about to plunge it into her breast, when the officer grasped her arm just in time to prevent the blow. He took the dagger from her, and then examined her clothes to see that there were no other secret weapons concealed there.

Cleopatra Made Octavian's Prisoner – Treatment of the Queen

The capture of the queen being reported to Octavian, he appointed an officer to take her into close custody. This officer was charged to treat her with all possible courtesy, but to keep a close and constant watch over her, and particularly to guard against allowing her any possible means or opportunity for self-destruction.

Octavian Seizes Alexandria

In the meantime, Octavian took formal possession of the city, marching in at the head of his troops with the most imposing pomp and parade. A chair of state, magnificently decorated, was set up for him on a high elevation in a public square; and here he sat, with circles of guards around him, while the people of the city, assembled before him in the dress of suppliants, and kneeling upon the pavement, begged his forgiveness, and implored him to spare the city. These petitions the great conqueror graciously condescended to grant.

Cleopatra's Transfers Her Treasury To Octavian

Many of the princes and generals who had served under Antony came next to beg the body of their commander, that they might give it an honourable burial. These requests, however, Octavian would not accede to, saying that he could not take the body away from Cleopatra. He, however, gave Cleopatra leave to make such arrangements for the obsequies as she thought fit, and allowed her to appropriate such sums of money from her treasures for this purpose as she desired. Cleopatra accordingly made the necessary arrangements, and superintended the execution of them; not, however, with any degree of calmness and composure, but in a state, on the contrary, of extreme agitation and distress. In fact, she had been living now so long under the unlimited and unrestrained dominion of caprice and passion, that reason was pretty effectually dethroned, and all self-control was gone. She was now nearly forty years of age, and, though traces of her inexpressible beauty remained, her bloom was faded, and her countenance was wan with the effects of weeping, anxiety, and despair. She was, in a word, both in body and mind, only the wreck and ruin of what she once had been.

Antony's Funeral – Cleopatra Resolves to Starve Herself to Death

When the burial ceremonies were performed, and she found that all was over – that Antony was for ever gone, and she herself hopelessly and irremediably ruined – she gave herself up to a perfect frenzy of grief. She beat her breast, and scratched and tore her flesh so dreadfully, in the vain efforts which she made to kill herself, in the paroxysms of her despair, that she was soon covered with contusions and wounds, which, becoming inflamed and swelled, made her a shocking spectacle to see, and threw her into a fever. She then conceived the idea of pretending to be more sick than she was, and so refusing food and starving herself to death. She attempted to execute this design. She rejected every medical remedy that was offered her, and would not eat, and lived thus some days without food. Octavian, to whom everything relating to his captive was minutely reported by her attendants, suspected her design. He was very unwilling that she should die, having set his heart on exhibiting her to the Roman people, on his return to the capital, in his triumphal procession. He accordingly sent her orders, requiring that she should submit to the treatment prescribed by the physician, and take her food, enforcing these his commands with a certain threat which he imagined might have some influence over her. And what threat does the reader imagine could possibly be devised to reach a mind so sunk, so desperate, so wretched as hers? Everything seemed already lost but life, and life was only an insupportable burden. What interests, then, had she still remaining upon which a threat could take hold?

Octavian's Threats

Octavian, in looking for some avenue by which he could reach her, reflected that she was a mother. Caesarion, the son of Julius Caesar, and Alexander, Cleopatra, and Ptolemy, Antony's children, were still alive. Octavian imagined that in the secret recesses of her wrecked and ruined soul there might be some lingering principle of maternal affection remaining which he could goad into life and action. He accordingly sent word to her that, if she did not yield to the physician and take her food, he would kill every one of her children.

Impact of Octavian's Threats

The threat produced its effect. The crazed and frantic patient became calm. She received her food. She submitted to the physician. Under his treatment her wounds began to heal, the fever was allayed, and at length she appeared to be gradually recovering.

Octavian Visits Cleopatra – Her Wretched Condition

When Octavian learned that Cleopatra had become composed, and seemed to be in some sense convalescent, he resolved to pay her a visit. As he entered the room where she was confined, which seems to have been still the upper chamber of her tomb, he found her lying on a low and miserable bed, in a most wretched condition, and exhibiting such a spectacle of disease and wretchedness that he was shocked at beholding her. She appeared, in fact, almost wholly bereft of reason. When Octavian came in, she suddenly leaped out of the bed, half naked as she was, and covered with bruises and wounds, and crawled miserably along to her conqueror's feet in the attitude of a suppliant. Her hair was torn from her head, her limbs were swollen and disfigured, and great bandages appeared here and there, indicating that there were still worse injuries than these concealed. From the midst of all this squalidness and misery there still beamed from her sunken eyes a great portion of their former beauty, and her voice still possessed the same inexpressible charm that had characterized it so strongly in the days of her prime. Octavian made her go back to her bed again and lie down.

The False Inventory

Cleopatra then began to talk and excuse herself for what she had done, attributing all the blame of her conduct to Antony. Octavian, however, interrupted her, and defended Antony from her criminations, saying to her that it was not his fault so much as hers. She then suddenly changed her tone, and acknowledging her sins, piteously implored mercy. She begged Octavian to pardon and spare her, as if now she were afraid of death and dreaded it, instead of desiring it as a boon. In a word, her mind, the victim and the prey alternately of the most dissimilar and inconsistent passions, was now overcome by fear. To propitiate Octavian, she brought out a list of all her private treasures and delivered it to him as a complete inventory of all that she had. One of her treasurers, however, named Zeleucus, who was standing by, said to Octavian that that list was not complete. Cleopatra had, he alleged, reserved several things of great value, which she had not put down upon it.

Cleopatra in a Rage

This assertion, thus suddenly exposing her duplicity, threw Cleopatra into a violent rage. She sprang from her bed and assaulted her secretary in a most furious manner. Octavian and the others who were there interposed, and compelled Cleopatra to lie down again, which she did, uttering all the time the most grievous complaints at the wretched degradation to which she was reduced, to be insulted thus by her own servant at such a time. If she had reserved anything, she said, of her private treasures, it was only for presents to some of her faithful friends, to induce them the more zealously to intercede with Octavian on her behalf. Octavian replied by urging her to feel no concern on the subject whatever. He freely gave her, he said, all that she had reserved, and he promised in other respects to treat her in the most honourable and courteous manner.

Octavian Plans His Departure – Cleopatra Advised to Prepare to Go to Rome

Octavian was much pleased at the result of this interview. It was obvious, as it appeared to him, that Cleopatra had ceased to desire to die; that she now, on the contrary, wished to live, and that he should accordingly succeed in his desire of taking her with him to grace his triumph at Rome. He accordingly made his arrangements for departure, and Cleopatra was notified that in three days she was to set out, together with her children, to go into Syria. Octavian said Syria, as he did not wish to alarm Cleopatra by speaking of Rome. She, however, understood well where the journey, if once commenced, would necessarily end, and she was fully determined in her own mind that she would never go there.

Cleopatra's Determination – She Visits Antony's Tomb

She asked to be allowed to pay one parting visit to Antony's tomb. This request was granted; and she went to the tomb with a few attendants, carrying with her chaplets and garlands of flowers. At the tomb her grief broke forth anew and was as violent as ever. She bewailed her lover's death with loud cries and lamentations, uttered while she was placing the garlands upon the tomb, and offering the oblations and incense, which were customary in those days, as expressions of grief. "These," said she, as she made the offerings, "are the last tributes of affection that I can ever pay thee, my dearest, dearest lord. I cannot join thee, for I am a captive and a prisoner, and they will not let me die. They watch me every hour, and are going to bear me far away, to exhibit me to thine enemies, as a badge and trophy of their triumph over thee. Oh intercede, dearest Antony, with the gods where thou art now, since those that reign here on earth have utterly forsaken me; implore them to save me from this fate, and let me die here in my native land, and be buried by thy side in this tomb."

Cleopatra's Composure on Her Return

When Cleopatra returned to her apartment again after this melancholy ceremony, she seemed to be more composed than she had been before. She went to the bath, and then she attired herself handsomely for supper. She had ordered supper that night to be very sumptuously served. She was at liberty to make these arrangements, for the restrictions upon her movements, which had been imposed at first, were now removed, her appearance and demeanour having been for some time such as to lead Octavian to suppose that there was no longer any danger that she would attempt self-destruction. Her entertainment was arranged, therefore, according to her directions, in a manner corresponding with the customs of her court when she had been a queen. She had many attendants, and among them were two of her own women. These women were long-tried and faithful servants and friends.

Cleopatra's Supper – The Basket of Figs – Her Letter to Octavian

While she was at supper, a man came to the door with a basket, and wished to enter. The guards asked him what he had in his basket. He opened it to let them see; and, lifting up some green leaves which were laid over the top, he showed the soldiers that the basket was filled with figs. He said that they were for Cleopatra's supper. The soldiers admired the appearance of the figs, saying that they were very fine and beautiful. The man asked the soldiers to take some of them. This they declined, but allowed the man to pass in. When the supper was ended, Cleopatra sent all of her attendants away except the two women. They remained. After a little time, one of these women came out with a letter for Octavian, which Cleopatra had written, and which she wished to have immediately delivered. One of the soldiers from the guard stationed at the gates was accordingly dispatched to carry the letter. Octavian, when it was given to him, opened the envelope at once and read the letter, which was written, as was customary in those days, on a small tablet of metal. He found that it was a brief but urgent petition from Cleopatra, written evidently in agitation and excitement, praying that he would overlook her offence, and allow her to be buried with Antony. Octavian immediately inferred that she had destroyed herself. He sent off some messengers at once, with orders to go directly to her place of confinement and ascertain the truth, intending to follow them himself immediately.

Cleopatra Found Dead, 10 August 30 BCE

The messengers, on their arrival at the gates, found the sentinels and soldiers quietly on guard before the door, as if all were well. On entering Cleopatra's room, however, they beheld a shocking spectacle. Cleopatra was lying dead upon a couch. One of her women was upon the floor, dead too. The other, whose name was Charmian, was sitting over the body of her mistress, fondly caressing her, arranging flowers in her hair, and adorning her diadem. The messengers of Octavian, on witnessing this spectacle, were overcome with amazement, and demanded of Charmian what it could mean. "It is all right," said Charmian. "Cleopatra has acted in a manner worthy of a princess descended from so noble a line of kings." As Charmian said this, she began to sink herself, fainting, upon the bed, and almost immediately expired.

Amazement of the By-standers

The by-standers were not only shocked at the spectacle which was thus presented before them, but they were perplexed and confounded in their attempts to discover by what means Cleopatra and her women had succeeded in effecting their design. They examined the bodies, but no marks of violence were to be discovered. They looked all around the room, but no weapons, and no indication of any means of poison, were to be found. They discovered something that appeared like the slimy track of an animal on the wall, toward a window, which they thought might have been produced by an asp; but the reptile itself was nowhere to be seen. They examined the body with great care, but no marks of any bite or sting were to be found, except that there were two very slight and scarcely discernible punctures on the arm, which some persons fancied might have been so caused. The means and manner of her death seemed to be involved in impenetrable mystery.

Various Theories About Cleopatra's Death

There were various rumours on the subject subsequently in circulation both at Alexandria and at Rome, though the mystery was never fully solved. Some said that there was an asp concealed among the figs which the servant man brought in in the basket; that he brought it in that manner, by a preconcerted arrangement between him and Cleopatra, and that, when she received it, she placed the creature on her arm. Others say that she had a small steel instrument like a needle, with a poisoned point, which she had kept concealed in her hair, and that she killed herself with that, without producing any visible wound. Another story was that she had an asp in a box somewhere in her apartment, which she had reserved for this occasion, and when the time finally came, that she pricked and teased it with a golden bodkin to make it angry, and then placed it upon her flesh and received its sting. Which of these stories, if either of them, was true, could never be known. It has, however, been generally believed among mankind that Cleopatra died in some way or other by the self-inflicted sting of the asp, and paintings and sculptures without number have been made to illustrate and commemorate the scene.

Octavian's Opinion – His Triumph for His Conquest of Egypt, 15 August 29 BCE

This supposition in respect to the mode of her death is, in fact, confirmed by the action of Octavian himself on his return to Rome, which furnishes a strong indication of his opinion of the manner in which his captive at last eluded him. Disappointed in not being able to exhibit the queen herself in his triumphal train, he caused a golden statue representing her to be made, with an image of an asp upon the arm of it, and this sculpture he caused to be borne conspicuously before him in his grand triumphal entry into the capital, as the token and trophy of the final downfall of the unhappy Egyptian queen.

GEOGRAPHY BY STRABO

Strabo (Strabon, 64 or 63 BCE–*c.* 24 CE) was a Greek-speaking Roman geographer, philosopher and historian who lived in Asia Minor during the lifetime of Cleopatra.

Known for his extensive travels, Strabo journeyed to many places in the Roman world, including Kush, coastal Tuscany and Ethiopia; he moved to Rome in 44 BCE. His travels included a trip up the Nile to Philae around 25 BCE.

When Strabo began writing his *Geography* is uncertain (estimates range from 7 to 18 BCE), but he likely worked on it for many years. Certain comments in the text suggest that he completed the work during the reign of Emperor Tiberius (r. 14–37 CE). The latest dated reference is to the death of King Juba II in 23 CE.

Geography is an encyclopedic work covering the political, economic, social, cultural and geographic aspects of Europe and the Mediterranean, including North Africa. It remains the sole surviving source of information about societies and places in the Roman world during the time of Augustus (r. 27 BCE–14 CE). His description of Egypt and Alexandria are particularly valuable for the study of Cleopatra, as the places he saw were as the queen would have known them.

These extracts are taken from the translation of H.L. Jones, made from 1917 to 1932.

Note: Strabo uses the measures of his time. The cubit (*pekhys*) is an ancient unit of length. It represents the distance from the elbow to the tip of the middle finger, which by the time of the Ancient Greeks measured approximately 46 centimetres (18 in). The Ancient Greek foot (*pous*, pl. *podes*) measured around 30 centimetres (approximately 1 imperial foot). The *stadion* (pl. *stadia*) was an ancient Greek unit of length that comprised 600 *podes*, the exact length of which is now unknown but modern historians estimate was between 150 metres (492 ft) and 210 (689 ft) metres. The *plethron* is an ancient unit of Greek measurement equal to between 97 and 100 *podes*, and a square *plethron* measure of 10,000 *podes*, *c.* 30 metres by 30 metres (98 ft by 98 ft).

FROM THE SEVENTEENTH BOOK

The Nile

Now according to him [Eratosthenes] the Nile is nine hundred or a thousand *stadia* distant towards the west from the Arabian Gulf, and is similar in shape to the letter 'N' written reversed; for after flowing, he says, from Meroê towards the north about two thousand seven hundred *stadia*, it turns back towards the south and the winter sunset about three thousand seven hundred *stadia*, and after almost reaching the same parallel as that of the region of Meroê and projecting far into Libya and making the second turn, flows towards the north five thousand three hundred *stadia* to the great cataract, turning aside slightly towards the east, and then one thousand two hundred *stadia* to the smaller cataract at Syenê, and then five thousand three hundred more to the sea.

Tributaries of the Nile

Two rivers empty into it, which flow from some lakes on the east and enclose Meroê, a rather large island. One of these rivers, which flows on the eastern side of the island, is called Astaboras and the other is called Astapus, though some call it Astasobas and say that another river, which flows from some lakes in the south, is the Astapus and that this river forms almost all the straight part of the body of the Nile, and that it is filled by the summer rains. Above the confluence of the Astaboras and the Nile, he says, at a distance of seven hundred *stadia*, lies Meroê, a city bearing the same name as the island; and there is another island above Meroê which is held by the Egyptian fugitives who revolted in the time of Psammitichus, and are called *Sembritae*, meaning "foreigners". They are ruled by a queen, but they are subject to the kings of Meroê. The lower parts of the country on either side of Meroê, along the Nile towards the Red Sea, are inhabited by Megabari and Blemmyes, who are subject to the Aethiopians and border on the Egyptians, and, along the sea, by Troglodytes (the Troglodytes opposite Meroê are a ten or twelve days' journey distant from the Nile), but the parts on the left side of the course of the Nile, in Libya, are inhabited by Nubae, a large tribe, who, beginning at Meroê, extend as far as the bends of the river, and are not subject to the Aethiopians but are divided into several separate kingdoms. The extent of Egypt along the sea from the Pelusiac to the Canopic mouth is one thousand three hundred *stadia*. This, then, is what Eratosthenes says.

Egypt and Its Neighbour Aethiopia

But it is necessary to speak at greater length, and first of the parts about Egypt, in order to proceed from those that are better known to those that come in order thereafter; for the Nile effects certain common results in this country and in that which is continuous with it and lies above it, I mean the country of the Aethiopians, in that it waters them at the time of its rise and also leaves also those parts of them habitable which have been covered during the overflows, and in that it merely passes through all the higher parts that are at a greater altitude than its current, leaving them uninhabited and desert on both sides because of the same lack of water. However, the Nile does not pass through the whole of Aethiopia, nor alone, nor in a straight line, but it alone passes through Egypt, through the whole of it and in a straight line, beginning from the little cataract above Syenê and Elephantinê, which are the boundaries of Egypt and Aethiopia, to its outlets on the seacoast. And indeed the Aethiopians lead for the most part a nomadic and resourceless life, on account of the barrenness of the country and of the unseasonableness of its climate and of its remoteness from us, whereas with the Egyptians the contrary is the case in all these respects; for from the outset they have led a civic and cultivated life and have been settled in well-known regions, so that their organisations are a matter of comment. And they are commended in that they are thought to have used worthily the good fortune of their country, having divided it well and having taken good care of it; for when they had appointed a king they divided the people into three classes, and they called one class soldiers, another farmers, and another priests; and the last class had the care of things sacred and the other two of things relating to man; and some had charge of the affairs of war, and others of all the affairs of peace, both tilling soil and following trades, from which sources the revenues were gathered for the king. The priests devoted themselves both to philosophy and to astronomy; and they were companions of the king.

The Nomes

The country was first divided into Nomes, the Thebaïs containing ten, the country in the Delta ten, and the country between them sixteen (according to some, the number of the Nomes all told was the same as that of the halls in the Labyrinth, but the number of these is less than thirty); and again the Nomes were divided into other sections, for most of them were divided into toparchies, and these also into other sections; and the smaller portions were the *arourae*. There was need of this accurate and minute division on account of the continuous confusion of the boundaries caused by the Nile at the time of its increases, since the Nile takes away and adds soil, and changes conformations of lands, and in general hides from view the signs by which one's own land is distinguished from that of another. Of necessity, therefore, the lands must be re-measured again and again. And here it was, they say, that the science of geometry originated, just as accounting and arithmetic originated with the Phoenicians, because of their commerce. Like the people as a whole, the people in each Nome were also divided into three parts, since the land had been divided into three equal parts. The activity of people in connection with the river goes so far as to conquer nature through diligence. For by nature the land produces more fruit than do other lands, and still more when watered; but diligence has oftentimes, when nature has failed, availed to bring about the watering of as much land even at the time of the smaller rises of the river as at the greater rises, that is, through the means of canals and embankments. At any rate, in the times before Petronius the crop was the largest and the rise the highest when the Nile would rise to fourteen cubits, and when it would rise to only eight a famine would ensue; but in the time of his reign over the country, and when the Nilometer registered only twelve cubits, the crop was the largest, and once, when it registered only eight cubits, no one felt hunger. Such is the organisation of Egypt; but let me now describe the things that come next in order.

The Nile Delta

The Nile flows from the Aethiopian boundaries towards the north in a straight line to the district called *Delta*, and then, being "split at the head," as Plato says, the Nile makes this place as it were the vertex of a triangle, the sides of the triangle being formed by the streams that split in either direction and extend to the sea – the one on the right to the sea at Pelusium and the other on the left to the sea at Canopus and the neighbouring Heracleium, as it is called – and the base by the coast-line between Pelusium and the Heracleium. An island, therefore, has been formed by the sea and the two streams of the river; and it is called Delta on account of the similarity of its shape; and the district at the vertex has been given the same name because it is the beginning of the above-mentioned figure; and the village there is also called Delta.

Pelusiac and Canopic Mouths of the Nile

Now these are two mouths of the Nile, of which one is called Pelusiac and the other Canopic or Heracleiotic; but between these there are five other outlets, those at least that are worth mentioning, and several that are smaller; for, beginning with the first parts of the Delta, many branches of the river have been split off throughout the whole island and have formed many streams and islands, so that the whole Delta has become navigable – canals on canals having been cut, which are navigated with such ease that some people even use earthenware ferry-boats. Now the island as a whole is as much as three thousand *stadia* in perimeter; and they also call it, together with the opposite river-lands of the Delta, Lower Egypt; but at the rising of the Nile the whole country is under water and becomes a lake, except the settlements; and these are situated on natural hills or on artificial mounds, and contain cities of considerable size and villages, which, when viewed from afar, resemble islands. The water stays more than forty days in summer and then goes down gradually just as it rose; and in sixty days the plain is completely bare and begins to dry out; and the sooner the drying takes place, the sooner the ploughing and the sowing; and the drying takes place sooner in those parts where the heat is greater. The parts above the Delta are also watered in the same way, except that the river flows in a straight course about four thousand *stadia* through only one channel, except where some island intervenes, of which the most noteworthy is that which comprises the Heracleiotic Nome, or except where the river is diverted to a greater extent than usual by a canal into a large lake or a territory which it can water, as, for instance, in the case of the canal which waters the

Arsinoïte Nome and Lake Moeris and of those which spread over Lake Mareotis.

River-Land

In short, Egypt consists of only the river-land, I mean the last stretch of river-land on either side of the Nile, which, beginning at the boundaries of Aethiopia and extending to the vertex of the Delta, scarcely anywhere occupies a continuous habitable space as broad as three hundred *stadia*. Accordingly, when it is dried, it resembles lengthwise a girdle-band, the greater diversions of the river being excepted. This shape of the river-land of which I am speaking, as also of the country, is caused by the mountains on either side, which extend from the region of Syenê down to the Egyptian Sea; for in proportion as these mountains lie together or at a distance from one another, in that proportion the river is contracted or widened, and gives to the lands that are habitable their different shapes. But the country beyond the mountains is for a great distance uninhabited.

Flooding of the Nile

Now the ancients depended mostly on conjecture, but the men of later times, having become eyewitnesses, perceived that the Nile was filled by summer rains, when Upper Aethiopia was flooded, and particularly in the region of its farthermost mountains, and that when the rains ceased the inundation gradually ceased. This fact was particularly clear to those who navigated the Arabian Gulf as far as the Cinnamon-bearing country, and to those who were sent out to hunt elephants or upon any other business which may have prompted the Ptolemaic kings of Egypt to despatch men thither. For these kings were concerned with things of this kind; and especially the Ptolemy surnamed Philadelphus, since he was of an enquiring disposition, and on account of the infirmity of his body was always searching for novel pastimes and enjoyments. But the kings of old were not at all concerned with such things, although they proved themselves congenial to learning, both they and the priests, with whom they spent the greater part of their lives; and therefore we may well be surprised, not only on this account, but also by the fact that Sesostris traversed the whole of Aethiopia as far as the Cinnamon-bearing country, and that memorials of his expedition, pillars and inscriptions, are to be seen even to this day. Further, when Cambyses took possession of Egypt, he advanced with the Egyptians even as far as Meroê; and indeed, this name was given by him to both the island and the city, it is said, because his sister Meroê – some say his wife – died there. The name, at any rate, he bestowed upon the place in honour of the woman.

It is surprising, therefore, that the men of that time, having such knowledge to begin with, did not possess a perfectly clear knowledge of the rains, especially since the priests rather meticulously record in their sacred books, and thus store away, all facts that reveal any curious information; for they should have investigated, for they made any investigations at all, the question, which even to this day is still being investigated, I mean why in the world rains fall in summer but not in winter, and in the southernmost parts but not in Thebaïs and the country round Syenê; but the fact that the rising of the river results from rains should not have been investigated, nor yet should this matter have needed such witnesses as Poseidonius mentions; for instance, he says that it was Callisthenes who states that the summer rains are the cause of the risings, though Callisthenes took the assertion from Aristotle, and Aristotle from Thrasyalces the Thasian (one of the early physicists), and Thrasyalces from someone else, and he from Homer, who calls the Nile "heaven-fed": "And back again to the land of Egypt, heaven-fed river."

But I dismiss this subject, since it has been discussed by many writers, of whom it will suffice to report only the two who in my time have written the book about the Nile, I mean Eudorus and Ariston the Peripatetic philosopher; for except in the matter of arrangement everything found in the two writers is the same as regards both style and treatment. I, at any rate, being in want of copies with which to make a comparison, compared the one work with the other; but which of the two men it was who appropriated to himself the other's work might be discovered at Ammon's temple! Eudorus accused Ariston; the style, however, is more like that of Ariston.

Extent of Egypt

Now the early writers gave the name Egypt to only the part of the country that was inhabited and watered by the Nile, beginning at the region of Syenê and extending to the sea; but the later writers down to the present time have added on the eastern side approximately all the parts between the Arabian Gulf and the Nile (the Aethiopians do not use the Red Sea at all), and on the western side the parts extending as far as the oases, and on the sea-coast the parts extending from the Canopic mouth to Catabathmus and the domain of the Cyrenaeans. For the kings after Ptolemy became so powerful that they took possession of Cyrenaea itself and even united Cypros with Egypt. The Romans, who succeeded the Ptolemies, separated their three dominions and have kept Egypt within its former limits. The

Egyptians call *oases* the inhabited districts which are surrounded by large deserts, like islands in the open sea. There is many an oasis in Libya, and three of them lie close to Egypt and are classed as subject to it. This, then, is my general, or summary, account of Egypt, and I shall now discuss the separate parts and the excellent attributes of the country.

Since Alexandria and its neighbourhood constitute the largest and most important part of this subject, I shall begin with them. The seacoast, then, from Pelusium, as one sails towards the west, as far as the Canopic mouth, is about one thousand three hundred *stadia* – the "base" of the Delta, as I have called it; and thence to the island Pharos, one hundred and fifty *stadia* more. Pharos is an oblong isle, is very close to the mainland, and forms with it a harbour with two mouths; the shore of the mainland forms a bay, since it thrusts two promontories into the open sea, and between these is situated the island, which closes the bay, for it lies lengthwise parallel to the shore.

The Pharos Lighthouse

Of the extremities of Pharos, the eastern one lies closer to the mainland and to the promontory opposite it (the promontory called Lochias), and thus makes the harbour narrow at the mouth; and in addition to the narrowness of the intervening passage there are also rocks, some under the water, and others projecting out of it, which at all hours roughen the waves that strike them from the open sea. And likewise the extremity of the isle is a rock, which is washed all round by the sea and has upon it a tower that is admirably constructed of white marble with many stories and bears the same name as the island. This was an offering made by Sostratus of Cnidus, a friend of the kings, for the safety of mariners, as the inscription says: for since the coast was harbourless and low on either side, and also had reefs and shallows, those who were sailing from the open sea thither needed some lofty and conspicuous sign to enable them to direct their course aright to the entrance of the harbour.

The Eunostus Harbour

And the western mouth is also not easy to enter, although it does not require so much caution as the other. And it likewise forms a second harbour, that of Eunostus, as it is called, which lies in front of the closed harbour which was dug by the hand of man. For the harbour which affords the entrance on the side of the above-mentioned tower of Pharos is the Great Harbour, whereas these two lie continuous with that harbour in their innermost recess, being separated from it only by the embankment called the Heptastadium. The embankment forms a bridge extending from the mainland to the western portion of the island, and leaves open only two passages into the harbour of Eunostus, which are bridged over. However, this work formed not only a bridge to the island but also an aqueduct, at least when Pharos was inhabited. But in these present times it has been laid waste by the deified Caesar in his war against the Alexandrians since it had sided with the kings. A few seamen, however, live near the tower.

The Great Harbour

As for the Great Harbour, in addition to its being beautifully enclosed both by the embankment and by nature, it is not only so deep close to the shore that the largest ship can be moored at the steps, but also is cut up into several harbours. Now the earlier kings of the Egyptians, being content with what they had and not wanting foreign imports at all, and being prejudiced against all who sailed the seas, and particularly against the Greeks (for owing to scarcity of land of their own the Greeks were ravagers and coveters of that of others), set a guard over this region and ordered it to keep away any who should approach; and they gave them as a place of abode Rhacotis, as it is called, which is now that part of the city of the Alexandrians which lies above the ship-houses, but was at that time a village; and they gave over the parts round about the village to herdsmen, who likewise were able to prevent the approach of outsiders. But when Alexander visited the place and saw the advantages of the site, he resolved to fortify the city on the harbour. Writers record, as a sign of the good fortune that has since attended the city, an incident which occurred at the time of tracing the lines of the foundation: When the architects were marking the lines of the enclosure with chalk, the supply of chalk gave out; and when the king arrived, his stewards furnished a part of the barley-meal which had been prepared for the workmen, and by means of this the streets also, to a larger number than before, were laid out. This occurrence, then, they are said to have interpreted as a good omen.

Favourable Location of Alexandria

The advantages of the city's site are various; for, first, the place is washed by two seas, on the north by the Egyptian Sea, as it is called, and on the south by Lake Mareia, also called Mareotis. This is filled by many canals from the Nile, both from above and on the sides, and through these canals the imports are much larger than those from the sea, so that the harbour on the lake was in fact richer than that on the sea; and here the exports from Alexandria also are larger than the imports; and anyone might judge, if he were at either Alexandria or Dicaearchia and saw the merchant vessels both at their arrival and at their departure, how much heavier or lighter they sailed thither or therefrom. And in addition to the great value of the things brought down from both directions, both into the harbour on the sea and into that on the lake, the salubrity of the air is also worthy of remark. And this likewise results from the fact that the land is washed by water on both sides and because of the timeliness of the Nile's risings; for the other cities that are situated on lakes have heavy and stifling air in the heats of summer, because the lakes then become marshy along their edges because of the evaporation caused by the sun's rays, and, accordingly, when so much filth-laden moisture rises, the air inhaled is noisome and starts pestilential diseases, whereas at Alexandria, at the beginning of summer, the Nile, being full, fills the lake also, and leaves no marshy matter to corrupt the rising vapours. At that time, also, the Etesian winds blow from the north and from a vast sea, so that the Alexandrians pass their time most pleasantly in summer.

Shape and Plan of Alexandria

The shape of the area of the city is like a *chlamys* [a type of an ancient Greek cloak]; the long sides of it are those that are washed by the two waters, having a diameter of about thirty *stadia*, and the short sides are the isthmuses, each being seven or eight *stadia* wide and pinched in on one side by the sea and on the other by the lake. The city as a whole is intersected by streets practicable for horse-riding and chariot-driving, and by two that are very broad, extending to more than a *plethrum* in breadth, which cut one another into two sections and at right angles. And the city contains most beautiful public precincts and also the royal palaces, which constitute one-fourth or even one-third of the whole circuit of the city; for just as each of the kings, from love of splendour, was wont to add some adornment to the public monuments, so also he would invest himself at his own expense with a residence, in addition to those already built, so that now, to quote the words of the poet, "there is building upon building." All, however, are connected with one another and the harbour, even those that lie outside the harbour.

The Museum

The Museum is also a part of the royal palaces; it has a public walk, an Exedra with seats, and a large house, in which is the common mess-hall of the men of learning who share the Museum. This group of men not only hold property in common, but also have a priest in charge of the Museum, who formerly was appointed by the kings, but is now appointed by Caesar [Augustus]. The Sema also, as it is called, is a part of the royal palaces. This was the enclosure which contained the burial-places of the kings and that of Alexander; for Ptolemy, the son of Lagus, forestalled Perdiccas by taking the body away from him when he was bringing it down from Babylon and was turning aside towards Egypt, moved by greed and a desire to make that country his own. Furthermore, Perdiccas lost his life, having been slain by his soldiers at the time when Ptolemy attacked him and hemmed him up in a desert island. So Perdiccas was killed, having been transfixed by his soldiers' *sarissae* [pikes] when they attacked him; but the kings who were with him, both Aridaeus and the children of Alexander, and also Rhoxanê, Alexander's wife, departed for Macedonia; and the body of Alexander was carried off by Ptolemy and given sepulture in Alexandria, where it still now lies – not, however, in the same sarcophagus as before, for the present one is made of glass, whereas the one wherein Ptolemy laid it was made of gold. The latter was plundered by the Ptolemy nicknamed "Cocces" and "Pareisactus", who came over from Syria but was immediately expelled, so that his plunder proved unprofitable to him.

The Artificial Harbour

In the Great Harbour at the entrance, on the right hand, are the island and the tower Pharos, and on the other hand are the reefs and also the promontory Lochias, with a royal palace upon it; and on sailing into the harbour one comes, on the left, to the inner royal palaces, which are continuous with those on Lochias and have groves and numerous lodges painted in various colours. Below these lies the harbour that was dug by the hand of man and is hidden from view, the private property of the kings, as also Antirrhodos, an isle lying off the artificial harbour, which has both a royal palace and a small harbour. They so called it as being a rival of Rhodes. Above the artificial harbour lies the theatre; then the Poseidium – an elbow, as it were, projecting from the Emporium, as it is called, and containing a temple of Poseidon. To this elbow of land Antony added a mole projecting still farther, into the middle of a harbour, and on the extremity of it built a royal lodge which he called Timonium. This was his last act, when, forsaken by his friends, he sailed away to Alexandria after his misfortune at Actium, having chosen to live the life of Timon to the end of his days, which he intended to spend in solitude from all those friends. Then one comes to the Caesarium and the Emporium and the warehouses; and after these to the ship-houses, which extend as far as the Heptastadium. So much for the Great Harbour and its surroundings.

The Canals

Next, after the Heptastadium, one comes to the Harbour of Eunostus, and, above this, to the artificial harbour, which is also called Cibotus; it too has ship-houses. Farther in there is a navigable canal, which extends to Lake Mareotis. Now outside the canal there is still left only a small part of the city; and then one comes to the suburb Necropolis, in which are many gardens and groves and halting-places fitted up for the embalming of corpses, and, inside the canal, both to the Sarapium and to other sacred precincts of ancient times, which are now almost abandoned on account of the construction of the new buildings at Nicopolis; for instance, there are an amphitheatre and a stadium at Nicopolis, and the quinquennial games are celebrated there; but the ancient buildings have fallen into neglect.

Nicopolis

In short, the city is full of public and sacred structures; but the most beautiful is the Gymnasium, which has porticoes more than a *stadium* in length. And in the middle are both the court of justice and the groves. Here, too, is the Paneium, a "height," as it were, which was made by the hand of man; it has the shape of a fir-cone, resembles a rocky hill, and is ascended by a spiral road; and from the summit one can see the whole of the city lying below it on all sides. The broad street that runs lengthwise extends from Necropolis past the Gymnasium to the Canopic Gate; and then one comes to the Hippodrome, as it is called, and to the other (streets?) that lie parallel, extending as far as the Canopic Canal. Having passed through the Hippodrome, one comes to Nicopolis, which has a settlement on the sea no smaller than a city. It is thirty *stadia* distant from Alexandria. Caesar Augustus honoured this place because it was here that he conquered in battle those who came out against him with Antony; and when he had taken the city at the first onset, he forced Antony to put himself to death and Cleopatra to come into his power alive; but a little later she too put herself to death secretly, while in prison, by the bite of an asp or (for two accounts are given) by applying a poisonous ointment; and the result was that the empire of the sons of Lagus, which had endured for many years, was dissolved.

ROMAN HISTORY BY CASSIUS DIO

Cassius Dio (Lucius Cassius Dio, *c.* 164–*c.* 229/235 CE) wrote *Roman History*, spanning the millennium from the foundation of the city (753 BCE) to his own time (around 233 CE). Of the 80 volumes, about one-third survive, but large parts of them are only known in Byzantine excerpts. The most complete texts cover the period 69 BCE–46 CE.

Writing fully two centuries after the events in Cleopatra's life, Dio's work draws upon earlier published histories. Dio's *Roman History* is chronological, with Books 42 through 51 of *Roman History* providing one of the most complete narratives of the events of Cleopatra's life and times. The chapter that explores how Cleopatra died highlights the Romans' fascination in trying to understand what happened to one of their most powerful and clever adversaries.

The text includes lines of dialogue spoken by various historical people. These are unlikely to have been the actual words spoken on the reported occasions, but were instead created by Dio. This was a rhetorical device used by Ancient Greek and Roman historians, who were trained in oratory, to explain an individual's position on a matter of substantive importance to the reader and to elevate the drama of the story.

These extracts are from the translation by Earnest Cary, which was published in 1917.

FROM THE FORTY-SECOND BOOK

Chapter XXXIV
Cleopatra Seeks Julius Caesar's Support

These were the events which occurred in Rome during Caesar's absence. Now the reasons why he was so long in coming there and did not arrive immediately after Pompey's death were as follows. The Egyptians were discontented at the levies of money and indignant because not even their temples were left untouched. For they are the most religious people on earth in many respects and wage wars even against one another on account of their beliefs, since they are not all agreed in their worship, but are diametrically opposed to each other in some matters. As a result, then, of their vexation at this and, further, of their fear that they might be surrendered to Cleopatra, who had great influence with Caesar, they began a disturbance.

Cleopatra, it seems, had at first urged with Caesar her claim against her brother by means of agents, but as soon as she discovered his disposition (which was very susceptible, to such an extent that he had his intrigues with ever so many other women – with all, doubtless, who chanced to come in his way) she sent word to him that she was being betrayed by her friends and asked that she be allowed to plead her case in person. For she was a woman of surpassing beauty, and at that time, when she was in the prime of her youth, she was most striking; she also possessed a most charming voice and a knowledge of how to make herself agreeable to everyone. Being brilliant to look upon and to listen to, with the power to subjugate everyone, even a love-sated man already past his prime, she thought that it would be in keeping with her role to meet Caesar, and she reposed in her beauty all her claims to the throne. She asked therefore for admission to his presence, and on obtaining permission adorned and beautified herself so as to appear before him in the most majestic and at the same time pity-inspiring guise. When she had perfected her schemes, she entered the city (for she had been living outside of it) and, by night without Ptolemy's knowledge, went into the palace.

Chapter XXXV
Julius Caesar Reads Ptolemy XII Auletes' Will

Caesar, upon seeing her and hearing her speak a few words was forthwith so completely captivated that he at once, before dawn, sent for Ptolemy and tried to reconcile them, thus acting as advocate for the very woman whose judge he had previously assumed to be. For this reason, and because the sight of his sister within the palace was so unexpected, the boy was filled with wrath and rushed out among the people crying out that he was being betrayed, and at last he tore the diadem from his head and cast it away. In the great tumult which thereupon arose Caesar's troops seized the person of the prince and the Egyptian populace continued to be in an uproar. They assaulted the palace by land and sea at the same time and might have taken it without a blow, since the Romans had no adequate force present, owing to the apparent friendship of the natives; but Caesar in alarm came out before them, and standing in a safe place, promised to do for them whatever they wished.

Afterwards he entered an assembly of theirs, and producing Ptolemy and Cleopatra, read their father's will, in which it was directed that they should live together according to the custom of the Egyptians and rule in common, and that the Roman people should exercise a guardianship over them. When he had done this and had added that it belonged to him as dictator, holding all the power of the people, to have an oversight of the children and to fulfil their father's wishes, he bestowed the kingdom upon them both and granted Cyprus to Arsinoë and Ptolemy the Younger, a sister and a brother of theirs. For so great fear possessed him, it would seem, that he not only laid hold on none of the Egyptian domain, but actually gave them some of his own besides.

Chapter XXXVI
Pothinus and Achillas Go to Alexandria

By this action they were temporarily calmed, but not long afterwards were roused even to the point of making war. For Pothinus, a eunuch who was charged with the management of Ptolemy's funds and who had taken a leading part in stirring up the Egyptians, became afraid that he might sometime have to pay the penalty for his conduct, and he accordingly sent secretly to Achillas, who was still at this time near Pelusium, and by frightening him and at the same time inspiring him with hopes he made him his associate, and next won over also all the rest who bore arms. To all of them alike it seemed a shame to be ruled by a woman – for they suspected that Caesar on the occasion mentioned had given the kingdom ostensibly to both the children merely to quiet the people, and that in the course of time he would offer it to Cleopatra alone – and they thought themselves a match for the army he then had present. So, they set out at once and proceeded toward Alexandria.

Chapter XXXVII
Achillas Rouses the Egyptian Troops to Support Ptolemy XIII Against Cleopatra

Caesar, learning of this and feeling afraid of their numbers and daring, sent some men to Achillas, not in his own, but in Ptolemy's name, bidding him keep the peace. Achillas, however, realizing that this was not the boy's command, but Caesar's, so far from giving it any attention, was filled with contempt for the sender, believing him afraid. So, he called his soldiers together and by haranguing them at length in favour of Ptolemy and against Caesar and Cleopatra he finally roused their anger against the messengers, though these were Egyptians, so that they should defile themselves with their murder and thus be forced into a relentless war. Caesar, apprised of this, summoned his soldiers from Syria and fortified the palace and the other buildings near it by a moat and wall reaching to the sea.

Chapter XXXVIII
The Library Destroyed by Fire

Meanwhile Achillas arrived with the Romans and the others who had been left behind with Septimius by Gabinius to keep guard over Ptolemy; for these troops as a result of their stay there had changed their habits and had adopted those of the natives. And he immediately won over the larger part of the Alexandrines and made himself master of the most advantageous positions. After this many battles occurred between the two forces both by day and by night, and many places were set on fire, with the result that the docks and the storehouses of grain among other buildings were burned, and also the library, whose volumes, it is said, were of the greatest number and excellence. Achillas was in possession of the mainland, with the exception of what Caesar had walled off, and the latter of the sea except the harbour. Caesar, indeed, was victorious in a sea-fight, and when the Egyptians, consequently, fearing that he would sail into their harbour, had blocked up the entrance with the exception of a narrow passage, he cut off that outlet also by sinking freight ships loaded with stones; so they were unable to stir, no matter how much they might desire to sail out. After this achievement provisions, and water in particular, were brought in more easily; for Achillas had deprived them of the local water-supply by cutting the pipes.

Chapter XXXIX
Arsinoë Declared Queen of Egypt

While these events were taking place, one Ganymedes, a eunuch, secretly brought Arsinoë to the Egyptians, as she was not very well guarded. They declared her queen and proceeded to prosecute the war more vigorously, inasmuch as they now had as leader a representative of the family of the Ptolemies. Caesar, therefore, in fear that Pothinus might kidnap Ptolemy, put the former to death and guarded the latter strictly without any further dissimulation. This served still more to incense the Egyptians, to whose party numbers were being added continually, whereas the Roman soldiers from Syria were not yet present. Caesar was therefore anxious to win the people's friendship, and so he led Ptolemy up to a place from which they could hear his voice, and then bade him say to them that he was unharmed and did not desire war; and he urged them toward peace, and moreover promised to arrange it for them. Now if he had talked to them thus of his own accord, he might have persuaded them to become reconciled; but as it was, they suspected that it was all prearranged by Caesar, and so did not yield.

Chapter XL
Egyptians Attack the Romans

As time went on a dispute arose among the followers of Arsinoë, and Ganymedes prevailed upon her to put Achillas to death, on the ground that he was going to betray the fleet. When this had been done, he assumed command of the soldiers and gathered all the boats that were in the river and lake, besides constructing others; and he conveyed them all through the canals to the sea, where he attacked the Romans while off their guard, burned some of their freight ships to the water's edge and towed others away. Then he cleared out the entrance to the harbour and by lying in wait for vessels there he caused the Romans great annoyance. So, Caesar, having waited for a time when they were acting carelessly by reason of their success, suddenly sailed into the harbour, burned a large number of vessels, and disembarking on Pharos, slew the inhabitants of the island. When the Egyptians on the mainland saw this, they rushed over the bridges to the aid of their friends, and after killing many of the Romans in turn drove the remainder back to the ships. While the fugitives were forcing their way into these in crowds anywhere they could, Caesar and many others fell into the sea. He would have perished miserably, being weighed down by his robes and pelted by the Egyptians (for his garments, being of purple, offered a good mark), had he not thrown off his clothing and then succeeded in swimming out to where a skiff lay, which he boarded. In this way he was saved, and that, too, without wetting one of the documents of which he held up a large number in his left hand as he swam. The Egyptians took his clothing and hung it upon the trophy which they set up to commemorate this rout, just as if they had captured him himself. They also kept a close watch upon the landings, since the legions which had been sent for from Syria were already drawing near and were doing the Romans much injury. For while Caesar could defend in a fashion those of them who came ashore on the Libyan side, yet near the mouth of the Nile the Egyptians deceived many of his men by means of signal fires, as if they too were Romans, and thus captured them, so that the rest no longer ventured to come to land, until Tiberius Claudius Nero [father of the future Emperor Tiberius] at this time sailed up the river itself, conquered the foe in battle, and made it safer for his followers to come to land.

Chapter XLI
Mithridates of Pergamum Captures Pelusium

Thereupon Mithridates, called the Pergamenian, undertook to go up with his ships into the mouth of the Nile opposite Pelusium; but when the Egyptians barred his entrance with their vessels, he betook himself by night to the canal, hauled the ships over into it, since it does not empty into the sea, and through it sailed up into the Nile. After that he suddenly attacked, from both sea and river at once, those who were guarding the mouth of the river, and thus breaking up their blockade, he assaulted Pelusium with his infantry and his fleet simultaneously and captured it.

Advancing then toward Alexandria, and learning that a certain Dioscorides was coming to confront him, he ambushed and destroyed him.

Chapter XLII
Julius Caesar Releases Ptolemy XIII to the Egyptians

But the Egyptians on receiving the news would not end the war even then; yet they were irritated at the rule of the eunuch and of the woman and thought that if they could put Ptolemy at their head they would be superior to the Romans. So then, finding themselves unable to seize him in any way, inasmuch as he was skilfully guarded, they pretended that they were worn out by their disasters and desired peace; and they sent to Caesar, making overtures and asking for Ptolemy, in order, as they claimed, that they might consult with him about the terms on which a truce could be effected. Now Caesar believed that they had in very truth changed their mind, since he heard that they were cowardly and fickle in general and perceived that at this time they were terrified in the face of their defeats; but even in case they should be planning some trick, in order that he might not be regarded as hindering peace, he said that he approved their request, and sent them Ptolemy. For he saw no source of strength in the lad, in view of his youth and lack of education, and hoped that the Egyptians would either become reconciled with him on the terms he wished or else would more justly deserve to be warred upon and subjugated, so that there might be some reasonable excuse for delivering them over to Cleopatra; for of course he had no idea that he would be defeated by them, particularly now that his troops had joined him.

Chapter XLIII
Ptolemy XIII Drowns

But the Egyptians, when they secured the lad, took not a thought for peace, but straightway set out against Mithridates, as if they were sure to accomplish some great achievement by the name and by the family of Ptolemy; and they surrounded Mithridates near the lake, between the river and the marshes, and routed his forces. Now Caesar did not pursue them, through fear of being ambushed, but at night he set sail as if he were hurrying to some outlet of the Nile, and kindled an enormous fire on each vessel, so that it might be widely believed that he was going thither. He started at first, then, to sail away, but afterwards extinguished the fires, returned, passed alongside the city to the peninsula on the Libyan side, where he came to land; and there he disembarked the soldiers, went around the lake, and fell upon the Egyptians unexpectedly about dawn. They were immediately so dismayed that they made overtures for peace, but since he would not listen to their entreaty, a fierce battle later took place in which he was victorious and slew great numbers of the enemy. Ptolemy and some others tried in their haste to escape across the river and perished in it.

Chapter XLIV
Julius Caesar Commands Cleopatra to Marry Her Younger Brother Ptolemy XIV Philopator

In this way Caesar overcame Egypt. He did not, however, make it subject to the Romans, but bestowed it upon Cleopatra, for whose sake he had waged the conflict. Yet, being afraid that the

Egyptians might rebel again, because they were delivered over to a woman to rule, and that the Romans might be angry, both on this account and because he was living with the woman, he commanded her to "marry" her other brother, and gave the kingdom to both of them, at least nominally. For in reality Cleopatra was to hold all the power alone, since her husband was still a boy, and in view of Caesar's favour there was nothing that she could not do. Hence her living with her brother and sharing the rule with him was a mere pretence which she accepted, whereas in truth she ruled alone and spent her time in Caesar's company.

FROM THE FIFTY-FIRST BOOK

Chapter XI

Octavian (Caesar) Seeks an Audience with Cleopatra

So, Antony died there in Cleopatra's bosom; and she now felt a certain confidence in Caesar, and immediately informed him of what had taken place; still, she was not altogether convinced that she would suffer no harm. She accordingly kept herself within the building, in order that, even if there should be no other motive for her preservation, she might at least purchase pardon and her kingdom through his fear for the money. So thoroughly mindful was she even then, in the midst of her dire misfortune, of her royal rank, and chose rather to die with the name and dignity of a sovereign than to live in a private station. At all events, she kept at hand fire to consume her wealth, and asps and other reptiles to destroy herself, and she had the latter tried on human beings, to see in what way they killed in each case.

Now Caesar was anxious not only to get possession of her treasures but also to seize her alive and to carry her back for his triumph, yet he was unwilling to appear to have tricked her himself after having given her a kind of pledge, since he wished to treat her as a captive and to a certain extent subdued against her will. He therefore sent to her Caius Proculeius, a knight, and Epaphroditus, a freedman, giving them directions as to what they were to say and do. Following out this plan, they obtained an audience with Cleopatra, and after discussing with her some moderate proposals they suddenly seized her before any agreement was reached. After this they put out of her way everything by means of which she could cause her own death and allowed her to spend some days where she was, occupied in embalming Antony's body; then they took her to the palace, but did not remove any of her accustomed retinue or attendants, in order that she should entertain more hope than ever of accomplishing all she desired, and so should do no harm to herself. At any rate, when she expressed a desire to appear before Caesar and to have an interview with him, she gained her request; and to deceive her still more, he promised that he would come to her himself.

Chapter XII
Octavian Meets Cleopatra

She accordingly prepared a splendid apartment and a costly couch, and moreover arrayed herself with affected negligence – indeed, her mourning garb wonderfully became her – and seated herself upon the couch; beside her she placed many images of his father, of all kinds, and in her bosom she put all the letters that his father had sent her. When, after this, Caesar entered, she leaped gracefully to her feet and cried: "Hail, master – for Heaven has granted you the mastery and taken it from me. But surely you can see with your own eyes how your father looked when he visited me on many occasions, and you have heard people tell how he honoured me in various ways and made me queen of the Egyptians. That you may, however, earn something about me from him himself, take and read the letters which he wrote me with his own hand."

After she had spoken thus, she proceeded to read many passionate expressions of Caesar's. And now she would lament and kiss the letters, and again she would fall before his images and do them reverence. She kept turning her eyes toward Caesar and bewailing her fate in musical accents. She spoke in melting tones, saying at one time, "Of what avail to me, Caesar, are these your letters?" and at anyone, "But in this man here you also are alive for me"; again, "Would that I had died before you," and still again, "But if I have him, I have thee."

Such were the subtleties of speech and of attitude which she employed, and sweet were the glances she cast at him and the words she murmured to him. Now Caesar was not insensible to the ardour of her speech and the appeal to his passions, but he pretended to be; and letting his eyes rest upon the ground, he merely said: "Be of good cheer, woman, and keep a stout heart; for you shall suffer no harm." She was greatly distressed because he would neither look at her nor say anything about the kingdom nor even utter a word of love, and falling at his knees, she said with an outburst of sobbing: "I neither wish to live nor can I live, Caesar. But this favour I beg of you in memory of your father, that, since Heaven gave me to Antony after him, I may also die with Antony. Would that I had perished then, straightway after Caesar! But since it was decreed by fate that I should suffer this affliction also, send me to Antony; grudge me not burial with him, in order that, as it is because of him I die, so I may dwell with him even in Hades."

Chapter XIII
Despite Having Assured Octavian, Cleopatra Commits Suicide

Such words she uttered, expecting to move him to pity, but Caesar made no answer to them; fearing, however, that she might destroy herself, he exhorted her again to be of good cheer, and not only did not remove any of her attendants but also took special care of her, that she might add brilliance to his triumph. This purpose she suspected, and regarding that fate as worse than a thousand deaths, she conceived a genuine desire to die, and not only addressed many entreaties to Caesar that she might perish in some manner or other, but also devised many plans herself. But when she could accomplish nothing, she feigned a change of heart, pretending to set great hopes in him and also in Livia [his wife]. She said she would sail of her own free will, and she made ready some treasured articles of adornment to use as gifts, in the hope that by these means she might inspire belief that it was not her purpose to die, and so might be less closely guarded and thus be able to destroy herself. And so it came about. For as soon as the others and Epaphroditus, to whose charge she had been committed, had come to believe that she really felt as she pretended to, and neglected to keep a careful watch, she made her preparations to die as painlessly as possible. First, she gave a sealed paper, in which she begged Caesar to order that she be buried beside Antony, to Epaphroditus himself to deliver, pretending that it contained some other matter, and then, having by this excuse freed herself of his presence, she set to her task. She put on her most beautiful apparel, arranged her body in most seemly fashion, took in her hands all the emblems of royalty, and so died.

Chapter XIV
Speculations on How Cleopatra Died

No one knows clearly in what way she perished, for the only marks on her body were slight pricks on the arm. Some say she applied to herself an asp which had been brought in to her in a water-jar, or perhaps hidden in some flowers. Others declare that she had smeared a pin, with which she was wont to fasten her hair, with some poison possessed of such a property that in ordinary circumstances it would not injure the body at all, but if it came into contact with even a drop of blood would destroy the body very quietly and painlessly; and that previous to this time she had worn it in her hair as usual, but now had made a slight scratch on her arm and had dipped the pin in the blood. In this or in some very similar way she perished, and her two handmaidens with her. As for the eunuch, he had of his own accord delivered himself up to the serpents at the very time of Cleopatra's arrest, and after being bitten by them had leaped into a coffin already prepared for him. When Caesar heard of Cleopatra's death, he was astounded, and not only viewed her body but also made use of drugs and Psylli in the hope that she might revive. These Psylli are males, for there is no woman born in their tribe, and they have the power to suck out any poison of any reptile, if use is made of them immediately, before the victim dies; and they are not harmed themselves when bitten by any such creature. They are propagated from one another, and they test their offspring either by having them thrown among serpents as soon as they are born or else by having their swaddling-clothes thrown upon serpents; for the reptiles in the one case do no harm to the child, and in the other case are benumbed by its clothing. So much for this matter. But Caesar, when he could not in any way resuscitate Cleopatra, felt both admiration and pity for her, and was excessively grieved on his own account, as if he had been deprived of all the glory of his victory.

Chapter XV
Insatiable Cleopatra, Would-be Queen of the Romans

Thus, Antony and Cleopatra, who had caused many evils to the Egyptians and many to the Romans, made war and met their death in the manner I have described; and they were both embalmed in the same fashion and buried in the same tomb. Their qualities of character and the fortunes of their lives were as follows. Antony had no superior in comprehending his duty, yet he committed many acts of folly. He sometimes distinguished himself for bravery, yet often failed through cowardice. He was characterized equally by greatness of soul and by servility of mind. He would plunder the property of others and would squander his own. He showed compassion to many without cause and punished even more without justice. Consequently, though he rose from utter weakness to great power, and from the depths of poverty to great riches, he derived no profit from either circumstance, but after hoping to gain single-handed the empire of the Romans, he took his own life. Cleopatra was of insatiable passion and insatiable avarice; she was swayed often by laudable ambition, but often by overweening effrontery. By love she gained the title of Queen of the Egyptians, and when she hoped by the same means to win also that of Queen of the Romans, she failed of this and lost the other besides. She captivated the two greatest Romans of her day, and because of the third she destroyed herself. Such were these two and such was their end.

THE CIVIL WARS BY APPIAN

Appian (Appianus of Alexandria, *c.* 95–*c.* 165 CE) was not a historian who wrote chronologically. Instead his *Civil Wars* is ethnographical. It explains, by region, the conflicts between peoples in which Roman armies fought, ranging from the very beginning of Roman history to the time of Emperor Trajan (r. 98–117 CE).

Of the 24 volumes, 11 have survived complete or in part, namely those on the Spanish, Hannibalic, Punic (or Sicilian), Illyrian, Syrian and Mithridatic Wars, as well as five books on the Civil Wars. The events leading to the fall of Cleopatra and the annexation of Egypt were so pivotal in Roman history that Appian cites them in the Introduction to his work.

Appian wrote in Greek. His clear, unembellished style is preserved in this translation by Horace White, published in 1913.

FROM THE FIRST BOOK

Historian's Introduction

Out of multifarious civil commotions, the Roman state passed into solidarity and monarchy. To show how these things came about I have written and compiled piled this narrative, which is well worth the study of those who wish to know the measureless ambition of men, their dreadful lust of power, their unwearying perseverance, and the countless forms of evil.

It is especially necessary for me to describe these things beforehand since they are the preliminaries of my Egyptian history, and end where that begins, for Egypt was seized in consequence of this last civil commotion, Cleopatra having joined forces with Antony. On account of its magnitude I have divided the work, first taking up the events that occurred from the time of Sempronius Gracchus to that of Cornelius Sulla; next, those that followed to the death of Caesar. The remaining books of the civil wars treat of those waged by the triumvirs against each other and the Roman people, until the end of these conflicts, and the greatest achievement, the Battle of Actium, fought by [Octavian] Caesar against Antony and Cleopatra together, which will be the beginning of the Egyptian history.

FROM THE SECOND BOOK

Chapter XV
Julius Caesar's Four Triumph, 46 BCE

When Caesar returned to Rome he had four triumphs together: one for his Gallic wars, in which he had added many great nations to the Roman sway and subdued others that had revolted; one for the Pontic war against Pharnaces;

one for the war in Africa against the African allies of L. Scipio, in which the historian Juba (the son of King Juba), then an infant, was led a captive. Between the Gallic and the Pontic triumphs, he introduced a kind of Egyptian triumph, in which he led some captives taken in the naval engagement on the Nile. Although he took care not to inscribe any Roman names in his triumph (as it would have been unseemly in his eyes and base and inauspicious in those of the Roman people to triumph over fellow-citizens), yet all these misfortunes were represented in the processions and the men also by various images and pictures, all except Pompey, the only one whom he did not venture to exhibit, since the latter was still greatly regretted by all. The people, although restrained by fear, groaned over their domestic ills, especially when they saw the picture of Lucius Scipio, the general-in-chief, wounded in the breast by his own hand, casting himself into the sea, and Petreius committing self-destruction at the banquet, and Cato torn open by himself like a wild beast. They applauded the death of Achillas and Pothinus, and laughed at the flight of Pharnaces.

It is said that money to the amount of 60,500 talents [of silver] was borne in the procession and 2,822 crowns of gold weighing 20,414 pounds, from which wealth Caesar made apportionments immediately after the triumph, paying the army all that he had promised and more. Each soldier received 5,000 Attic drachmas, each centurion double, and each tribune of infantry and prefect of cavalry fourfold that sum. To each plebeian citizen also was given an Attic mina. He gave also various spectacles with horses and music, a combat of foot-soldiers, 1,000 on each side, and a cavalry fight of 200 on each side. There was also another combat of horse and foot together.

There was a combat of elephants, twenty against twenty, and a naval engagement of 4,000 oarsmen, where 1,000 fighting men contended on each side. He erected a temple to Venus, his ancestress, as he had vowed to do when he was about to begin the Battle of Pharsalus, and he laid out ground around the temple which he intended to be a forum for the Roman People, not for buying and selling, but a meeting-place for the transaction of public business, like the public squares of the Persians, where the people assemble to seek justice or to learn the laws. He placed a beautiful image of Cleopatra by the side of the goddess, which stands there to this day. He caused an enumeration of the people to be made, and it is said that it was found to be only one-half of the number existing before this war. To such a degree had the rivalry of these two men reduced the city.

FROM THE FIFTH BOOK

Chapter I

Antony Plans to Meet Cleopatra

After the death of Cassius and Brutus, Octavian returned to Italy, but Antony proceeded to Asia, where he met Cleopatra, Queen of Egypt, and succumbed to her charms at first sight. This passion brought ruin upon them and upon all Egypt besides. For this reason, a part of this book will treat of Egypt – a small part, however, not worth mentioning in the title, since it is incidental to the narrative of the civil wars, which constitutes much the larger portion. Other similar civil wars took place after Cassius and Brutus, but there was no one in command of all the forces as they had been. The latter wars were sporadic, till finally Sextus Pompeius, the younger son of Pompey the Great, the last remaining leader of that faction, was slain, as Brutus and Cassius had been, Lepidus was deprived of his share of the *triumvirate*, and the whole government of the Romans was centred in two only, Antony and Octavian. These events came about in the following manner.

Chapter VIII

Antony Meets Cleopatra in Cilicia, 41 BCE

Cleopatra came to meet him [Antony] in Cilicia, and he blamed her for not sharing their labours in avenging Caesar. Instead of apologising she enumerated to him the things she had done, saying that she had sent the four legions that had been left with her to Dolabella forthwith, and that she had another fleet in readiness, but had been prevented from sending it by adverse winds and by the misfortune of Dolabella, whose defeat came suddenly; but that she did not lend assistance to Cassius, who had threatened her twice; that while the war was going on she had set sail for the Adriatic in person with a powerful fleet to assist them, in defiance of Cassius, and disregarding Murcus, who was lying in wait for her; but that a tempest shattered the fleet and prostrated herself with illness, for which reason she was not able to put to sea again till they had already gained her victory. Antony was amazed at her wit as well as her good looks and became her captive as though he were a young man, although he was forty years of age. It is said that he was always very susceptible in this way, and that he had fallen in love with her at first sight long ago when she was still a girl, and he was serving as master of horse under Gabinius at Alexandria.

Chapter IX

Cleopatra's Influence over Antony

Straightway Antony's former interest in public affairs began to dwindle. Whatever Cleopatra ordered was done, regardless of laws, human or divine. While her sister Arsinoë was a suppliant in the temple of Artemis Leucophryne at Miletus, Antony sent assassins thither and put her to death; and Serapion, Cleopatra's prefect in Cyprus, who had assisted Cassius and was now a suppliant at Tyre, Antony ordered the Tyrians to deliver to her. He commanded the Aradians to deliver up another suppliant, who when Ptolemy, the brother of Cleopatra, disappeared at the battle with Caesar on the Nile, said that he was Ptolemy, and whom the Aradians now held. He ordered the priest of Artemis at Ephesus, whom they called the Megabyzus, and who had once received Arsinoë as queen, to be brought before him, but in response to the supplications of the Ephesians, addressed to Cleopatra herself, released him. So swiftly was Antony transformed, and this passion was the beginning and the end of evils that afterwards befell him. When Cleopatra returned home Antony sent a cavalry force to Palmyra, situated not far from the Euphrates, to plunder it, bringing the trifling accusation against its inhabitants, that being on the frontier between the Romans and the Parthians, they had avoided taking sides between them; for, being merchants, they bring the products of India and Arabia from Persia and dispose of them in the Roman territory; but in fact, Antony's intention was to enrich his horsemen. However, the Palmyreans were forewarned, and they transported their property across the river, and, stationing themselves on the bank, prepared to shoot anybody who should attack them, for they are expert bowmen. The cavalry found nothing in the city. They turned round and came back, having met no foe, and empty-handed.

Chapter X
Antony Joins Cleopatra After the Parthian War

It seems that this course on Antony's part caused the outbreak of the Parthian war not long afterwards, as many of the rulers expelled from Syria had taken refuge with the Parthians. Syria, until the reign of Antiochus Pius and his son, Antiochus, had been ruled by the descendants of Seleucus Nicator, as I have related in my Syrian history. Pompey added it to the Roman sway, and Scaurus was appointed praetor over it. After Scaurus the Senate sent others, including Gabinius, who made war against the Alexandrians, and after Gabinius, Crassus, who lost his life in the Parthian war, and after Crassus, Bibulus. At the time of Caesar's death and the intestine strife which followed, tyrants had possession of the cities one by one, and they were assisted by the Parthians, who made an irruption into Syria after the disaster to Crassus and co-operated with the tyrants. Antony drove out the latter, who took refuge in Parthia. He then imposed very heavy tribute on the masses and committed the outrage already mentioned against the Palmyreans and did not wait for the disturbed country to become quiet but distributed his army in winter quarters in the provinces, and himself went to Egypt to join Cleopatra.

Chapter XI
Antony Goes Native

She gave him a magnificent reception, and he spent the winter there without the insignia of his office and with the habit and mode of life of a private person, either because he was in a foreign jurisdiction, in a city under royal sway, or because he regarded his wintering as a festal occasion; for he even laid aside the cares and escort of a general, and wore the square-cut garment of the Greeks instead of the costume of his own country, and the white Attic shoe of the Athenian and Alexandrian priests, which they call the *phaecasion*. He went out only to the temples, the schools, and the discussions of the learned, and spent his time with Greeks, out of deference to Cleopatra, to whom his sojourn in Alexandria was wholly devoted.

JEWISH ANTIQUITIES BY FLAVIUS JOSEPHUS

Flavius Josephus (Yosef ben Matityahu, *c.* 37–*c.* 100 CE) was a commander of the Jewish resistance forces in Galilee. At the end of the siege of Yodfat in 67 CE he surrendered to Titus Flavius Vespasian, leader of the Roman counterinsurgency. When Vespasian became emperor (r. 69–79 CE), Josephus was freed and took the family name of his Roman patron. He is famous for *The Jewish War*, which documents the struggle between the Jews and Romans for supremacy in Judaea (67–73 CE).

In his *Jewish Antiquities*, Josephus was attempting to write a complete, authoritative history of the Jewish people that could be considered by his gentile patrons as the equal of the histories of the Greeks by Herodotus and Thucydides, or of the Romans by Livy and Sallust. Written in 94 CE in Greek, the work consists of 20 books. The first ten follow the events of the Hebrew Bible, beginning with the creation of Adam and Eve.

As a contemporary of King Herod, Queen Cleopatra appears throughout the events described in Books 13 through 16. It is a reminder of the complex connections between the empires of the Ancient World; their leading families interacted through diplomatic exchanges and, when those failed, through war. A one-time client king of Cleopatra, Herod was an ally of

Antonius until the queen sent him back to Judaea on the eve of the Battle of Actium. Soon after Herod became a loyal ally of the victor who would become Caesar Augustus.

This extract is taken from the translation by William Whiston, which dates back to before 1737.

FROM THE FIFTEENTH BOOK XV

Chapter IV

Cleopatra's Visit to Judea and Meeting with King Herod, 36 BCE

Now at this time the affairs of Syria were in confusion, by Cleopatra's constant persuasions to Antony to make an attempt upon everybody's dominions. For she persuaded him to take those dominions away from their several princes and bestow them upon her. And she had a mighty influence upon him; by reason of his being enslaved to her by his affections.

She was also by nature very covetous; and stuck at no wickedness. She had already poisoned her brother; because she knew that he was to be King of Egypt: and this when he was but fifteen years old. And she got her sister Arsinoë to be slain, by the means of Antony; when she was a supplicant at Diana's temple at Ephesus. For if there were but any hopes of getting money, she would violate both temples and sepulchres. Nor was there any holy place, that was esteemed the most inviolable, from which she would not fetch the ornaments it had in it: nor any place so profane, but was to suffer the most flagitious treatment possible from her, if it could but contribute somewhat to the covetous humour of this wicked creature: Yet did not all this suffice so extravagant a woman, who was a slave to her lusts. But she still imagined that she wanted everything she could think of; and did her utmost to gain it. For which reason she hurried Antony on perpetually to deprive others of their dominions and give them to her. And as she went over Syria with him, she contrived to get it into her possession. So, he slew Lysanias, the son of Ptolemy, accusing him of his bringing the Parthians upon those countries. She also petitioned Antony to give her Judea and Arabia: and in order thereto desired him to take these countries away from their present governors. As for Antony, he was so entirely overcome by this woman that one would not think her conversation only could do it, but that he was some way or other bewitched to do whatsoever she would have him. Yet did the grossest parts of her injustice make him so ashamed that he would not always hearken to her, to do those flagrant enormities she would have persuaded him to. That therefore he might not totally deny her; nor, by doing everything that she enjoined him, appear openly to be an ill man; he took some parts of each of those countries away from their former governors, and gave them to her. Thus, he gave her the cities that were within the River Eleutherus, as far as Egypt, excepting Tyre and Sidon, which he knew to have been free cities from their ancestors: although she pressed him very often to bestow those on her also.

When Cleopatra had obtained thus much, and had accompanied Antony in his expedition to Armenia, as far as Euphrates; she returned back, and came to Apamia, and Damascus, and passed on to Judea, where Herod met her; and farmed of her her parts of Arabia, and those revenues that came to her from the region about Jericho. This country bears that balsam, which is the most precious drug that is there, and grows there alone. The place bears also palm trees, both many in number and those excellent in their kind. When she was there, and was very often with Herod, she endeavoured to have criminal conversation with the King. Nor did she affect secrecy in the indulgence of such sort of pleasures. And perhaps she had in some measure, a passion of love to him; or rather, what is most probable, she laid a treacherous snare for him, by aiming to obtain such adulterous conversation from him. However, upon the whole, she seemed overcome with love to him. Now Herod had a great while born no good will to Cleopatra: as knowing that she was a woman irksome to all; and at that time, he thought her particularly worthy of his hatred, if this attempt proceeded out of lust: he had also thought of preventing her intrigues, by putting her to death, if such were her endeavours.

However, he refused to comply with her proposals: and called a counsel of his friends to consult with them, "Whether he should not kill her, now he had her in his power? For that he should thereby deliver all those from a multitude of evils to whom she was already become irksome, and was expected to be still so for the time to come: and that this very thing would be much for the advantage of Antony himself: since she would certainly not be faithful to him, in case any such season or necessity should come upon him as that he should stand in need of her fidelity."

But when he thought to follow this advice, his friends would not let him; and told him that, "In the first place, it was not right to attempt so great a thing and run himself thereby into the utmost danger. And they laid hard at him and begged of him to undertake nothing rashly. For that Antony would never bear it: no not though anyone should evidently lay before his eyes that it was for his own advantage. And that the appearance of depriving him of her conversation by this violent and treacherous method, would probably set his affections more on a flame than before. Nor did it appear that he could offer anything of tolerable weight in his defence. This attempt being against such a woman, as was of the highest dignity of any of her sex at that time in the world. And as to any advantage to be expected from such an undertaking, if any such could be supposed in this case, it would appear to deserve condemnation, on account of the insolence he must take upon him in doing it. Which considerations made it very plain, that in so doing he would find his government filled with mischiefs, both great and lasting, both to himself and his posterity. Whereas it was still in his power to reject that wickedness she would persuade him to; and to come off honourably at the same time." So, by thus affrighting Herod, and representing to him the hazard he must, in all probability, run by this undertaking, they restrained him from it. So, he treated Cleopatra kindly, and made her presents, and conducted her on her way to Egypt.

But Antony subdued Armenia, and sent Artabazes, the son of Tigranes, in bonds, with his children, and procurators to Egypt; and made a present of them, and of all the royal ornaments which he had taken out of that Kingdom to Cleopatra. And Artaxias the eldest of his sons, who had escaped at that time, took the Kingdom of Armenia. Who yet was ejected by Archelaus, and Nero Cesar, when they restored Tigranes his younger brother to that Kingdom. But this happened a good while afterwards.

But then, as to the tributes which Herod was to pay Cleopatra for that country which Antony had given her, he acted fairly with her: as deeming it not safe for him to afford any cause for

Cleopatra to hate him. As for the King of Arabia, whose tribute Herod had undertaken to pay her; for some time, indeed, he paid him as much as came to two hundred talents. But he afterwards became very miserly, and slow in his payments; and could hardly be brought to pay some parts of it: and was not willing to pay even them without some deductions.

NATURAL HISTORY BY PLINY THE ELDER

Pliny the Elder (Caius Plinius Secundus, 23 or 24–79 CE) was an accomplished man of his times. He served variously in the Roman army as a cavalry commander and as admiral of the Roman fleet at Misenum. It was while attempting to rescue a friend and his family from the eruption of Mount Vesuvius, in which the cities of Pompeii and Herculaneum were destroyed, that Pliny the Elder died.

The author of several books, Pliny is best known for his *Natural History*. Written in Latin, this encyclopedia in 37 books set out to describe anything that could be found in the world, including living things, geology, astronomy, geography, art and humanity itself. It is brim full of fun facts and anecdotes about the Ancient World. These often provide details or stories missing from the other extant accounts, which help to humanize the people of history – not least Cleopatra herself.

These extracts are from the translation by John Bostock and H.T. Riley, dating from 1855.

FROM THE NINTH BOOK

Chapter LVIII
Cleopatra's Wager Involving Dissolved Pearls

There were formerly two pearls, the largest that had been ever seen in the whole world: Cleopatra, the last of the queens of Egypt, was in possession of them both, they having come to her by descent from the kings of the East.

When Antony had been sated by her, day after day, with the most exquisite banquets, this queenly courtesan, inflated with vanity and disdainful arrogance, affected to treat all this sumptuousness and all these vast preparations with the greatest contempt; upon which Antony enquired what there was that could possibly be added to such extraordinary magnificence. To this she made answer, that on a single entertainment she would expend ten millions of sesterces. Antony was extremely desirous to learn how that could be done but looked upon it as a thing quite impossible; and a wager was the result.

On the following day, upon which the matter was to be decided, in order that she might not lose the wager, she had an entertainment set before Antony, magnificent in every respect, though no better than his usual repast. Upon this, Antony joked her, and enquired what was the amount expended upon it; to which she made answer that the banquet which he then beheld was only a trifling appendage to the real banquet, and that she alone would consume at the meal to the ascertained value of that amount, she herself would swallow the ten millions of sesterces; and so ordered the second course to be served.

In obedience to her instructions, the servants placed before her a single vessel, which was filled with vinegar, a liquid, the sharpness and strength of which is able to dissolve pearls. At this moment she was wearing in her ears those choicest and most rare and unique productions of Nature; and while Antony was waiting to see what she was going to do, taking one of them from out of her ear, she threw it into the vinegar, and directly it was melted, swallowed it.

Lucius Plancus, who had been named umpire in the wager, placed his hand upon the other at the very instant that she was making preparations to dissolve it in a similar manner, and declared that Antony had lost – an omen which, in the result, was fully confirmed. The fame of the second pearl is equal to that which attends its fellow. After the queen, who had thus come off victorious on so important a question, had been seized, it was cut asunder, in order that this, the other half of the entertainment, might serve as pendants for the ears of Venus, in the Pantheon at Rome.

FROM THE NINETEENTH BOOK

Chapter V
When Linen Was First Dyed and Used to Identify Warships

Attempts, *too*, have even been made to dye linen, and to make it assume the frivolous colours of our cloths. This was first done in the fleet of Alexander the Great, while sailing upon the river Indus; for, upon one occasion, during a battle that was being fought, his generals and captains distinguished their vessels by the various tints of their sails and astounded the people on the shores by giving their many colours to the breeze, as it impelled them on. It was with sails of purple, too, that Cleopatra accompanied Mark Antony to the Battle of Actium, and it was by their aid that she took to flight: such being the distinguishing mark of the royal ship.

FROM THE TWENTY-FIRST BOOK

Chapter IX
Scent from the Flowers of a Chaplet Affect Cleopatra

Among the Greeks, the physicians Mnesitheus and Callimachus have written separate treatises on the subject of chaplets, making mention of such flowers as are injurious to the head. For, in fact, the health is here concerned to some extent, as it is at the moments of carousal and gaiety in particular that penetrating odours steal insidiously upon the brain – witness an instance in the wicked cunning displayed upon one occasion by Cleopatra.

PARALLEL LIVES BY PLUTARCH

Plutarch (Lucius Mestrius Plutarchus, c. 46–after 119 CE) wrote about famous Greeks and Romans in his series of biographical portraits entitled *Parallel Lives*. This paired a famous Greek with an equally famous Roman to illuminate their common moral virtues and vices.

His subjects included Julius Caesar (Caius Iulius Caesar) and Mark Antony (Marcus Antonius), two 'strong men' of the first century BCE who were instrumental in changing for ever the fortunes of Cleopatra and of Egypt.

Plutarch is well regarded by modern historians and biographers. Each subject of his *Parallel Lives* is described in moral terms. He emphasized captivating anecdotes and incidental details, believing that these often revealed more about his subjects than their most renowned achievements. He aimed to create comprehensive portraits, likening his approach to that of a painter. The adventures of Caesar and Antony respectively with Cleopatra are prime sources of such triviality.

These extracts are taken from the translation by Bernadotte Perrin, which dates back to 1923 or earlier.

THE LIFE OF JULIUS CAESAR

Chapter XLVIII
Pothinus Plots Against Julius Caesar

As for the war in Egypt, some say that it was not necessary, but due to Julius Caesar's passion for Cleopatra, and that it was inglorious and full of peril for him. But others blame the king's party for it, and especially the eunuch Pothinus, who had most influence at court, and had recently killed Pompey; he had also driven Cleopatra from the country and was now secretly plotting against Caesar. On this account they say that from this time on Caesar passed whole nights at drinking parties in order to protect himself.

But in his open acts also Pothinus was unbearable, since he said and did many things that were invidious and insulting to Caesar. For instance, when the soldiers had the oldest and worst grain measured out to them, he bade them put up with it and be content, since they were eating what belonged to others; and at the state suppers he used wooden and earthen dishes, on the ground that Caesar had taken all the gold and silver ware in payment of a debt. For the father of the present king owed Caesar seventeen million five hundred thousand drachmas, of which Caesar had formerly remitted a part to his children, but now demanded payment of ten millions for the support of his army. When, however, Pothinus bade him go away now and attend to his great affairs, assuring him that later he would get his money with thanks, Caesar replied that he had no need whatever of Egyptians as advisers, and secretly sent for Cleopatra from the country.

Chapter XLIX
Caesar Leaves for Syria Having Appointed Cleopatra as Queen of Egypt, 48–47 BCE

So, Cleopatra, taking only Apollodorus the Sicilian from among her friends, embarked in a little skiff and landed at the palace when it was already getting dark; and as it was impossible to escape notice otherwise, she stretched herself at full length inside a bed-sack, while Apollodorus tied the bed-sack up with a cord and carried it indoors to Caesar.

It was by this device of Cleopatra's, it is said, that Caesar was first captivated, for she showed herself to be a bold coquette, and succumbing to the charm of further intercourse with her, he reconciled her to her brother on the basis of a joint share with him in the royal power. Then, as everybody was feasting to celebrate the reconciliation, a slave of Caesar's, his barber, who left nothing unscrutinized, owing to a timidity in which he had no equal, but kept his ears open and was here, there, and everywhere, perceived that Achillas the general and Pothinus the eunuch were hatching a plot against Caesar.

After Caesar had found them out, he set a guard about the banqueting-hall, and put Pothinus to death; Achillas, however, escaped to his camp, and raised about Caesar a war grievous and difficult for one who was defending himself with so few followers against so large a city and army.

In this war, to begin with, Caesar encountered the peril of being shut off from water, since the canals were dammed up by the enemy; in the second place, when the enemy tried to cut off his fleet, he was forced to repel the danger by using fire, and this spread from the dockyards and destroyed the great library; and thirdly, when a battle arose at Pharos, he sprang from the mole into a small boat and tried to go to the aid of his men in their struggle, but the Egyptians sailed up against him from every side, so that he threw himself into the sea and with great difficulty escaped by swimming. At this time, too, it is said that he was holding many papers in his hand and would not let them go, though missiles were flying at him and he was immersed in the sea, but held them above water with one hand and swam with the other; his little boat had been sunk at the outset. But finally, after the king had gone away to the enemy, he marched against him and conquered him in a battle where many fell and the king himself disappeared. Then, leaving Cleopatra on the throne of Egypt (a little later she had a son by him whom the Alexandrians called Caesarion), he set out for Syria.

THE LIFE OF ANTONY

Chapter X

Antony, His Wife Fulvia and Suitor Cleopatra

These things are also thought to have augmented the discord, and to have incited the soldiery to deeds of violence and rapacity. For this reason, too, when Julius Caesar came back, he pardoned Dolabella, and, on being chosen consul for the third time, selected Lepidus as his colleague, and not Antony. Pompey's house, when put up for sale, was bought by Antony; but when he was asked to pay the price for it, he was indignant. And he says himself that this was the reason why he did not go with Caesar on his African campaign, since he got no recompense for his private successes. However, it would seem that Caesar cured him of most of his prodigality and folly by not allowing his errors to pass unnoticed. For Antony put away his reprehensible way of living, and turned his thoughts to marriage, taking to wife Fulvia, the widow of Clodius the demagogue. She was a woman who took no thought for spinning or housekeeping, nor would she deign to bear sway over a man of private station, but she wished to rule a ruler and command a commander. Therefore, Cleopatra was indebted to Fulvia for teaching Antony to endure a woman's sway, since she took him over quite tamed, and schooled at the outset to obey women.

However, Antony tried, by sportive ways and youthful sallies, to make even Fulvia more light-hearted. For instance, when many were going out to meet Caesar after his victory in Spain, Antony himself went forth. Then, on a sudden, a report burst upon Italy that Caesar was dead and his enemies advancing upon the country, and Antony turned back to Rome. He took the dress of a slave and came by night to his house, and on saying that he was the bearer of a letter to Fulvia from Antony, was admitted to her presence, his face all muffled. Then Fulvia, in great distress, before taking the letter, asked whether Antony was still alive; and he, after handing her the letter without a word, as she began to open and read it, threw his arms about her and kissed her.

Chapter XXV
Antony Meets Cleopatra in Cilicia, 41 BCE

Such, then, was the nature of Antony, where now as a crowning evil his love for Cleopatra supervened, roused and drove to frenzy many of the passions that were still hidden and quiescent in him, and dissipated and destroyed whatever good and saving qualities still offered resistance. And he was taken captive in this manner. As he was getting ready for the Parthian War, he sent to Cleopatra, ordering her to meeting him in Cilicia in order to make answer to the charges made against her of raising and giving to Cassius much money for the war. But Dellius, Antony's messenger, when he saw how Cleopatra looked, and noticed her subtlety and cleverness in conversation, at once perceived that Antony would not so much as think of doing such a woman any harm, but that she would have the greatest influence with him. He therefore resorted to flattery and tried to induce the Egyptian to go to Cilicia "decked out in fine array" (as Homer would say), and not to be afraid of Antony, who was the most agreeable and humane of commanders. She was persuaded by Dellius and, judging by the proofs which she had had before this of the effect of her beauty upon Julius Caesar and Cnaeus the son of Pompey, she had hopes that she would more easily bring Antony to her feet. For Caesar and Pompey had known her when she was still a girl and inexperienced in affairs, but she was going to visit Antony at the very time when women have the most brilliant beauty and are at the acme of intellectual power. Therefore, she provided herself with many gifts, much money, and such ornaments as high position and prosperous kingdom made it natural for her to take; but she went putting her greatest confidence in herself, and in the charms and sorceries of her own person.

Chapter XXVI
Cleopatra Entertains Antony Aboard Her Opulent Barge

Though she received many letters of summons both from Antony himself and from his friends, she so despised and laughed the man to scorn as to sail up the River Cydnus in a barge with gilded poop, its sails spread purple, its rowers urging it on with silver oars to the sound of the flute blended with pipes and lutes. She herself reclined beneath a canopy spangled with gold, adorned like Venus in a painting, while boys like Loves in paintings stood on either side and fanned her. Likewise, also the fairest of her serving-maidens, attired like Nereïds and Graces, were stationed, some at the rudder-sweeps, and others at the reefing-ropes. Wondrous odours from countless incense-offerings diffused themselves along the riverbanks. Of the inhabitants, some accompanied her on either bank of the river from its very mouth, while others went down from the city to behold the sight. The throng in the marketplace gradually streamed away, until at last, Antony himself, seated on his tribunal, was left alone. And a rumour spread on every hand that Venus was come to revel with Bacchus for the good of Asia.

Antony sent, therefore, and invited her to supper; but she thought it meet that he should rather come to her. At once, then, wishing to display his complacency and friendly feelings, Antony obeyed and went. He found there a preparation that beggared description but was most amazed at the multitude of lights. For, as we are told, so many of these were let down and displayed on all sides at once, and they were arranged and ordered with so many inclinations and adjustments to each other in the form of rectangles and circles, that few sights were so beautiful or so worthy to be seen as this.

Chapter XXVII
Cleopatra's Beauty and Talent for Languages

On the following day Antony feasted her in his turn, and was ambitious to surpass her splendour and elegance, but in both regards he was left behind, and vanquished in these very points, and was first to rail at the meagreness and rusticity of his own arrangements. Cleopatra observed in the jests of Antony much of the soldier and the common man, and adopted this manner also towards him, without restraint now, and boldly. For her beauty, as we are told, was in itself not altogether incomparable, nor such as to strike those who saw her; but converse with her had an irresistible charm, and her presence, combined with the persuasiveness of her discourse and the character, which was somehow diffused about her behaviour towards others, had something stimulating about it. There was sweetness also in the tones of her voice; and her tongue, like an instrument of many strings, she could readily turn to whatever language she pleased, so that in her interviews with Barbarians she very seldom had need of an interpreter, but made her replies to most of them herself and unassisted, whether they were Ethiopians, Troglodytes, Hebrews, Arabians, Syrians, Medes or Parthians. Nay, it is said that she knew the speech of many other peoples also, although the kings of Egypt before her had not even made an effort to learn the native language, and some actually gave up their Macedonian dialect.

Chapter XXIX
Cleopatra Tricks Antony into Thinking He Catches a Fish

But Cleopatra, distributing her flattery, not into the four forms of which Plato speaks, but into many, and ever contributing some fresh delight and charm to Antony's hours of seriousness or mirth, kept him in constant tutelage, and released him neither night nor day. She played at dice with him, drank with him, hunted with him, and watched him as he exercised himself in arms; and when by night he would station himself at the doors or windows of the common folk and scoff at those within, she would go with him on his round of mad follies, wearing the garb of a serving maiden. For Antony also would try to array himself like a servant. Therefore, he always reaped a harvest of abuse, and often of blows, before coming back home; though most people suspected who he was. However, the Alexandrians took delight in their graceful and cultivated way; they liked him and said that he used the tragic mask with the Romans, but the comic mask with them.

Now, to recount the greater part of his boyish pranks would be great nonsense. One instance will suffice. He was fishing once, and had bad luck, and was vexed at it because Cleopatra was there to see. He therefore ordered his fishermen to dive down and secretly fasten to his hook some fish that had been previously caught and pulled up two or three of them. But the Egyptian saw through the trick, and pretending to admire her lover's skill, told her friends about it, and invited them to be spectators of it the following day. So great numbers of them got into the fishing boats, and when Antony had let down his line, she ordered one of her own attendants to get the start of him by swimming onto his hook and fastening on it a salted Pontic herring. Antony thought he had caught something, and pulled it up, whereupon there was great laughter, as was natural, and Cleopatra said: "*Imperator* [Commander], hand over your fishing-rod to the fishermen of Pharos and Canopus; your sport is the hunting of cities, realms, and continents."

Chapter XXX
Octavian Caesar, Antony and Lepidus Divide Up the Roman Empire, 40 BCE

While Antony was indulging in such trifles and youthful follies, he was surprised by reports from two quarters: one from Rome, that Lucius his brother and Fulvia his wife had first quarrelled with one another, and then had waged war with Octavian Caesar [Julius Caesar's heir], but had lost their cause and were in flight from Italy; and another, not a whit more agreeable than this, that Labienus at the head of the Parthians was subduing Asia from the Euphrates and Syria as far as Lydia and Ionia. At last, then, like a man roused from sleep after a deep debauch, he set out to oppose the Parthians, and advanced as far as Phoenicia; but on receiving from Fulvia a letter full of lamentations, he turned his course towards Italy, at the head of two hundred ships. On the voyage, however, he picked up his friends who were in flight from Italy and learned from them that Fulvia had been to blame for the war, being naturally a meddlesome and headstrong woman, and hoping to draw Antony away from Cleopatra in case there should be a disturbance in Italy. It happened, too, that Fulvia, who was sailing to meet him, fell sick and died at Sicyon. Therefore, there was even more opportunity for a reconciliation with Caesar. For when Antony reached Italy, and Caesar manifestly intended to make no charges against him, and Antony himself was ready to put upon Fulvia the blame for whatever was charged against himself, the friends of the two men would not permit any examination of the proffered excuse, but reconciled them, and divided up the empire, making the Ionian Sea a boundary, and assigning the

East to Antony, and the West to Caesar; they also permitted Lepidus to have Africa, and arranged that, when they did not wish for the office themselves, the friends of each should have the consulship by turns.

Chapter XXXI
Antony Marries Octavian's Sister, Octavia, 40 BCE

These arrangements were thought to be fair, but they needed a stronger security, and this security Fortune offered. Octavia was a sister of Caesar, older than he, though not by the same mother; for she was the child of Ancharia, but he, by a later marriage, of Atia. Caesar was exceedingly fond of his sister, who was, as the saying is, a wonder of a woman. Her husband, Caius Marcellus, had died a short time before, and she was a widow. Antony, too, now that Fulvia was gone, was held to be a widower, although he did not deny his relations with Cleopatra; he would not admit, however, that she was his wife, and in this matter his reason was still battling with his love for the Egyptian. Everybody tried to bring about this marriage, for they hoped that Octavia, who, besides her great beauty, had intelligence and dignity, when united to Antony and beloved by him, as such a woman naturally must be, would restore harmony and be their complete salvation. Accordingly, when both men were agreed, they went up to Rome and celebrated Octavia's marriage, although the law did not permit a woman to marry before her husband had been dead ten months. In this case, however, the Senate passed a decree remitting the restriction in time.

Chapter XXXII
Pompey the Great's Son Sextus Makes a Pact with Octavian and Antony, 39 BCE

Now, Sextus Pompeius was holding Sicily, was ravaging Italy, and, with his numerous piratical ships under the command of Menas the corsair and Menecrates, had made the sea unsafe for sailors. But he was thought to be kindly disposed to Antony, since he had given refuge to Antony's mother when she fled from Rome with Fulvia, and so it was decided to make terms with him. The men met at the promontory and mole of Misenum, near which Pompey's fleet lay at anchor and the forces of Antony and Caesar were drawn up. After it had been agreed that Pompey should have Sardinia and Sicily, should keep the sea clear of robbers, and should send up to Rome a stipulated amount of grain, they invited one another to supper. Lots were cast, and it was the lot of Pompey to entertain the others first. And when Antony asked him where the supper would be held, "There," said he, pointing to his admiral's ship with its six banks of oars, "for this is the ancestral house that is left to Pompey." This he said by way of reproach to Antony, who was now occupying the house which had belonged to the elder Pompey. So, he brought his ship to anchor, made a sort of bridge on which to cross to it from the headland, and gave his guests a hearty welcome on board. When their good fellowship was at its height and the jokes about Antony and Cleopatra were in full career, Menas the pirate came up to Pompey and said, so that the others could not hear, "Shall I cut the ship's cables and make you master, not of Sicily and Sardinia, but of the whole Roman Empire?" Pompey, on hearing this, communed with himself a little while, and then said: "Menas, you ought to have done this without speaking to me about it beforehand; but now let us be satisfied with things as they are; for perjury is not my way." Pompey, then, after being feasted in his turn by Antony and Caesar, sailed back to Sicily.

Chapter XXXIII
Antony Takes Octavia to Athens, Winter 39-38 BCE

After this settlement, Antony sent Ventidius on ahead into Asia to oppose the further progress of the Parthians, while he himself, as a favour to Caesar, was appointed to the priesthood of the elder Caesar [Pontifex Maximus]; everything else also of the most important political nature they transacted together and in a friendly spirit. But their competitive diversions gave Antony annoyance, because he always came off with less than Caesar. Now, there was with him a seer from Egypt, one of those who cast nativities. This man, either as a favour to Cleopatra, or dealing truly with Antony, used frank language with him, saying that his fortune, though most great and splendid, was obscured by that of Caesar; and he advised Antony to put as much distance as possible between himself and that young man. "For your guardian genius," said he, "is afraid of his; and though it has a spirited and lofty mien when it is by itself, when his comes near, thine is cowed and humbled by it." And, indeed, events seemed to testify in favour of the Egyptian, for we are told that whenever, by way of diversion, lots were cast or dice thrown to decide matters in which they were engaged, Antony came off worse. They would often match cocks, and often fighting quails, and Caesar's would always be victorious. At all this Antony was annoyed, though he did not show it, and giving rather more heed now to the Egyptian, he departed from

Italy, after putting his private affairs in the hands of Caesar; and he took Octavia with him as far as Greece (she had borne him a daughter [Antonia the Younger]). It was while he was spending the winter at Athens that word was brought to him of the first successes of Ventidius, who had conquered the Parthians in battle and slain Labienus, as well as Pharnapates, the most capable general of King Hyrodes. To celebrate this victory Antony feasted the Greeks and acted as *gymnasiarch* [administrator of the gymnasia] for the Athenians. He left at home the insignia of his command, and went forth carrying the wands of a gymnasiarch, in a Greek robe and white shoes, and he would take the young combatants by the neck and part them.

Chapter XXXVI
Antony Gives Cleopatra Roman Territories, including Cyprus and Judaea, 37 BCE

But the dire evil which had been slumbering for a long time, namely, his passion for Cleopatra, which men thought had been charmed away and lulled to rest by better considerations, blazed up again with renewed power as he drew near to Syria. And finally, like the stubborn and unmanageable beast of the soul, of which Plato speaks, he spurned away all saving and noble counsels and sent Fonteius Capito to bring Cleopatra to Syria. And when she was come, he made her a present of no slight or insignificant addition to her dominions, namely, Phoenicia, Coele Syria, Cyprus, and a large part of Cilicia; and still further, the balsam-producing part of Judaea, and all that part of Arabia Nabataea which slopes toward the outer sea. These gifts particularly annoyed the Romans. And yet he made presents to many private persons of tetrarchies and realms of great peoples, and he deprived many monarchs of their kingdoms, as, for instance, Antigonus the Jew, whom he brought forth and beheaded, though no other king before him had been so punished. But the shamefulness of the honours conferred upon Cleopatra gave most offence. And he heightened the scandal by acknowledging his two children by her, and called one Alexander Helios and the other Cleopatra Selene, with the surname for the first of Sun, and for the other of Moon. However, since he was an adept at putting a good face upon shameful deeds, he used to say that the greatness of the Roman Empire was made manifest, not by what the Romans received, but by what they bestowed; and that noble families were extended by the successive begettings of many kings. In this way, at any rate, he said, his own progenitor was begotten by Heracles, who did not confine his succession to a single womb, nor stand in awe of laws like Solon's for the regulation of conception, but gave free course to nature, and left behind him the beginnings and foundations of many families.

Chapter XXXVII
Antony Negotiates Phraates' Offer of Peace, Advances to Armenia

And now Phraates put Hyrodes his father to death and took possession of his kingdom, other Parthians ran away in great numbers, and particularly Monaeses, a man of distinction and power, who came in flight to Antony. Antony likened the fortunes of the fugitive to those of Themistocles, compared his own abundant resources and magnanimity to those of the Persian kings, and gave him three cities, Larissa, Arethusa, and Hierapolis, which used to be called Bambycé. But when the Parthian king made an offer of friendship to Monaeses, Antony gladly sent Monaeses back to him, determined to receive Phraates with a prospect of peace, and demanding back the standards captured in the campaign of Crassus, together with such of his men as still survived. Antony himself, however, after sending Cleopatra back to Egypt, proceeded through Arabia and Armenia to the place where his forces were assembled, together with those of the allied kings. These kings were very many in number, but the greatest of them all was Artavasdes, king of Armenia, who furnished six thousand horse and seven thousand foot. Here Antony reviewed his army. There were, of the Romans themselves, sixty thousand foot-soldiers, together with the cavalry classed as Roman, namely, ten thousand Iberians and Celts; of the other nations there were thirty thousand, counting alike horsemen and light-armed troops. And yet we are told that all this preparation and power, which terrified even the Indians beyond Bactria and made all Asia quiver, was made of no avail to Antony by reason of Cleopatra. For so eager was he to spend the winter with her that he began the war before the proper time and managed everything confusedly. He was not master of his own faculties, but, as if he were under the influence of certain drugs or of magic rites, was ever looking eagerly towards her, and thinking more of his speedy return than of conquering the enemy.

Chapter XL
Phraates' Stratagem to Degrade the Romans' Morale

The war was full of hardship for both sides, and its future course was still more to be dreaded. Antony expected a famine; for it was no longer possible to get provisions without having many men wounded and killed. Phraates, too, knew that his Parthians were able to do anything rather than to undergo hardships and encamp in the open during winter, and he was afraid that if the Romans persisted and remained, his men would desert him, since already the air was getting sharp after the summer solstice. He therefore contrived the following stratagem. Those of the Parthians who were most acquainted with the Romans attacked them less vigorously in their forays for provisions and other encounters, allowing them to take some things, praising their valour, and declaring that they were capital fighting men and justly admired by their own king. After this, they would ride up nearer, and quietly putting their horses alongside the Romans, would revile Antony because, when Phraates wished to come to terms and spare so many such excellent men, Antony would not give him an opportunity, but sat there awaiting those grievous and powerful enemies, famine and winter, which would make it difficult for them to escape even though the Parthians should escort them on their way. Many persons reported this to Antony, but though his hope inclined him to yield, he did not send heralds to the Parthians until he had enquired of the Barbarians who were showing such kindness whether what they said represented the mind of their king. They assured him that it did, and urged him to have no fear or distrust, whereupon he sent some of his companions with a renewed demand for the return of the standards and the captives, that he might not be thought altogether satisfied with an escape in safety. But the Parthian told him not to urge this matter and assured him of peace and safety as soon as he started to go away; whereupon, within a few days Antony packed up his baggage and broke camp.

But though he was persuasive in addressing a popular audience and was better endowed by nature than any man of his time for leading an army by force of eloquence, he could not prevail upon himself, for shame and dejection of spirits, to make the usual speech of encouragement to the army but ordered Domitius Ahenobarbus to do it. Some of the soldiers were incensed at this and felt that he had held them in contempt; but the majority of them were moved to the heart as they comprehended the reason. Therefore, they thought they ought to show all the more respect and obedience to their commander.

Chapter L
Antony Reviews the Army

There [on the bank of the Araxes River, which forms the boundary between Media and Armenia] Antony held a review of his troops and found that twenty thousand of the infantry and four thousand of the cavalry had perished, not all at the hands of the enemy, but more than half by disease. They had, indeed, marched twenty-seven days from Phraata, and had defeated the Parthians in eighteen battles, but their victories were not complete or lasting because the pursuits which they made were short and ineffectual. And this more than all else made it plain that it was Artavasdes the Armenian who had robbed Antony of the power to bring that war to an end. For if the sixteen thousand horsemen who were led back from Media by him had been on hand, equipped as they were like the Parthians and accustomed to fighting with them, and if they, when the Romans routed the fighting enemy, had taken off the fugitives, it would not have been in the enemy's power to recover themselves from defeat and to venture again so often. Accordingly, all the army, in their anger, tried to incite Antony to take vengeance on the Armenian. But Antony, as a measure of prudence, neither reproached him with his treachery nor abated the friendliness and respect usually shown to him being now weak in numbers and in want of supplies. But afterwards, when he once more invaded Armenia, and by many invitations and promises induced Artavasdes to come to him, Antony seized him, and took him in chains down to Alexandria, where he celebrated a triumph. And herein particularly did he give offence to the Romans, since he bestowed the honourable and solemn rites of his native country upon the Egyptians for Cleopatra's sake. This, however, took place at a later time.

Chapter LI
Antony Waits for Cleopatra at White Village

But now, hastening on through much wintry weather, which was already at hand, and incessant snowstorms, he lost eight thousand men on the march. He himself, however, went down with a small company to the sea, and in a little place between Berytus and Sidon, called White Village, he waited for Cleopatra to come; and since she was slow in coming he was beside himself with distress, promptly resorting to drinking and intoxication, although he could not hold out long at table, but in the midst of the drinking would often rise or spring up to look out, until she put into port, bringing an abundance of clothing and money for the soldiers. There are some, however, who say that he received the clothing from Cleopatra, but took the money from his own private funds, and distributed it as a gift from her.

Chapter LIII
Cleopatra Sees Octavia as a Rival, 35 BCE

But at Rome Octavia was desirous of sailing to Antony, and Caesar gave her permission to do so, as the majority say, not as a favour to her, but in order that, in case she were neglected and treated with scorn, he might have plausible ground for war. When Octavia arrived at Athens, she received letters from Antony in which he bade her remain there and told her of his expedition. Octavia, although she saw through the pretext and was distressed, nevertheless wrote Antony asking where he would have the things sent which she was bringing to him. For she was bringing a great quantity of clothing for his soldiers, many beasts of burden, and money and gifts for the officers and friends about him; and besides this, two thousand picked soldiers equipped as Praetorian Cohorts with splendid armour. These things were announced to Antony by a certain Niger, a friend of his who had been sent from Octavia, and he added such praises of her as was fitting and deserved. But Cleopatra perceived that Octavia was coming into a contest at close quarters with her, and feared lest, if she added to the dignity of her character and the power of Caesar her pleasurable society and her assiduous attentions to Antony, she would become invincible and get complete control over her husband. She therefore pretended to be passionately in love with Antony herself and reduced her body by slender diet; she put on a look of rapture when Antony drew near, and one of faintness and melancholy when he went away. She would contrive to be often seen in tears, and then would quickly wipe the tears away and try to hide them, as if she would not have Antony notice them. And she practised these arts while Antony was intending to go up from Syria to join the Mede. Her flatterers, too, were industrious on her behalf, and used to revile Antony as hard-hearted and unfeeling, and as the destroyer of a mistress who was devoted to him and him alone. For Octavia, they said, had married him as a matter of public policy and for the sake of her brother, and enjoyed the name of wedded wife; but Cleopatra, who was queen of so many people, was called Antony's beloved, and she did not shun this name nor disdain it, as long as she could see him and live with him; but if she were driven away from him she would not survive it. At last, then, they so melted and enervated the man that he became fearful lest Cleopatra should throw away her life, and went back to Alexandria, putting off the Mede until the summer season, although Parthia was said to be suffering from internal dissensions. However, he went up and brought the king once more into friendly relations, and after betrothing to one of his sons by Cleopatra one of the king's daughters who was still small, he returned, his thoughts being now directed towards the civil war.

Chapter LIV
Antony Recognizes Ptolemy XV Caesarion as Co-Regent with Cleopatra

As for Octavia, she was thought to have been treated with scorn, and when she came back from Athens [Octavian] Caesar ordered her to dwell in her own house. But she refused to leave the house of her husband, nay, she even entreated Caesar himself, unless on other grounds he had determined to make war upon Antony, to ignore Antony's treatment of her, since it was an infamous thing even to have it said that the two greatest imperators in the world plunged the Romans into civil war, the one out of passion for, and the other out of resentment on behalf of, a woman. These were her words, and she confirmed them by her deeds. For she dwelt in her husband's house, just as if he were at home, and she cared for his children, not only those whom she herself, but also those whom Fulvia had borne him, in a noble and magnificent manner; she also received such friends of Antony as were sent to Rome in quest of office or on business, and helped them to obtain from Caesar what they wanted. Without meaning it, however, she was damaging Antony by this conduct of hers; for he was hated for wronging such a woman. He was hated, too, for the distribution which he made to his children in Alexandria; it was seen to be theatrical and arrogant, and to evince hatred of Rome. For after filling the gymnasium with a throng and placing on a tribunal of silver two thrones of gold, one for himself and the other for Cleopatra, and other lower thrones for his sons, in the first place he declared Cleopatra Queen of Egypt, Cyprus, Libya, and Coele Syria, and she was to share her throne with Caesarion. Caesarion was believed to be a son of the former [Julius] Caesar, by whom Cleopatra was left pregnant. In the second place, he proclaimed his own sons by Cleopatra Kings of Kings, and to Alexander he allotted Armenia, Media and Parthia (when he should have subdued it), to Ptolemy Phoenicia, Syria, and Cilicia. At the same time, he also produced his sons, Alexander arrayed in Median garb, which included a tiara and upright head-dress, Ptolemy in boots, short cloak, and broad-brimmed hat surmounted by a diadem. For the latter was the dress of the kings who followed Alexander, the former that of Medes and Armenians. And when the boys had embraced their parents, one was given a bodyguard of Armenians, the other of

Macedonians. Cleopatra, indeed, both then and at other times when she appeared in public, assumed a robe sacred to Isis, and was addressed as the New Isis.

Chapter LVI
Antony and Cleopatra Meet at Ephesus, 33 BCE

Antony heard of this while he was tarrying in Armenia; and at once he ordered Canidius to take sixteen legions and go down to the sea. But he himself took Cleopatra with him and came to Ephesus. It was there that his naval force was coming together from all quarters, eight hundred ships of war with merchant vessels, of which Cleopatra furnished two hundred, besides twenty thousand talents, and supplies for the whole army during the war. But Antony, listening to the advice of Domitius and sundry others, ordered Cleopatra to sail to Egypt and there await the result of the war. Cleopatra, however, fearing that Octavia would again succeed in putting a stop to the war, persuaded Canidius by large bribes to plead her cause with Antony, and to say that it was neither just to drive away from the war a woman whose contributions to it were so large, nor was it for the interest of Antony to dispirit the Egyptians, who formed a large part of his naval force; and besides, it was not easy to see how Cleopatra was inferior in intelligence to anyone of the princes who took part in the expedition, she who for a long time had governed so large a kingdom by herself, and by long association with Antony had learned to manage large affairs. These arguments (since it was destined that everything should come into Caesar's hands) prevailed; and with united forces they sailed to Samos and there made merry. For just as all the kings, dynasts, tetrarchs, nations, and cities between Syria, the Maeotic

Lake, Armenia, and Illyria had been ordered to send or bring their equipment for the war, so all the dramatic artists were compelled to put in an appearance at Samos; and while almost all the world around was filled with groans and lamentations, a single island for many days resounded with flutes and stringed instruments; theatres there were filled, and choral bands were competing with one another. Every city also sent an ox for the general sacrifice, and kings vied with one another in their mutual entertainments and gifts. And so, men everywhere began to ask: "How will the conquerors celebrate their victories if their preparations for the war are marked by festivals so costly?"

Chapter LVII
Antony and Cleopatra in Athens, 32 BCE

When these festivities were over, Antony gave the dramatic artists Priene as a place for them to dwell, and sailed himself to Athens, where sports and theatres again engaged him. Cleopatra, too, jealous of Octavia's honours in the city (for Octavia was especially beloved by the Athenians), tried by many splendid gifts to win the favour of the people. So, the people voted honours to her, and sent a deputation to her house carrying the vote, of whom Antony was one, for was he not a citizen of Athens? And standing in her presence he delivered a speech on behalf of the city. To Rome, however, he sent men who had orders to eject Octavia from his house. And we are told that she left it taking all his children with her except his eldest son by Fulvia, who was with his father; she was in tears of distress that she herself also would be regarded as one of the causes of the war. But the Romans felt pity for Antony, not for her, and especially those who had seen Cleopatra and knew that neither in youthfulness nor beauty was she superior to Octavia.

Chapter LVIII
Octavian Caesar Reads Certain Clauses in Antony's Will to the Senate

When Caesar heard of the rapidity and extent of Antony's preparations, he was much disturbed, lest he should be forced to settle the issue of the war during that summer. For he was lacking in many things, and people were vexed by the exactions of taxes. The citizens were generally compelled to pay one fourth of their income, and the freedmen one eighth of their property, and both classes cried out against Caesar, and disturbances arising from these causes prevailed throughout all Italy. Wherefore, among the greatest mistakes of Antony men reckon his postponement of the war. For it gave Caesar time to make preparations and put an end to the disturbances among the people. For while money was being exacted from them, they were angry, but when it had been exacted and they had paid it, they were calm. Moreover, Titius and Plancus, friends of Antony and men of consular rank, being abused by Cleopatra (for they had been most opposed to her accompanying the expedition) ran away to Caesar, and they gave him information about Antony's will, the contents of which they knew. This will was on deposit with the Vestal Virgins, and when Caesar asked for it, they would not give it to him; but if he wanted to take it, they told him to come and do so. So, he went and took it; and to begin with, he read its contents through by himself; and marked certain reprehensible passages; then he assembled the Senate and read it aloud to them, although most of them were displeased to hear him do so. For they thought it a strange and grievous matter that a man should be called to account while alive for what he wished to have done after his death. Caesar laid most stress on the clause in the will relating to Antony's burial. For it directed that Antony's body, even if he should die in Rome, should be borne in state through the forum and then sent away to Cleopatra in Egypt. Again, Calvisius, who was a companion of Caesar, brought forward against Antony the following charges also regarding his behaviour towards Cleopatra: he had bestowed upon her the libraries from Pergamum, in which there were two hundred thousand volumes; at a banquet where there were many guests he had stood up and rubbed her feet, in compliance with some agreement and compact which they had made; he had consented to have the Ephesians in his presence salute Cleopatra as mistress; many times, while he was seated on his tribunal and dispensing justice to tetrarchs and kings, he would receive love-billets from her in tablets of onyx or crystal, and read them; and once when Furnius was speaking, a man of great worth and the ablest orator in Rome, Cleopatra was carried through the forum on a litter, and Antony, when he saw her, sprang up from his tribunal and forsook the trial, and hanging on to Cleopatra's litter escorted her on her way.

Chapter LIX
Friends of Antony Plead with him to Return to Rome

However, most of the charges thus brought by Calvisius were thought to be falsehoods; but the friends of Antony went about in Rome beseeching the people on his behalf, and they sent one of their number, Geminius, with entreaties that Antony would not suffer himself to be voted out of his office and proclaimed an enemy of Rome. But Geminius, after his voyage to Greece, was an object of suspicion to Cleopatra, who thought that he was acting in the interests of Octavia; he was always put upon with jokes at supper and insulted with places of no honour at table, but he endured all this and waited for an opportunity to confer with Antony. Once, however, at a supper, being bidden to tell the reasons for his coming, he replied that the rest of his communication required a sober head, but one thing he knew, whether he was drunk or sober, and that was all would be well if Cleopatra was sent off to Egypt. At this, Antony was angry, and Cleopatra said: "You have done well, Geminius, to confess the truth without being put to the torture." Geminius, accordingly, after a few days, ran away to Rome. And Cleopatra's flatterers drove away many of the other friends of Antony also who could not endure their drunken tricks and scurrilities. Among these were Marcus Silanus and Dellius the historian. And Dellius says that he was also afraid of a plot against him by Cleopatra, of which Glaucus the physician had told him. For he had offended Cleopatra at supper by saying that while sour wine was served to them, Sarmentus, at Rome, was drinking Falernian. Now, Sarmentus was one of the youthful favourites of Caesar, such as the Romans call *deliciae* ('luxury').

Chapter LX
Roman Senate Votes for War Against Cleopatra, 32 BCE

When Caesar had made sufficient preparations, a vote was passed to wage war against Cleopatra, and to take away from Antony the authority which he had surrendered to a woman. And Caesar said in addition that Antony had been drugged and was not even master of himself, and that the Romans were carrying on war with Mardion the eunuch, and Pothinus, and Iras, and the tire-woman of Cleopatra, and Charmion, by whom the principal affairs of the government were managed. The following signs are said to have been given before the war. Pisaurum, a city colonized by Antony situated near the Adriatic, was swallowed by chasms in the earth. From one of the marble statues of Antony near Alba sweat oozed for many days, and though it was wiped away it did not cease. In Patrae, while Antony was staying there, the Heracleium was destroyed by lightning; and at Athens the Dionysus in the Battle of the Giants was dislodged by the winds and carried down into the theatre. Now, Antony associated himself with Heracles in lineage, and with Dionysus in the mode of life which he adopted, as I have said, and he was called *Neos Dionysos* ('New Dionysus'). The same tempest fell upon the colossal figures of Eumenes and Attalus at Athens, on which the name of Antony had been inscribed, and prostrated them, and them alone out of many. Moreover, the admiral's ship of Cleopatra was called *Antonius*, and a dire sign was given with regard to it. Some swallows, namely, made their nest under its stern; but other swallows attacked these, drove them out and destroyed their nestlings.

Chapter LXII
Opposing Fleets Gather at Actium, 31 BCE

But to such an extent, now, was Antony an appendage of the woman that although he was far superior on land, he wished the decision to rest with his navy, to please Cleopatra, and that too when he saw that for lack of crews his trierarchs were haling together out of long-suffering Greece wayfarers, mule-drivers, harvesters, and *ephebi* [young men approaching full military age, who were enrolled for preliminary training and service] and that even then their ships were not fully manned, but most of them were deficient and sailed wretchedly. Caesar's fleet, on the other hand, was perfectly equipped, and consisted of ships which had not been built for a display of height or mass, but were easily steered, swift, and fully manned. This fleet Caesar kept assembled at Tarentum and Brundisium, and he sent to Antony a demand to waste no time, but to come with his forces; Caesar himself would furnish his armament with unobstructed road steads and harbours and would withdraw with his land forces a day's journey for a horseman from the seashore, until Antony should have safely landed and fixed his camp. This boastful language Antony matched by challenging Caesar to single combat, although he was an older man than Caesar; and if Caesar declined this, Antony demanded that they should fight out the issue at Pharsalus, as Caesar and Pompey had once done. But while Antony was lying at anchor off Actium, where now Nicopolis stands, Caesar got the start of him by crossing the Ionian Sea and occupying a place in Epirus called Toruné (that is, 'ladle'); and when Antony and his friends were disturbed by this, since their infantry forces were belated, Cleopatra, jesting, said: "What is there dreadful in Caesar's sitting at a ladle?"

Chapter LXIII
Defections from the Camp of Antony and Cleopatra

But Antony, when the enemy sailed against him at daybreak, was afraid lest they should capture his ships while they had no fighting crews, and therefore armed the rowers and drew them up on the decks so as to make a show; then he grouped his ships at the mouth of the gulf near Actium, their ranks of oars on either side lifted and poised as for the stroke, and their prows towards the enemy, as if they were fully manned and prepared to fight. Caesar, thus outwitted and deceived, withdrew. Antony was also thought to have shown great skill in enclosing the potable water within certain barriers and thus depriving the enemy of it, since the places round about afforded little, and that of bad quality. He also behaved with magnanimity towards Domitius, contrary to the judgment of Cleopatra. For when Domitius, who was already in a fever, got into a small boat and went over to Caesar, Antony, though deeply chagrined, nevertheless, sent off to him all his baggage, together with his friends and servants. And Domitius, as if repenting when his faithlessness and treachery became known, straightway died.

There were also defections among the kings, and Amyntas and Deiotarus went over to Caesar. Besides, since his navy was unlucky in everything and always too late to be of assistance, Antony was again compelled to turn his attention to his land forces. Canidius also, the commander of the land forces, changed his mind in presence of the danger, and advised Antony to send Cleopatra away, to withdraw into Thrace or Macedonia, and there to decide the issue by a land battle. For Dicomes the king of the Getae promised to come to their aid with a large force; and it would be no disgrace, Canidius urged, for them to give up the sea to Caesar, who had practised himself there in the Sicilian war; but it would be a strange thing for Antony, who was most experienced in land conflicts, not to avail himself of the strength and equipment of his numerous legionary soldiers, but to distribute his forces among ships and so fritter them away.

However, Cleopatra prevailed with her opinion that the war should be decided by the ships, although she was already contemplating flight, and was disposing her own forces, not where they would be helpful in winning the victory, but where they could most easily get away if the cause was lost. Moreover, there were two long walls extending down to the naval station from the camp, and between these Antony was wont to pass without suspecting any danger. But a slave told Caesar that it was possible to seize Antony as he went down between the walls, and Caesar sent men to lie in ambush for him. These men came near accomplishing their purpose, but seized only the man who was advancing in front of Antony, since they sprang up too soon; Antony himself escaped with difficulty by running.

Chapter LXIV
Antony Provisions the Largest Ships in His Fleet

When it had been decided to deliver a sea battle, Antony burned all the Egyptian ships except sixty; but the largest and best, from those having three to those having ten banks of oars, he manned, putting on board twenty thousand heavy-armed soldiers and two thousand archers. It was on this occasion, we are told, that an infantry centurion, a man who had fought many a battle for Antony and was covered with scars, burst into laments as Antony was passing by, and said: "*Imperator*, why do you distrust these wounds and this sword and put thy hopes in miserable logs of wood? Let Egyptians and Phoenicians do their fighting at sea, but give us land, on which we are accustomed to stand and either conquer our enemies or die." To this Antony made no reply, but merely encouraged the man by a gesture and a look to be of good heart and passed on. He had no good hopes himself, since, when the masters of his ships wished to leave their sails behind, he compelled them to put them on board and carry them, saying that not one fugitive of the enemy should be allowed to make his escape.

Chapter LXV
The Battle of Actium, 2 September 31 BCE

During that day, then, and the three following days the sea was tossed up by a strong wind and prevented the battle; but on the fifth, the weather becoming fine and the sea calm, they came to an engagement. Antony had the right wing, with Publicola, Coelius the left, and in the centre were Marcus Octavius and Marcus Insteius. Caesar posted Marcus Agrippa on the left and reserved the right wing for himself. Of the land forces, that of Antony was commanded by Canidius, that of Caesar by Taurus, who drew them up along the sea and remained quiet. As for the leaders themselves, Antony visited all his ships in a row-boat, exhorting the soldiers, owing to the weight of their ships, to fight without changing their position, as if they were on land; he also ordered the masters of the ships to receive the attacks of the enemy as if their ships were lying quietly at anchor, and to maintain their position at the mouth of the gulf, which was narrow and difficult. Caesar, we are told, who had left his tent while it was still dark and was going round to visit his ships, was met by a man driving an ass. Caesar asked the man his name, and he, recognizing Caesar, replied: "My name is Prosper, and my ass's name is Victor." Therefore, when Caesar afterwards decided the place with the beaks of ships, he set up bronze figures of an ass and a man. After surveying the rest of his line of battle, he was carried in a small boat to his right wing, and there was astonished to see the enemy lying motionless in the narrows; indeed, their ships had the appearance of riding at anchor. For a long time, he was convinced that this was really the case, and kept his own ships at a distance of about eight furlongs from the enemy. But it was now the sixth hour, and since a wind was rising from the sea, the soldiers of Antony became impatient at the delay, and, relying on the height and size of their own ships as making them unassailable, they put their left wing in motion. When Caesar saw this, he was delighted, and ordered his right wing to row backwards, wishing to draw the enemy still farther out from the gulf and the narrows, and then to surround them with his own agile vessels and come to close quarters with ships which, owing to their great size and the smallness of their crews, were slow and ineffective.

Chapter LXVI
Cleopatra Flees the Battle

Though the struggle was beginning to be at close range, the ships did not ram or crush one another at all, since Antony's, owing to their weight, had no impetus, which chiefly gives effect to the blows of the beaks, while Caesar's not only avoided dashing front to front against rough and hard bronze armour, but did not even venture to ram the enemy's ships in the side. For their beaks would easily have been broken off by impact against vessels constructed of huge square timbers fastened together with iron. The struggle was therefore like a land battle; or, to speak more truly, like the storming of a walled town. For three or four of Caesar's vessels were engaged at the same time about one of Antony's, and the crews fought with wicker shields and spears and punting-poles and fiery missiles; the soldiers of Antony also shot with catapults from wooden towers.

And now, as Agrippa was extending the left wing with a view to encircling the enemy, Publicola was forced to advance against him, and so was separated from the centre. The centre falling into confusion and engaging with Arruntius, although the sea-fight was still undecided and equally favourable to both sides, suddenly the sixty ships of Cleopatra were seen hoisting their sails for flight and making off through the midst of the combatants; for they had been posted in the rear of the large vessels and threw them into confusion as they plunged through. The enemy looked on with amazement, seeing that they took advantage of the wind and made for Peloponnesus. Here, indeed, Antony made it clear to all the world that he was swayed neither by the sentiments of a commander nor of a brave man, nor even by his own, but, as someone in pleasantry said that the soul of the lover dwells in another's body, he was dragged along by the woman as if he had become incorporate with her and must go where she did. For no sooner did he see her ship sailing off than he forgot everything else, betrayed and ran away from those who were fighting and dying in his cause, got into a five-oared galley, where Alexas the Syrian and Scellius were his only companions, and hastened after the woman who had already ruined him and would make his ruin still more complete.

Chapter LXVII
Antony Flees the Battle

Cleopatra recognized him and raised a signal on her ship; so, Antony came up and was taken on board, but he neither saw nor was seen by her. Instead, he went forward alone to the prow and sat down by himself in silence, holding his head in both hands. At this point, Liburnian ships were seen pursuing them from Caesar's fleet; but Antony ordered the ship's prow turned to face them, and so kept them off, except the ship of Eurycles the Laconian, who attacked vigorously, and brandished a spear on the deck as though he would cast it at Antony. And when Antony, standing at the prow, asked, "Who is this that pursues Antony?" the answer was, "I am Eurycles, the son of Lachares, whom the fortune of Caesar enables to avenge the death of his father." Now, Lachares had been beheaded by Antony because he was involved in a charge of robbery. However, Eurycles did not hit Antony's ship, but smote the other admiral's ship (for there were two of them) with his bronze beak and whirled her round, and one of the other ships also, which contained costly equipment for household use. When Eurycles was gone, Antony threw himself down again in the same posture and did not stir. He spent three days by himself at the prow, either because he was angry with Cleopatra, or ashamed to see her, and then put in at Taenarum. Here the women in Cleopatra's company at first brought them into a parley, and then persuaded them to eat and sleep together.

Presently not a few of their heavy transport ships and some of their friends began to gather about them after the defeat, bringing word that the fleet was destroyed, but that, in their opinion, the land forces still held together. So Antony sent messengers to Canidius, ordering him to retire with his army as fast as he could through Macedonia into Asia; he himself, however, since he purposed to cross from Taenarum to Libya, selected one of the transport ships which carried much coined money and very valuable royal utensils in silver and gold, and made a present of it to his friends, bidding them divide up the treasure and look out for their own safety. They refused his gift and were in tears, but he comforted them and besought them with great kindness and affection, and finally sent them away, after writing to Theophilus, his steward in Corinth, that he should keep the men in safe hiding until they could make their peace with Caesar. This Theophilus was the father of Hipparchus, who had the greatest influence with Antony, was the first of Antony's freedmen to go over to Caesar, and afterwards lived in Corinth.

Chapter LXVIII
Antony's and Cleopatra's Fleet Surrenders to Octavian Caesar

This, then, was the situation of Antony. But at Actium his fleet held out for a long time against Caesar, and only after it had been most severely damaged by the high sea which rose against it did it reluctantly, and at the tenth hour, give up the struggle. There were not more than five thousand dead, but three hundred ships were captured, as Caesar himself has written. Only a few were aware that Antony had fled, and to those who heard of it the story was at first an incredible one, that he had gone off and left nineteen legions of undefeated men-at-arms and twelve thousand horsemen, as if he had not many times experienced both kinds of fortune and were not exercised by the reverses of countless wars and fighting. His soldiers, too, had a great longing for him, and expected that he would presently make his appearance from some quarter or other; and they displayed so much fidelity and bravery that even after his flight had become evident, they held together for seven days, paying no heed to the messages which Caesar sent them. But at last, after Canidius their general had run away by night and forsaken the camp, being now destitute of all things and betrayed by their commanders, they went over to the conqueror.

In consequence of this, Caesar sailed to Athens, and after making a settlement with the Greeks, he distributed the grain which remained over after the war among their cities; these were in a wretched plight, and had been stripped of money, slaves, and beasts of burden. At any rate, my great-grandfather Nicarchus used to tell how all his fellow-citizens were compelled to carry on their shoulders a stipulated measure of wheat down to the sea at Anticyra, and how their pace was quickened by the whip; they had carried one load in this way, he said, the second was already measured out, and they were just about to set forth, when word was brought that Antony had been defeated, and this was the salvation of the city; for immediately the stewards and soldiers of Antony took to flight, and the citizens divided the grain among themselves.

Chapter LXIX
As Antony Lands at Libya, Cleopatra Plans to Leave Egypt

After Antony had reached the coast of Libya and sent Cleopatra forward into Egypt from Paraetonium, he had the benefit of solitude without end, roaming and wandering about with two friends, one a Greek, Aristocrates a rhetorician, and the other a Roman, Lucilius, about whom I have told a story elsewhere. He was at Philippi, and in order that Brutus might make his escape, pretended to be Brutus and surrendered himself to his pursuers. His life was spared by Antony on this account, and he remained faithful to him and steadfast up to the last crucial times. When the general to whom his forces in Libya had been entrusted brought about their defection, Antony tried to kill himself, but was prevented by his friends and brought to Alexandria. Here he found Cleopatra venturing upon a hazardous and great undertaking. The isthmus, namely, which separates the Red Sea from the Mediterranean Sea off Egypt and is considered to be the boundary between Asia and Libya, in the part where it is most constricted by the two seas and has the least width, measures three hundred furlongs. Here Cleopatra undertook to raise her fleet out of water and drag the ships across, and after launching them in the Arabian Gulf with much money and a large force, to settle in parts outside of Egypt, thus escaping war and servitude. But since the Arabians about Petra burned the first ships that were drawn up, and Antony still thought that his land forces at Actium were holding together, she desisted, and guarded the approaches to the country. And now Antony forsook the city and the society of his friends and built for himself a dwelling in the sea at Pharos, by throwing a mole out into the water. Here he lived an exile from men and declared that he was contentedly imitating the life of Timon, since, indeed, his experiences had been like Timon's; for he himself also had been wronged and treated with ingratitude by his friends, and therefore hated and distrusted all mankind.

Chapter LXXI
Cleopatra Evaluates Different Poisons

These are a few things out of many concerning Timon. As for Antony, Canidius in person brought him word of the loss of his forces at Actium, and he heard that Herod the Jew, with sundry legions and cohorts, had gone over to Caesar, and that the other dynasts in like manner were deserting him and nothing longer remained of his power outside of Egypt. However, none of these things greatly disturbed him, but, as if he gladly laid aside his hopes, that so he might lay aside his anxieties also, he forsook that dwelling of his in the sea, which he called Timoneum, and after he had been received into the palace by Cleopatra, turned the city to the enjoyment of suppers and drinking-bouts and distributions of gifts, inscribing in the list of *ephebi* the son of Cleopatra and Caesar, and bestowing upon Antyllus the son of Fulvia the *toga virilis* (all-white *toga* of manhood) without purple hem, in celebration of which, for many days, banquets and revels and feastings occupied Alexandria. Cleopatra and Antony now dissolved their famous society of Inimitable Livers, and founded another, not at all inferior to that in daintiness and extravagant outlay, which they called the society of Partners in Death. For their friends enrolled themselves as those who would die together and passed the time delightfully in a round of suppers. Moreover, Cleopatra was getting together collections of all sorts of deadly poisons, and she tested the painless working of each of them by giving them to prisoners under sentence of death. But when she saw that the speedy poisons enhanced the sharpness of death by the pain they caused, while the milder poisons were not quick, she made trial of venomous animals, watching with her own eyes as they were set upon another. She did this daily, tried them almost all; and she found that the bite of the asp alone induced a sleepy torpor and sinking, where there was no spasm or groan, but a gentle perspiration on the face, while the perceptive faculties were easily relaxed and dimmed, and resisted all attempts to rouse and restore them, as is the case with those who are soundly asleep.

Chapter LXXII
Antony and Cleopatra Try and Negotiate with Octavian Caesar

At the same time, they also sent an embassy to Caesar in Asia, Cleopatra asking the realm of Egypt for her children, and Antony requesting that he might live as a private person at Athens, if he could not do so in Egypt. But owing to their lack of friends and the distrust which they felt on account of desertions, Euphronius, the teacher of the children, was sent on the embassy. For Alexas the Laodicean, who had been made known to Antony in Rome through Timagenes and had more influence with him than any other Greek, who had also been Cleopatra's most effective instrument against Antony and had overthrown the considerations arising in his mind in favour of Octavia, had been sent to keep Herod the king from apostasy; but after remaining there and betraying Antony he had the audacity to come into Caesar's presence, relying on Herod. Herod, however, could not help him, but the traitor was at once confined and carried in fetters to his own country, where he was put to death by Caesar's orders. Such was the penalty for his treachery which Alexas paid to Antony while Antony was yet alive.

Chapter LXXIII
Octavian Caesar Makes an Offer to Cleopatra

Caesar would not listen to the proposals for Antony, but he sent back word to Cleopatra that she would receive all reasonable treatment if she either put Antony to death or cast him out. He also sent with the messengers one of his own freedmen, Thyrsus, a man of no mean parts, and one who would persuasively convey messages from a young general to a woman who was haughty and astonishingly proud in the matter of beauty. This man had longer interviews with Cleopatra than the rest, and was conspicuously honoured by her, so that he roused suspicion in Antony, who seized him and gave him a flogging, and then sent him back to Caesar with a written message stating that Thyrsus, by his insolent and haughty airs, had irritated him, at a time when misfortunes made him easily irritated. "But if you do not like the thing," he said, "you have my freedman Hipparchus; hang him up and give him a flogging, and we shall be quits." After this, Cleopatra tried to dissipate his causes of complaint and his suspicions by paying extravagant court to him; her own birthday she kept modestly and in a manner becoming to her circumstances, but she celebrated his with an excess of all kinds of splendour and costliness, so that many of those who were bidden to the supper came poor and went away rich. Meanwhile Caesar was being called home by Agrippa, who frequently wrote him from Rome that matters there greatly needed his presence.

Chapter LXXIV
Octavian Caesar Reaches Pelusium

Accordingly, the war was suspended for the time being; but when the winter was over, Caesar again marched against his enemy through Syria, and his generals through Libya. When Pelusium was taken there was a rumour that Seleucus had given it up, and not without the consent of Cleopatra; but Cleopatra allowed Antony to put to death the wife and children of Seleucus, and she herself, now that she had a tomb and monument built surpassingly lofty and beautiful, which she had erected near the temple of Isis, collected there the most valuable of the royal treasures, gold, silver, emeralds, pearls, ebony, ivory, and cinnamon; and besides all this she put there great quantities of torch-wood and tow, so that Caesar was anxious about the reason, and fearing lest the woman might become desperate and burn up and destroy this wealth, kept sending on to her vague hopes of kindly treatment from him, at the same time that he advanced with his army against the city. But when Caesar had taken up position near the hippodrome, Antony sallied forth against him and fought brilliantly and routed his cavalry and pursued them as far as their camp. Then, exalted by his victory, he went into the palace, kissed Cleopatra, all armed as he was, and presented to her the one of his soldiers who had fought most spiritedly. Cleopatra gave the man as a reward of valour a golden breastplate and a helmet. The man took them, of course – and in the night deserted to Caesar.

Chapter LXXVI
Antony Commits Suicide, 1 August 31 BCE

At daybreak, Antony in person posted his infantry on the hills in front of the city and watched his ships as they put out and attacked those of the enemy; and as he expected to see something great accomplished by them, he remained quiet. But the crews of his ships, as soon as they were near, saluted Caesar's crews with their oars, and on their returning the salute changed sides, and so all the ships, now united into one fleet, sailed up towards the city prows on. No sooner had Antony seen this than he was deserted by his cavalry, which went over to the enemy, and after being defeated with his infantry he retired into the city, crying out that he had been betrayed by Cleopatra to those with whom he waged war for her sake. But she, fearing his anger and his madness, fled for refuge into her tomb and let fall the drop-doors, which were made strong with bolts and bars; then she sent messengers to tell Antony that she was dead. Antony believed that message, and saying to himself, "Why do you longer delay, Antony? Fortune has taken away thy sole remaining excuse for clinging to life," he went into his chamber. Here, as he unfastened his breastplate and laid it aside, he said: "O Cleopatra, I am not grieved to be bereft of thee, for I shall straightway join you; but I am grieved that such an *imperator*, as I am, has been found to be inferior to a woman in courage." Now, Antony had a trusty slave named Eros. Him Antony had long before engaged, in case of need, to kill him, and now demanded the fulfilment of his promise. So, Eros drew his sword and held it up as though he would smite his master, but then turned his face away and slew himself. And as he fell at his master's feet Antony said: "Well done, Eros! Though you were not able to do it yourself, you teach me what I must do"; and running himself through the belly he dropped upon the couch. But the wound did not bring a speedy death. Therefore, as the blood ceased flowing after he had lain down, he came to himself and besought the bystanders to give him the finishing stroke. But they fled from the chamber, and he lay writhing and crying out, until Diomedes the secretary came from Cleopatra with orders to bring him to her in the tomb.

Chapter LXXVII
Dying Antony Taken to Cleopatra's Tomb

Having learned, then, that Cleopatra was alive, Antony eagerly ordered his servants to raise him up, and he was carried in their arms to the doors of her tomb. Cleopatra, however, would not open the doors, but showed herself at a window, from which she let down ropes and cords. To these Antony was fastened, and she drew him up herself, with the aid of the two women whom alone she had admitted with her into the tomb. Never, as those who were present tell us, was there a more piteous sight. Smeared with blood and struggling with death he was drawn up, stretching out his hands to her even as he dangled in the air, for the task was not an easy one for the women, and scarcely could Cleopatra, with clinging hands and strained face, pull up the rope, while those below called out encouragement to her and shared her agony. And when she had thus got him in and laid him down, she rent her garments over him, beat and tore her breasts with her hands, wiped off some of his blood upon her face, and called him master, husband, and imperator;

indeed, she almost forgot her own ills in her pity for his. But Antony stopped her lamentations and asked for a drink of wine, either because he was thirsty, or in the hope of a speedier release. When he had drunk, he advised her to consult her own safety, if she could do it without disgrace, and among all the companions of Caesar to put most confidence in Proculeius, and not to lament him for his last reverses, but to count him happy for the good things that had been his, since he had become most illustrious of men, had won greatest power, and now had been not ignobly conquered, a Roman by a Roman.

Chapter LXXVIII
Told of Antony's Death, Octavian Caesar Demands Cleopatra Be Taken Alive

Scarcely was he dead when Proculeius came from Caesar. For after Antony had smitten himself and while he was being carried to Cleopatra, Dercetaeus, one of his bodyguard, seized Antony's sword, concealed it, and stole away with it; and running to Caesar, he was the first to tell him of Antony's death, and showed him the sword all smeared with blood. When Caesar heard these tidings, he retired within his tent and wept for a man who had been his relation by marriage, his colleague in office and command, and his partner in many undertakings and struggles. Then he took the letters which had passed between them, called in his friends, and read the letters aloud, showing how reasonably and justly he had written, and how rude and overbearing Antony had always been in his replies. After this, he sent Proculeius, bidding him, if possible, above all things to get Cleopatra into his power alive; for he was fearful about the treasures in her funeral pyre, and he thought it would add greatly to the glory of his triumph if she were led in the procession. Into the hands of Proculeius, however, Cleopatra would not put herself; but she conferred with him after he had come close to the tomb and stationed himself outside at a door which was on a level with the ground. The door was strongly fastened with bolts and bars but allowed a passage for the voice. So, they conversed, Cleopatra asking that her children might have the kingdom, and Proculeius bidding her be of good cheer and trust Caesar in everything.

Chapter LXXIX
Proculeius Prevents Cleopatra from Stabbing Herself

After Proculeius had surveyed the place, he brought back word to Caesar, and Gallus was sent to have another interview with the queen; and coming up to the door he purposely prolonged the conversation. Meanwhile Proculeius applied a ladder and went in through the window by which the women had taken Antony inside. Then he went down at once to the very door at which Cleopatra was standing and listening to Gallus, and he had two servants with him. One of the women imprisoned with Cleopatra cried out, "Wretched Cleopatra, you are taken alive," whereupon the queen turned about, saw Proculeius, and tried to stab herself; for she had at her girdle a dagger such as robbers wear. But Proculeius ran swiftly to her, threw both his arms about her, and said: "O Cleopatra, you are wronging both yourself and Caesar, by trying to rob him of an opportunity to show great kindness, and by fixing upon the gentlest of commanders the stigma of faithlessness and implacability." At the same time, he took away her weapon, and shook out her clothing, to see whether she was concealing any poison. And there was also sent from Caesar one of his freedmen, Epaphroditus, with injunctions to keep the queen alive by the strictest vigilance, but otherwise to make any concession that would promote her ease and pleasure.

Chapter LXXX
Alexandrians Prostrate Themselves Before Octavian

And now Caesar himself drove into the city, and he was conversing with Areius the philosopher, to whom he had given his right hand, in order that Areius might at once be conspicuous among the citizens and be admired because of the marked honour shown him by Caesar. After he had entered the gymnasium and ascended a tribunal there made for him, the people were beside themselves with fear and prostrated themselves before him, but he bade them rise up, and said that he acquitted the people of all blame, first, because of Alexander, their founder; second, because he admired the great size and beauty of the city; and third, to gratify his companion, Areius. This honour Caesar bestowed upon Areius and pardoned many other persons also at his request. Among these was Philostratus, a man more competent to speak extempore than any sophist who ever lived, but he improperly represented himself as belonging to the school of the Academy. Therefore Caesar, abominating his ways, would not listen to his entreaties. So Philostratus, having a long white beard and wearing a dark robe, would follow behind Areius, ever declaiming this verse:

"A wise man will a wise man save, if wise he be."

When Caesar heard of this, he pardoned him, wishing rather to free Areius from odium than Philostratus from fear.

Chapter LXXXI
Ptolemy XV Caesarion Escapes

As for the children of Antony, Antyllus, his son by Fulvia, was betrayed by Theodorus his tutor and put to death; and after the soldiers had cut off his head, his tutor took away the exceeding precious stone which the boy wore about his neck and sewed it into his own girdle; and though he denied the deed, he was convicted of it and crucified. Cleopatra's children, together with their attendants, were kept under guard and had generous treatment. But Caesarion, who was said to be Cleopatra's son by Julius Caesar, was sent by his mother, with much treasure, into India, by way of Ethiopia. There Rhodon, another tutor like Theodorus, persuaded him to go back on the grounds that Caesar invited him to take the kingdom. But while Caesar was deliberating on the matter, we are told that Areius said:

"Not a good thing were a Caesar too many."

Chapter LXXXII
Antony Buried with Honour

As for Caesarion, then, he was afterwards put to death by Caesar – after the death of Cleopatra; but as for Antony, though many generals and kings asked for his body that they might give it burial,

Caesar would not take it away from Cleopatra, and it was buried by her hands in sumptuous and royal fashion, such things being granted her for the purpose as she desired. But in consequence of so much grief as well as pain (for her breasts were wounded and inflamed by the blows she gave them) a fever assailed her, and she welcomed it as an excuse for abstaining from food and so releasing herself from life without hindrance. Moreover, there was a physician in her company of intimates, Olympus, to whom she told the truth, and she had his counsel and assistance in compassing her death, as Olympus himself testifies in a history of these events which he published. But Caesar was suspicious and plied her with threats and fears regarding her children, by which she was laid low, as by engines of war, and surrendered her body for such care and nourishment as was desired.

Chapter LXXXIII
Octavian Meets Cleopatra

After a few days Caesar himself came to talk with her and give her comfort. She was lying on a mean pallet-bed, clad only in her tunic but sprang up as he entered and thew herself at his feet; her hair and face were in terrible disarray, her voice trembled, and her eyes were sunken. There were also visible many marks of the cruel blows upon her bosom; in a word, her body seemed to be no better off than her spirit. Nevertheless, the charm for which she was famous, and the boldness of her beauty, were not altogether extinguished, but, although she was in such a sorry plight, they shone forth from within and made themselves manifest in the play of her features. After Caesar had bidden her to lie down and had seated himself near her, she began a sort of justification of her course, ascribing it to necessity and fear of Antony; but as Caesar opposed and refuted her on every point, she quickly changed her tone and sought to move his pity by prayers, as one who above all things clung to life. And finally, she gave him a list which she had of all her treasures; and when Seleucus, one of her stewards, showed conclusively that she was stealing away and hiding some of them, she sprang up, seized him by the hair, and showered blows upon his face. And when Caesar, with a smile, stopped her, she said: "But is it not a monstrous thing, O Caesar, that when you have deigned to come to me and speak to me though I am in this wretched plight, my slaves denounce me for reserving some women's adornments – not for myself, indeed, unhappy woman that I am – but that I may make trifling gifts to Octavia and thy Livia, and through their intercession find you merciful and more gentle?" Caesar was pleased with this speech, being altogether of the opinion that she desired to live. He told her, therefore, that he left these matters for her to manage, and that in all other ways he would give her more splendid treatment than she could possibly expect. Then he went off, supposing that he had deceived her, but the rather deceived by her.

Chapter LXXXIV
Cleopatra Pours a Libation to Antony

Now, there was a young man of rank among Caesar's companions, named Cornelius Dolabella. This man was not without a certain tenderness for Cleopatra; and so now, in response to her request, he secretly sent word to her that Caesar himself was preparing to march with his land forces through Syria and had resolved to send off her and her children within three days. After Cleopatra had heard this, in the first place, she begged Caesar that she might be permitted to pour libations for Antony; and when the request was granted, she had herself carried to the tomb, and embracing the urn which held his ashes, in company with the women usually about her, she said: "Dear Antony, I buried you but lately with hands still free; now, however, I pour libations for you as a captive, and so carefully guarded that I cannot either with blows or tears disfigure this body of mine, which is a slave's body, and closely watched that it may grace the triumph over you. Do not expect other honours or libations; these are the last from Cleopatra the captive. For though in life nothing could part us from each other, in death we are likely to change places; you, the Roman, lying buried here, while I, the hapless woman, lie in Italy, and get only so much of your country as my portion. But if indeed there is any might or power in the gods of that country (for the gods of this country have betrayed us), do not abandon your own wife while she lives, nor permit a triumph to be celebrated over myself in my person, but hide and bury me here with yourself, since out of all my innumerable ills not one is so great and dreadful as this short time that I have lived apart from you."

Chapter LXXXV
Cleopatra Dies, 10 August 30 BCE

After such lamentations, she wreathed and kissed the urn, and then ordered a bath to be prepared for herself. After her bath, she reclined at table and was making a sumptuous meal. And there came a man from the country carrying a basket; and when the guards asked him what he was bringing there, he opened the basket, took away the leaves, and showed them that the dish inside was full of figs. The guards were amazed at the great size and beauty of the figs, whereupon the man smiled and asked them to take some; so they felt no mistrust and bade him take them in. After her meal, however, Cleopatra took a tablet which was already written upon and sealed, and sent it to Caesar, and then, sending away all the rest of the company except her two faithful women, she closed the doors.

But Caesar opened the tablet, and when he found there lamentations and supplications of one who begged that he would bury her with Antony, he quickly knew what had happened. At first he was minded to go himself and give aid; then he ordered messengers to go with all speed and investigate. But the mischief had been swift. For though his messengers came on the run and found the guards as yet aware of nothing, when they opened the doors they found Cleopatra lying dead upon a golden couch, arrayed in royal state. And of her two women, the one called Iras was dying at her feet, while Charmion, already tottering and heavy-handed, was trying to arrange the diadem which encircled the queen's brow. Then somebody said in anger: "A fine deed, this, Charmion!" "It is indeed most fine," she said, "and befitting the descendant of so many kings." Not a word more did she speak but fell there by the side of the couch.

Chapter LXXXVI
The Asp

It is said that the asp was brought with those figs and leaves and lay hidden beneath them, for thus Cleopatra had given orders, that the reptile might fasten itself upon her body without her being aware of it. But when she took away some of the figs and saw it, she said: "There it is, you see," and baring her arm she held it out for the bite. But others say that the asp was kept carefully shut up in a water jar, and that while Cleopatra was stirring it up and irritating it with a golden distaff it sprang and fastened itself upon her arm. But the truth of the matter no one knows; for it was also said that she carried about poison in a hollow comb and kept the comb hidden in her hair; and yet neither spot nor other sign of poison broke out upon her body. Moreover, not even was the reptile seen within the chamber, though people said they saw some traces of it near the sea, where the chamber looked out upon it with its windows. And some also say that Cleopatra's arm was seen to have two slight and indistinct punctures; and this Caesar also seems to have believed. For in his triumph an image of Cleopatra herself with the asp clinging to her was carried in the procession. These, then, are the various accounts of what happened.

But Caesar, although vexed at the death of the woman, admired her lofty spirit; and he gave orders that her body should be buried with that of Antony in splendid and regal fashion. Her women also received honourable interment by his orders. When Cleopatra died, she was forty years of age save one, and had shared her power with Antony more than fourteen. Antony was fifty-six years of age, according to some, according to others, fifty-three. Now, the statues of Antony were torn down, but those of Cleopatra were left standing, because Archibius, one of her friends, gave Caesar two thousand talents, in order that they might not suffer the same fate as Antony's.

Chapter LXXXVII
The Children and Descendants of Antony and Cleopatra

Antony left seven children by his three wives, of whom Antyllus, the eldest, was the only one who was put to death by Caesar; the rest were taken up by Octavia and reared with her own children. Cleopatra, the daughter of Cleopatra, Octavia gave in marriage to Juba, the most accomplished of kings, and Antony, the son of Fulvia, she raised so high that, while Agrippa held the first place in Caesar's estimation, and the sons of Livia the second, Antony was thought to be and really was third. By Marcellus Octavia had two daughters, and one son, Marcellus, whom Caesar made both his son and his son-in-law, and he gave one of the daughters to Agrippa. But since Marcellus died very soon after his marriage and it was not easy for Caesar to select from among his other friends a son-in-law whom he could trust, Octavia proposed that Agrippa should take Caesar's daughter to wife and put away her own. First Caesar was persuaded by her, then Agrippa, whereupon she took back her own daughter and married her to young Antony, while Agrippa married Caesar's daughter. Antony left two daughters by Octavia, of whom one was taken to wife by Domitius Ahenobarbus, and the other, Antonia, famous for her beauty and discretion, was married to Drusus, who was the son of Livia and the stepson of Caesar. From this marriage sprang Germanicus and Claudius; of these, Claudius afterwards came to the throne, and of the children of Germanicus, Caius [Caligula] reigned with distinction, but for a short time only, and was then put to death with his wife and child, and Agrippina, who had a son by Ahenobarbus, Lucius Domitius, became the wife of Claudius Caesar. And Claudius, having adopted Agrippina's son, gave him the name of Nero Germanicus. This Nero came to the throne in my time. He killed his mother, and by his folly and madness came near subverting the Roman Empire. He was the fifth in descent from Antony.

ANCIENT KINGS & LEADERS

Ancient cultures often traded with and influenced each other, while others grew independently. This section provides the key leaders from a number of regions, to offer comparative insights into developments across the ancient world.

ANCIENT NEAR EAST LEADER LIST

This list concentrates on leaders with at least some proven legitimate claim. Dates are based on archaeological evidence as far as possible but are approximate. Where dates of rule overlap, rulers either ruled jointly or ruled in opposition to one another. There may also be differences in name spellings between different sources.

SUMER

The Sumerian list that follows is based on the *Sumerian King List* or *Chronicle of the One Monarchy*. The lists were often originally carved into clay tablets and several versions have been found, mainly in southern Mesopotamia. Some of these are incomplete and others contradict one another. Nevertheless, the lists remain an invaluable source of information.

After the kingship descended from heaven, the kingship was in Eridug.

Alulim	28,800 years (8 *sars**)
Alalngar	36,000 years (10 *sars*)

Then Eridug fell and the kingship was taken to Bad-tibira.

En-men-lu-ana	43,200 years (12 *sars*)
En-mel-gal-ana	28,800 years (8 *sars*)
Dumuzid the Shepherd (or Tammuz)	36,000 years (10 *sars*)

Then Bad-tibira fell and the kingship was taken to Larag.

En-sipad-zid-ana	28,800 years (8 *sars*)

Then Larag fell and the kingship was taken to Zimbir.

En-men-dur-ana	21,000 years (5 *sars* and 5 *ners*)

Then Zimbir fell and the kingship was taken to Shuruppag.

Ubara-Tutu	18,600 years (5 *sars* and 1 *ner**)

Then the flood swept over.

*A *sar* is a numerical unit of 3,600; a *ner* is a numerical unit of 600.

FIRST DYNASTY OF KISH

After the flood had swept over, and the kingship had descended from heaven, the kingship was in Kish.

Jushur	1,200 years	Kullassina-bel	960 years

Nangishlisma	1,200 years
En-tarah-ana	420 years
Babum	300 years
Puannum	840 years
Kalibum	960 years
Kalumum	840 years
Zuqaqip	900 years
Atab (or A-ba)	600 years
Mashda (son of Atab)	840 years
Arwium (son of Mashda)	720 years
Etana the Shepherd	1,500 years
Balih (son of Etana)	400 years
En-me-nuna	660 years
Melem-Kish (son of Enme-nuna)	900 years
Barsal-nuna (son of Enme-nuna)	1,200 years
Zamug (son of Barsal-nuna)	140 years
Tizqar (son of Zamug)	305 years
Ilku	900 years
Iltasadum	1,200 years
Enmebaragesi (earliest proven ruler based on archaeological sources; Early Dynastic Period, 2900–2350 BCE)	900 years
Aga of Kish (son of Enmebaragesi) (Early Dynastic Period, 2900–2350 BCE)	625 years

Then Kish was defeated and the kingship was taken to E-anna.

FIRST RULERS OF URUK

Mesh-ki-ang-gasher (son of Utu)	324 years (Late Uruk Period, 4000–3100 BCE)
Enmerkar (son of Mesh-ki-ang-gasher)	420 years (Late Uruk Period, 4000–3100 BCE)
Lugal-banda the shepherd	1200 years (Late Uruk Period, 4000–3100 BCE)

Dumuzid the fisherman	100 years (Jemdet Nasr Period, 3100–2900 BCE)
Gilgamesh	126 years (Early Dynastic Period, 2900–2350 BCE)
Ur-Nungal (son of Gilgamesh)	30 years
Udul-kalama (son of Ur-Nungal)	15 years
La-ba'shum	9 years
En-nun-tarah-ana	8 years
Mesh-he	36 years
Melem-ana	6 years
Lugal-kitun	36 years

Then Unug was defeated and the kingship was taken to Urim (Ur).

FIRST DYNASTY OF UR

Mesh-Ane-pada	80 years
Mesh-ki-ang-Nuna (son of Mesh-Ane-pada)	36 years
Elulu	25 years
Balulu	36 years

Then Urim was defeated and the kingship was taken to Awan.

DYNASTY OF AWAN

Three kings of Awan	356 years

Then Awan was defeated and the kingship was taken to Kish.

SECOND DYNASTY OF KISH

Susuda the fuller	201 years
Dadasig	81 years
Mamagal the boatman	360 years
Kalbum (son of Mamagal)	195 years
Tuge	360 years
Men-nuna (son of Tuge)	180 years
Enbi-Ishtar	290 years
Lugalngu	360 years

Then Kish was defeated and the kingship was taken to Hamazi.

DYNASTY OF HAMAZI

Hadanish	360 years

Then Hamazi was defeated and the kingship was taken to Unug (Uruk).

SECOND DYNASTY OF URUK

En-shag-kush-ana	60 years (*c.* 25th century BCE)
Lugal-kinishe-dudu	120 years
Argandea	7 years

Then Unug was defeated and the kingship was taken to Urim (Ur).

SECOND DYNASTY OF UR

Nanni	120 years
Mesh-ki-ang-Nanna II (son of Nanni)	48 years

Then Urim was defeated and the kingship was taken to Adab.

DYNASTY OF ADAB

Lugal-Ane-mundu	90 years (*c.* 25th century BCE)

Then Adab was defeated and the kingship was taken to Mari.

DYNASTY OF MARI

Anbu	30 years
Anba (son of Anbu)	17 years
Bazi the leatherworker	30 years
Zizi of Mari, the fuller	20 years
Limer the 'gudug' priest	30 years
Sharrum-iter	9 years

Then Mari was defeated and the kingship was taken to Kish.

THIRD DYNASTY OF KISH

Kug-Bau (Kubaba)	100 years (*c.* 25th century BCE)

Then Kish was defeated and the kingship was taken to Akshak.

DYNASTY OF AKSHAK

Unzi	30 years	Ishu-Il	24 years
Undalulu	6 years	Shu-Suen (son of Ishu-Il)	7 years
Urur	6 years		
Puzur-Nirah	20 years		

Then Akshak was defeated and the kingship was taken to Kish.

FOURTH DYNASTY OF KISH

Puzur-Suen (son of Kug-bau)	25 years (*c.* 2350 BCE)
Ur-Zababa (son of Puzur-Suen)	400 years (*c.* 2300 BCE)
Zimudar	30 years
Usi-watar (son of Zimudar)	7 years
Eshtar-muti	11 years
Ishme-Shamash	11 years
Shu-ilishu	15 years
Nanniya the jeweller	7 years

Then Kish was defeated and the kingship was taken to Unug (Uruk).

THIRD DYNASTY OF URUK

Lugal-zage-si	25 years (*c.* 2296–2271 BCE)

Then Unug was defeated and the kingship was taken to Agade (Akkad).

DYNASTY OF AKKAD

Sargon of Akkad	56 years (c. 2270–2215 BCE)
Rimush of Akkad (son of Sargon)	9 years (c. 2214–2206 BCE)
Manishtushu (son of Sargon)	15 years (c. 2205–2191 BCE)
Naram-Sin of Akkad (son of Manishtushu)	56 years (c. 2190–2154 BCE)
Shar-kali-sharri (son of Naram-Sin)	24 years (c. 2153–2129 BCE)

Then who was king? Who was not the king?

Irgigi, Nanum, Imi and Ilulu	3 years (four rivals who fought to be king during a three-year period; c. 2128–2125 BCE)
Dudu of Akkad	21 years (c. 2125–2104 BCE)
Shu-Durul (son of Duu)	15 years (c. 2104–2083 BCE)

Then Agade was defeated and the kingship was taken to Unug (Uruk).

FOURTH DYNASTY OF URUK

Ur-ningin	7 years (c. 2091?–2061? BCE)
Ur-gigir (son of Ur-ningin)	6 years
Kuda	6 years
Puzur-ili	5 years
Ur-Utu (or Lugal-melem; son of Ur-gigir)	6 years

Unug was defeated and the kingship was taken to the army of Gutium.

GUTIAN RULE

Inkišuš	6 years (c. 2147–2050 BCE)
Sarlagab (or Zarlagab)	6 years
Shulme (or Yarlagash)	6 years
Elulmeš (or Silulumeš or Silulu)	6 years
Inimabakeš (or Duga)	5 years
Igešauš (or Ilu-An)	6 years
Yarlagab	3 years
Ibate of Gutium	3 years
Yarla (or Yarlangab)	3 years
Kurum	1 year
Apilkin	3 years
La-erabum	2 years
Irarum	2 years
Ibranum	1 year
Hablum	2 years
Puzur-Suen (son of Hablum)	7 years
Yarlaganda	7 years
Si'um (or Si-u)	7 years
Tirigan	40 days

Then the army of Gutium was defeated and the kingship taken to Unug (Uruk).

FIFTH DYNASTY OF URUK

Utu-hengal	427 years / 26 years / 7 years (conflicting dates; c. 2055–2048 BCE)

THIRD DYNASTY OF UR

Ur-Namma (or Ur-Nammu)	18 years (c. 2047–2030 BCE)
Shulgi (son of Ur-Namma)	48 years (c. 2029–1982 BCE)
Amar-Suena (son of Shulgi)	9 years (c. 1981–1973 BCE)
Shu-Suen (son of Amar-Suena)	9 years (c. 1972–1964 BCE)
Ibbi-Suen (son of Shu-Suen)	24 years (c. 1963–1940 BCE)

Then Urim was defeated. The very foundation of Sumer was torn out. The kingship was taken to Isin.

DYNASTY OF ISIN

Ishbi-Erra	33 years (c. 1953–1920 BCE)
Shu-Ilishu (son of Ishbi-Erra)	20 years
Iddin-Dagan (son of Shu-Ilishu)	20 years
Ishme-Dagan (son of Iddin-Dagan)	20 years
Lipit-Eshtar (son of Ishme-Dagan or Iddin Dagan)	11 years
Ur-Ninurta (son of Ishkur)	28 years
Bur-Suen (son of Ur-Ninurta)	21 years
Lipit-Enlil (son of Bur-Suen)	5 years
Erra-imitti	8 years
Enlil-bani	24 years
Zambiya	3 years
Iter-pisha	4 years
Ur-du-kuga	4 years
Suen-magir	11 years
Damiq-ilishu (son of Suen-magir)	23 years

BABYLON

FIRST DYNASTY OF BABYLON (AMORITE, *C.* 1894–1595 BCE)

Sumu-abum	1894–1881 BCE
Sumulael	1880–1845 BCE
Sabium	1844–1831 BCE
Apil-Sin	1830–1813 BCE
Sin-muballit	1812–1793 BCE
Hammurapi	1792–1750 BCE
Samsu-iluna	1749–1712 BCE
Abi-eshuh	1711–1684 BCE
Ammi-ditana	1683–1647 BCE
Ammi-saduqa	1646–1626 BCE
Samsu-ditana	1625–1595 BCE

KASSITE DYNASTY (*C.* 1729–1155 BCE)

Gandash	1729–1704 BCE
Agum I	1703–1682 BCE
Kashtiliashu I	1681–1660 BCE
Abi-Rattash?	
Kashtiliash II?	
Urzigurumash	
Harba-Shipak?	
Shipta'ulzi?	
Burna-Buriash I	
Ulamburiash?	

Kashtiliash III?	
Agum III?	
Kara-indash	
Kadashman-Harbe I	
Kurigalzu I	
Kadashman-Enlil I	1374–1360 BCE
Burna-Buriash II	1359–1333 BCE
Kara-hardash	1333 BCE
Nazi-Bugash	1333 BCE
Kurigalzu II	1332–1308 BCE
Nazi-Maruttash	1307–1282 BCE
Kadashman-Turgu	1281–1264 BCE
Kadashman-Enlil II	1263–1255 BCE
Kudur-Enlil	1254–1246 BCE
Shagarakti-Shuriash	1245–1233 BCE
Kashtiliashu IV	1232–1225 BCE
Tukulti-Ninurta I of Assyria	1225 BCE
Enlin-nadin-shumi	1224 BCE
Kadashman-Harbe II	1223 BCE
Adad-shuma-iddina	1222–1217 BCE
Adad-shuma-usur	1216–1187 BCE
Meli-Shipak	1186–1172 BCE
Merodach-Baladan I	1171–1159 BCE
Zababa-shuma-iddina	1158 BCE
Enlil-nadin-ahi	1157–1155 BCE

DYNASTY OF ISIN (*C.*1157–1026 BCE)

Marduk-kabit-ahheshu	1157–1140 BCE

Itti-Marduk-balatu	1139–1132 BCE
Ninurta-nadin-shumi	1131–1126 BCE
Nebuchadrezzar I	1125–1104 BCE
Enlil-nadin-apli	1103–1100 BCE
Marduk-nadin-ahhe	1099–1082 BCE
Marduk-shapik-zeri	1081–1069 BCE
Adad-apla-iddina	1068–1047 BCE
Marduk-ahhe-eriba	1046 BCE
Marduk-zer-X?	1045–1034 BCE
Nabu-shumu-libur	1033–1026 BCE

SECOND DYNASTY OF THE SEALAND (*C.* 1025–1005 BCE)

Simbar-Shipak	1025–1008 BCE
Ea-mukin-zeri	1008 BCE
Kashshu-nadin-ahhe	1007–1005 BCE

DYNASTY OF BAZI (*C* .1004–985 BCE)

Eulmash-shakin-shumi	1004–988 BCE
Ninurta-kudurri-usur I	987–985 BCE
Shirikti-Shuqamuna	985 BCE

DYNASTY OF ELAM (*C.* 984–979 BCE)

Mar-biti-apla-usur	984–979 BCE

PERIOD OF MIXED DYNASTIES (*C.* 978–732 BCE)

Nabu-mukin-apli	978–943 BCE
Ninurta-kudurri-usur II	943 BCE
Mar-biti-ahhe-iddina	942–? BCE
Shamash-mudammiq	
Nabu-shuma-ukin I	
Nabu-apla-iddina	(33+ years)
Marduk-zakir-shumi I	(27+ years)
Marduk-balassu-iqbi	?–813 BCE
Baha-aha-iddina	812–? BCE
(interregnum)	
Ninruta-apl-X?	
Marduk-apla-usur	
Eriba-Marduk	(9+ years)
Nabu-shuma-ishkun	?–748 BCE (13+ years)
Nabonassar	747–734 BCE
Nabu-nadin-zeri	733–732 BCE
Nabu-shuma-ukin	732 BCE

NINTH DYNASTY OF BABYLON (*C.* 731–626 BCE)

Nabu-mukin-zeri	731–729 BCE
Tiglath-Pileser III of Assyria	728–727 BCE
Shalmaneser V of Assyria	726–722 BCE
Merodach-Baladan II	721–710 BCE
Sargon II of Assyria	709–705 BCE
Sennacherib of Assyria (first reign)	704–703 BCE
Marduk-zakir-shumi II	703 BCE

Merodach-Baladan II	703 BCE
Bel-ibni	702–700 BCE
Ashur-nadin-shumi	699–694 BCE
Nergal-ushezib	693 BCE
Mushezib-Marduk	692–689 BCE
Sennecherib of Assyria (second reign)	688–681 BCE
Esarhaddon of Assyria	680–669 BCE
Ashurbanipal of Assyria	668 BCE
Shamash-shuma-ukin	667–648 BCE
Kandalanu	647–627 BCE
(interregnum)	626 BCE

NEO-BABYLONIAN DYNASTY (*C.* 625–539 BCE)

Nabopolassar	625–605 BCE
Nebuchadrezzar II	604–562 BCE
Amel-Marduk	561–560 BCE
Neriglissar	559–556 BCE
Labashi-Marduk	556 BCE
Nabonius (co-ruler)	555–539 BCE
Belshazzar (co-ruler/regent)	555–539 BCE

ASSYRIA

DUZUR-ASHUR DYNASTY (2025–1809 BCE)

Puzur-Ashur I

Shalim-ahum	
Ilu-shuma	
Erishum I	1974–1935 BCE
Ikunum	1934–1921 BCE
Sargon I	1920–1881 BCE
Puzur-Ashur II	1880–1873 BCE
Naram-Sim	1872–1829 or 1819 BCE
Erishum II	1828 or 1818–1809 BCE

SHAMSHI-ADAD DYNASTY (1808–1736 BCE)

Shamshi-Adad I	1808–1776 BCE
Ishme-Dagan I	1775–1765 BCE
Mut-Ashkur	
Rimush	
Asinum	

NON-DYNASTIC USURPERS (1735–1701 BCE)

Puzur-Sin
Ashur-dugul
Ashur-apla-idi
Nasir-Sin
Sin-namir
Ipqi-Ishtar
Adad-salulu
Adasi

ADASIDE DYNASTY (1700–722 BCE)

Belu-bani	1700–1689 BCE
Libaya	1688–1672 BCE
Sharma-Adad I	1671–1660 BCE
Iptar-Sin	1659–1648 BCE
Bazaya	1647–1620 BCE
Lullaya	1619–1614 BCE
Shu-Ninua	1613–1600 BCE
Sharma-Adad II	1599–1597 BCE
Erishum III	1596–1584 BCE
Shamshi-Adad II	1583–1578 BCE
Ishme-Dagan II	1577–1562 BCE
Sharmshi-Adad III	1561–1546 BCE
Ashur-nirari I	1545–1520 BCE
Puzur-Ashur III	1519–1496 BCE
Enlil-nasir I	1495–1483 BCE
Nur-ili	1482–1471 BCE
Ashur-shaduni	1471 BCE
Ashur-rabi I	1470–1451 BCE
Ashur-nadin-ahhe I	1450–1431 BCE
Enlil-nasir II	1430–1425 BCE
Ashur-nirari II	1424–1418 BCE
Ashur-bel-nisheshu	1417–1409 BCE
Ashur-ra'im-nisheshu	1408–1401 BCE
Ashur-nadin-ahhe II	1400–1391 BCE
Eriba-Adid I	1390–1364 BCE

MIDDLE ASSYRIAN EMPIRE (1363–912 BCE)

Ashur-uballit I	1363–1328 BCE
Enlil-nirari	1327–1318 BCE
Arik-den-ili	1317–1306 BCE
Adad-nirari I	1305–1274 BCE
Shalmaneser I	1273–1244 BCE
Tukulti-Ninurta I	1243–1207 BCE
Ashur-nadin-apli	1206–1203 BCE
Ashur-nirari III	1202–1197 BCE
Enlil-kudurri-usur	1196–1192 BCE
Ninurta-apil-Ekur	1191–1179 BCE
Ashur-dan I	1178–1133 BCE
Ninurta-tukulti-Ashur	1132 BCE
Mutakkil-Nusku	1132 BCE
Ashur-resh-ishi I	1132–1115 BCE
Tiglath-Pileser I	1114–1076 BCE
Ashared-apil-Ekur	1075–1074 BCE
Ashur-bel-kala	1073–1056 BCE
Eriba-Adad II	1055–1054 BCE
Shamshi-Adad IV	1053–1050 BCE
Ashurnasirpal I	1049–1031 BCE
Shalmaneser II	1030–1019 BCE
Ashur-nirari IV	1018–1013 BCE
Ashur-rabi II	1012–972 BCE
Ashur-resh-ishi	971–967 BCE
Tiglath-Pileser II	966–935 BCE
Ashur-dan II	934–912 BCE

NEO-ASSYRIAN EMPIRE (911–609 BCE)

Adad-nirari II	911–891 BCE
Tukulti-Ninurta II	890–884 BCE
Ashurnasirpal II	883–859 BCE
Shalmaneser III	858–824 BCE
Shamshi-Adad V	823–811 BCE
Adad-nirari III	810–783 BCE
Shalmaneser IV	782–773 BCE
Ashur-dan III	772–755 BCE
Ashur-nirari V	754–745 BCE
Tiglath-Pileser III	744–727 BCE
Shalmaneser V	726–722 BCE

SARGONID DYNASTY (722–609 BCE)

Sargon II	721–705 BCE
Sennacherib	704–681 BCE
Esarhaddon	680–669 BCE
Ashurbanipal	668–627 BCE
Ashur-etil-ilani	626–623 BCE
Sin-shumu-lishir	623 BCE
Sin-shar-ishkun	622–612 BCE
Ashur-uballit II	611–609 BCE

(fall of Assyrian Empire 609 BCE*)*

PERSIA

ACHAEMENID DYNASTY (559–330 BCE)

Cyrus the Great	559–530 BCE
Cambyses	529–522 BCE
Smerdis	522 BCE
Darius I the Great	521–486 BCE
Xerxes I	485–465 BCE
Ataxerxes I (Longimanus)	464–424 BCE
Xerxes II	424 BCE
Sogdianus	424 BCE
Darius II (Nothus)	423–405 BCE
Ataxerxes II (Mnemon)	404–359 BCE
Ataxerxes III (Ochus)	358–338 BCE
Arses	337–336 BCE
Darius III (Codomannus)	335–330 BCE

(The Persian Empire ended when Alexander the Great invaded in 330 BCE)

PHOENICIA

ANCIENT TYRIAN LEADERS (MYTHOLOGICAL), (2050–1450 BCE)

Agenor (son of Posiedon or Belus)	*c.*2050–1450 BCE
Phoenix (son of Agenor, gave his name to Phoenicia)	?

LATE BRONZE AGE (1350–1335 BCE)

Abi-Milku	*c.*1350–1335 BCE

KINGS OF TYRE AND SIDON (990–785 BCE)

Abibaal	*c.*993–981 BCE
Hiram I	980–947 BCE
Baal-Eser I	946–930 BCE
Abdastartus	929–921 BCE
Astartus	920–901 BCE
Deleastartus	900–889 BCE
Astarymus	888–880 BCE
Phelles	879 BCE
Ithobaal I	878–847 BCE
Baal-Eser II	846–841 BCE
Mattan I	840–832 BCE
Pygmalion (Dido's brother, who formed Carthage in 814 BCE)	831–785 BCE

UNDER ASSYRIAN CONTROL (*C.* 750–660 BCE)

Ithobaal II	750–739 BCE
Hiram II	739–730 BCE
Mattan II	730–729 BCE
Elulaios	729–694 BCE
Abd Melqart	694–680 BCE
Baal I	680–660 BCE

AFTER ASSYRIAN CONTROL (*C.* 592–573 BCE)

Ithobaal III	591–573 BCE

(Overthrow of monarchy in favour of oligarchic government)

RESTORATION OF MONARCHY (551–532 BCE)

Hiram III	551–532 BCE

UNDER PERSIAN CONTROL (539–411 BCE)

Mattan IV	*c.*490–480 BCE
Boulomenus	*c.*450 BCE
Abdemon	*c.*420–411 BCE

UNDER CYPRIOT CONTROL (SALAMIS, 411–374 BCE)

Evagoras of Salamis	411–374 BCE

UNDER PERSIAN CONTROL (374–332 BCE)

Eugoras	*c.*340s
Azemilcus	*c.*340–332 BCE

(The Phoenician Empire ended when Alexander the Great invaded in 332 BCE)

ANCIENT EGYPTIAN PHARAOHS

There is dispute about the dates and position of pharaohs within dynasties due to several historical sources being incomplete or inconsistent. This list aims to provide an overview of the ancient Egyptian dynasties, but is not exhaustive and dates are approximate. There may also be differences in name spellings between different sources. Also please note that the throne name is given first, followed by the personal name – more commonly they are known by the latter.

ANCIENT EGYPTIAN DEITIES

Ancient Egyptian gods and goddesses were worshipped as deities. They were responsible for maat (divine order or stability), and different deities represented different natural forces, such as Ra the Sun God. After the Egyptian state was first founded in around 3100 BCE, pharaohs claimed to be divine representatives of these gods and were thought to be successors of the gods.

While there are many conflicting Egyptian myths, some of the significant gods and goddesses and their significant responsibilities are listed here.

Amun/Amen/Amen-Ra	Creation
Atem/Tem	Creation, the sun

Ra	The sun
Isis	The afterlife, fertility, magic
Osiris	Death and resurrection, agriculture
Hathor	The sky, the sun, motherhood
Horus	Kingship, the sky
Set	Storms, violence, deserts
Maat	Truth and justice, she personifies *maat*
Anubis	The dead, the underworld

PREDYNASTIC AND EARLY DYNASTIC PERIODS (*c.* 3000–2686 BCE)

First Dynasty (*c.* 3150–2890 BCE)

The first dynasty begins at the unification of Upper and Lower Egypt.

Narmer (Menes/M'na?)	*c*. 3150 BCE
Aha (Teti)	*c*. 3125 BCE
Djer (Itej)	54 years
Djet (Ita)	10 years
Merneith (possibly the first female Egyptian pharaoh)	*c*. 2950 BCE
Khasti (Den)	42 years
Merybiap (Adjib)	10 years
Semerkhet (Iry)	8.5 years
Qa'a (Qebeh)	34 years
Sneferka	*c*. 2900 BCE
Horus-Ba (Horus Bird)	*c*. 2900 BCE

Second Dynasty (*c.* 2890–2686 BCE)

Little is known about the second dynasty of Egypt.

Hetepsekhemwy (Nebtyhotep)	15 years
Nebra	14 years
Nynetjer (Banetjer)	43–45 years
Ba	unknown
Weneg-Nebty	c. 2740 BCE
Wadjenes (Wadj-sen)	c. 2740 BCE
Nubnefer	unknown
Senedj	c. 47 years
Peribsen (Seth-Peribsen)	unknown
Sekhemib (Sekhemib-Perenmaat)	c. 2720 BCE
Neferkara I	25 years
Neferkasokkar	8 years
Horus Sa	unknown
Hudejefa (real name missing)	11 years
Khasekhemwy (Bebty)	18 years

OLD KINGDOM (*c.* 2686–2181 BCE)

Third Dynasty (*c.* 2686–2613 BCE)

The third dynasty was the first dynasty of the Old Kingdom. Its capital was at Memphis.

Djoser (Netjerikhet)	c. 2650 BCE
Sekhemkhet (Djoser-Teti)	2649–2643 BCE
Nebka? (Sanakht)	c. 2650 BCE
Qahedjet (Huni?)	unknown
Khaba (Huni?)	2643–2637 BCE
Huni	2637–2613 BCE

Fourth Dynasty (*c.* 2613–2498 BCE)

The fourth dynasty is sometimes known as the 'golden age' of Egypt's Old Kingdom.

Snefru (Nebmaat)	2613–2589 BCE
Khufu, or Cheops (Medjedu)	2589–2566 BCE
Djedefre (Kheper)	2566–2558 BCE
Khafre (Userib)	2558–2532 BCE
Menkaure (Kakhet)	2532–2503 BCE
Shepseskaf (Shepeskhet)	2503–2498 BCE

Fifth Dynasty (*c.* 2498–2345 BCE)

There is some doubt over the succession of pharaohs in the fifth dynasty, especially Shepseskare.

Userkaf	2496/8–2491 BCE
Sahure	2490–2477 BCE
Neferirkare-Kakai	2477–2467 BCE
Neferefre (Izi)	2460–2458 BCE
Shepseskare (Netjeruser)	few months between 2458 and 2445 BCE
Niuserre (Ini)	2445–2422 BCE
Menkauhor (Kaiu)	2422–2414 BCE
Djedkare (Isesi)	2414–2375 BCE
Unis (Wenis)	2375–2345 BCE

Sixth Dynasty (*c.* 2345–2181 BCE)

Teti	2345–2333 BCE
Userkare	2333–2332 BCE
Meryre (Pepi I)	2332–2283 BCE

Merenre I (Nemtyemsaf I)	2283–2278 BCE
Neferkare (Pepi II)	2278–2183 BCE
Merenre II (Nemtyemsaf II)	2183 or 2184 BCE
Netjerkare (Siptah I) or Nitocris	2182–2179 BCE

FIRST INTERMEDIATE PERIOD (*c.* 2181–2040 BCE)

Seventh and Eighth Dynasties (*c.* 2181–2160 BCE)

There is little evidence on this period in ancient Egyptian history, which is why many of the periods of rule are unknown.

Menkare	*c.* 2181 BCE
Neferkare II	unknown
Neferkare III (Neby)	unknown
Djedkare (Shemai)	unknown
Neferkare IV (Khendu)	unknown
Merenhor	unknown
Sneferka (Neferkamin I)	unknown
Nikare	unknown
Neferkare V (Tereru)	unknown
Neferkahor	unknown
Neferkare VI (Peiseneb)	unknown to 2171 BCE
Neferkamin (Anu)	*c.* 2170 BCE
Qakare (Ibi)	2175–2171 BCE
Neferkaure	2167–2163 BCE
Neferkauhor (Khuwihapi)	2163–2161 BCE
Neferiirkkare (Pepi)	2161–2160 BCE

Ninth Dynasty (*c.* 2160–2130 BCE)

There is little evidence on this period in ancient Egyptian history which is why many of the periods of rule are unknown.

Maryibre (Khety I)	2160 BCE to unknown
Name unknown	unknown
Naferkare VII	unknown
Seneh (Setut)	unknown

The following pharaohs and their dates of rule are unknown or widely unconfirmed.

Tenth Dynasty (*c.* 2130–2040 BCE)

Rulers in the Tenth dynasty were based in Lower Egypt.

Meryhathor	2130 BCE to unknown
Neferkare VIII	2130–2040 BCE
Wahkare (Khety III)	unknown
Merykare	unknown to 2040 BCE
Name unknown	unknown

Eleventh Dynasty (*c.* 2134–1991 BCE)

Rulers in the eleventh dynasty were based in Upper Egypt.

Intef the Elder	unknown
Tepia (Mentuhotep I)	unknown to 2133 BCE
Sehertawy (Intef I)	2133–2117 BCE
Wahankh (Intef II)	2117–2068 BCE
Nakhtnebtepefer (Intef III)	2068–2060/40 BCE

MIDDLE KINGDOM (c. 2040–1802 BCE)

Eleventh Dynasty Continued (c. 2134–1991 BCE)

This period is usually known as the beginning of the Middle Kingdom.

Nebhepetre (Mentuhotep II) 2060–2040 BCE as king of Upper Egypt, 2040–2009 BCE as King of Upper and Lower Egypt
Sankhkare (Mentuhotep III) 2009–1997 BCE
Nebtawyre (Mentuhotep IV) 1997–1991 BCE

Twelfth Dynasty (c. 1991–1802 BCE)

The twelfth dynasty was one of the most stable prior to the New Kingdom, and is often thought to be the peak of the Middle Kingdom.

Sehetepibre (Amenemhat I)	1991–1962 BCE
Kheperkare (Senusret I / Sesostris I)	1971–1926 BCE
Nubkaure (Amenemhat II)	1929–1895 BCE
Khakheperre (Senusret II / Sesostris II)	1898–1878 BCE
Khakaure (Senusret III / Sesostris III)	1878–1839 BCE
Nimaatre (Amenemhat III)	1860–1815 BCE
Maakherure (Amenemhat IV)	1815–1807 BCE
Sobekkare (Sobekneferu/Nefrusobek)	1807–1802 BCE

SECOND INTERMEDIATE PERIOD (c. 1802–1550 BCE)

Thirteenth Dynasty (c. 1802–c. 1649 BCE)

There is some ambiguity on the periods of rule of the thirteenth dynasty, but it is marked by a period of several short rules. This dynasty is often combined with the eleventh, twelfth and fourteenth dynasties under the Middle Kingdom.

Sekhemre Khutawy (Sobekhotep I)	1802–1800 BCE
Mehibtawy Sekhemkare (Amenemhat Sonbef)	1800–1796 BCE
Nerikare (Sobek)	1796 BCE
Sekhemkare (Amenemhat V)	1796–1793 BCE
Ameny Qemau	1795–1792 BCE
Hotepibre (Qemau Siharnedjheritef)	1792–1790 BCE
Lufni	1790–1788 BCE
Seankhibre (Amenemhat VI)	1788–1785 BCE
Semenkare (Nebnuni)	1785–1783 BCE
Sehetepibre (Sewesekhtawy)	1783–1781 BCE
Sewadijkare I	1781 BCE
Nedjemibre (Amenemhat V)	1780 BCE
Khaankhre (Sobekhotep)	1780–1777 BCE
Renseneb	1777 BCE
Awybre (Hor)	1777–1775 BCE
Sekhemrekhutawy Khabaw	1775–1772 BCE
Djedkheperew	1772–1770 BCE
Sebkay	unknown
Sedjefakare (Kay Amenemhat)	1769–1766 BCE
Khutawyre (Wegaf)	c. 1767 BCE
Userkare (Khendjer)	c. 1765 BCE
Smenkhkare (Imyremeshaw)	started in 1759 BCE
Sehetepkare (Intef IV)	c. 10 years
Meribre (Seth)	ended in 1749 BCE
Sekhemresewadjtawy (Sobekhotep III)	1755–1751 BCE
Khasekhemre (Neferhotep I)	1751–1740 BCE

Menwadjre (Sihathor)	1739 BCE
Khaneferre (Sobekhotep IV)	1740–1730 BCE
Merhotepre (Sobekhotep V)	1730 BCE
Knahotepre (Sobekhotep VI)	c. 1725 BCE
Wahibre (Ibiau)	1725–1714 BCE
Merneferre (Ay I)	1714–1691 BCE
Merhotepre (Ini)	1691–1689 BCE
Sankhenre (Sewadjtu)	1675–1672 BCE
Mersekhemre (Ined)	1672–1669 BCE
Sewadjkare II (Hori)	c. 5 years
Merkawre (Sobekhotep VII)	1664–1663 BCE
Seven kings (names unknown)	1663–? BCE

Note: the remaining pharaohs of the thirteenth dynasty are not listed here as they are either unknown or there is a lot of ambiguity about when they ruled.

Fourteenth Dynasty (*c.* 1805/1710–1650 BCE)

Rulers in the fourteenth dynasty were based at Avaris, the capital of this dynasty.

Sekhaenre (Yakbim)	1805–1780 BCE
Nubwoserre (Ya'ammu)	1780–1770 BCE
Khawoserre (Qareh)	1770–1745 BCE
Aahotepre ('Ammu)	1760–1745 BCE
Maaibre (Sheshi)	1745–1705 BCE
Aasehre (Nehesy)	c. 1705 BCE
Khakherewre	unknown
Nebefawre	c. 1704 BCE
Sehebre	1704–1699 BCE

Merdjefare	c. 1699 BCE

Note: the remaining pharaohs of the fourteenth dynasty are not listed here as they are either unknown or there is a lot of ambiguity about when they ruled.

Fifteenth Dynasty (*c.* 1650–1544 BCE)

The fifteenth dynasty was founded by Salitas and covered a large part of the Nile region.

Salitas	c. 1650 BCE
Semqen	1649 BCE to unknown
'Aper-'Anat	unknown
Sakir-Har	unknown
Seuserenre (Khyan)	c. 30 to 35 years
Nebkhepeshre (Apepi)	1590 BCE?
Nakhtyre (Khamudi)	1555–1544 BCE

Sixteenth Dynasty (*c.* 1650–1580 BCE)

Rulers in the sixteenth dynasty were based at Thebes, the capital of this dynasty. The name and date of rule of the first pharaoh is unknown.

Sekhemresementawy (Djehuti)	3 years
Sekhemresemeusertawy (Sobekhotep VIII)	16 years
Sekhemresankhtawy (Neferhotep III)	1 year
Seankhenre (Mentuhotepi)	less than a year
Sewadjenre (Nebiryraw)	26 years
Neferkare (?) (Nebiryraw II)	c. 1600 BCE
Semenre	c. 1600 BCE

Seuserenre (Bebiankh)	12 years
Djedhotepre (Dedumose I)	*c*. 1588–1582 BCE
Djedneferre (Dedumose II)	*c*. 1588–1582 BCE
Djedankhre (Montensaf)	*c*. 1590 BCE
Merankhre (Mentuhotep VI)	*c*. 1585 BCE
Seneferibre (Senusret IV)	unknown
Sekhemre (Shedwast)	unknown

Seventeenth Dynasty (*c*. 1650–1550 BCE)

Rulers in the seventeenth dynasty ruled Upper Egypt.

Sekhemrewahkhaw (Rahotep)	*c*. 1620 BCE
Sekhemre Wadjkhaw (Sobekemsaf I)	*c*. 7 years
Sekhemre Shedtawy (Sobekemsaf II)	unknown to *c*. 1573 BCE
Sekhemre-Wepmaat (Intef V)	*c*. 1573–1571 BCE
Nubkheperre (Intef VI)	*c*. 1571–1565 BCE
Sekhemre-Heruhirmaat (Intef VII)	late 1560s BCE
Senakhtenre (Ahmose)	*c*. 1558 BCE
Seqenenre (Tao I)	1558–1554 BCE
Wadkheperre (Kamose)	1554–1549 BCE

NEW KINGDOM (*c*. 1550–1077 BCE)

Eighteenth Dynasty (*c*. 1550–1292 BCE)

The first dynasty of Egypt's New Kingdom marked the beginning of ancient Egypt's highest power and expansion.

Nebpehtire (Ahmose I)	*c*. 1550–1525 BCE
Djeserkare (Amenhotep I)	1541–1520 BCE

Aakheperkare (Thutmose I)	1520–1492 BCE
Aakheperenre (Thutmose II)	1492–1479 BCE
Maatkare (Hatshepsut)	1479–1458 BCE
Menkheperre (Thutmose III)	1458–1425 BCE
Aakheperrure (Amenhotep II)	1425–1400 BCE
Menkheperure (Thutmose IV)	1400–1390 BCE
Nebmaatre 'the Magnificent' (Amehotep III)	1390–1352 BCE
Neferkheperure Waenre (Amenhotep IV)	1352–1336 BCE
Ankhkheperure (Smenkhkare)	1335–1334 BCE
Ankhkheperure mery Neferkheperure (Neferneferuaten III)	1334–1332 BCE
Nebkheperure (Tutankhamun)	1332–1324 BCE
Kheperkheperure (Aya II)	1324–1320 BCE
Djeserkheperure Setpenre (Haremheb)	1320–1292 BCE

Nineteenth Dynasty (*c.* 1550–1292 BCE)

The nineteenth dynasty is also known as the Ramessid dynasty as it includes Ramesses II, one of the most famous and influential Egyptian pharaohs.

Menpehtire (Ramesses I)	1292–1290 BCE
Menmaatre (Seti I)	1290–1279 BCE
Usermaatre Setpenre 'the Great', 'Ozymandias' (Ramesses II)	1279–1213 BCE
Banenre (Merneptah)	1213–1203 BCE
Menmire Setpenre (Amenmesse)	1203–1200 BCE
Userkheperure (Seti II)	1203–1197 BCE
Sekhaenre (Merenptah Siptah)	1197–1191 BCE
Satre Merenamun (Tawosret)	1191–1190 BCE

Twentieth Dynasty (*c.* 1190–1077 BCE)

This, the third dynasty of the New Kingdom, is generally thought to mark the start of the decline of ancient Egypt.

Userkhaure (Setnakht)	1190–1186 BCE
Usermaatre Meryamun (Ramesses III)	1186–1155 BCE
Heqamaatre Setpenamun (Ramesses IV)	1155–1149 BCE
Heqamaatre Setpenamun (Ramesses IV)	1155–1149 BCE
Usermaatre Sekheperenre (Ramesses V)	1149–1145 BCE
Nebmaatre Meryamun (Ramesses VI)	1145–1137 BCE
Usermaatre Setpenre Meryamun (Ramesses VII)	1137–1130 BCE
Usermaatre Akhenamun (Ramesses VIII)	1130–1129 BCE
Neferkare Setpenre (Ramesses IX)	1128–1111 BCE
Khepermaatre Setpenptah (Ramesses X)	1111–1107 BCE
Menmaatre Setpenptah (Ramesses XI)	1107–1077 BCE

Twenty-first Dynasty (*c.* 1077–943 BCE)

Rulers in the twenty-first dynasty were based at Tanis and mainly governed Lower Egypt.

Hedjkheperre-Setpenre (Nesbanadjed I)	1077–1051 BCE
Neferkare (Amenemnisu)	1051–1047 BCE
Aakkheperre (Pasebakhenniut I)	1047–1001 BCE
Usermaatre (Amenemope)	1001–992 BCE
Aakheperre Setepenre (Osorkon the Elder)	992–986 BCE
Netjerikheperre-Setpenamun (Siamun)	986–967 BCE
Titkheperure (Pasebakhenniut II)	967–943 BCE

Twenty-second Dynasty (*c.* 943–728 BCE)

Sometimes called the Bubastite dynasty. Its pharaohs came from Libya.

Hedjkheneperre Setpenre (Sheshonq I)	943–922 BCE
Sekhemkheperre Setepenre (Osorkon I)	922–887 BCE
Heqakheperre Setepenre (Sheshonq II)	887–885 BCE
Tutkheperre (Sheshonq Llb)	c. the 880s BCE
Hedjkheperre Setepenre (Takelot I Meriamun)	885–872 BCE
Usermaatre Setpenre (Sheshonq III)	837–798 BCE
Hedjkheperre Setepenre (Sheshonq IV)	798–785 BCE
Usermaatre Setpenre (Pami Meriamun)	785–778 BCE
Aakheperre (Sheshonq V)	778–740 BCE
Usermaatre (Osorkon IV)	740–720 BCE

Twenty-third and Twenty-fourth Dynasties (*c.* 837–720 BCE)

These dynasties were led mainly by Libyans and mainly ruled Upper Egypt.

Hedjkheperre Setpenre (Takelot II)	837–813 BCE
Usermaatre Setpenamun (Meriamun Pedubaste I)	826–801 BCE
Usermaatre Meryamun (Sheshonq VI)	801–795 BCE
Usermaatre Setpenamun (Osorkon III)	795–767 BCE
Usermaatre-Setpenamun (Takelot III)	773–765 BCE
Usermaatre-Setpenamun (Meriamun Rudamun)	765–762 BCE
Shepsesre (Tefnakhte)	732–725 BCE
Wahkare (Bakenrenef)	725–720 BCE

Twenty-fifth Dynasty (*c.* 744–656 BCE)

Also known as the Kushite period, the twenty-fifth dynasty follows the Nubian invasions.

Piankhy (Piye)	744–714 BCE
Djedkaure (Shebitkku)	714–705 BCE
Neferkare (Shabaka)	705–690 BCE
Khuinefertemre (Taharqa)	690–664 BCE

LATE PERIOD (*c.* 664–332 BCE)

Twenty-sixth Dynasty (*c.* 664 – 525 BCE)

Also known as the Saite period, the twenty-sixth dynasty was the last native period before the Persian invasion in 525 BCE.

Wahibre (Psamtik I)	664–610 BCE
Wehemibre (Necho II)	610–595 BCE
Neferibre (Psamtik II)	595–589 BCE
Haaibre (Apreis)	589–570 BCE
Khemibre (Amasis II)	570–526 BCE
Ankhkaenre (Psamtik III)	526–525 BCE

Twenty-seventh Dynasty (*c.* 525–404 BCE)

The twenty-seventh dynasty is also known as the First Egyptian Satrapy and was ruled by the Persian Achaemenids.

Mesutre (Cambyses II)	525–1 July 522 BCE
Seteture (Darius I)	522–November 486 BCE
Kheshayarusha (Xerxes I)	November 486–December 465 BCE
Artabanus of Persia	465–464 BCE
Arutakhshashas (Artaxerxes I)	464–424 BCE
Ochus (Darius II)	July 423–March 404 BCE

Twenty-eighth Dynasty (*c.* 404–398 BCE)

The twenty-eighth dynasty consisted of a single pharaoh.

Amunirdisu (Amyrtaeus)	404–398 BCE

Twenty-ninth Dynasty (*c.* 398–380 BCE)

The twenty-ninth dynasty was founded following the overthrow of Amyrtaeus.

Baenre Merynatjeru (Nepherites I)	398–393 BCE
Khnemmaatre Setepenkhnemu (Hakor)	c. 392–391 BCE
Userre Setepenptah (Psammuthis)	c. 391 BCE
Khnemmaatre Setepenkhnemu (Hakor)	c. 390–379 BCE
Nepherites II	c. 379 BCE

Thirtieth Dynasty (*c.*379–340 BCE)

The thirtieth dynasty is thought to be the final native dynasty of ancient Egypt.

Kheperkare (Nectanebo I)	c. 379–361 BCE
Irimaatenre (Teos)	c. 361–359 BCE
Snedjemibre Setepenanhur (Nectanebo II)	c. 359–340 BCE

Thirty-first Dynasty (*c.* 340–332 BCE)

The thirty-first dynasty is also known as the Second Egyptian Satrapy and was ruled by the Persian Achaemenids.

Ochus (Artaxerxes III)	c. 340–338 BCE
Arses (Artaxerxes IV)	338–336 BCE
Darius III	336–332 BCE

MACEDONIAN/ARGEAD DYNASTY (*c.* 332–309 BCE)

Alexander the Great conquered Persia and Egypt in 332 BCE.

Setpenre Meryamun (Alexander III of Macedon 'the Great')	332–323 BCE
Setpenre Meryamun (Philip Arrhidaeus)	323–317 BCE
Khaibre Setepenamun (Alexander IV)	317–309 BCE

PTOLEMAIC DYNASTY (*c.* 305–30 BCE)

The Ptolemaic dynasty in Egypt was the last dynasty of ancient Egypt before it became a province of Rome.

Ptolemy I Soter	305–282 BCE
Ptolemy II Philadelphos	284–246 BCE
Arsinoe II	*c.* 277–270 BCE
Ptolemy III Euergetes	246–222 BCE
Berenice II	244/243–222 BCE
Ptolemy IV Philopater	222–204 BCE
Arsinoe III	220–204 BCE
Ptolemy V Epiphanes	204–180 BCE
Cleopatra I	193–176 BCE
Ptolemy VI Philometor	180–164, 163–145 BCE
Cleopatra II	175–164 BCE, 163–127 BCE and 124–116 BCE
Ptolemy VIII Physcon	171–163 BCE, 144–131 BCE and 127–116 BCE
Ptolemy VII Neos Philopator	145–144 BCE

Cleopatra III	142–131 BCE, 127–107 BCE
Ptolemy Memphites	113 BCE
Ptolemy IX Soter	116–110 BCE
Cleopatra IV	116–115 BCE
Ptolemy X Alexander	110–109 BCE
Berenice III	81–80 BCE
Ptolemy XI Alexander	80 BCE
Ptolemy XII Auletes	80–58 BCE, 55–51 BCE
Cleopatra V Tryphaena	79–68 BCE
Cleopatra VI	58–57 BCE
Berenice IV	58–55 BCE
Cleopatra VII	52–30 BCE
Ptolemy XIII Theos Philopator	51–47 BCE
Arsinoe IV	48–47 BCE
Ptolemy XIV Philopator	47–44 BCE
Ptolemy XV Caesar	44–30 BCE

In 30 BCE, Egypt became a province of the Roman Empire.

ANCIENT GREEK MONARCHS

This list is not exhaustive and dates are approximate. Where dates of rule overlap, emperors either ruled jointly or ruled in opposition to one another. There may also be differences in name spellings between different sources.

Because of the fragmented nature of Greece prior to its unification by Philip II of Macedon, this list includes mythological and existing rulers of Thebes, Athens and Sparta as some of the leading ancient Greek city-states. These different city-states had some common belief in the mythological gods and goddesses of ancient Greece, although their accounts may differ.

KINGS OF THEBES (c. 753–509 BCE)

These rulers are mythological. There is much diversity over who the kings actually were, and the dates they ruled.

Calydnus (son of Uranus)
Ogyges (son of Poseidon, thought to be king of Boeotia or Attica)
Cadmus (Greek mythological hero known as the founder of Thebes, known as Cadmeia until the reign of Amphion and Zethus)
Pentheus (son of Echion, one of the mythological Spartoi, and Agave, daughter of Cadmus)

Polydorus (son of Cadmus and Harmonia, goddess of harmony)
Nycteus (like his brother Lycus, thought to be the son of a Spartoi and a nymph, or a son of Poseidon)
Lycus (brother of Nyceteus)
Labdacus (grandson of Cadmus)
Lycus (second reign as regent for Laius)
Amphion and Zethus (joint rulers and twin sons of Zeus, constructed the city walls of Thebes)
Laius (son of Labdacus, married to Jocasta)
Oedipus (son of Laius, killed his father and married his mother, Jocasta)
Creon (regent after the death of Laius)
Eteocles and Polynices (brothers/sons of Oedipus; killed each other in battle)
Creon (regent for Laodamas)
Laodamas (son of Eteocles)
Thersander (son of Polynices)
Peneleos (regent for Tisamenus)
Tisamenus (son of Thersander)
Autesion (son of Tisamenes)
Damasichthon (son of Peneleos)
Ptolemy (son of Damasichton, 12 century BCE)
Xanthos (son of Ptolemy)

KINGS OF ATHENS

Early legendary kings who ruled before the mythological flood caused by Zeus, which only Deucalion (son of Prometheus) and a few others survived (date unknown).

Periphas (king of Attica, turned into an eagle by Zeus)
Ogyges (son of Poseidon, thought to be king of either Boeotia or Attica)
Actaeus (king of Attica, father-in-law to Cecrops I)

Erechtheid Dynasty (1556–1127 BCE)

Cecrops I (founder and first king of Athens; half-man, half-serpent who married Actaeus' daughter)	1556–1506 BCE
Cranaus	1506–1497 BCE
Amphictyon (son of Deucalion)	1497–1487 BCE
Erichthonius (adopted by Athena)	1487–1437 BCE
Pandion I (son of Erichthonius)	1437–1397 BCE
Erechtheus (son of Pandion I)	1397–1347 BCE
Cecrops II (son of Erechtheus)	1347–1307 BCE
Pandion II (son of Cecrops II)	1307–1282 BCE
Aegeus (adopted by Pandion II, gave his name to the Aegean Sea)	1282–1234 BCE
Theseus (son of Aegeus, killed the minotaur)	1234–1205 BCE
Menestheus (made king by Castor and Pollux when Theseus was in the underworld)	1205–1183 BCE
Demophon (son of Theseus)	1183–1150 BCE
Oxyntes (son of Demophon)	1150–1136 BCE
Apheidas (son of Oxyntes)	1136–1135 BCE
Thymoetes (son of Oxyntes)	1135–1127 BCE

Melanthid Dynasty (1126–1068 BCE)

Melanthus (king of Messenia, fled to Athens when expelled)	1126–1089 BCE
Codrus (last of the semi-mythological Athenian kings)	1089–1068 BCE

LIFE ARCHONS OF ATHENS (1068–753 BCE)

These rulers held public office up until their deaths.

Medon	1068–1048 BCE	Pherecles	864–845 BCE
Acastus	1048–1012 BCE	Ariphon	845–825 BCE
Archippus	1012–993 BCE	Thespieus	824–797 BCE
Thersippus	993–952 BCE	Agamestor	796–778 BCE
Phorbas	952–922 BCE	Aeschylus	778–755 BCE
Megacles	922–892 BCE	Alcmaeon	755–753 BCE
Diognetus	892–864 BCE		

From this point, archons led for a period of 10 years up to 683 BCE, then a period of one year up to 485 CE. Selected important leaders – including archons and tyrants – in this later period are as follows:

SELECTED LATER LEADERS OF ATHENS

Peisistratos 'the Tyrant of Athens'	561, 559–556, 546–527 BCE
Cleisthenes (archon)	525–524 BCE
Themistocles (archon)	493–492 BCE
Pericles	*c.* 461–429 BCE

KINGS OF SPARTA

These rulers are mythological and are thought to be descendants of the ancient tribe of Leleges. There is much diversity over who the kings actually were, and the dates they ruled.

Lelex (son of Poseidon or Helios, ruled Laconia)	*c*. 1600 BCE
Myles (son of Lelex, ruled Laconia)	*c*. 1575 BCE
Eurotas (son of Myles, father of Sparta)	*c*. 1550 BCE

From the Lelegids, rule passed to the Lacedaemonids when Lacedaemon married Sparta.

Lacedaemon (son of Zeus, husband of Sparta)
Amyklas (son of Lacedaemon)
Argalus (son of Amyklas)
Kynortas (son of Amyklas)
Perieres (son of Kynortas)
Oibalos (son of Kynortas)
Tyndareos (first reign; son of Oibalos, father of Helen of Troy)
Hippocoon (son of Oibalos)
Tyndareos (second reign; son of Oibaos, father of Helen of Troy)

From the Lacedaemons, rule passed to the Atreids when Menelaus married Helen of Troy.

Menelaus (son of Atreus, king of Mycenae, and husband of Helen)	*c*. 1250 BCE
Orestes (son of Agamemnon, Menelaus' brother)	*c*. 1150 BCE
Tisamenos (son of Orestes)	
Dion	*c*. 1100 BCE

From the Atreids, rule passed to the Heraclids following war.

Aristodemos (son of Aristomachus, great-great-grandson of Heracles)

Theras (served as regent for Aristodemes' sons, Eurysthenes and Procles)	
Eurysthenes	*c*. 930 BCE

From the Heraclids, rule passed to the Agiads, founded by Agis I. Only major kings during this period are listed here.

Agis I (conceivably the first historical Spartan king)	*c*. 930–900 BCE
Alcamenes	*c*. 740–700 BCE, during First Messenian War
Cleomenes I (important leader in the Greek resistance against the Persians)	524 – 490 BCE
Leonidas I (died while leading the Greeks – the 300 Spartans – against the Persians in the Battle of Thermopylae, 480 BCE)	490–480 BCE
Cleomenes III (exiled following the Battle of Sellasia)	*c*. 235–222 BCE

KINGS OF MACEDON

Argead Dynasty (808–309 BCE)

Karanos	*c*. 808–778 BCE	Alcetas I	*c*. 576–547 BCE
Koinos	*c*. 778–750 BCE	Amyntas I	*c*. 547–498 BCE
Tyrimmas	*c*. 750–700 BCE	Alexander I	*c*. 498–454 BCE
Perdiccas I	*c*. 700–678 BCE	Alcetas II	*c*. 454–448 BCE
Argaeus I	*c*. 678–640 BCE	Perdiccas II	*c*. 448–413 BCE
Philip I	*c*. 640–602 BCE	Archelaus I	*c*. 413–339 BCE
Aeropus I	*c*. 602–576 BCE	Craterus	*c*. 399 BCE

Orestes	*c.* 399–396 BCE
Aeropus II	*c.* 399–394/93 BCE
Archelaus II	*c.* 394–393 BCE
Amyntas II	*c.* 393 BCE
Pausanias	*c.* 393 BCE
Amyntas III	*c.* 393 BCE; first reign
Argeus II	*c.* 393–392 BCE
Amyntas III	*c.* 392–370 BCE
Alexander II	*c.* 370–368 BCE
Perdiccas III	*c.* 368–359 BCE
Amyntas IV	*c.* 359 BCE
Philip II	*c.* 359–336 BCE
Alexander III 'the Great' (also King of Persia and Pharaoh of Egypt by end of reign)	*c.* 336–323 BCE
Philip III	*c.* 323–317 BCE
Alexander IV	*c.* 323/317–309 BCE

Note: the Corinthian League or Hellenic League was created by Philip II and was the first time that the divided Greek city-states were unified under a single government.

Post-Argead Dynasty (309–168 BCE, 149–148 BCE)

Cassander	*c.* 305–297 BCE
Philip IV	*c.* 297 BCE
Antipater II	*c.* 297–294 BCE
Alexpander V	*c.* 297–294 BCE

Antigonid, Alkimachid and Aeacid Dynasties (294–281 BCE)

Demetrius	*c.* 294–288 BCE
Lysimachus	*c.* 288–281 BCE
Pyrrhus	*c.* 288–285 BCE; first reign

Ptolemaic Dynasty (281–279 BCE)

Ptolemy Ceraunus (son of Ptolemy I of Egypt)	*c.* 281–279 BCE
Meleager	279 BCE

Antipatrid, Antigonid, Aeacid Dynasties, Restored (279–167 BCE)

Antipater	c. 279 BCE
Sosthenes	c. 279–277 BCE
Antigonus II	c. 277–274 BCE; first reign
Pyrrhus	c. 274–272 BCE; second reign
Antigonus II	c. 272–239 BCE; second reign
Demetrius II	c. 239–229 BCE
Antigonus III	c. 229–221 BCE
Philip V	c. 221–179 BCE
Perseus (deposed by Romans)	c. 179–168 BCE
Revolt by Philip VI (Andriskos)	c. 149–148 BCE

SELEUCID DYNASTY (*c.* 320 BCE–63 CE)

Seleucus I Nicator	c. 320–315, 312–305, 305–281 BCE
Antiochus I Soter	c. 291, 281–261 BCE
Antiochus II Theos	c. 261–246 BCE
Seleucus II Callinicus	c. 246–225 BCE
Seleucus III Ceraunus	c. 225–223 BCE
Antiochus III 'the Great'	c. 223–187 BCE
Seleucus IV Philopator	c. 187–175 BCE
Antiochus (son of Seleucus IV)	c. 175–170 BCE
Antiochus IV Epiphanes	c. 175–163 BCE
Antiochus V Eupater	c. 163–161 BCE
Demetrius I Soter	c. 161–150 BCE
Alexander I Balas	c. 150–145 BCE
Demetrius II Nicator	c. 145–138 BCE; first reign
Antiochus VI Dionysus	c. 145–140 BCE

Diodotus Tryphon	*c*. 140–138 BCE
Antiochus VII Sidetes	*c*. 138–129 BCE
Demetrius II Nicator	*c*. 129–126 BCE; second reign
Alexander II Zabinas	*c*. 129–123 BCE
Cleopatra Thea	*c*. 126–121 BCE
Seleucus V Philometor	*c*. 126/125 BCE
Antiochus VIII Grypus	*c*. 125–96 BCE
Antiochus IX Cyzicenus	*c*. 114–96 BCE
Seleucus VI Epiphanes	*c*. 96–95 BCE
Antiochus X Eusebes	*c*. 95–92/83 BCE
Demetrius III Eucaerus	*c*. 95–87 BCE
Antiochus XI Epiphanes	*c*. 95–92 BCE
Philip I Philadelphus	*c*. 95–84/83 BCE
Antiochus XII Dionysus	*c*. 87–84 BCE
Seleucus VII	*c*. 83–69 BCE
Antiochus XIII Asiaticus	*c*. 69–64 BCE
Philip II Philoromaeus	*c*. 65–63 BCE

PTOLEMAIC DYNASTY (305–30 BCE)

The Ptolemaic dynasty was a Greek-Macedonian dynasty that ruled Egypt before it became a province of Rome. See pages 395–96 for the Ptolemaic leaders. In 27 BCE, Caesar Augustus annexed Greece and it became integrated into the Roman Empire.

ANCIENT ROMAN LEADERS

This list is not exhaustive and some dates are approximate. The legitimacy of some rulers is also open to interpretation. Where dates of rule overlap, emperors either ruled jointly or ruled in opposition to one another. There may also be differences in name spellings between different sources.

KINGS OF ROME (753–509 BCE)

Romulus (mythological founder and first ruler of Rome)	753–716 BCE
Numa Pompilius (mythological)	715–672 BCE
Tullus Hostilius (mythological)	672–640 BCE
Ancus Marcius (mythological)	640–616 BCE
Lucius Tarquinius Priscus (mythological)	616–578 BCE
Servius Tullius (mythological)	578–534 BCE
Lucius Tarquinius Superbus (Tarquin the Proud; mythological)	534–509 BCE

ROMAN REPUBLIC (509–27 BCE)

During this period, two consuls were elected to serve a joint one-year term. Therefore, only a selection of significant consuls are included here.

Lucius Junius Brutus (semi-mythological)	509 BCE
Marcus Porcius Cato (Cato the Elder)	195 BCE
Scipio Africanus	205 and 194 BCE
Caius Marius	107, 104, 103, 102, 101, 100 and 86 BCE
Cnaeus Pompeius Magnus (Pompey the Great)	70, 55 and 52 BCE
Marcus Linius Crassus	70 and 55 BCE
Marcus Tullius Cicero	63 BCE
Caius Julius Caesar	59, 48 and 46–44 BCE
Marcus Aemilius Lepidus	46 and 42 BCE
Marcus Antonius (Mark Anthony)	44, 34 and 31 BCE
Marcus Agrippa	37, 28 and 27 BCE

PRINCIPATE (27 BCE–284 CE)

Julio-Claudian Dynasty (27 BCE–68 CE)

Augustus (Caius Octavius Thurinus, Caius Julius Caesar, Imperator Caesar Divi filius)	27 BCE–14 CE
Tiberius (Tiberius Julius Caesar Augustus)	14–37 CE
Caligula (Caius Caesar Augustus Germanicus)	37–41 CE
Claudius (Tiberius Claudius Caesar Augustus Germanicus)	41–54 CE
Nero (Nero Claudius Caesar Augustus Germanicus)	54–68 CE

Year of the Four Emperors (68–69 CE)

Galba (Servius Sulpicius Galba Caesar Augustus)	68–69 CE
Otho (Marcus Salvio Otho Caesar Augustus)	Jan–Apr 69 CE
Vitellius (Aulus Vitellius Germanicus Augustus)	Apr–Dec 69 CE

Note: the fourth emperor, Vespasian, is listed below.

Flavian Dynasty (66–96 CE)

Vespasian (Caesar Vespasianus Augustus)	69–79 CE
Titus (Titus Caesar Vespasianus Augustus)	79–81 CE
Domitian (Caesar Domitianus Augustus)	81–96 CE

Nerva-Antonine Dynasty (69–192 CE)

Nerva (Nerva Caesar Augustus)	96–98 CE
Trajan (Caesar Nerva Traianus Augustus)	98–117 CE
Hadrian (Caesar Traianus Hadrianus Augustus)	117–138 CE
Antonius Pius (Caesar Titus Aelius Hadrianus Antoninus Augustus Pius)	138–161 CE
Marcus Aurelius (Caesar Marcus Aurelius Antoninus Augustus)	161–180 CE
Lucius Verus (Lucius Aurelius Verus Augustus)	161–169 CE
Commodus (Caesar Marcus Aurelius Commodus Antoninus Augustus)	180–192 CE

Year of the Five Emperors (193 CE)

Pertinax (Publius Helvius Pertinax)	Jan–Mar 193 CE
Didius Julianus (Marcus Didius Severus Julianus)	Mar–Jun 193 CE

Note: Pescennius Niger and Clodius Albinus are generally regarded as usurpers, while the fifth, Septimius Severus, is listed below

Severan Dynasty (193–235 CE)

Septimius Severus (Lucius Septimus Severus Pertinax) 193–211 CE
Caracalla (Marcus Aurelius Antonius) 211–217 CE
Geta (Publius Septimius Geta) Feb–Dec 211 CE
Macrinus (Caesar Marcus Opellius Severus Macrinus Augustus) 217–218 CE
Diadumenian (Marcus Opellius Antonius Diadumenianus) May–Jun 218 CE
Elagabalus (Caesar Marcus Aurelius Antoninus Augustus) 218–222 CE
Severus Alexander (Marcus Aurelius Severus Alexander) 222–235 CE

Crisis of the Third Century (235–285 CE)

Maximinus 'Thrax' (Caius Julius Verus Maximus) 235–238 CE
Gordian I (Marcus Antonius Gordianus Sempronianus Romanus) Apr–May 238 CE
Gordian II (Marcus Antonius Gordianus Sempronianus Romanus) Apr–May 238 CE
Pupienus Maximus (Marcus Clodius Pupienus Maximus) May–Aug 238 CE
Balbinus (Decimus Caelius Calvinus Balbinus) May–Aug 238 CE
Gordian III (Marcus Antonius Gordianus) Aug 238–Feb 244 CE
Philip I 'the Arab' (Marcus Julius Philippus) 244–249 CE
Philip II 'the Younger' (Marcus Julius Severus Philippus) 247–249 CE
Decius (Caius Messius Quintus Traianus Decius) 249–251 CE
Herennius Etruscus (Quintus Herennius Etruscus Messius Decius) May/Jun 251 CE

Trebonianus Gallus (Caius Vibius Trebonianus Gallus)	251–253 CE
Hostilian (Caius Valens Hostilianus Messius Quintus)	Jun–Jul 251 CE
Volusianus (Caius Vibius Afinius Gallus Veldumnianus Volusianus)	251–253 CE
Aemilian (Marcus Aemilius Aemilianus)	Jul–Sep 253 CE
Silbannacus (Marcus Silbannacus)	Sep/Oct 253 CE
Valerian (Publius Licinius Valerianus)	253–260 CE
Gallienus (Publius Licinius Egnatius Gallienus)	253–268 CE
Saloninus (Publius Licinius Cornelius Saloninus Valerianus)	Autumn 260 CE
Claudius II Gothicus (Marcus Aurelius Claudius)	268–270 CE
Quintilus (Marcus Aurelius Claudias Quintillus)	Apr–May/Jun 270 CE
Aurelian (Luciua Domitius Aurelianus)	270–275 CE
Tacitus (Marcus Claudius Tacitus)	275–276 CE
Florianus (Marcus Annius Florianus)	276–282 CE
Probus (Marcus Aurelius Probus Romanus; in opposition to Florianus)	276–282 CE
Carus (Marcus Aurelias Carus)	282–283 CE
Carinus (Marcus Aurelius Carinus)	283–285 CE
Numerian (Marcus Aurelius Numerianus)	283–284 CE

DOMINATE (284–610)

Tetrarchy (284–324)

Diocletian 'Lovius' (Caius Aurelius Valerius Diocletianus)	284–305
Maximian 'Herculius' (Marcus Aurelius Valerius Maximianus; ruled the western provinces)	286–305/late 306–308

Galerius (Caius Galerius Valerius Maximianus; ruled the eastern provinces)	305–311
Constantius I 'Chlorus' (Marcus Flavius Valerius Constantius; ruled the western provinces)	305–306
Severus II (Flavius Valerius Severus; ruled the western provinces)	306–307
Maxentius (Marcus Aurelius Valerius Maxentius)	306–312
Licinius (Valerius Licinanus Licinius; ruled the western, then the eastern provinces)	308–324
Maximinus II 'Daza' (Aurelius Valerius Valens; ruled the western provinces)	316–317
Martinian (Marcus Martinianus; ruled the western provinces)	Jul–Sep 324

Constantinian Dynasty (306–363)

Constantine I 'the Great' (Flavius Valerius Constantinus; ruled the western provinces then whole)	306–337
Constantine II (Flavius Claudius Constantinus)	337–340
Constans I (Flavius Julius Constans)	337–350
Constantius II (Flavius Julius Constantius)	337–361
Magnentius (Magnus Magnentius)	360–353
Nepotianus (Julius Nepotianus)	Jun 350
Vetranio	Mar–Dec 350
Julian 'the Apostate' (Flavius Claudius Julianus)	361–363
Jovian (Jovianus)	363–364

Valentinianic Dynasty (364–392)

Valentinian I 'the Great' (Valentinianus)	364–375
Valens (ruled the eastern provinces)	364–378

Procopius (revolted against Valens)	365–366
Gratian (Flavius Gratianus Augustus; ruled the western provinces then whole)	375–383
Magnus Maximus	383–388
Valentinian II (Flavius Valentinianus)	388–392
Eugenius	392–394

Theodosian Dynasty (379–457)

Theodosius I 'the Great' (Flavius Theodosius)	Jan 395
Arcadius	383–408
Honorius (Flavius Honorius)	395–432
Constantine III	407–411
Theodosius II	408–450
Priscus Attalus; usurper	409–410
Constantius III	Feb–Sep 421
Johannes	423–425
Valentinian III	425–455
Marcian	450–457

Last Emperors in the West (455–476)

Petronius Maximus	Mar–May 455
Avitus	455–456
Majorian	457–461
Libius Severus (Severus III)	461–465
Anthemius	467–472
Olybrius	Apr–Nov 472
Glycerius	473–474
Julius Nepos	474–475
Romulus Augustulus (Flavius Momyllus Romulus Augustulus)	475–476

Leonid Dynasty (East, 457–518)

Leo I (Leo Thrax Magnus)	457–474
Leo II	Jan–Nov 474
Zeno	474–475
Basiliscus	475–476
Zeno (second reign)	476–491
Anastasius I 'Dicorus'	491–518

Justinian Dynasty (East, 518–602)

Justin I	518–527
Justinian I 'the Great' (Flavius Justinianus, Petrus Sabbatius)	527–565
Justin II	565–578
Tiberius II Constantine	578–582
Maurice (Mauricius Flavius Tiberius)	582–602
Phocas	602–610

LATER EASTERN EMPERORS (610–1059)

Heraclian Dynasty (610–695)

Heraclius	610–641
Heraclius Constantine (Constantine III)	Feb–May 641
Heraclonas	Feb–Nov 641
Constans II Pogonatus ('the Bearded')	641–668
Constantine IV	668–685
Justinian II	685–695

Twenty Years' Anarchy (695–717)

Leontius	695–698
Tiberius III	698–705

Justinian II 'Rhinometus' (second reign)	705–711
Philippicus	711–713
Anastasius II	713–715
Theodosius III	715–717

Isaurian Dynasty (717–803)

Leo III 'the Isaurian'	717–741
Constantine V	741–775
Artabasdos	741/2–743
Leo V 'the Khazar'	775–780
Constantine VI	780–797
Irene	797–802

Nikephorian Dynasty (802–813)

Nikephoros I 'the Logothete'	802–811
Staurakios	July–Oct 811
Michael I Rangabé	813–820

Amorian Dynasty (820–867)

Michael II 'the Amorian'	820–829
Theophilos	829–842
Theodora	842–856
Michael III 'the Drunkard'	842–867

Macedonian Dynasty (867–1056)

Basil I 'the Macedonian'	867–886
Leo VI 'the Wise'	886–912
Alexander	912–913
Constantine VII Porphyrogenitus	913–959
Romanos I Lecapenus	920–944

Romanos II	959–963
Nikephoros II Phocas	963–969
John I Tzimiskes	969–976
Basil II 'the Bulgar-Slayer'	976–1025
Constantine VIII	1025–1028
Romanus III Argyros	1028–1034
Michael IV 'the Paphlagonian'	1034–1041
Michael V Kalaphates	1041–1042
Zoë Porphyrogenita	Apr–Jun 1042
Theodora Porphyrogenita	Apr–Jun 1042
Constantine IX Monomachos	1042–1055
Theodora Porphyrogenita (second reign)	1055–1056
Michael VI Bringas 'Stratioticus'	1056–1057
Isaab I Komnenos	1057–1059